THE
SIEGE

Ismail Kadare was born in 1936 in Gjirokastër, in the south of Albania. He studied in Tirana and Moscow, returning to Albania in 1960 after the country broke ties with the Soviet Union. Translations of his novels have since been published in more than forty countries, and in 2005 he became the first winner of the Man Booker International Prize.

David Bellos, Director of the Program in Translation at Princeton University, is also the translator of Georges Perec's *Life: A User's Manual* and a winner of the Goncourt Prize for biography. He has translated seven of Ismail Kadare's novels, and in 2005 was awarded the Man Booker International Prize for his translations of Kadare's work.

Translated works by Ismail Kadare

THE
SIEGE

ISMAIL KADARE

Translated from the French of
Jusuf Vrioni by David Bellos

CANONGATE

This Canons edition published in Great Britain in 2018 by Canongate Books

First published in Great Britain in 2008 by Canongate Books Ltd,
14 High Street, Edinburgh, EH1 1TE

First published in Albanian in 1970 as *Kështjella. Roman*,
by Shtëpia Botuese Naim Frashëri, Tirana

canongate.co.uk

1

This translation made from the definitive edition of the text published as *Les Tambours de la pluie* in Ismail Kadare, *OEuvres complètes*, t. II. Paris: Fayard, 1994, translated from the Albanian by Jusuf Vrioni

Amendments (2008) translated from the Albanian by Elidor Mehilli and David Bellos

British Library Cataloguing-in-Publication Data
A catalogue record for this book is available on
request from the British Library

ISBN 978 1 78689 394 9

Typeset by Palimpsest Book Production Ltd, Falkirk, Stirlingshire

Printed and bound in Great Britain by Clays Ltd, Elcograf S.p.A.

GUIDE TO PRONUNCIATION

All but a few of the named characters in this novel are Ottoman Turks, or members of the Ottoman Army. Where no conventional English transcriptions of their names, ranks or units exist, the spellings adopted by Ismail Kadare in the original Albanian text of this novel, or else those approved by him for this English edition, have been used. In some cases the spelling is identical between modern Turkish, modern Albanian, and modern English. For other cases, the following table of the main differences between the Albanian and the English alphabet may be helpful:

c	*ts* as in *curtsy*
ç	*ch* as in *church*
gj	*gy* as in *hogyard*
j	*y* as in *year*
q	*ky* as in *stockyard* or the *t* in *mature*
x	*dz* as in *adze*
xh	*j* as in *joke*
zh	*s* as in *measure*

THE
SIEGE

As winter fell away and the Sultan's envoys departed, we realised that war was our ineluctable fate. They had pressured us in every way to accept being vassals of the Sultan. First they used flattery, promising us a part in governing their vast empire. Then they accused us of being renegades in the pay of the Frankish knights, that is to say, slaves of Europe. Finally, as was to be expected, they made threats.

You seem mighty sure of your fortresses, they said to us, but even if they are as sturdy as you think, we'll throttle you with an altogether more fearsome iron band — hunger and thirst. At each season of harvest and threshing, the only seeded field you'll see will be the sky, and your only sickle the moon.

And then they left. All through March their couriers galloped as fast as the wind bearing messages to the Sultan's Balkan vassals, telling them either to persuade us to give in, or else to cut off all relations with us. As was to be expected, all were obliged to take the latter course.

We were alone and knew that sooner or later they would come. Many times in the past we had faced attacks from our enemies, but lying in wait of the mightiest army the world had ever known was a different matter. Our own minds were perpetually abuzz, but our prince, George Castrioti, was preoccupied beyond easy imagining. The inland castles and coastal keeps were ordered to repair their watchtowers and above all to build up stocks of arms and supplies. We did not yet know from which direction they would come, but in early June we heard that they had

3

begun to march along the old Roman road, the Via Egnatia, so they were heading straight towards us.

One week later, as fate decreed that our castle would be the first defence against the invasion, the icon of the Virgin from the great church at Shkodër was brought to us. A hundred years before it had given the defenders of Durrës the strength to repulse the Normans. We all gave thanks to Our Immaculate Lady and felt calmer and stronger for it.

Their army moved slowly. It crossed our border in mid-June. Two days later George Castrioti came with Count Musaka to inspect the garrison one last time, and to give it his blessing. After issuing final instructions, he left the castle on Sunday afternoon, followed by his escort and the officers' womenfolk and children, so as to place them in safety in the mountains.

We walked alongside them for a while without speaking. Then we made our adieus with much feeling and went back into the keep. From look-outs on our towers we watched them climb up to the Plain of the Cross, then we saw them re-emerge on the Evil Slope and finally disappear into the Windy Ravine. Then we closed the heavy outer doors, and the fortress seemed to have gone mute now that we could no longer hear the voices of our youngsters inside it. We also battened down the inner sets of doors and let silence reign over us.

On June 18, at daybreak, we heard the tolling of the bell. The sentinel on the East Tower announced that a yellowish cloud could be seen in the far distance. It was the dust kicked up by their horses.

CHAPTER ONE

The first Turkish troops came beneath the walls of the fortress on June 18. They spent the day pitching camp. By evening the entire army had still not arrived. New units kept on coming in. A thick layer of dust lay on men, shields, flags and drums, horses and wagons, and on the camels laden with bronze and heavy equipment. As soon as each marching group came on to the plain that lay before the garrison, officers from a special battalion would allocate a specific camping site, and the weary soldiers, under orders from their leaders, would busy themselves with setting up the tents before collapsing inside them, half-dead from fatigue.

Ugurlu Tursun Pasha, the commander-in-chief, stood alone outside his pink pavilion. He was watching the sun set. The huge camp throbbed with the noise of horseshoes and a thousand voices, and with its long lines of tents, it looked to him like a giant octopus which would stretch out one tentacle after another and slowly but surely encircle and suffocate the castle. The nearest tents were less than a hundred paces from the ramparts, the furthest were beyond the horizon. The Pasha's lieutenants had insisted his pavilion be placed at least a thousand paces from the castle walls.

But he had refused to be so far away. Some years earlier, when he had been still a young man and of less elevated rank, he had often slept less than fifty paces from the ramparts, almost at the foot of the besieged citadel. Later on, however, in successive wars and sieges, as he rose in rank, the colour of his tent and its distance from the walls had changed in tandem. It was now pitched at a distance slightly more than half of what his lieutenants recommended, that is, at six hundred paces. That was a lot less than a thousand, all the same.

The Pasha sighed. He often did that when he took up quarters before a fortress that had to be taken. It was a reflex prompted by the first impression, always the deepest, before he became accustomed to the situation — it was rather like getting used to a woman. Each of his apprehensions began the same way, and they always also ended with another sigh, a sigh of relief, when he cast his last glance at a vanquished fortress, waiting, like a small and dusky widow, for the order for restoration, or for final demolition.

On this occasion, the citadel that soared up before him looked particularly gloomy, like most of the fortresses of the Christians. There was something odd, or even sinister, in the shape and lay-out of its towers. He had had that same impression two months earlier, when the surveyors responsible for planning the campaign had brought him drawings of the structure. He had spread out the charts on his knees many times, for hours on end, after dinner, when everyone else in his great house at Bursa was sleeping. He knew every detail of the lay-out by heart, and yet, now that he was at last seeing it with his own eyes, it aroused in him a sense of foreboding.

He glanced up at the cross on the top of the citadel's church. Then at the fearsome banner, the two-headed black eagle whose outline he could barely make out. The vertical drop beneath the

East Tower, the wasteland around the gallows, the crenellated keep, all these other sights gradually grew dark. He raised his eyes to take another look at the cross, which seemed to him to give off an eerie glow.

The moon had not yet risen. It struck him as rather odd that the Christians, having seen Islam take possession of the moon, had not promptly made their own emblem the sun, but had taken instead a mere instrument of torture, the cross. Apparently they weren't as clever as people claimed. But they had been even less bright in times when they believed in several gods.

The sky was now black. If everything was decided up on high, why did Allah put them through so many trials, why did he allow them to spill so much blood? To one camp He had given ramparts and iron doors to defend itself, and to the other, ladders and ropes to try to overcome them, and He was content just to be a spectator of the ensuing butchery.

But the Pasha didn't rebel against fate and he turned around to look at his own camp. The plain was gradually being drowned in darkness and the myriad white tents appeared to hover above the ground like a bank of fog. He could see the different corps of the army laid out according to the plan that had been agreed. From where he was standing, he could see the snow-white flags of the janissaries, and the copper cauldron they hung on top of a tall pole. The raiders, or *akinxhis*, were taking their horses to drink in the nearby stream. Further on lay the endless tents of the *azabs*, as the infantry units were called; beyond them were the tents of the *eshkinxhis*, the cavalry recruited for this campaign; then, further on still, the tents of the swordsmen known as *dalkiliç*, then the quarters of the *serden geçti*, the soldiers of death, then the *müslüman* or Muslim troops, and the prettier abodes of the *sipahi*, the regular cavalry. Spread out behind them were the Kurdish units, then the

Persians, the Tartars, the Caucasians and the Kalmyks, and, even further off, where the commander's eye could no longer make out any clear shapes, there must have been the motley horde of the irregular volunteers, the exact number of whom was known to no man. Everything was gradually falling into order. A large part of the army was already sleeping. The only noise to be heard was the sound of quartermasters unloading supplies from the camel trains. Crates of bronze pieces, cauldrons, innumerable sacks bursting with victuals, gourds of oil and honey, fat cartons full of all kinds of equipment, iron bars, stakes, forks, hempen ropes with hooks on their ends, clubs, whetstones, bags of sulphur, and a whole array of metal tools he could not even name — all now came to rest in growing piles on the ground.

At the moment the army was swathed in darkness but at the crack of dawn it would shimmer like a Persian carpet as it spread itself out in all directions. Plumes, tents, manes, white and blue flags, and crescents — hundreds and hundreds of brass, silver, and silk crescents — would burst into flower. The pageant of colour would make the citadel look even blacker beneath its symbolic instrument of torture, the cross. He had come to the end of the earth to topple that sign.

In the deepening silence the sound of the *azabs* at work on the ditches became more noticeable. He was well aware that many of his officers were cursing through their teeth and hoping that as he was himself half-dead from fatigue he would give the order to halt work on the drains. He clenched his jaw just as he had when he had first spoken about latrines at a meeting of the high command. An army, he said, before it was a marching horde, or a swathe of flags, or blood to be spilled, or a victory or a defeat — an army was in the first place an ocean of piss. They had listened to him open-mouthed as he explained that in many cases an army may begin to fail not on the field of battle, but in mundane details of unsuspected importance, details no one thought about, like stench and filth, for instance.

In his mind's eye he saw the drains moving ever closer to the river, which would wake in the morning looking dull and yellow . . . In fact, that was how war really began, and not as the *hanums* in the capital — the ladies of high society — imagined it.

He almost laughed at the thought of those fine ladies, but oddly, a sense of nostalgia stopped him. It was the first time he'd noticed himself having feelings of that kind. He shook his head as if to make fun of his own plight. Yes, he really did miss the *hanums* of Bursa, but that was only part of it. What he missed was his distant homeland, Anatolia. He had often thought of its peaceful, lazy plains during the long march through the Balkans. He had thought of it most of all when his army had entered the land of the Shqipetars and first seen its fearsome peaks. One morning before noon, when he was drowsing on horseback, he had heard the cry from all around: "*daglar, daglar*", but said in a special way, as if expressing fear. His officers raised their heads and looked to the left, then to the right, as if they were trying to get a better view. He too gazed at the mountains at length. He'd never seen any like them before. They reminded him of ghastly nightmares unrelieved by waking up. The ground and the rocks seemed to be scrambling madly towards the sky in mockery of the laws of nature. Allah must have been very angry when he created this land, he thought, and for the hundredth time since the start of the campaign he wondered if his leadership of the army had been won for him by his friends, or by his enemies.

In the course of the journey he had noticed that the mere sight of these mountains could make his officers agitated. They spoke more and more often of the plain they hoped to see before them as soon as possible. The army moved slowly, for now it hauled not only its arms and supplies, but also the heavy shadow of the Albanian mountains. The worst of it was that there was nothing he could do to be rid of it. His only resource was to summon the campaign chronicler and to ask him how he was going to describe the mountainous terrain. Trembling with fear, the chronicler had said that in order to portray the Albanian landscape he had assembled a series of terrifying epithets. But they hadn't met with the Pasha's approval, and he ordered the scribbler to think again. Next morning, the historian appeared before him, his eyes bloodshot from the sleepless night he had spent, and read him out his new description. High mountains, he declaimed, that reached even higher than crows can fly; the devil himself could barely climb up them, the demon would rip his sandals on their rocks, and even hens had to have their claws shod with iron to scale them.

The Pasha had found these images pleasing. The march was now over, night had fallen, and he tried to recall the phrases used, but he was tired and his weary mind could think of nothing but rest. It had been the longest and most exhausting expedition of his soldiering life. The ancient road, which was impassable in several places and which his engineers had repaired as fast as they could, bore the strange name of Egnatia. It went back to Roman times, but seemed to go on for ever. Sometimes, in the narrow gorges, his troops had stayed stuck until sappers cut a detour. Then the road became passable once more, and his army resumed its slow and dusty advance, as it had on the first, third, fifth and eighth day prior. Even now, when it was all over, that thick and unpleasant layer of grey dust still hung over his memory.

He heard horses neigh behind him. The closed carriage which had brought four women from his harem was still there, parked beside his tent.

Before leaving he had wondered several times whether he should bring his wives with him. Some of his friends had advised against it. It was a well-known fact, they said, that women bring ill fortune to a military campaign. Others took the opposite view and said that he should take them with him if he wanted to feel calm and relaxed and to sleep well (insofar as anyone can sleep well during war). Usually pashas did not take women with them in similar circumstances. But this expedition aimed to reach a very distant land; in addition, according to all forecasts, the siege was likely to last a long time. But those weren't the real reasons, because on all campaigns, however far-flung or long-drawn-out they might be, captives were always taken, and women won at the cost of soldiers' blood were indisputably more alluring than any member of a harem. However, friends had warned him that where he was going it would be difficult to take any female prisoners. The girls there were certainly very beautiful, but in the words of a poet who had accompanied an earlier raid into those lands, they were also as enticing and, alas! as unattainable as a dream. To escape from pursuit they would often throw themselves off a cliff. That's just poetic licence, some said, but the Pasha's closest friends shook their heads to say it was no such thing. In the end, as he was taking his leave, the Grand Vizier had noticed the small carriage with barred windows, and asked him why he was taking women to a land famed for the beauty of its own. Avoiding the Vizier's sly glance, he replied that he didn't want to have any share in the prisoners his valiant soldiers would take by their own efforts and blood.

During the march he hadn't had a thought for his wives. They must now surely be asleep in their lilac-coloured tent, worn out by the length of the journey.

Before feeling them on his own skin, he heard the raindrops

falling on the tent. Then, after a short while, from somewhere inside the camp there rose the familiar sound of the rain drum. Its ominous roll, so different from the banging of heavy crates or the blare of the trumpets of war, summoned up the image of his soldiers who, despite their exhaustion, had to haul out the heavy tarpaulins to cover up the equipment, cursing at the weather as they laboured. He had heard it said that no foreign army except the Mongols had a special unit, as theirs did, whose job was to announce the coming of rain. Everything that's any use in the art of war, he said to himself, comes from the Mongols. Then he went inside his tent.

Orderlies had set up the Pasha's bed, placed the divans around it, and were now laying carpets on the floor. A strip of cloth embroidered with verses from the Koran had been hung at the entrance. Hooks had been hung in the customary manner from the top of the main pole so he could stow his scabbard and his cape. Contrary to what he had always expected, the more he rose in rank, the more gloomy his tent became.

He sat down on one of the divans and put his head between his hands as he waited for his chef-de-camp to finish his report. Almost all troops had now arrived, they had been allocated their proper camping places, guards, sentries and scouts had been posted all around — in sum, everything necessary had been done and was in order. The commander-in-chief could sleep peacefully.

The Pasha listened without interrupting. He didn't even take his head out of his hands, so that the chef-de-camp couldn't see his eyes, but only the ruby on his commander's middle finger. It was a ruby of the kind that because of its hue is called a blood-stone.

When his subaltern had left, Tursun Pasha stood up and went out once again. The rain was lighter than he had thought it was from the noise it made inside the tent. His ears were still ringing with the chef-de-camp's litany of guards, sentries and scouts, but instead of calming him down, it had made him even more agitated. Night always bears a litter, he thought. He had heard the saying somewhere or other in his youth, but only when he was much older had he discovered that it did not refer to the consequences of love or lust, but to nasty surprises.

The night was pregnant and he was in its belly, all alone. He could see a faint glow leaking out of tents to the right of his own. Others were still awake, as he was. Maybe they were quartermasters, or exorcists or sorcerers warding off evil spirits. Normally, the astrologer, the chronicler, the spell-caster, the exorcists and the dream-interpreters had tents set next to each other. All of them knew more than he did about what lay in store, that was certain. Nevertheless, he did not trust them entirely.

The patter of raindrops was getting louder. The Pasha felt he was quite close to the sky and separated from it only by the feeble crown of his tent. A strange nostalgia overcame him as he thought of his bedroom at home, in his palace, where you could barely hear the sound of bad weather. He was usually more prone to longing for war. At home, lying in a room soundproofed by carpets, he would think eagerly of his campaign tent with the wind howling around it . . . Had he not now reached the age when he should don his slippers and retire to his peaceful Anatolian home? Should he not let go before the fall?

He knew it was not a practicable proposition. He was still young, but that was not the main reason. He had attained a rank where it was impossible to stand still. He was condemned either to rise even higher, or else to fall. The Empire was growing by the day. Whoever could prove himself the most energetic and courageous could have it all. Thousands of ambitious men were clawing their way like wild beasts towards wealth and fame. They were shoving others aside, often by intelligent manoeuvring, but even more often by plot and by poison.

He had recently felt the ground shifting under his own feet. There was no obvious cause for that uncertain sensation, which made it all the less easy to deal with. Like one of those mysterious diseases no one knows how to cure.

He had used all the means at his disposal to find out which hidden circles were plotting against him. A waste of time. He had not uncovered anything at all. His friends had begun to look at him pityingly. Especially after receiving his latest gift from the Sultan — a collection of armour. Everybody knew it was a bad omen. People were expecting him to fall, when, all of a sudden, news went round that he had been appointed commander of a huge expedition due to set off in short order against the Albanians. People said he must have still had some friends in high places, even if he had enemies aplenty. At the same time, however, it was clear that by sending him off to fight Skanderbeg, the Sultan was giving him one last chance.

It wasn't the first time the Padishah had acted in that way. He always appointed men who were playing their last card to head the most hazardous expeditions, well aware that the fiercest of warriors are those with their backs to the wall.

The Pasha rose and began to pace up and down on the plush carpet of his tent. Then he sat down again and took a thick swatch of papers and cardboard from a large leather satchel. Among the documents was the map of the fortress. The Pasha put it on his lap and pored over it. It contained very full details of the location and especially the height of the ramparts and the towers, the slope of the ground on every side, the specifications of the main door and of the secondary entrance to the south-west, the gully on the west side, and the river. The draftsman had put question marks in red ink in three or four places to mark the probable locations where the aqueduct entered and left the fortress. The Pasha stared fixedly at these marks.

One of his orderlies brought him his dinner on a tray, but he didn't touch it. His fingers ran through his worry-beads but the faint noise they made did no more than the patter of raindrops to dissipate the feeling of emptiness inside him.

He clapped his hands, and a eunuch appeared at the tent door.

"Bring me Exher," he said without even looking at the man.

The eunuch bowed to the ground but stayed where he was. He seemed to have something to say, but was too scared to open his mouth.

"What is it?" the Pasha asked, seeing the man was still there.

The eunuch mouthed something but made no sound.

"Is she ill?" the Pasha asked.

"No, Pasha, but you know that the hammam . . . and perhaps she . . ."

The Pasha motioned him to keep quiet. He looked at his beads once again. The night was going to be as long as a winter night.

"Bring her to me all the same," he blurted out.

The eunuch bowed again and then vanished like a shadow.

He came back a few moments later holding a young woman by the hand. Her hair had been done up in haste and she looked as if she was still asleep. She was the youngest of the women in his harem. Nobody knew her age, and nor did she. She couldn't have been more than sixteen.

The Pasha motioned to her. She sat on the bed. She did not arouse him one bit, but he lay down beside her nonetheless. She apologised for not having been able to perform her ablutions that night, for reasons beyond her control. The Pasha grasped that the sentence had been put in her mouth by the eunuch. He didn't answer. As he smelled the familiar perfume of the girl, which for the first time was blended with the smell of dust, it occurred to him briefly that maybe he should not lay his hand on a woman on the night before a battle, but the thought left his mind as casually as it had come into it.

He gazed at her pubis and was almost surprised by the vigorous tuft that the eunuch had not had time to shave, as he usually did. With this shadow over her sexual organ, the girl looked slightly foreign, and all the more desirable for it. He often told himself that he should abstain from making love when an affair of State was on his mind, but swung just as often to the opposite view, that it would help him cope. On this night, he overcame his hesitation.

He opened her legs with a gentle touch and, contrary to habit, as if he were afraid of bruising his young wife, he penetrated her with similar tenderness. The unusual consideration he showed did not surprise him; he guessed vaguely that it was connected to the long journey the girl had put up with alongside his soldiers, which made her almost part of his army.

He moved clumsily, as if his desire lay outside of his body, and it was only when he felt his seed spurt from him into the girl's warm belly that he livened up. His pleasure was brief but intense and sharp, as if it were all concentrated in itself, like the trunk of a tree with no branches.

The girl realised he had made love without desire. As she ascribed his coldness to the black tufts of her pubic hair rather than to her not having been bathed beforehand, she apologised once again. He didn't respond. He propped himself on his elbow, leaned back on the cushions, and started counting out his beads again. With a blush in her cheeks and her head on the pillow, she marvelled at the harsh and rough-hewn face of the man to whom she belonged.

He forgot all about her. He reached over to the pile of documents and extracted the map of the fortress from it. He drew two signs on it, and then a third, in black ink. The girl raised herself on an elbow and with her beautiful eyes cast a quizzical glance at the paper and its multitude of strange marks. Her master's cold, grey eyes did not budge from it. She made a small movement, as carefully as she could, so as not to disturb him. However, when she shifted her elbow, which was going numb, the bed moved, and one of its heavy pendants almost fell on to the sketch. She held her breath — but he hadn't noticed a thing. He was completely absorbed by the map.

She looked alternately at the Pasha's face and at the marks he was making on the map. She was extremely curious, and just as bold, for she asked:

"Is that what war is, then?"

He looked up and stared at her, as if surprised to see her lying there, then turned away and went back to poring over the map.

He carried on marking up the map for a long time. When he turned around, she had fallen asleep. She was breathing deeply, with her lips half-parted. She looked even younger than her years.

Rain was still falling and drumming on the tent.

As the Pasha gazed at the eyelashes and pale long neck of his fourth wife, his mind went back — who knows why? — to the latrines that had been constructed at top speed. The first ditch would now be creeping up to the river, like a water-snake . . . He lifted the blanket and, against his normal practice, took a look at his partner's delta, with its lips still wet. He thought he might have impregnated her. In nine months' time, she might give him a son . . . Approaching sleep made his mind wander to the *matériel* that should by now be under the tarpaulins, to the sentries, tomorrow's meeting of the war council, and back again to that woman's belly where his son may just have been engendered. When he grew up, would he ever imagine he had been conceived in a campaign tent, in the pouring rain, at the foot of a sinister citadel, far beyond the setting sun . . . ? Maybe he too would become a soldier, and as he rose in rank, maybe his tent too would move two hundred, six hundred, twelve hundred paces from the ramparts . . . "Allah! Why hast Thou made us thus?" he sighed as his head nodded, as if over a bottomless pit.

Their white tents have surrounded our citadel in the shape of an immense crown. At dawn on the morning after their arrival, the plain looked as if it were covered by a thick layer of snow. You could see no ground, no grass, no rocks. We climbed up to the battlements to get a view of this wintry scene. That was when we realised what a huge conflict our Castrioti had entered into with Murad Han, the most powerful prince of the age.

Their camp stretches out as far as the eye can see. The ground has vanished from sight and our hearts sink. We are now alone with only the clouds for company, as it were, while at our feet, like some nightmare vision, a myriad tents are forging a new landscape, a nowhere world, so to speak.

From here you can see the pink pavilion of the commander-in-chief. The day before yesterday he sent a delegation to seek our surrender. They stated their conditions quite clearly: they would not touch any of us, they would let us leave the citadel with our arms and chattels, and we could go wherever we chose. In return all they wanted were the keys to the castle so they could take down the black bird-flag (which is what they call our eagle) from the tower where it flies, for in their view it offends the firmament. In its place they want to raise the true son of the heavenly world, the crescent.

That is what they have been doing everywhere in recent times: they pretend to be pursuing a symbol when their real aim is conquest. They kept the issue of religion to the end, since they were sure it would be their winning bid. Their chief pointed to the bell-tower and said that as far as the instrument of torture was concerned (that is what they call the Holy Cross), we could, if we wished, hang on to it, and also, obviously, keep our Christian faith. You'll renounce it yourselves in due course, he added, because no nation could possibly prefer martyrdom to the peace of Islam.

Our answer was short and firm: neither the eagle nor the cross would ever be removed from our firmament; they were the symbols and the fate we had elected, and we would remain faithful to them. And so that each of us may keep his own symbols and fate according to the dispositions of the Lord, they had no alternative but to leave.

They did not wait for the interpreter to translate our last words before rising hurriedly to their feet in fury. They called us blind, said they had parleyed enough already, and that it was now time for arms to speak. Then they hastened towards the rear gate, taking a path through the centre of the courtyard so as to show off their magnificent costumes.

CHAPTER TWO

Mevla Çelebi, the chronicler, halted at fifty paces from the Pasha's tent. He stared with interest at the members of the council going into the pavilion one by one. Before the tent stood a metal pole with a brass crescent – the imperial emblem — perched atop. As he gazed at the high-ranking officers he tried to summon up the adjectives he would use to describe them in his chronicle. But all he could find were a few weak words, most of which had been worn out by his predecessors. Moreover, if he set aside those he had to use for the commander-in-chief, there were precious few left, and he would have to take care not to use them up too quickly. It was as if he had in his fist a bunch of jewels which he would have to distribute parsimoniously among these countless combatants.

Kurdisxhi, the captain of the *akinxhis*, had hardly got off his horse. His big ruddy head seemed to be still asleep. After him came the captain of the janissaries, the old but still ferocious Tavxha Tokmakhan, whose short legs looked as if they had been broken and badly put back together again. The commander of the *azabs*, Kara-Mukbil, strode in together with the army Mufti and two provincial commanders, or sanxhakbeys. Then along came Aslanhan, Deli Burxhuba, Ullu Bekbey, Olça Karaduman, Hatai, Uç Kurtogmuz and Uç Tunxhkurt, Bakerhanbey, Tahanka the deaf-mute, and the Alaybey of the army. It occurred to Çelebi that he would have to mention in his chronicle every one of these famous captains whose names echoed with the clash of steel, wild beasts, the black dust of long marches, storms, lightning and other such-like subjects of fear.

With the exceptions of the commander-in-chief and Kara-Mukbil, whose oval faces were agreeable to the eye, and also of the Alaybey who, like most officers of his army, was a fine figure of a man, all the leaders had features that seemed to have been designed solely in order to make it harder for him to write his chronicle. Traits unworthy of appearing in a battle epic automat-ically came into his mind: Olça Karaduman's sty, the Mufti's asthma, Uç Kurtogmuz's extra tooth, the chilblains of his name-sake, Uç Tunxhkurt, and the humped backs, short necks, scare-crow arms and sciatic shoulders of many others, and especially the coarse hairs sticking out of Kurdisxhi's nose.

He was musing on those nasal hairs, for who knows what reason, when he heard someone calling his name.

"Greetings, Mevla Çelebi!"

The chronicler turned round and bowed obsequiously down to the ground. The man who had hailed him was the army's Quartermaster General. He was coming towards him accompa-nied by Engineer Saruxha, the famous caster of cannon. Pale of skin, with eyes that were bloodshot from many sleepless nights, the engineer was the only member of the council who wore a black cloak, which accorded well with the aura of mystery surrounding his work.

"What are you doing here?" the Quartermaster asked Çelebi.

"I am observing the members of our illustrious council," the chronicler replied in a pompous tone, as if to justify his presence.

The Quartermaster General smiled at him, and walked on with Saruxha towards the door of the tent where sentries stood guard like statues.

Feeling guilty once again for the thoughts he had just had, the chronicler watched the tall, slim figure of the Quartermaster General, whom he had got to know during the long march. Quite unusually, this time he gave an impression of haughtiness.

The last to turn up for the meeting was Giaour, the architect. Çelebi tracked him and was struck by how unnatural his gait appeared. Nobody rightly knew the origins or the nationality of the man who was acquainted with every secret of the structures of fortresses. He had no known family, which was not surprising for a foreigner, but he seemed doubly alone because of the way he spoke — in a peculiar kind of Turkish that few could fully understand. As his chin was smooth, many suspected he was really a woman, or at least half-man and half-woman — a hermaphrodite, as people say.

The architect went in last. The duty guards were the only people left outside, and they started playing dice. The chronicler was burning to know what was being said inside the tent. Now, if he had been appointed secretary to the council of war as well as campaign chronicler, he would have been in a position to know everything. It was normal for the same man to occupy both positions. He accounted for his own limited station in various ways, depending on his mood. Sometimes he thought they had done him a favour by not overloading him with work and thus allowing him to concentrate entirely on the chronicle, which was intended to be an immortal record of the campaign. But at other times, such as now, as he looked at the Pasha's pavilion from a distance, he guessed the real reason for his exclusion, and felt bitter and disappointed.

He was about to move off when he saw several council members emerge from the tent. The Quartermaster General was among them. He saw Çelebi and called out to him.

"Come on, Mevla, come for a walk, we'll be able to chat. The council is now going over the details of the attack and those of us not directly involved have been asked to leave."

"When will the assault begin?" Çelebi asked shyly.

"In a week, I think. As soon as the two big cannon have been cast."

They sauntered slowly, with the Quartermaster's orderly following them like a shadow.

"Let's go into my tent for a drink and escape from all this racket," the Quartermaster said, making a wide gesture with his arm.

Çelebi put his hand on his heart and bowed low once more.

"You do me great honour."

Being invited into the tent to talk about history and philosophy once more, as he had done a few days ago, filled him with a joy that evaporated instantly at the fear of disappointing his eminent friend.

"My head's bursting," the high official said, "and I need some respite. I've still got a pile of things to settle."

The chronicler listened to him with a guilty air.

"It's very odd," the Quartermaster said. "You historians usually attribute all the glory of conquest to military leaders. But mark my words, Mevla, mark them well: after the commander-in-chief's, it's this here head," he said, tapping his forehead with his index finger, "that has more worries than any other."

Çelebi bowed in homage.

"Supplying food to an army is the key problem in war," the Quartermaster went on, in a tone close to irritation. "Anybody can wave a sword about, but keeping forty thousand men fed and watered in a foreign, unpopulated and uncultivated land, now that's a hard nut to crack."

"How very true," the chronicler commented.

"Shall I tell you a secret?" the Quartermaster said all of a sudden. "The army you can see camped all around you has got supplies for only fifteen days!"

Çelebi raised his eyebrows, but thought they were insufficiently bushy to give adequate expression to his amazement.

"According to the plan," the officer went on, "supply trains are supposed to leave Edirne every two weeks. Granted, but given the huge distance they have to cover, can I rely on them? Provisions . . . If you ever hear that I've gone out of my mind, you'll know why!"

The chronicler wanted to protest: Whatever are you saying? He nodded his head, even raised his arms — but they seemed too short to say what he now wanted to say.

"So all the responsibility falls on our shoulders," the other man went on. "If the cooks come and say one fine day that they've nothing left to fill their pots, who is the Pasha going to call to order? Obviously not Kurdisxhi, nor old Tavxha, nor any other captain. Only me!" And he stuck a finger into his breast as if it was a dagger.

Çelebi's face, on which deference and attentiveness were painted like a mask, now also expressed commiseration, which wasn't difficult, seeing that in its normal state it was deeply lined and wrinkled.

The Quartermaster General's tent was pitched at the very heart of the camp so that as they drew nearer to it they were walking among throngs of soldiers. Some of them were sitting outside their tents undoing their packs, others were picking their fleas without the slightest embarrassment. Çelebi recalled that no chronicle ever mentioned the tying and untying of soldier's backpacks. As for flea hunting, that was never spoken of either.

"What about the *akinxhis*?" he enquired, trying to banish all reprehensible thoughts from his mind. "Aren't they going to be allowed to pillage in the environs?"

"Of course they are," the officer replied. "However, the booty they take usually covers less than a fifth of the needs of the troops. And only in the early stages of a siege."

"That's odd . . ." the chronicler opined.

"There's only one solution: Venice."

Çelebi started with surprise.

"The Sultan has made an agreement with the Serenissima. Venetian merchants are supposed to supply us with food and *matériel*."

The chronicler was astounded, but nodded his head.

"I understand why you are amazed," the Quartermaster said. "You must find it bizarre that we accuse Skanderbeg of being in the pay of Westerners while we do deals with Venice behind Skanderbeg's back. If I were in your shoes, I admit I would find that shocking."

The Quartermaster General put a formal smile on his lips, but his eyes were not smiling at all.

"That's politics for you, Mevla!"

The chronicler lowered his head. It was his way of taking cover whenever a conversation wandered into dangerous terrain.

A long line of *azabs* went past, carrying rushes on their backs. The Quartermaster watched them go by.

"That's what they use, I believe, to weave the screens the

soldiers use to shield themselves from burning projectiles. Have you really never seen a siege before?"

The chronicler blushed and said, "I have not had that good fortune."

"Oh! It's an impressive sight."

"I can imagine."

"Believe me," the general said in a more informal way. "I've taken part in many sieges, but this," he waved towards the castle walls, "is where the most fearful carnage of our times will take place. And you surely know as well as I do that great massacres always give birth to great books." He took a deep breath. "You really do have an opportunity to write a thundering chronicle redolent with pitch and blood, and it will be utterly different from the graceful whines composed at the fireside by squealers who never went to war."

Çelebi blushed again as he recalled the opening of his chronicle. "One day, if you like, I could read you some passages from what I have written," he said. "I would like to hope they will not disappoint you."

"Accepted! You know how much I like history."

A squad of janissaries marched past noisily.

"They're in a good mood," the Quartermaster said. "Today is pay day."

Çelebi remembered that pay was also never mentioned in that kind of narrative.

Troopers were setting out some oval tents. Further off, carters were unloading beams and rushes beside a ditch that had just been dug. The camp looked less like military quarters than a construction site.

"Look, there are the old hags from Rumelia," the Quartermaster said.

The chronicler turned his head to the left, where he could see a score and more of old women in an enclosure; they were busying themselves with pots hung over a campfire.

"What are they cooking up?" Çelebi asked.

"Balms for wounds, especially burns."

The chronicler looked at the tanned, impassive and aged faces of the women.

"Our warriors are going to suffer horrible injuries," the Quartermaster said sadly. "But they don't yet know the real function of the Rumelian women. They're reputed to be witches."

Çelebi looked away so as not to see the soldiers picking out their fleas. Many of them were in fact sitting cross-legged so as to examine the corns on the soles of their feet.

"Their feet are sore from the long march," the Quartermaster said with sympathy. "I've still never read a historical work that even mentions soldiers' feet."

The chronicler was sorry to have displayed his distaste, but the harm was done now.

"In truth, the vast Empire of which we are all so proud was enlarged only by these blistered and torn feet," the officer said with a touch of grandiloquence. "A friend often said to me: I am willing to kneel and kiss these stinking feet."

The chronicler didn't know what to do with himself. Fortunately for him, they had just got to the Quartermaster General's tent.

"So here's my den," the general said in a different tone of voice. "Come in, Mevla Çelebi. Do you like pomegranate syrup? In such scorching weather there's nothing better than the juice of a pomegranate to cool you down. And then, a conversation with a friend on matters of high interest is like a violet blooming among thorns. Isn't that so, Çelebi?"

The chronicler's mind flashed back to the soldiers' blisters and filthy feet, but he soon took solace in the thought that man is so great that all can be permitted him.

"I am overwhelmed by the friendship you bestow on me, a mere chronicler."

"Not at all!" the Quartermaster interrupted. "Your trade is most honourable: you are a historian. Only the uneducated could fail to grant you their esteem. Now, my dear friend, are you going to read me a few passages from your work, as you promised?"

Çelebi would have blushed with contentment had he not been so scared. After the whole exchange of courtesies, the chronicler, who knew the start of his work by heart, began to recite slowly as follows:

"At the behest of the Padishah, master of the universe, to whom men and genies owe total obedience, a myriad harems were abandoned and the lions set forth for the land of the Shqipetars . . ."

The Quartermaster General explained that this overture was not entirely lacking in poetry, but he would have preferred the idea of abandoned harems to be linked to some more basic element of human life, something more vital to the economy, such as, for example, the plough or the vine. He added that a few figures would give it more substance.

At that moment the general's secretary appeared at the tent door. His master signalled to him to come nearer, and the servant whispered something in the general's ear. The Quartermaster said "yes" several times, and "no" an equal number of times.

"What were we saying?" he asked the chronicler as soon as the secretary had left. "Ah yes, figures! But you mustn't take too much notice of me on this issue, because I'm obsessed with numbers. All day long I do nothing but count and reckon!"

The secretary reappeared.

"A messenger from the Pasha," he blurted out as soon as he saw his master scowl.

The courier came close to the general, bent down to speak in his ear, and went on whispering in that position for a long while. Then he put his own ear to the Quartermaster's mouth to collect the reply.

"Let's go out," the Quartermaster suggested when the courier had left. "We'll have a better chance to talk outdoors. Otherwise the thorns of everyday business will throttle the violet of our conversation!"

Dusk was falling. The camp was in a state of lively activity. *Akinxhis* were coming from all directions, leading their horses to water. Standards rustled in the wind from the tips of the tent poles. With the addition of a handful of flowers to add their smell, the many-coloured camp would have looked less like a military installation than a blooming garden. The chronicler remembered that none of his colleagues had ever described an army as a flower garden — a *gulistan* — but that was what he was going to do. He would liken it to a meadow, or else to a polychrome kilim, but one from which, as soon as the order to move forward was given, would emerge the black fringes of death.

They had almost reached the centre-point of the camp when they ran into the engineer, Saruxha. He was wandering around looking absent-minded.

"Is the meeting over?" the Quartermaster General enquired.

"Yes, it's just ended. I'm dead tired," Saruxha replied, rubbing his red-rimmed eyes. "We've not had a wink of sleep for three nights in a row. Today the Pasha gave us final orders to ready the cannon for next week . . . In eight days, he said, he wants to hear their blast."

"Will you manage?"

"I don't know. We might. But you can't imagine how difficult the work will be. Especially as we're using a new kind of weapon, one which has never been made before, so I have to attend to every detail of manufacture."

"I understand," the Quartermaster said.

"Do you want to have a look at the foundry?" Saruxha asked, and, without waiting for an answer, he led them off across waste ground.

The chronicler was delighted to be given so much trust. Before leaving the capital he had heard all kinds of rumours about the new weapon. People spoke of it alternately with admiration and horror, as is normal with a secret weapon. They said its roar would make you deaf for the rest of your life, and its blast would topple everything around it within a radius of several leagues.

During the long march he had noticed the camels that were alleged to be carrying pieces of the barrel destined to serve the big cannon. The soldiers who marched silently alongside never took their eyes off the rain-soaked black tarpaulins hiding the mortal secret.

Çelebi itched to learn more about the camels' packs but he was frightened of arousing suspicion. When at last he overcame his shyness and questioned the Quartermaster, whom he had just got to know, the latter burst out laughing, with his hands on hips. Those heavy packs, he said, don't have any tubes in them at all. All that was in them were bars of iron and bronze, and a special kind of coal. "So you're going to ask me, where then is the secret weapon? I'll tell you, Mevla Çelebi. The big, fearsome cannon are in a tiny little satchel . . . as tiny as the one over my shoulder, here . . . Don't look at me like that, I'm not pulling your leg!" Now he whispered it into Mevla's ear, nodding towards a waxen-faced man wrapped in a black cloak: "The secret cannon really is in a satchel." It took the chronicler a little while to grasp that in that wan figure's shoulder bag were to be found secret designs and formulae that would be used for casting the big gun.

The foundry had been set up away from the camp in an area that was entirely fenced off and under heavy guard. It was separated from the stream by a hillock, and at twenty paces from the gate stood a sign saying: "Forbidden Zone".

"It's well guarded, day and night," the engineer said. "Spies might try to steal our secret."

The engineer acted as their tour guide through the long shack that had been thrown up and gave them copious explanations of what could be seen. The forge and the ovens had just been lit, and the flames gave off stifling heat. Shirtless, soot-blackened men dripping with sweat were busy at work.

Heaps of iron and bronze ingots and huge clay moulds covered most of the floor.

The engineer showed them the designs for the giant cannon.

The visitors looked with wonderment at the mass of straight lines, arcs and circles meticulously traced out on the blueprints.

"This one's the biggest," Saruxha said as he showed them one of the drawings. "My artificers have already dubbed it *balyemeztop*!"

"The gun that eats no honey? Why call it by such a strange name?" the Quartermaster asked.

"Because it prefers to eat men!" Saruxha replied. "It's a whimsical cannon, if I may say, a bit like a spoiled child who says to its mother one fine morning, 'I'm fed up with honey!' . . . Now come and see the place where it will be cast," he added as he moved off in another direction. "Here's the great hole where the clay moulds will be laid down, and over there are the six furnaces where the metal will be melted. A standard cannon takes one furnace, but for this one, six will barely suffice! That's one of the main secrets of the casting. All six furnaces have to produce molten metal at exactly the same degree of fusion at precisely the same time. If there's the tiniest crack, the tiniest bubble, so to speak, then the cannon will burst apart when it's fired."

The Quartermaster General gave a whistle of astonishment.

Although he too was amazed at what he had heard, Mevla Çelebi was sufficiently astute not to turn his head towards the general in case the latter, once he had regained his poise, might feel annoyed at having been caught in a moment of weakness by a mere chronicler, or, in other words, at having let himself be seen to be astonished, when he was supposed to be far above such emotions.

But the Quartermaster General wasn't trying to hide his bewilderment. The chronicler, for his part, trembled at the thought that Engineer Saruxha was engaged on God's work, or else the Devil's own, by having his furnaces produce a fiery liquid that Allah himself caused the earth to spew out through the mouths of volcanoes. Labour of that kind usually brought severe punishment.

As the engineer went on explaining how the casting would be done, in their eyes he slowly turned into a wizard, wrapped in his black cloak, about to perform some ancient, mysterious ritual.

"It is the first time that cannon of this kind are to be used in the whole military history of humankind," Saruxha finally declared with pride. "An earthquake will sound like a lullaby next to their terrible thunder."

They looked at him with admiration.

"This is where the most modern war the world has ever known is about to be waged," he concluded, staring at the chronicler.

Çelebi was worried.

"The Padishah's priority at present is to force the Balkans

into submission," the Quartermaster commented. "Obviously, he will spare no expense to achieve his aim."

"This is my right-hand man," Saruxha said as he turned towards a tall, pale and worn-out young man who was coming towards them.

The young man glanced nonchalantly at the visitors, made a gesture that could barely be understood as a greeting, and then whispered a few words in the engineer's ear.

"You're amazed I picked that lad as my first assistant, aren't you?" Saruxha asked when the youngster had walked off. "Most people share your view. He doesn't look the part, but he is extremely able."

They said nothing.

"In this shed we will cast four other, smaller cannon, but they will be no less fearsome than the big one," the engineer went on. "They are called mortars, and they shoot cannon-balls in a curved trajectory. Unlike cannon which hit the walls straight on, mortars can rain down on the castle's inner parts from above, like a calamity falling from the heavens."

He picked up a lump of coal and piece of board from the ground.

"Let's suppose this is the castle wall. We put the cannon here. Its shot takes a relatively straight path" — he drew a line — "and hits the wall here. But the shot from the mortar or bombard rises high in the sky, almost innocently, if I may say so, as if it had no intention of hitting the wall — and then falls almost vertically behind it." With his hand, which the chronicler thought he saw shaking a little, he made out the shape of the two arcs in the air. "Bombards make a noise that sounds like the moaning of a stormy sea."

"Allah!" the chronicler cried out.

"Where did you learn how to do all this?" the Quartermaster General asked.

The engineer looked at him evasively.

"From my master, Saruhanli. I was his first assistant."

"He's in prison now, isn't he?"

"Yes," Saruxha replied. "The Sultan had him put away in the fortress of Bogazkezen."

"And nobody knows why?" the chronicler ventured timidly.

"I know why," the engineer replied.

The Quartermaster General raised his eyes and glanced at Saruxha with surprise.

"Recently, the poor old man's mind began to wander. He refused to make cannon of larger calibre. He claimed it was impossible, but in fact, as he told me, he didn't want to do it. If we make them even bigger, he would say, then the cannon will become a terrible scourge that will decimate the human race. The monster has come into the world, he said by way of explanation, and we can't put it back where it came from. The best we can do is to keep its barrel no bigger than it is now. If we enlarge it further, the cannon will devour the world. The old man stopped experimenting. That's why the Sultan had him arrested."

The engineer picked up a piece of clay and rubbed it until it turned to dust, and said, "That's what's happened to him."

The other two men nodded.

"But I have a different view of the matter," the engineer explained. "I think that if we give in to scruples of that kind, then science will come to a halt. War or no war, science must advance. I don't really mind who uses this weapon, or against whom it is used. What matters to me is that it should hurl a cannon-ball along a path identical to my calculation of the trajectory. The rest of it is your business." And on that abrupt note, he stopped.

"I've been given to understand that the money for making this weapon was donated by one of the Sultan's wives for the salvation of her soul," the Quartermaster General said, obviously intending to change the topic of conversation.

"For the salvation of her soul?" Çelebi asked, thinking the detail worthy of figuring in his chronicle. "Is it expensive?" he added after a pause, astounded at his own temerity.

"He's the one to know," the engineer said, pointing at the Quartermaster. "All I can tell you about is the gun's range and firepower."

The chronicler smiled.

"Oh yes, the big gun costs a lot of money," the Quartermaster said. "A very great deal. Especially now that we are at war, and the price of bronze has soared."

He narrowed his eyes and made a quick mental calculation.

"Two million silver aspers," he blurted out.

The chronicler was awe-struck. But the figure made no impact whatever on the master caster.

"To pay that much for the salvation of one's soul may seem prohibitively expensive," the Quartermaster said, "but if the cannon-balls break through those ramparts in a few days' time, they'll be worth their weight in gold."

An ironical smile hovered over his face.

"At the siege of Trabzon," he continued, "when the first cannon, which was much smaller than this one, shot its first ball, many of those present thought the barrel had grunted 'Allah!' But what I thought I heard though the roar, maybe because I think about it all the time, was the word 'Taxation!'"

Once again the chronicler was struck dumb. The engineer, for his part, started to laugh out loud.

"You don't realise the full meaning of that word, nor how

many things, including the siege of this fortress, depend on it," the Quartermaster observed.

"Well, when the gun fires," the engineer said, "I don't hear it say 'Allah!' or 'Taxation' at all. All I think about is that the power and noise of the explosion are the product of the amount of gunpowder packed behind the cannon-ball combined with the precise diameter and length of the barrel."

The Quartermaster General smiled. Çelebi, for his part, pondered on his having become friendly with powerful and learned men, and wondered how long he could keep up conversations of this kind, which rose into spheres he had never previously encountered.

"Let's go outside for a breath of air," the Quartermaster suggested.

Saruxha walked with them as far as the door.

"People say that these new weapons will change the nature of war," the chronicler said. "That they'll make citadels redundant."

Saruxha shook his head doubtfully.

"Indeed they might. People also say they will make other weapons obsolete."

"Who are the 'people' saying these things?" the Quartermaster butted in. "You don't believe these cannon can overcome the fortress all by themselves, do you?"

"I certainly wish they could," Saruxha replied, "because they are, at bottom, my creations. However, I take a rather different view. I think that although the guns will play a role in the victory, what really matter are the soldiers of our great Padishah. It is they who will storm the fortress."

"Quite right," the Quartermaster General said.

"The cannon will have at least one other effect," Saruxha added. "Their thunderous noise will spread panic among the besieged and break their courage. That's a considerable help, isn't it?"

"It's very important," the Quartermaster agreed. "And I'm not thinking only of those wretches. The whole of Christendom trembles when it hears speak of our new weapon. It has already become a legend."

"I would walk with you for a while," Saruxha said, "but this evening I've still got a thousand things to do. Casting should begin around midnight."

"Don't apologise, and thank you," the visitors replied almost in unison.

Meanwhile night had fallen and fires had been lit here and there around the camp. Beside one of them, somewhere out there in the dark, someone was singing a slow and sorrowful chant. Further off, two ragged dervishes were mumbling their prayers.

They walked on in silence. The chronicler thought how strange it was that men of such different kinds should all be serving the Padishah, brought together by war in this god-forsaken spot at the end of the world.

They could still hear chanting in the far distance, and could just about make out the refrain: "O Fate, O Fate . . ."

Dead calm. But the calm weighs heavily on us, as it always does in times that are pregnant with the unknown. Sometimes it seems to us that the army camped all around has nothing to do with us. You could easily imagine that our citadel and the Ottoman camp just happen to find themselves facing one another in the middle of the peneplain and that they will soon stop taunting each other. But we know it is too late already. Of the citadel and the army, one will be annihilated.

They are ready for the assault. From our position we can see them preparing their ladders, ropes, hooks, rams, pikes — in short, all the engines of war, from the most ancient to those that have been invented in the last three or four years.

Smoke rises day and night from their foundry. That is where they are casting the new weapon which is apparently going to be tried out on us for the first time. We told our men that a new device is never as terrible as feared, but it's clear they're shaken. At night our partisans send us messages of encouragement from beacons they light on the mountains. But in bad weather we can see neither the mountains nor the beacons, and we feel as if we are suspended over a black abyss.

Sometimes, when we are tired of spying on the camp, we keep our eyes fixed on the sky for hours on end. It seems that this prolonged concentration has induced barely credible visions in some among us. They insist they have seen the Good Fairy of Albania flitting through the clouds as well as other gods armed with spears and pitchforks or *else holding the scales of Fate in their hands. Others claim they have also seen the Bad Fairy.*

These hallucinations, no doubt caused by weariness and waiting, are perhaps distant reminiscences of the time when the Albanians, like all other peoples of the Balkan Peninsula, believed in a multiplicity of gods. Many of us are convinced that these divinities are not only gathered in the heavens above us, but will sway the outcome of battle, as they did in the past. They hope that the heavens which have been less clement to us, for who knows what reason, will look on us more kindly and take our side, as they did long ago. We shall hear the rumbling of the wheels of the celestial chariots and the rustling of their wings, so they say, and we no longer know whether the outcome of the fight and the fate of each of us will be fixed on this blackish earth or up on high, among the clouds.

CHAPTER THREE

The council met on Sunday afternoon. When the Pasha came into the pavilion, the functionaries were already present, seated in a semicircle on cushions laid against the sides of the tent. With sombre visage, without glancing at anyone, he strode to his seat.

The scribe dipped his quill in the inkpot and then held it in mid-air over the sheets of paper laid out before him. He shifted slightly to make himself more comfortable but as he did so, knocked his elbow, and a drop of black ink spilled on to the sheaf. He quickly wiped the blot with the cuff of his sleeve so no one would notice it, because a black spot could be interpreted as a bad omen intentionally put upon the paper by fate.

"I want your final views on the most auspicious moment for launching the assault. But before we make a decision on this matter, I want to tell you that, though I am touched by your shared concern for my personal safety," pointing to Aslanhan Begbey and the Mufti of the army, "I definitely reject your proposal to provide me with a decoy, or body double, as they are called these days."

He looked straight into the faces of the two men he had named, searching for the slightest trace of malice, but he was quickly persuaded that they had no ulterior motive and had come up with the idea of a double only because it was the fashion of the day.

The Pasha thought the two soldiers looked a little upset. I don't think they are really worried about keeping me alive, he thought. But despite that, he had no reason to be cross. He had been an officer himself, and he knew that soldiers are perfectly happy to have doubles of their commander whom they can allow themselves to despise and even to insult under their breaths without taking too great a risk. What they wouldn't think about was that by sneering at the commander-in-chief's stand-in they would acquire a habit of disrespect. When, one day, the real commander appeared before them, he might get unexpected reactions . . . if not worse, he thought. Any old time they could claim that Tursun Pasha was his other . . . that's to say, just a shadow . . . while his corpse, buried under two yards of earth . . .

The commander-in-chief massaged his forehead with the palm of his hand. He had slept badly, tossing and turning all night long, and now he had a migraine.

"Let's get back to the attack," he said sternly. "Speak!"

He did not like long meetings and made his distaste quite clear. He crossed his arms on his chest and waited. There was such silence that you could hear the scratching of the scribe's quill as he wrote down the Pasha's words.

Saruxha was the first to speak. Without any of the usual courtly preambles — council members were not accustomed to his informal manner — he declared:

"My cannon can be ready by tomorrow, but the mortars won't be there until Tuesday. That's the day when I'll be able to set off the cannonade. I'll need a full day to take down those walls."

"Next!"

It was the Mufti's turn. He had first consulted the astrologer on the position of the celestial bodies.

"Gazi Tursun Pasha!" he said with an obsequious bow of his head. "After listening to the dream-interpreter and the astrologer," he went on, waving at the latter, who was squatting in the corner looking scared, "I am of the opinion that the attack should be launched tomorrow."

"What an idiot!" the engineer muttered.

"Tomorrow, the position of the stars with respect to the moon will be particularly favourable," the Mufti went on. "Whereas on Tuesday, it will turn unfavourable. In addition, Allah granted me a dream last night. I saw a moonlit scene in which a crocodile attacked a black ox and ate its heart. The black ox must represent the fortress, and, as you know, tomorrow the moon is full."

"Dolt!" Saruxha muttered once again. The Quartermaster General had to tug on his sleeve.

"Next!" the Pasha said.

"I don't understand," the engineer butted in. "What does the Mufti really believe? That we'll bombard the citadel before we attack it, or afterwards?"

The Quartermaster almost tore the engineer's sleeve off.

The Mufti didn't even bother to reply. He and Saruxha exchanged frankly hostile stares. The Pasha's dark glance barely touched them before alighting on the Alaybey. He wanted his opinion as well. The Alaybey did not have a vote on the war council and his official position was subordinate to many of its formal members, but he was the Sultan's special envoy and for that reason feared by all. He guessed that the Pasha wanted the dispute quashed, and he made a skilful contribution to the debate.

"As for the bombardment, I think it should be less drawn out than Saruxha proposes. If our firepower has not breached the walls by the middle of the day, it will not do so in the afternoon. If the cannonade begins at first light, I think we should storm the citadel a few hours later, as soon as the guns have stopped firing, so as not to give the enemy time to recover from the terror that our new arm will have struck into its heart."

The Alaybey had skirted round the issue and not committed himself to any one of the positions being advanced. Tursun Pasha thought he had spoken sensibly, but at that moment what he wanted above all else was to settle the timing of the attack.

"Next!" he said.

"My janissaries are weary of waiting," Old Tavxha declared. "We must attack tomorrow!"

"Tomorrow!" Kurdisxhi echoed, in an extremely high-pitched voice.

The rush of blood to his face demonstrated his exasperation even more than his voice. He was unhappy that Tursun Pasha had still not allowed his *akinxhis* out of camp to sack the surrounding countryside. But the Pasha knew from experience that if they were allowed to pillage before the day of the assault, then the booty they would gather would bring the instinct of preservation to the fore and thus diminish their thirst for battle. He wanted the citadel to be not just a monster to be vanquished, but a prize that all would hanker after.

The Quartermaster General asked to speak.

He bowed low, and then, in carefully chosen words and with compliments to those who had spoken before him, he cleverly demolished all their arguments, save the engineer's. He deplored the fact that men did not behave in accordance with the signs that Allah gave them. They do not do this knowingly, but because heavenly messages are often beyond the capacity of our feeble minds, and unable to penetrate our blind eyes and deaf ears!

The Pasha noticed the flashes of hatred darting from the eyes of the Mufti towards the speaker. Kurdisxhi and Old Tavxha looked on wide-eyed as they concentrated on finding the treasonable flaw that might be hidden in such orotund words.

The Pasha realised that two opposing groups had now constituted themselves among his council. Hatred, scorn and irony were now being expressed almost openly by each group towards the other. He reckoned that the engineer and the Quartermaster General were thinking correctly, but for all the confidence he had in their intelligence, he was not sure of their hearts. As for the captains, it was the other way round, he trusted their courage more than their wisdom. But it was no use being convinced that the experts were right when he could not easily join their camp against the opinion of the Mufti and his two powerful captains. He was now waiting for the third military leader, Kara-Mukbil, and for the architect Giaour to speak out. It wasn't hard to guess which side they would take. The soldier would side with his comrades, and the architect would join the experts. The position was not going to change. He was going to have to take the decision himself, because he did not usually take any more account of the opinion of the sanxhakbeys than he did of the *eshkinxhi* commander, the deaf-mute Tahanka, who always looked as fierce as a man about to launch an assault, even one bound to lead to defeat. Since the Alaybey had got himself off the hook, the Pasha realised he would have to cut the knot himself.

The captain of the *azabs* asked to be allowed to speak. To the Pasha's astonishment, Kara-Mukbil gave his support to the engineer. He did not say much. He reckoned the citadel should not be stormed until it had suffered a major bombardment from every one of the available guns. That way many lives would be saved. In conclusion he recommended that the assault should not begin before the walls had been breached in several places to a significant width. His last words were:

"The greater the wounds in the wall, the lighter our men's injuries will be."

"Shame on you, Kara-Mukbil, for speaking thus!" Old Tavxha cried out in his deep-throated voice.

Kara-Mukbil went puce with anger. He was the youngest of the captains, and Tavxha's reproach cut him to the quick.

"And what should I be ashamed of?" he roared angrily. "You're in favour of attacking because you know my *azabs* will be the first in line. They will fall like flies, and your janissaries will walk over their dead bodies to take the castle."

Old Tavxha waved his short arm agitatedly.

Although he was not a resentful man, Kara-Mukbil's eyes flamed with anger. When he grasped that Tursun Pasha was not going to intervene, he raised the tone of his onslaught on Tavxha.

"You wouldn't say that if the order of battle was the reverse. If your janissaries made up the front line, I'm sure you'd think as I do, and not pretend to be indignant."

"The rules of war were established by the great Padishah," Tavxha replied curtly. "It is not for us to doubt them."

Kara-Mukbil said nothing.

If the architect were now to put forward a convincing reason for delaying the assault, the Pasha now thought, he would take the experts' side.

"Let us hear the architect!" he said.

Giaour began to speak, and not a muscle moved in his mask-like face. Anyone hearing him for the first time would be flabbergasted. He didn't have a speech defect or a stammer, but the words he uttered in his toneless voice issued from his lips like a string of icy, shiny beads.

"Cannon hit main junction point second tower and also right wall middle main door left wall first tower . . ."

He was pointing out the weaknesses in the citadel's construction, which were invisible to the untutored eye but which his studies had taught him to see as through a pane of glass. As he amputated the suffixes and prefixes from some of his words, moreover, his speech reminded the soldiers present, who had experience of great carnage, of the remains of mutilated bodies.

The architect came to the end of his contribution as abruptly as if he had cut it off with a knife. What emerged from the long string of his lifeless words was a single point: he did not support the view of his usual allies. Tursun Pasha was barely able to stifle a sigh. Everything was going the wrong way in his council of war. As he listened to the sanxhakbeys, who stuck to the "hard" line, as was to be expected, since they knew it was the only way of protecting themselves from any consequential mistake, the Pasha watched the Alaybey's face out of the corner of his eye. Clearly, even now that a divergence of views was manifest, the Alaybey had no intention of swaying the debate to one side or the other. The thought that this attitude might have been laid down for him by secret orders from above froze Tursun Pasha's heart. Yes, they must have suggested what attitude he should adopt, even if it hadn't been said in so many words: if there's a quarrel, don't take sides.

Fifteen hundred, maybe two thousand of his fighters' lives hung on the Alaybey's lips. May they also lie on your conscience! Tursun Pasha thought, and forthwith he uttered his decision.

"Tomorrow before first light the cannon will launch a barrage of fire at the fortress walls. We will storm the citadel in the afternoon, as soon as the heat of the day begins to slacken. Troops are to be forewarned tonight. Let the drums sound throughout the camp, let the *shehs* address the soldiers and may the spirit of battle be enhanced by all the usual means. Troops will be sent to rest at midnight."

He paused for a moment, and then concluded.

"I have spoken."

Everyone stood up, bowed to their commander, and filed out of the tent. The astrologer, who thought he was the principal cause of the dispute that had arisen, made himself scarce. He knew that even when they suffer temporary defeat the mighty are always more powerful than their subordinates, and it seemed to him more prudent to keep out of sight than to flaunt his pride in the fact that his own prediction had prevailed.

Night had fallen.

The astrologer wandered around the camp for quite a while without encountering any familiar figure. It was a huge camp, and there was little likelihood he would bump into anyone he knew just by chance. In addition, so many paths had been hastily laid out in identical fashion as to make finding the tent of a friend, even one you had been to before, quite a challenge. All the same he was bursting to meet someone to whom he could tell "the latest news from the pavilion". But as if on purpose, nobody came into sight. All the tents were the same. Only officers' tents were distinguished by little pennants stitched over the door indicating their inhabitants' rank. Even the faces that he made out by the light of torches lit inside the tents, whenever he put his head through the flap, seemed interchangeable.

He heard someone calling him. It was the poet Sadedin, who was coming towards him. The astrologer was delighted.

"Where are you going?" Sadedin asked.

"I was walking around in the hope of finding a friend. Where have you all been hiding?"

As the poet opened his mouth to reply the astrologer smelled a heavy odour of raki.

"So, have you heard?" Sadedin asked. "The attack is for tomorrow! At last! Thank goodness!"

The astrologer was dumbfounded.

"But how do *you* know?"

"Everyone knows. Are you out of the loop?"

"Me?" the astrologer said with a touch of pique. "I was the first to know! I was in the Pasha's tent when the decision was made. In fact, I actually knew it beforehand . . . from the stars!"

"Mm . . ." Sadedin replied.

"In the pavilion, things almost got out of hand . . ."

"I've got a gourd," the poet interrupted. "Come on, let's have a drink."

Coming from anyone else, such familiarity would have offended the astrologer. But he felt quite disarmed by Sadedin.

"People will see us."

"So what? It's party night."

The astrologer grabbed the gourd from the poet's hand, turned around so his face would not be seen by passers-by, and took a few swigs.

Somewhere in the distance a drum sounded. Then another.

"They've started the drumming. The news has got around," the astrologer observed.

"I told you so."

Now drumming could be heard in every quarter. Soldiers came out of their tents in groups. Great fires were being lit all over the camp.

"It's going to be a wild night!" the poet said.

They crossed the centre of the camp, then turned right at the point where the janissaries had laid out their tents. One of them walked past, stopped, turned around to follow them for a few paces, and then grabbed the poet by his sleeve.

The poet turned round, thinking he had been accosted by one of his friends, but before he could get over his surprise, the janissary hissed:

"Brother, spare me a drink, you've still got a drop left in the bottom."

The poet arched his eyebrows.

"How do you know I've got raki on me?"

"The smell of your breath, brother," the janissary replied. "But don't be afraid, a janissary never rats on anyone."

"You're an odd kind of janissary!" the poet exclaimed, and put his hand inside his tunic.

"Wait. Don't get it out until we can't be seen."

"What's your name?" the poet asked.

"Tuz Okçan!"

"That's a fine name, a real soldier's name!"

Once he had made sure no one could see them, the poet handed his gourd to the stranger.

Sadedin took a swig too, and passed it on to the astrologer. Then the three of them walked on through the growing tumult.

The moon appeared in a cleft between the mountains, like the yellowish face of a wild beast keeping watch on what was going on down on the valley floor. It spilled its cold light over thousands of white tents.

"Mevla Çelebi!" the poet suddenly cried out.

He had seen the chronicler from afar.

"Are you out for a walk?" the latter asked.

"Yes, we're having a stroll," Sadedin said. "May I introduce Tuz Okçan, a valiant young janissary whose acquaintance we have just made." Then he turned towards the soldier. "Mevla Çelebi, a scholar and historian by trade. As for me, I'm called Sadedin, I'm a poet, and my friend here is the army's astrologer. That's to say, he gets the stars to talk to him."

The janissary was aghast at finding himself in the company of such important people.

"Where did you find the raki?" Çelebi enquired.

"I've got my own," Sadedin said, putting his hand inside his tunic. "Here you are, have some yourself."

"Wait a moment," the chronicler said. "Let's get behind a corner."

"Well, I prefer to drink as I walk," Sadedin said.

Çelebi turned to the astrologer and asked, "Were you at the war council meeting?"

Delighted to be able to show off his inside information, the astrologer started whispering. The poet and the janissary walked on a little ahead of the pair.

Almost the entire plain was now bathed in moonlight. It shone down on turbaned hoxhas scuttling in all directions with Korans in their hands. The dervishes were getting ready for their dance.

The drums went on beating.

"Haven't you finished your tittle-tattle yet?" the poet asked as he turned round to face his two companions. "So, what do you say? Time for a drink?"

"Does he really talk to the stars?" the janissary asked with awe, nodding towards the astrologer.

"So it seems," Sadedin replied.

The janissary looked out of the corner of his eye at the three stars engraved on the brass plate the astrologer wore around his neck.

A little further on they stepped out of the main path once again and handed round the gourd. The raki made them merrier.

The poet had his arm around the janissary's shoulder and was calling him "my brother soldier" now. At the bonfire sites hoxhas were reciting suras from the Koran. Soldiers sat in an arc around them and listened. Further on, there were *shehs* and old soldiers making heated speeches in voices so impassioned that they almost drowned out the sound of the drums.

"Look at their flag at the top of the main tower," one of the *shehs* yelled, pointing to the fortress. "Look at it! You can almost see it shaking with fear!"

The soldiers turned their heads in the direction suggested. Although the emblem was very far away and looked quite pale in the moonlight, they really did think they could see it quivering. They had seen so many pennants waving in the wind these last weeks and months that they often saw flags in their dreams.

"Our flags tremble too," someone said in the ill-lit night.

The *sheh* glanced ferociously towards where the voice had come from.

"Indeed they do!" he thundered. "Our flags tremble with impatience as they wait for the start of combat, just as lions' manes quiver before the attack!"

They went on their way and the poet carried on muttering between his teeth. Apparently he was composing a verse. The janissary gaped at him. He'd never seen a poet before, and even less a poet in the process of composition.

"Have you ever seen any Albanian girls?" Sadedin suddenly asked the janissary.

"No, but I've heard speak about them."

"What extraordinary girls they are!" Sadedin said, striking his forehead with the flat of his hand. "I can tell you about them. I've seen them."

"So what are they like?" Tuz Okçan asked.

"Ah! I was forgetting you are a janissary. I pity you. The Sultan has granted you many privileges, but what good are they if the pleasure of women is forbidden to you?"

"That's true," Tuz Okçan sighed.

"Poor lad!" the poet sighed in turn.

"So what are they like?" the janissary asked once again.

The hubbub of the camp had grown ever louder, and now they had to shout to make themselves heard.

"Well, now," said Sadedin. "They are . . . They are . . . How can I describe them, brother? They are like clouds, and like milk . . . And on the surface of the milk you can see the clear black outline of a swallows' nest . . . When I found myself over one, I thought I would go mad . . . My hands trembled as I sought out the nest . . . And in that state, I came beforehand . . . I didn't manage anything. Janissary, you know what it means to drop your load before you've got to the door!"

"Will you buy one for yourself when we've taken the citadel?" the janissary asked.

"Sure I will. At any price. I've got money put aside." (He put his hand into his tunic.) "All I ever earned from my poems."

"You're a lucky man."

The poet reached for his gourd and put it to his lips.

"That's enough," the astrologer remonstrated. "You can't walk straight as it is."

Sadedin stuffed the gourd inside his tunic.

"It's going to be quite a night when we take the citadel! A real riot! Just wait to see the orgies we'll have! When the men have taken their pleasure they'll swap their captives. They'll keep them for an hour, then sell them on to buy others. The girls will go from tent to tent. There'll be brawls. Maybe even murders! Oh, we won't be short of fun!"

The janissary listened glumly.

They walked on further, along a path lined with *azabs* stretched out on the ground, in the even darker shadows thrown by the tents.

"These *azabs* are boring," Sadedin said. "I can guess what they're talking about as if I could hear them loud and clear."

"How do you know? I wouldn't have thought anybody could guess what goes through the mind of an *azab*."

"But I do know," Sadedin replied. "They dream of being granted a plot of land or a vineyard in the lands they conquer, then spending the rest of their days behind the plough."

"Everyone is free to dream," the astrologer said.

The poet was tempted to respond, but decided instead to have another swig of raki. He carried on mumbling as he made up his verses.

The crowds were getting thicker. Drums were being sounded in every quarter. Dervishes whirled and fell, prayed and screamed without respite.

"We shall teach the Sacred Koran to these accursed rebels," a *sheh* was proclaiming. "On their lands which are as humped as a demon's back, we shall raise minarets blessed by Allah! At dusk, from these high towers, the voices of our muezzins will fall on their untutored heads and take hold of their minds like hashish. We shall ensure that these infidels learn to bow towards Mecca five times a day. We shall wrap their sick and troubled skulls in the balmy turban of Islam."

"What a fine speaker he is," the astrologer commented.

"I want to recite a poem as well!" Sadedin declared, in a burst of passion. "I've got it in my head."

He began to mumble aloud a string of incomprehensible words:

Composing a poem would cause Okçan more pain
Than fighting his way through the Balkan campaign

It was hard to make any headway through the tightly packed crowds. Ragged dervishes belonging to different sects could be spotted all over the place. The Rufais had started their dance. Soldiers jostled to get a better view of them jumping up and down to the beat of the drum. It was a sinister, monotonous dance. They would squat on their heels, then rise up with a fast-paced, obsessive swaying movement, uttering loud screams that made your blood run cold. In a trance, their faces were pale and their eyes half-closed.

"It's quite a new dance," Sadedin explained to the janissary. "It's spreading all over. Do you like it?"

"Yes, I do rather like it," the janissary replied. "It gets you all excited."

The poet took another mouthful of raki and resumed his mumbling.

They next came across a group of collectors squabbling over their business as if they were at a souk. In recent years collectors had started devoting themselves to a whole variety of objects, and, according to their speciality, they hunted for teeth, fingers, locks of hair, ears, nails and eyelashes. After a battle, they would throw themselves on the corpses of slain enemies and fill whole sacks with the items they were after and then cart them off to the cities to sell. The most sought-after objects were human ears.

They usually spent the night before a battle talking business, doing sums, and trying to forecast rising and falling prices and trends in the tastes of wealthy collectors. As they were obliged to spend long periods away from their markets in the cities, they were not always up to date on the latest fashions.

"Do you feel like a drink?" Sadedin asked the janissary.

Tuz Okçan said nothing, but took the gourd the poet held out to him, and had several swigs. All around them was turmoil, and no one noticed what they were doing.

"Where are we going?" the chronicler asked.

"Where our feet take us," the poet answered. "Wherever."

"Hand me the gourd."

The poet took it out of his tunic once more. It was almost empty now.

"You've got a very lovely name," he said to the janissary, moving closer to him to speak into his ear. "I'm jealous of it! Tuz Okçan! I'm fed up with my name. Everybody calls me Nightingale Sadedin, but I . . ."

The janissary was dumbfounded.

"When this war is over, I'm going to change my name. Do you know what I would like to be called? Sarperkan Tol-Keleç Olgunsoy! Do you like it?"

"*Sarperkan*, bitter blood. Yes, I think it's beautiful."

A crowd had assembled somewhere on their left.

"There's a fight," the astrologer said. "Let's take a look."

They moved towards the knot of men.

"What's going on?" Sadedin asked a janissary.

The soldier shrugged his shoulders. Seeing their unusual attire, the men let them through. Two soldiers of death were squabbling with a small group of *akinxhis*.

"Soldiers of death?" Tuz Okçan said. "Where are they?"

"It's those two over there," an *azab* said. "They nearly did each other in with knives."

At the janissary college, Tuz Okçan had often heard about the famous corps of the *serden geçti*. Their rule was never to return from an assault except as the victors. It was the first time he had seen any.

"They are the most glorious corps of the entire army, even more glorious than the *dalkiliç*."

"I think they're pretentious," the astrologer said.

"That's because of the privileges they are rightfully granted as soldiers of death," Sadedin said.

"Do they really have a rule that prevents them ever coming back from a defeat?" Tuz Okçan asked.

"They do," Sadedin replied curtly. "If they return in defeat, then they are murdered by their own comrades . . . I was once present at such a bloodbath. May I never see anything like it again!"

"We'd do better to move on," Mevla Çelebi butted in. "The fight could flare up again."

Voices among the crowd cried out: "*Chaouch-bashi! Chaouch-bashi!*"

The chef-de-camp rode up with a squad of military police in his wake.

"They'll put them in irons," a sapper said.

Sadedin turned round abruptly.

"Who's the donkey who said you can arrest a *serden geçti?*"

"I am," the sapper said.

"So clod-hoppers are allowed to have an opinion, are they?"

"I'd rather dig holes than lose my balls," the sapper shouted back, apparently taking their strange dress to mean they were eunuchs.

Men laughed in the half-light.

"Come and find out if I've got any, you cow-pat."

Mevla Çelebi began to pull at Sadedin's sleeve.

"Come on, you're not going to get into a fight with a peasant."

"Quite right, let's get out of here," the astrologer said.

From further off came again the sound of horses' hooves, and an order: "Shut your filthy mouth!"

Apparently the fighting had flared up again.

"They're taking a real hiding!" someone shouted out. "They're being fried alive!"

"Let's move on," the astrologer repeated.

They left without looking round.

The full moon had now risen high in the sky and dimmed the brilliance of the bonfires. The whole camp was humming and brimming over with life. Soldiers bumped into each other as they walked this way and that. Some had grown tired of listening to the hoxhas' prayers and were watching the dervishes dance, while others, having had enough of the show, had gone to listen to a pep-talk by a *sheh*. Sadedin stopped in front of a knot of men and then, all of a sudden, with shaking hands and eyes burning like coals, he began to declaim, or rather to bawl, his poem.

"Did you like it?" he asked his comrades as soon as he had finished.

"A lot," the janissary replied. "It warms your blood."

"That's exactly what I am after," Sadedin said. "I want to inflame our soldiers." He emptied the gourd. "On the one hand, there are poets who lisp tearful doggerel about pretty birds and paradise. On the other hand, I am a poet who seeks only to serve the great Padishah. My heaven is the hell of war!"

They weren't sure where they were any more. The camp area they had reached was occupied by a sizeable unit whose men spoke a language they could not understand.

"Caucasian troops," Çelebi whispered.

"What was that? Louder!" Sadedin shouted.

"Let's go back," the astrologer suggested. "We've gone quite far enough as it is."

They turned about and retraced their steps, making their way through the crowds with difficulty. Around the great campfires

veterans were telling young recruits about past wars and tales of
derring-do.

In the shadow of a large tent, set back from the milling throng,
they saw some men lying on the ground. They had propped their
heads on short-handled axes and were singing the same sorrowful
chant that they had heard once before. Apparently it was a recent
composition, originating in the marches of the Empire, which is
where the saddest dirges usually came from. The astrologer turned
towards the source of the singing, but the soldiers' faces could not
be made out in the dark. The beating of the drums and the thousand other noises of the camp also prevented him making out the
words. But as he moved off, he did catch a line:

"O Fate, O Fate, O cursed Fate . . ."

They wandered for a long while among the noisy crowds,
speaking barely a word, which they could hardly hear above the
tumult.

"Listen! I think that's a priest talking about the local women!"
the janissary said, drawing the poet closer to him. They slowed
their pace. It was true. A *sheh* was thundering on about Albanian
women. It was the same man they had heard a little earlier speaking
about flags.

"We shall strip their wives and daughters of their shameless
white garments and dress them in the noble black mantle blessed
by our faith. We shall cover their faces with a veil and stop their
sly eyes from casting licentious glances at men while offering themselves just as scabrously to their sight."

Tuz Okçan still had in his mind Sadedin's words about these
women's bellies. He had never before felt such burning desire.
Apparently, approaching battle heightened the desire for sensual
pleasure like nothing else.

"The most bewitching, the most lascivious parts of a woman," the *sheh* bawled on hoarsely, "are the eyes, alongside hair. The unveiled eyes of a woman are more entrancing than her naked body . . ."

Tuz Okçan suddenly felt like bursting into tears, for no reason he could fathom. He had never heard so many obscenities in his life. But nothing had stirred him up more than Sadedin's words.

". . . By tearing them from their barbaric customs and endowing them with our own grandiose costumes, we shall turn their souls away from the evil path, in whose wake their bodies will follow . . ."

The janissary was overcome once again with a need for tears. He almost leaned on Sadedin's arm and asked him: "So what will come of the swallows' nest?" The image of curly pubic hair was sucking up his whole mind like a whirlwind.

"Won't make a bit of difference," Sadedin said, putting his lips to the janissary's ear.

"What?"

"Changing customs . . . Bit by bit, with the passing years, their traditions will wilt and fall like apple blossom. They'll get used to our ways. So used to them, in fact, that if, God forbid, we ever had to leave these lands, they would find it very hard to re-adjust."

The poet continued to soliloquise for a long while. He had a fine deep voice, but the general racket and the noise of the drums made it hard for Tuz Okçan to grasp all that he said. The faces of the dervishes darkened and brightened in alternation. Fascinated soldiers stood round them in circles, clapping in time with the drums and screaming in unison with the dancers.

A number of the dervishes fell to the ground. Only some pulled themselves up to a squatting position, panting for lack of breath; the others stayed flat on the ground, as if in a cataleptic fit. Soldiers dripping with sweat started sobbing. Other men ran round and round.

"What a marvellous night!" Sadedin exclaimed, as if he had been blinded by it. He lifted his gourd to his lips for the last time, and then threw it at the feet of the crowd.

What we were given to witness on the eve of the attack was more horrible than any battle, worse than any carnage. When we heard their drums roll at dusk, we first thought that, contrary to all known principles of modern war, they were perhaps about to launch a night raid. But we soon saw that what they were trying to do, once they had got their equipment ready for the assault, was to raise their soldiers' morale.

At the first beats of their drums, the sight that greeted our eyes was unbearable. Such madness we had never imagined — neither in the orgies of ancient times, whose memory has come down to us through the generations, nor in the wildest carnival nights in our own villages. Shouting, screaming, praying and dancing, men offered themselves up for sacrifice, made exhibitions of themselves in which, as we were to learn later on, severed heads carried on talking as if still in delirium; soldiers wailed as if they were night owls and banged their drums dementedly. All those noises wafted up to our castle like stinking vapours.

The light of the moon seemed to trouble and excite them at the same time. What we saw spread out beneath us was Asia in all its mysticism and barbarity, a dark grave getting ready to swallow us all.

A putrid wind was blowing up from the plain. Despite going to pray before the icon of the Virgin, our hearts sank. The cross that rises above our chapel seemed very pale, as if it had gone white with fear. But these feelings did not weaken in the slightest our determination to fight to the end. On the contrary, never before had we felt so convinced that death would be far sweeter than the gloom and treachery laid out down below in plain sight.

Our low spirits had another cause as well. There were so many of them! As many as the pebbles on a beach. And they were trying to extend their empire so the sun would never set on it, that's to say, so that night and day would be perpetually and simultaneously contained within its boundaries. They believed that when they had achieved that objective (when they had "tied the yellow tigress and the black wolf to the same chain"), they would also rule over time itself.

That would really be the end of the world. The day God forbade, as people say in our land.

Towards midnight the hullabaloo stopped, and a deathly silence reigned.

Dawn had not quite risen when the East Tower raised the alarm. The sentinels had noticed the gleam of torches and suspicious movements around the cannon. Our men followed instructions and left their posts to gather in the underground shelters. There we prayed with great fervour to Christ and Our Lady right up to the moment when a mortal thunder seemed to shatter heaven and earth alike. Thereupon, an infernal explosion made the ground shake beneath us. Someone yelled: "The new weapon!" Then we heard screams, then the sound of men running who knows where.

The war had begun.

CHAPTER FOUR

Giaour the architect was pointing his finger at a particular spot on the great plan of the citadel he had laid out on his lap.

"Must strike again wall left side main door hope big breach that side."

The Pasha turned towards his aide-de-camp with a gesture of irritation. The architect's way of speaking, which gave him a migraine even in normal times, had become quite unbearable in the noise of cannon fire.

"What he's saying is that we need to shake the wall to the left of the main gate some more," the aide-de-camp translated in a low voice. "He hopes a few more direct hits will open a large breach at that point."

"Bring the engineer back," the Pasha ordered.

One of his orderlies galloped off.

The Pasha stared sullenly at the castle walls. In many places the parapet had been shattered. There were large cracks in the walls too, but he was not satisfied with them. He had expected more from those cannon. For the tenth time he took the chart from the architect's hands and pored over the spots marked in red ink. The cannon-balls had in fact come very near to hitting the targets directly. After each explosion the Pasha raised his eyes towards the wall that had been hit in the hope of seeing a gaping hole, which never materialised. It was past noon. The assault should begin in a couple of hours.

He handed the chart back to the architect with a gesture signifying that there was nothing more to say. The suspicion that the architect might have miscalculated merged instantly with the thought that he was maybe in the pay of the *giaours*, a thought prompted, without any real reason, by the man's very name. He had in fact already been arrested three times just because of his name, but it seems he was cleared of all charges as unceremoniously as he had been accused, the only difference for him now being that the elaborately constructed imputations of guilt had taken root and become difficult to pull out entirely. Not only had he been declared innocent three times in a row, but after each release from prison his personal standing had risen even higher.

Several members of the war council were standing behind the Pasha and the architect. They said nothing and merely looked in the same direction as their leader.

The engineer came in with his assistant, swearing under his breath. As he came close, everyone noticed that the fringe of his hair was singed. His assistant had a blackish patch between his eyebrows.

"Engineer!" Tursun Pasha said without even turning towards the man. "Where are the breaches we have been waiting for all day?"

"They're over there!" Saruxha said, waving his arm towards the citadel's walls.

The Quartermaster, standing behind the commander along

with the sanxhakbeys, bit his lip. The Pasha turned his bony face around abruptly.

"I don't see them."

Saruxha wiped his brow.

"I fired according to instructions," he said tartly. "My guns hit the designated spots. We've not shut our eyes for four days and four nights. I don't know what more you expect of me, sire."

The Pasha looked carefully for a moment at the worn-out faces of the master caster and his number two. He noticed the burned hair on Saruxha's forehead.

"I expect breaches," he said in a slightly more accommodating tone.

"You expect them to come from me alone, Pasha. But ask him for them as well," he replied, pointing to the architect.

Giaour was looking on with complete indifference, as if none of this concerned him at all.

"Must fire again wall left door . . ." he rattled on in his un-wavering voice.

"That's enough," the Pasha said. "Sort it out between your-selves. I need the walls breached."

The Quartermaster took a step forwards.

"Pasha, sire," he said in a honeyed tone, spying from the corner of his eye the slight quivering of the map that the commander-in-chief had between his fingers, "do not forget that huge breaches were made today by our cannon — in the hearts of those miserable rebels."

The Pasha sighed deeply. For maybe the hundredth time, his weary eyes scanned the vast plain where his innumerable soldiers were taking up their positions for the assault. Messengers on horse-back were darting all over the camp. Here and there the throng made way for rolls of thick rope, ladders, crowbars, defensive screens called testudos, sections of reed fencing, and battering rams. Kara-Mukbil rode up on horseback, passed a message to the Pasha, and rode off again at high speed. Saruxha and his assistant conferred with the architect for a few minutes and then moved off in their turn.

"Why can't we hear gun number two any more?" the Pasha asked without turning round.

Everyone shrugged. An orderly, standing at the ready, promptly galloped off towards the battery.

Clouds of dust hung over the walls. Not a soul could be seen behind the parapets. According to one of the doctors who specialised in nervous disorders, such a mind-numbing bombardment should have left the defenders suffering from the equivalent of a brain injury. With every blast of the cannon the Pasha hoped to see the white flag of surrender rise through the dust cloud. It was only a faint hope, but he clung to it nonetheless.

The orderly who had gone off to get news from the cannon came back.

"Gun number two missed its target three times in a row. The gunners are trying to find out why," he said without dismounting.

"The gun must have been possessed by the demon!" the Mufti declared, drawing closer to the Pasha's shoulder.

By age-old military tradition, that meant that the cannon would have to be fustigated. The Pasha didn't approve of the practice, but that did not stop him giving the order to apply the appropriate punishment.

The orderly set off once again to deliver the order.

Little time remained before the appointed hour for the storming of the citadel. Without a word to anyone, the Pasha went into his tent to have a short rest.

The Quartermaster General took the opportunity to leave the

sanxhakbeys and to go over to the artillery. After only a few steps he came across Çelebi standing at his usual position near the Pasha's tent, hoping to pick up a detail or two for his chronicle.

"Mevla, let's go and see what's up," he said.

The chronicler was only too happy to fall in behind. The Quartermaster General was worried about his friend Saruxha. He was sure the engineer would rebel against the Pasha's order, and he had to go and calm him down before it was too late.

"Today is my day off," the Quartermaster General said. "I was planning to watch the fight. I guess you were, too. It's your big day, after all. What you would rightly call a 'historic occasion'!"

The chronicler didn't know what to say so he just kept a smile on his face as long as he could. He was aware that when he kept his lips in a fixed position his expression turned into a gloomy scowl, but he couldn't help that.

When they reached the small enclosure watched over by sentries, they found that the gun's fustigation had already begun. Two bare-chested, Herculean Blacks were lashing the still-smoking barrel. Beneath the gun carriage, among the struts and props, lay Saruxha's assistant, banging away with a hammer, trying to loosen a moving part that seemed to have jammed. The master caster stood a few feet away, muttering curses.

"Can you see what they're doing?" he shouted out as he pointed to the gun. "It drives me mad. And don't forget to put this piece of unspeakable stupidity in your chronicle!" he added, to Çelebi.

"Calm down," the Quartermaster General said. "These things happen."

Saruxha started laughing like a hysteric.

"One of these days these ignoramuses will drive me crazy," he groaned, putting his hand to his forehead. Then, mumbling to himself: "Mother of mine, what have I got myself into? Woe is me! What am I going to do with these manifolds?"

The Quartermaster General looked at the engineer with friendly concern, and put his hand on the man's shoulder.

"Keep calm!" he said once more. Then he added: "Let's move away from here. It's getting dangerous."

They took a few steps away from the artillery. Looking over the fence that protected the forbidden zone, the chronicler noticed two young soldiers from the volunteer units lying on the grass. They were looking hard at the cannon, and as they talked they drew signs on the ground with a sharp stone. One of them was a redhead.

"They're curious lads," Saruxha said, seeing the Quartermaster General taking an interest in them. "They come almost every day and just sit there on the other side of the fence, staring at the cannon. Maybe they're dreaming of casting cannon themselves one day."

"When did you singe your hair?" the Quartermaster General asked.

"The first time we fired," the engineer answered, mechanically raising his hand to his scorched forehead. "I didn't get out the way in time."

"Be careful!"

At that instant, the largest gun fired again. The ground shook beneath them. The Quartermaster General and the chronicler held their hands to their ears. Saruxha's eyes gleamed with pride.

"It makes heaven and earth tremble!" he said.

"Yes," the Quartermaster General said slowly. "You've done something great, Saruxha. Your name will be remembered."

"For good or for bad?" the engineer asked with a touch of irony.

The Quartermaster General smiled.

"Does it matter? In this world nothing is either good or bad for all men."

Saruxha's assistant and the head gun-layer came over towards them.

"The cannon's been mended," the latter called out from a distance.

"Then fire it!" Saruxha commanded.

The assistant turned on his heels and moved off slowly on his long and scrawny legs.

"He's unusually bright," Saruxha said wearily. "There are some things he's even better at than I am. One day he'll be a great inventor, I'm sure of that."

"Saruxha, you've got a generous soul," the Quartermaster General said. "You're devoid of the poison of jealousy. In any case, the weapons that today appear to tear the sky in two are your work."

The gun roared. They blocked their ears once more. The master caster followed the trajectory of the cannon-ball and saw it crash into the citadel's wall, to the left of the main gate, where it made plumes of stone and dust spew up into the air.

"How do you think you'll describe that noise?" he asked Çelebi, who was stuck for an answer.

"Well, that's just what I was wondering. I'd like to represent the noise as accurately as possible, but words are powerless to describe such a terrible din."

The caster smiled.

"Of course they are," he said. "Cannon don't have much connection to poetry."

Suddenly the great drum could be heard. The storming of the castle was about to start.

"We'll leave you now," the Quartermaster General said. "You must have lots to do."

"The really dangerous work begins now," the master caster explained. "We have to rely on mortar fire only from now on. Their projectiles have to go over the parapet. If they fall short they will land on our own men."

"Farewell, Saruxha!"

"Farewell!"

They walked off at a smart pace.

"Come," the Quartermaster General said to Çelebi, "let's watch the assault from the command tent."

"I don't dare go near it."

"Stay by me, nobody will object."

The great drum went on thudding. As the cannon had stopped firing, the solitary drum-roll felt grave and overpowering. It moved ever further off as if aiming to envelop every soldier in the whole army. Near the pavilion, they saw the Pasha's white horse and alongside it the orderlies carrying his arms. The members of the war council who were not due to take part in the attack stood in line behind the horse. Among them were the Alaybey and Kurdisxhi. Further off stood a large group of junior officers and mounted heralds waiting for their orders. The Pasha was gazing at the top of the ramparts. There was nobody to be seen up there. He turned his head and looked at the sun, which had barely begun to go down from its zenith.

"Pasha, sire," an oily voice said from behind him. "Now is the time."

Tursun Pasha raised his right hand. The Mufti emerged from the group and stepped forwards. In his hand he held a gold-tooled Koran. He mumbled "*Bismillah!*", opened the book, and inclined his head towards the holy scripture. He stayed still in that position for a moment, then looked up, and all could see joy beaming from his eyes.

"Thanks be to Allah! I have just fallen upon the following passage: 'Victory is with the soldiers of Islam.'"

"Spread the good word," the commander-in-chief said in an icy tone.

Messengers raced off in all directions.

The great drum came to a halt. Silence reigned, as if the entire world had suddenly fallen into a deep sleep.

The Pasha raised his arm once more. The large ruby on his ring finger glinted in the sunlight. Someone was whispering something behind his back. Then the rustling of a silk flag being unfurled could be heard, and all of a sudden, the air filled with the hubbub of hundreds of kettle and hand drums banging, bagpipes wailing, horns and trumpets blaring, with calls to Allah and to the Padishah, with shouts of encouragement and bawled commands. The irregulars began to move, waving their lances and their standards in the wind. Behind them came the archers, whose job was to harass defenders on the tops of the walls during the attack. Then the unending column of the *azabs* set off, with their axes and shields gleaming in the sunlight. Ropes, ladders, shields, screens, pitchforks, stakes and instruments of every kind with names drawn from goats and scorpions, and some with no name at all, swam like flotsam over the turbid ocean of soldiers.

The *eshkinxhi* divisions were slow to start, and took up positions vacated by the *azabs* while waiting to attack. The sun glinted on the quivers they wore on their backs. The grave and imposing divisions of the janissaries were further off and had not yet started to move. Now the volunteers were getting near to the ditch before the main gate. For his part, the Pasha carried on staring hard at the parapet, where there was no sign of life. He was still hoping that the defenders would not appear behind the slits, but he knew it was a crazy idea. The volunteers had now got as far as the moat. The first men who rushed over filled it with a living torrent. They were sucked into it as by a whirlwind. From the distance it looked like a nightmare vision. Suddenly the Pasha imagined they were moving more slowly, too slowly in his view, and that silence had suddenly overcome them. They must now be climbing up the opposite bank. But they were advancing at a snail's pace. He still couldn't see them coming up and out on to the other side. But there's the first man up, then the second. Suddenly the Pasha thought he could hear a noise like the distant rustling of leaves in the breeze. It came from his archers, who had just let off the first volley aimed at the parapet. They had seen the defenders before he had. He closed his eyes and kept them shut for a minute. His head was throbbing and making him dizzy. When he opened his eyes, the volunteers who had climbed up out of the moat were now running towards the wall. At that moment, all four mortars fired and their cannon-balls fell somewhere over the other side of the wall. The cry of "Charge! Charge!" rose up from a thousand throats, and the great river of *azabs* dashed forwards. For a moment the ditch disappeared under the flood of soldiers. Then the men poured out of it and with their shields held before them raced for the wall. Many of them headed towards the main gate, and others went for the breaches that had been opened on the left of it. The mortars roared anew. Drums, big and small, and trumpets combined to make an ear-splitting racket. Where the ditch must have been, ladders could be seen waving in the air, resting on the attackers' shoulders. The first ladder was laid against the wall. It was a short one. Then came a gigantic ladder, which rose up slowly, and, as if bemused by the crowd of assailants, stopped in mid-air, plumb vertical, before gently resting itself against the wall. Struggling clumsily to get the ladder in the right position, the *azabs* put it off balance and it slid sideways, slowly at first, then fell on top of the swarming troops at the foot of the wall. Now more ladders had been laid by the sides of the various breaches. The giant ladder rose up once more like the long thin neck of a legendary beast and came to rest against the wall again. Hundreds of archers ceaselessly emptied quivers of arrows on to the spot where the ladder's top rung rested. A horde of *azabs* began to climb up it. Some fell, but most kept on going. A second long ladder was raised twenty paces further along, and two others could be seen being carried by a group of men. The first attackers had now reached the top of the citadel's outer wall. Thousands of arrows spilled over their heads to protect them from the besieged. The first man grabbed the edge of the parapet. He hauled himself up on to it, then stayed still, clutching the stone to his breast, as if he had suddenly dropped off to sleep.

"They've cut off his hands," the Quartermaster General murmured as he watched the body swoop down to the bottom again.

The second man was bent double and didn't even get to stretch out his arm. The soldier behind him clambered over his dead body with the skill of a cat and jumped over the parapet to the other side.

A Turkish fighter had at last set foot inside the fortress. Tursun Pasha closed his eyes. Don't retreat, my soldier! he implored silently.

When he opened his eyes two more fighters were on the parapet. One withdrew, and the other was thrown down, knocking another soldier off the ladder in his fall. The archers had stopped shooting now, for fear of hitting their own men. Taking advantage of the situation, dozens of defenders suddenly reappeared.

Tursun Pasha thought their lances were longer than ordinary ones. In any other circumstance he would have asked what this new weapon was and where it had been forged, but his curiosity was instantly dissipated.

"At the double, send in the *eshkinxhis*!" he shouted.

He watched the hindquarters of the horse bearing the herald who sped off to deliver the command.

The cheers of the *eshkinxhis* reached him in successive waves from somewhere near the right tower. At first he thought he could make out Tahanka's voice screaming above the others, but he soon realised it was only a buzzing in his own ears.

There were now dozens of ladders set against the wall, bearing more or less dense bunches of men. On some of them the bodies of the dead still hung on in strange poses.

"Look at those hanging corpses," the Quartermaster General said to the chronicler. "The carpenters did a hasty job, and left lots of nails sticking out."

Çelebi listened in amazement.

The forward thrust of the attackers grew more violent around the right tower. The bat-wing symbol on the crown of their helmets seemed to help them climb up. One ladder that was alive with soldiers swung back and fell into the void, but another one was put up straight away in its place.

"People who have heard Tahanka roar in battle say there is nothing more terrifying," the Quartermaster added.

"Ah! The demons!" someone from among the Pasha's silent retinue cried out.

At that moment several bright lights flashed on the ramparts, shot out like comets, and then fell, one by one, on to the attackers.

"Fire-bombing demons!" someone muttered. Now there was a phrase that would embellish his chronicle, Çelebi thought. He said it over to himself again: fire-bombing demons. He mustn't forget it.

The crowd at the foot of the wall swayed like a stormy sea each time one of these comets shot out from behind the parapet.

"They're balls of rags soaked in a mixture of resin, sulphur, wax and oil," the Quartermaster General explained to the chronicler. "They make burns that never heal up entirely."

The chronicler knew that, just as he knew many other things he pretended not to know, so as not to deprive his distinguished friend of the pleasure of explaining them to him.

"Never ever heal," he repeated with a deep frown.

The Quartermaster General pulled up his wide sleeve to show his bare left forearm. Çelebi could barely mask a grimace.

Some of the ladders now seemed deserted. Attackers carried on storming up the others, holding their shields over their heads for protection. Down below, men ran to take shelter beneath the testudos while waiting their turn to go to the wall. Some fighting had broken out on the top of the rampart. Two of the long ladders had caught fire in several places. Another one split in two down the middle. But the number of ladders increased by the minute.

A herald galloped up.

"Burxhuba has been killed!" he yelled from a distance.

Nobody said anything.

Cannon-balls fired by the mortars constantly whistled over the defenders' heads. They were still falling inside the citadel, but the fateful moment was not far off when they would start to fall on the wall itself.

"If Saruxha manages a direct strike on the parapet, then he's a genius," the Quartermaster General said. "But he's being cautious, and quite right too. Just a few paces off target, and our own men will be pulp."

A cannon-ball then hit the parapet dead on. The bunch of defenders preparing to repel a new wave of attackers was annihilated. Dismembered body parts rained down together with lumps of masonry.

"Bravo!" someone standing behind the Pasha cried out.

The almost entirely demolished parapet at the spot where the mortar had struck stayed empty for a moment or two. The *azabs* rushed into the breach and were quickly in command of the rampart walk. One of them unfurled a standard. Cheers rose from all around, in a deep-throated clamour. The flag fluttered for a moment, but then something happened: long black lances emerged from all around the men, a struggle ensued, and then the flag disappeared as if it had been whisked away by a gust of wind.

Meanwhile, to the left of the main gate, a horde of attackers thrust forwards towards the great breach. Some climbed along on wide ladders, others were moving screens towards the places where molten pitch and fireballs were hitting the ground. Many *azabs* had caught fire and were running away with their arms flailing, looking like giant torches. Some of them rolled themselves on the ground to put out the flames that were consuming them. Others pranced about like lunatics among the throng which parted in terror to leave them passage, then crawled along the ground, got up, fell again, and finally groaned until their last breath. Smoke still rose from the dead as if their souls were not finding it easy to quit the body.

Çelebi had been wondering for a while about how to find an image that would properly translate the sight of these burning men. He thought of comparing them to moths fluttering round a cresset, but the word "moth" hardly seemed adequate to suggest the ardour and heroism of these fighters. However nothing else occurred to him, and, in addition, if he likened the fires of a holy war to the candle of Islam, as he had read in ancient chronicles, then the word "moth" might do in the end. He could call these soldiers "the moths of the Sacred Candle".

Suddenly the earth shook and a terrific clap of thunder cut off the train of his thoughts. The Pasha and his retinue turned towards where the noise had come from. Something had happened somewhere near the artillery. A great column of black smoke rose into the sky in that quarter. An officer rushed off at a gallop.

Everyone behind the Pasha started asking questions in muffled tones.

A few moments later the officer came back.

"One of the mortars has exploded," he reported. "Many men killed, and many others wounded."

"And the master caster?" the Pasha asked.

"He is unharmed."

The Pasha turned back towards the citadel and nobody dared say another word.

He ordered fresh troops to move up to the assault. As he watched the Persian and Caucasian regiments dashing towards the walls to relieve the *azabs* and the *eshkinxhis* (as for the volunteers, they were for the most part no such thing), the commander-in-chief thought to himself that it was still too soon to send in the elite units of the *dalkiliç*, which he usually threw into battle after the janissaries.

The assault was now in progress along the entire length of the citadel's surrounding wall. There were hundreds of ladders large and small reaching up to the parapets or to the edges of the breaches opened in the masonry. They sucked up a proportion of the flood of soldiers swirling at their feet and raised them to the top of the wall. And as soon as those scorched and bloodied men clambered over the parapet or through the breach, they threw away their shields so as to brandish their adzes and swords. The shields, dripping with pitch and molten wax, fell on top of the soldiers following behind, and they screamed as they tried to avoid being hit by the falling objects.

"They've not stopped climbing," the Quartermaster General said pensively. His tone seemed to say: they are climbing, but what's the use? "It seems to me we are fighting a losing battle," he added in a dull voice.

"A losing battle," the chronicler repeated to himself. The words were so terrible as to stick in your throat.

The *eshkinxhis* pressed on obstinately up the escarpment. Many fell from their ladders into the void, but that didn't stop others from returning to the attack. Their red turbans looked as if they had been bloodstained in advance.

The strongest thrust was still being played out at the main gate. The assailants had massed around it, and in the midst of that awful swarm there arose, incomprehensibly, a kind of wooden hut. The *azabs* threw wetted goatskins on top of it to stop it catching fire. Men rushed under it and used a great iron battering ram to try to knock a hole in the gate, while sappers and *müslümans* attempted to smash the hinges with huge metal bars.

Another messenger, black with dust, came back from the battle zone.

"Begbey Bozkurtoglu is dead!" he shouted.

No one uttered any comment, but everyone's face froze on hearing the word "dead" used by the messenger instead of "killed". Apparently he was a Kalmyk who had had trouble learning Turkish properly.

"Wait!" Tursun Pasha called out when the courier had already turned his horse around to ride off. "Repeat what you just said."

"Begbey Bozkurtoglu is dead," the messenger yelled out as loud as he could. "Died of a fit . . ." he added after a pause.

"A heart attack," the Quartermaster General murmured. "May his soul rest in peace."

The three remaining mortars were now firing uninterruptedly and their cannon-balls were still falling inside the citadel, but the screams of the wounded and burned were so loud that they could be heard from the observation platform. The sun had begun to go down. The Pasha could not take his eyes off the huge shapeless mass of his army, writhing and palpitating around the citadel like a living, warm-blooded and bleeding beast. The smell of burned flesh was awful.

A horseman came riding towards them at a gallop. The Pasha recognised the rider at a hundred paces. It was Kara-Mukbil. He held the reins in one hand, for the other was holding his blood-soaked jaw.

"My *azabs* are being wiped out," he shouted without dismounting. "Where are the janissaries?" His voice was rough and harsh.

Tursun Pasha looked at him severely and waved his arm towards the ramparts.

"Your place is over there, Kara-Mukbil," he said.

Kara-Mukbil was on the point of answering back, but instead pulled in the reins, put one hand back to his jaw, made his horse circle in a fit of rage, and raced off, with his orderly following, towards the place he had come from.

The Pasha waved his hand. An aide-de-camp came up to him.

"Send in the janissaries," he said without moving his head.

A few moments later the elite units began to move, slowly at first, then at ever-greater speed, towards the great wall. Their hurrahs rang out. As they drew near to the ditch, they began to run, brandishing lances and all their weaponry.

The racket of tambourines and kettle-drums rose to a peak. The janissaries crossed the ditch that was now half-choked with the corpses of *azabs* and volunteers. Like an avalanche of steel splitting in two, half of them rushed towards the battlements, and the other half threw themselves at the main gate. Their appeals to Allah and to the Padishah drowned the hubbub for a moment. They did not stop at the foot of the wall, they broke through the mass of *azabs*, braved the arrows and flaming resin raining down in a shower of sparks on to their helmets and shoulders, and leaped on to the soot-blackened, pitch-stained and now broken-toothed ladders. All who were watching from afar were anxious to see what would happen when the janissaries finally reached the parapet. More defenders suddenly appeared in the arrow slits when the first janissaries sprang over the top like wild cats. Behind them came an uninterrupted line of their comrades. A few ladders had caught fire. The attackers hastened up the rungs to get to the top before the ladder crumbled in flames. *Azabs* rushed to replace the charred ladders and knots of janissaries quickly sprang on to the new ones. Other soldiers pulled burning bodies off the roof of the shelter set up in front of the main gate. Despite being protected by wetted animal skins, it had caught fire several times, but the *azabs* had managed to extinguish it each time. From all around rose the cry: "The gate! The gate!" With streaks of pitch forming drips like black tears on it, the sombre, almost ghostly main door still held out against an ogre that it seemed no force in the world should be able to resist. The bludgeons falling on its hinges made a deafening noise. The thunderous crash of the battering ram was accompanied each time by a long-drawn-out "heave-ho!" An extended cheer meant that at last the main gate was beginning to yield.

The front line of janissaries did not even wait for the door to be demolished before rushing in through the first crack. More followed them in an irresistible surge. The onslaught was so forceful that within seconds the huge leaf of the main gate door had been swept aside as if it had been a piece of scrap.

Everyone in the Pasha's retinue began to pray under their breath. They were not averse to showing their enthusiasm more openly, but the unmoving back of their leader seemed to forbid them from raising their voice. Alone among them, the architect gave a desperate shout:

"Not go door there, dangerous trap, not go door, quick, about turn!"

"What's the old bird croaking about now?" someone blurted out.

But the Pasha had grasped what Giaour meant. He knew that the main gate gave on to a narrow, trapezoid internal courtyard, and at the bottom of the courtyard stood another door, a little smaller, but presumably just as strong as the outer gate. He also knew that his men would feel they were trapped like rats in a barrel. He expected them to be slaughtered and yet, as he saw the unstoppable wave of janissaries crashing onwards, he nurtured the hope that maybe his men could make a miracle happen. The janissaries, in their hundreds, carried on surging into the courtyard. Nobody could see what was happening inside. You could only hear muffled echoes of the screams from inside the citadel. They had a strange quality, no doubt caused by the walls surrounding the courtyard.

Another mounted messenger rode up in a cloud of dust.

"Hata has been killed," he said, and, like previous messengers, he promptly turned about and disappeared in the same direction he had come from.

Tursun Pasha knew that the decisive moment was upon him.

83

He now had to intensify the onslaught all along the main wall so as to draw the greatest possible number of defenders to the top of the citadel. It was the only way to relieve the janissaries caught in the rat-trap of the inner yard.

Now is the time, he thought, almost saying it aloud. Every battle reached a point of this kind, and a leader's luck consisted in recognising it amid the chaotic flow of time. Neither too soon nor too late, he repeated to himself. In his mind he felt a combination of clarity and void that scared him stiff.

He gave several orders in succession. The crack troops of the Tartars threw themselves into the fray, and in their wake came the Mongols and the Kalmyks, men whose fury was aroused by the mere sight of masonry, since in their view of the world war consisted solely of a confrontation between tents and walls.

For a while it seemed that the fresh troops committed to the battle were about to be swallowed up by it, as a river is swallowed by the sea, but a few minutes later their standards could be seen waving from the tops of the ladders.

The *dalkiliç*! He felt he was keeping them clenched between his teeth. And so he was. He just had to open his jaw to unleash their destructive fury. In his mind war often seemed like a many-storeyed building, with a frame, a roof, and a crown to top it all. As in all things the main requirement was to stick to the right order. To combine speed and advance.

"The *dalkiliç*!" he shouted, adding under his breath, "May it happen as it has been written!"

He did not have much material left after the *dalkiliç* to complete the building. His house was nearly finished.

The squads of *dalkiliç*, weighed down by the heavy fringes that their military rank required on their banners, raced towards the two towers, on the left and the right.

The Pasha looked towards the setting sun. It was late enough to look at the sun straight on. He knew that many of his badly wounded men would carry its fading image to the hereafter.

Tiger-striped yellow back-plates emerged on the parapet. Just one more push, Tursun Pasha thought. O Fate, give them just one more push!

All he had left to throw into battle was the mere handful of men who formed the death squads. They incarnated his last hope: the crown of the roof, the crowning glory of battle.

He hesitated. What then? he wondered. He closed his eyes and prayed silently: May Allah protect them! Then, in an almost muffled voice, he gave the order. "The *serden geçti*! First and second divisions!"

The chronicler could not believe his ears. A quiver of excitement ran through the small group gathered behind the Pasha. Bug-eyed, as if gazing at extraterrestrial creatures, they stared at the soldiers of death running forwards beneath their blue banners. Their crest-pieces and the plumes attached to their knee guards were similarly of the colour of the heavens.

Çelebi felt a lump in his throat. They were already wearing celestial signs, as if to make it easier for the All-Powerful to recognise them when He would choose to take them up on high.

Tursun Pasha thought that the noise of combat had slackened so as to allow the unique tone of the *serden geçtis'* clarions to ring out. He watched them until they merged with the human mass that had nothing more to expect. He imagined some of them giving them passage out of respect, and others grinding their teeth as they thought, You'll be losing your fame very soon too!

The death units had moved to the foot of the rampart and were beginning their ascent. "Now you'll see what stuff an Ottoman soldier is made of!" The Pasha uttered these words to a half-human, half-avian creature that had come to represent the Albanian in his mind when he was feeling downcast.

The sun was setting. It seemed that the attack, having become twice as violent, was achieving its objective. There were now many more defenders to be seen on the top of the wall. That should make things easier for the janissaries who thus far had been stuck in the inner courtyard. Old Tavxha had nothing to complain about. Nor would he be able to reproach the Pasha with having spared the princes of his army.

He caught sight of them out of the corner of his eye when they reached the right-hand tower. It occurred to him — but only faintly, palely — that he had perhaps sent them into battle too soon. He lowered his gaze towards the main gate. Attackers were still massing through it. Above the sea of men was a swarm of ladders, ropes and battering rams. Down below they must have already heard that the soldiers of death had reached the top of the ramparts. From its foundations to its summit, the enemy citadel was now entirely in the grip of his army.

The Pasha was on tenterhooks as he hoped to hear at any moment the shout announcing that the second door had fallen. But the noise from the courtyard was uniform and monotone, like a constant rumble of thunder. He knew that every minute spent inside the yard cost his army hundreds of men. He could see them in his mind's eye standing on top of their dead comrades, he could see the cobblestones already carpeted with blood and flesh. But he did not abandon hope of hearing the cry of victory. The huge crowd that had plunged into the castle must have had some effect. Yes, it must have.

He looked again at the walls. The sun had now gone down completely in the west and the men still fighting on the rampart looked more and more like shadows.

His eyes left them and returned to the main gate.

Most of the *serden geçti* must now have left the world of the living. So, are you pleased with yourself for having them slaughtered? he asked himself inwardly. He was no longer sure whether he had sent these soldiers of death into battle out of necessity, or whether he had sacrificed them to others' jealousy.

It was now almost night and the battered gateway looked like the mouth of an oven.

"It must be hell in there right now," the Quartermaster General whispered to the chronicler.

Çelebi was petrified. Now and again a whiff of charred flesh reached them on the wind.

"Our men won't be able to eat meat again for several days," the Quartermaster went on. "It's always like that after butchery of this kind."

"Allah!" the chronicler exclaimed. But he also wondered how the Quartermaster could be obsessed with logistics to the point of thinking about the savings he would make on food from such a horror.

Tursun Pasha had folded his arms and was looking at the plain. A courier with his visor down, as befits a man bearing bad news, was coming towards him, maybe to announce the death of Tavxha. Behind him came another messenger bearing who knows what news. But he didn't need dispatches to tell him that the fire of the attack was on the wane and could not be rekindled. He could see that the sad moment of all battles was upon him, when charred ladders, now almost entirely devoid of men, collapse as if they had had their legs cut off. He didn't cast another glance at the rest of the rampart. A constant muffled noise still emerged from the courtyard, sounding like a huge cauldron on the boil. For Tursun Pasha, not just the citadel, its walls and towers, but the whole world was concentrated in the glowing hole of the gateway, where his own fate lay nailed to the threshold, lit alternately by a sinister shadow and by a blood-flecked gleam.

God! he thought. What a catastrophe! What a disaster!

He stayed in that state for a long while.

When he finally admitted that he had no reason to hope any longer, he gave the order to retreat.

As he got back in the saddle he felt his nervous tension give way to a mortal torpor. Without a word to anyone he went back to his tent.

Bugles sounding long blasts with sharp pauses, as if their throats had been cut, gave the signal for retreat.

"Accursed citadel!" a sanxhakbey muttered gruffly.

Their first onslaught was as I shall tell it. God only knows what fate holds in store for us hereafter.

They began by bombarding us most dreadfully, and then they attacked the ramparts in rolling waves, like storm tides thrown up by an earthquake. Although we had been expecting it for months, many among us, when we saw them come upon us like a torrent of molten steel, screaming and waving their weapons, with their emblems and the instruments of death they had threatened us with for so long, reckoned we would never again see the light of day.

They surely imagined, for their part, that their fearsome thunder would drive many of us out of our minds. We were in fact stunned and almost deaf when we went up to the top of the wall while they set about climbing it from the outside. The first to cross swords with an Ottoman yatagan was Gjon Bardheci, whose soul has gone to meet our Holy Virgin. Men who were close to the duel report that the clash of blades made an unusual sound. Like church bells. Then came carnage, and many times we thought we were lost and would drag all our own people and our whole land down with us.

When their bugles sounded the retreat we kneeled and gave thanks to God and to the good fairies who had rescued us. Only then did we notice that the church was half-ruined and that the cross on the steeple had fallen off, as if it had sacrificed itself for us. Despite everything, in the midst of ruins, scorched and bloodied as we were, we sang a "Te Deum" and prayed for the salvation of the fallen.

Night has now come and those who are nearer to heaven than earth are making confession and taking communion. As we have not enough space to bury them we shall incinerate their bodies tomorrow and will keep their ashes in urns, in accordance with ancestral tradition.

Prince George sends us messages by means of beacons lit on the mountain-tops, but we can only see them dimly through the mist and clouds. Despite everything, we are different this evening from what we were in the morning and for us many things have changed for ever. We answered steel with steel, horror with horror, death with death. Often rivers of their blood fell on to our faces, just as we also rained blood down upon the enemy. Many events that can never be told or put into words have taken place, especially involving the soldiers of death who, in a blind fury, knowing that they could not return alive, fought with the savagery of wolves, but fell to our blades in the end.

Now their camp is shrouded in silence and darkness. All we can hear is the creaking of their tumbrels coming right up into our court-yard to collect their dead and wounded. The first cart flew a white flag, but we would not have attacked even if the sign had been absent: it is to our advantage to have the bodies taken away so that their miasma does not suffocate us and so that the wheeling crows stop driving us mad. Tomorrow we will perhaps make an exchange of the dead — those of our men who fell at the foot of the rampart against theirs who died at the top. But tomorrow is another day. Today is still night, and the silence of the dark is broken only by the groaning of dying men who lie all around and by the sound of burned-out ladders collapsing to the ground.

CHAPTER FIVE

When the Pasha left, the group of sanxhakbeys who had stood in line behind him throughout the assault broke up. The Quartermaster General and Çelebi found themselves alone. It was quite dark. The citadel could barely be made out. As soon as the bugles had sounded the retreat and no more pitch or flaming oil fell from the parapet, the fortress was swallowed up by the night as if by a magic spell. The shouting and hubbub of the fight gave way to a muted hum that sounded like giants mumbling. A huge beast with a thousand legs and arms seemed to be rubbing itself without interruption on the ground.

The Quartermaster General gave a deep sigh.

"Let's get going, Mevla!"

The chronicler followed him without saying a word. They took the main path through the centre of the camp. The Quartermaster General's orderly trotted behind them like a shadow. The camp was dark and quiet, and most of the tents were still empty.

They wandered for a while with no particular aim in mind. Now and again the chronicler heard the sound of voices giving orders, sending men to this place or that. Two mounted heralds passed by. Many carts moved about on creaky axles, and from further off came the beat of marching boots — hundreds of boots.

What's happening? Mevla Çelebi wondered. Who is giving the orders? Is it not all over?

A messenger went past in a rush of wind. Further on they heard the clap of galloping hooves, then anxious voices shouting orders. The chronicler's consternation subsided as a strange new feeling encroached upon it — that of admiration tinged with sorrow for his country's power. The commands and the ordered movements in the night demonstrated that even in this dark hour there were men in control of the situation, men in command.

A noise of wheels came nearer. All the chariots carried little torches fixed to the rear. Hundreds of them filed past, each with a flickering light that ravaged the heart.

A detachment of foot-soldiers followed behind. Çelebi noticed with surprise that they weren't carrying lances, as he had initially thought, but spades and picks.

"Sappers," the Quartermaster General said. "They're going to dig the graves to bury the dead."

"Will they be buried this night?"

"Looks like that's what's been ordered. In these circumstances burial is immediate, even at night."

Soon after, another detachment of sappers went by.

"How many do you think we have lost?" the chronicler asked timidly.

The Quartermaster General was deep in thought and didn't answer straight away. He was thinking that the two or three next days would, as usual, be days of cheating, false accounting and other kinds of fraud. Every day the deaths of thousands of wounded would change the total size of the army. In the general confusion and distress, nobody would remember the exact date of the death of each soldier, so that in the coming days the captains would collude with their units' quartermasters to produce fictional musters with such cleverness that even the great Ali Ibn Sin would never be able to get to the bottom of it.

"What were you saying?"

"How many do you think we have lost?"

The Quartermaster General pondered.

"To judge by the violence of the attack and its duration," he said matter-of-factly, as if he was talking about a quantity of money, "I think this business must have taken around three or four thousand men."

Another unit of sappers went by.

"We'll get a precise report tomorrow," the Quartermaster General added. Then, after a pause, he went on: "The only thing that's sure this evening is that we have suffered a major defeat."

The army had returned to camp. Paths, tents and pavilions slowly filled with its heavy, weary breath and with the dreary sound of thousands of trudging feet and countless groans. The two observers stopped by the side of a thoroughfare to watch the horde of shadows slowly moving through the darkness. At that point the moon appeared on the horizon. Its light first swept over the citadel's turrets, then bathed its high walls, then, like some great cloud of steam, enveloped everything, the plain, the camp, the crowns of the tents, and finally the Quartermaster General and the chronicler themselves.

Soldiers went on trudging past. Many had their arms round wounded comrades, others carried a man on their backs. Most of them moaned softly as they walked, and now and again let out a heart-rending shriek. In the moonlight it was hard to distinguish bloodstains from the marks made by hot pitch. Everything merged on bruised heads and shoulders, giving off a smell of oil, charred skin and scorching. Some fell down flat on their stomachs from sheer exhaustion as soon as they got to their tents, others — the most seriously wounded — were taken to field hospitals.

The Quartermaster General slowed his pace. The chronicler guessed he was doing a sum in his head. He could see the pale and evil glint in his eye that he had seen before.

"Some units must have lost about a third of their strength."

The chronicler did not know what to answer.

"Others seem to have been halved," the Quartermaster went on, staring at the long-drawn-out procession of returning men. Çelebi thought he saw the *dalkiliç* go by. Never before had he seen these previously unbeaten soldiers after a defeat, and he found them almost unrecognisable after such a terrible trial.

"The *serden geçti!*" the Quartermaster General exclaimed in a weird voice.

The chronicler shivered as if he had heard speak of ghosts. How is it possible? he thought. They are not supposed to return except as victors. They are surely going to be put to death.

"Where?" he asked, almost choking on his words.

The Quartermaster General had already stretched out his arm towards a cart. The chronicler's eyes bulged. There were many pale, sky-blue flags heaped up in the back. There was nobody following the cart.

Mevla Çelebi guessed what it meant. The brides of death, as they were called in the old chronicles, had kept their word. As the cart went by he saw that the standards were stained with blood and burns. He felt a lump rise in his throat and stifled a sob.

They had been watching the soldiers go by in silence for a long while when they saw the astrologer coming along, looking worried. The chronicler was tempted to hail him, but since he noticed a glint of scorn in the Quartermaster General's eyes he looked down, so as not to have to respond to any greeting from the magician. He knew the Quartermaster's hostile attitude towards the latter, and didn't want to witness their enmity.

A horse drew up behind them.

"Gazi," someone said.

They turned around. It was one of the Pasha's messengers.

"What is it?"

"The war council is to meet immediately. You are summoned." The messenger bowed respectfully and got back in the saddle.

"Mevla, I must leave you. What are you going to do now?"

"I'll hang around for a bit and then go to bed."

As soon as the Quartermaster General had gone, the chronicler plunged into the crowd and looked for the astrologer. He was glad to have relations in high places, but there were times like tonight when he needed close friends, people he could talk to naturally, without having to choose his words, without fearing that their faces would suddenly freeze into angular shapes like ancient inscriptions. Mevla Çelebi eventually caught up with the astrologer.

"So, how are you? Where were you going?"

The astrologer looked at him distractedly.

"I saw you a while back," the astrologer said, "but you were with the Quartermaster General. I imagine he's not too fond of me."

The chronicler shrugged his shoulders as if to say: That may well be, but what can I do about it?

They wandered around together for a while.

"What a wonderful evening it was yesterday," the astrologer said. "This evening everything is mournful."

"Allah chose not to grant us victory."

"If only He had not punished us with such a great defeat!"

"Accursed citadel!"

They watched the seemingly endless line of returning soldiers trudge past. The men passing by at that moment seemed particularly worn out. They must have been the ones who had carried the ladders and broken down the main gate with the battering rams.

"Look, there's Tuz, the janissary!" the astrologer cried out.

The young man looked up. He didn't seem to be wounded or marked with tar. Just a scratch on his forehead. He was holding up a comrade by the arm.

"God be praised, you are alive!" the chronicler exclaimed. "And who's the poor fellow with you?" he added, nodding towards the wounded man whose eyes were bandaged with a piece of turban. His face was blackened by pitch and his hair was scorched. "By Allah, is that not Sadedin?" he asked in a voice that broke.

Tuz Okçan nodded.

"He's lost his sight. His eyes were burned."

They bit their lips. The janissary spoke as if Sadedin couldn't hear them.

"I noticed him by chance in the crowd that rushed into the inner yard as soon as we'd broken down the main gate," the janissary explained. "He was among the first to get inside."

They could not help staring at the bandaged eyes.

"Then I saw him again in the thick of the fight with his hand over his forehead. It was hell in there. Everyone else was running for his life, but this fellow was just turning round and round in the smoke . . ."

The janissary's voice was weary and hoarse. He must have done a lot of shouting during the assault.

"When I saw him again, he still had one hand over his eyes but his other hand seemed to be seeking something in the air. He was being shoved about . . ." Tuz Okçan sighed deeply. "What was I saying?" he asked in a dull voice.

"That Sadedin was being shoved about . . . And that you saw him . . ."

"Ah, yes. He was being pushed around while he was waving one arm towards me, and I don't know why, but I suddenly recalled one of my aunts who when she wanted to curse someone never said 'May you go blind!' but 'May you look for the wall with your hands!' That's when I guessed what had happened to him," the janissary went on blankly. "When I got closer I saw molten pitch dripping down his cheeks. So I took him by the hand and struggled long and hard but finally managed to lead him out of that hell-hole."

Sadedin just stood there like a statue. If he hadn't been standing up he would have been taken for dead.

"I'm taking him to the doctors," the janissary said. "I know, there's little hope of saving his eyes, but maybe they'll be able to relieve him of some of the pain."

"We'll come along with you."

The hospital tents had only been set up the day before but they had already turned into slaughterhouses. Ragged soldiers were stacked right next to each other on sloping pallets, to allow the blood and gore to drain away. Dying groans mingled with entreaties — "Brother, finish me off!" "Dig the scalpel into my liver!" — which were themselves interrupted by gruff reproaches: "Shut up, you milksop!" The old hags from Rumelia were nearby, emptying bucketfuls of their potion on to the wounds. Further on, groans and exclamations came louder and sharper: "Water! Mamma mia!" "Kill me!" "Shut your trap!" "An Ottoman soldier does not snivel!"

It made the chronicler want to retch. He turned away so as

not to see these bloody bodies, but the knot in his stomach grew ever tighter.

They had to wait for a long time until any attention was paid to the poet. He was treated summarily. He didn't yell or moan. When his eyes had been bandaged again, his friends took him by the arm and led him to his tent. They laid him down and he fell instantly into a deep sleep.

They went outside and wandered for a while among the innumerable silhouettes without saying a word.

"You were there," the chronicler said, waving towards the citadel that was now lost in darkness. "Tell us."

The janissary looked at him with wild eyes. His answer was long in coming. Only after walking along for a while in complete silence did he mumble, as if he was talking to himself: "Dreadful."

"What was dreadful?"

"Over there," he replied, waving towards the same place the chronicler had gestured at a few minutes before.

"I'm thinking of the wonderful evening we had yesterday," the astrologer said.

Shapes of soldiers moved around them in every direction. None spoke. There was nothing but low mumbles and evasions.

"I can't get his look out of my mind!" Tuz Okçan suddenly cried out. "Last night, when he was talking, how his eyes sparkled!"

"He was planning on writing a great poem about this campaign," the chronicler blurted out, thinking of his own work.

"That is perhaps why he was the first to come forward, so as to be in the front row when the door came down," the astrologer surmised.

"It's really sad," Çelebi said. "He was talented — and courageous."

"God! How his eyes sparkled last night!" the janissary said again, softly.

"Yes," Mevla Çelebi chimed in melancholically. "They shone as if they guessed they were looking on the world for the last time."

"The fallacious world," the astrologer corrected him.

"Pitch has covered that gleam with a black veil for ever."

Who had said something last night about a black veil? The chronicler was tired, and his memory was getting confused.

The astrologer looked at the sky.

"What fate do the stars foretell?" the janissary asked.

Since he had taken part in the assault, the janissary had lost his shyness and he now spoke to them like old friends.

"Sad prophecies!" the astrologer answered. "Some crazy wind seems to be swirling them around all the time."

In fact the astrologer had a migraine and a temperature, so that the stars really did seem to him to be on the point of falling out of the sky. "Do not fall, my star . . ." Had he not read that somewhere? He had banked heavily on this campaign. If his predictions turned out right, he would be able to see about getting a much better position, even an eminent one, on his return to the capital. Palace astrologer, why not? It was the most important campaign for years. The whole empire had its eyes on these misty mountains. He was bored with his life in the muddy backwater where he had spent the last two years going to see the portly wife of the wali every Friday to predict when the next letter from Akhashir would come. He liked the liveliness of the capital, its crowded streets, days packed full of things to do, fashion, women. Heaven may make him a gift of all that, but it could turn him down too. "Stay by me, my star . . ." When he had seen the burned-out ladders crashing to the foot of the ramparts he saw his own future fall. Ill-starred: all afternoon that word had been pressing like a rusty nail into his soul.

The only things that came into his mind now were curses of every kind, and it began to frighten him.

"Tuz Okçan, what did you say a moment ago? 'May you look for the wall with your hands?' Our curses are different. For example, we say: 'Go cold!'"

"What's that got to do with me?" the janissary answered. "What is this business about cursing? Why do you want to involve me in that kind of thing?"

The janissary was starting to weep. The chronicler grabbed the astrologer by the sleeve.

"Stop it," he whispered. "Can't you see he's in distress?"

"Actually, he needs taking care of. Maybe even more than Sadedin does . . ."

During his long saunter through the camp Mevla Çelebi had heard about a special unit in the army, consisting of priestly men who were part healers and part sorcerers, and whose task it was to calm soldiers afflicted with mental disturbances after battle. In the old days they were killed, like any man who could not hold back his tears, but in the course of the last year the rules had been made less harsh.

"Yesterday evening there were four of us," Mevla Çelebi observed thoughtfully. "Tonight we are only three."

Cartwheels could be heard creaking not far away. It wasn't the same sound as had been heard earlier on, when the carts were making their way towards the citadel. The lower, duller noise of the axles suggested that the carts were now fully loaded.

"Let's go and see our dead being buried," the chronicler said. They walked a long while in silence before they caught up with the tumbrels. Heaped-up corpses were lit by the pale rays of the moon. One of them slipped and fell to the ground. The following vehicle halted, then someone came to pick up the body and heaved it into the back.

Empty wagons passed by in the opposite direction, on their way to collect another load. Their floorboards were stained red and black by the blood. The three men looked at the ground and saw that it too was soaked in blood.

"Are you alright?" the astrologer asked the chronicler. "You're as pale as a ghost. Do you want us to go back?"

"No! I must see the burial of our dead. I have to describe it in my chronicle."

That was all they said to each other for the entire journey. From afar they heard the lugubrious, drawn-out murmur of hoxhas praying. As they drew nearer the voices became more distinct and drowned out the sounds of spades and picks.

When they got to the burial ground sappers had already dug out three large rectangular pits, and were working on four others. Tumbrels drew to a halt at the edge of a pit, the bodies were given a cursory inspection by a doctor, and were then thrown into their grave. The first was already full and sappers had started covering it. The hoxhas bowed again and again, casting clumps of earth into the mass grave as it was being filled in. Bodies were now being piled up in the second grave. Shirtless dervishes with blood-stained forearms grasped corpses by their hands and feet and swung them energetically over the edge. The tumbrels were emptied one by one. Horses snorted and stamped at the smell of blood, which disturbed them. Hoxhas went on reciting prayers. Now and again a doctor would have a body taken out of the heap — a survivor put among the dead by mistake.

The astrologer and Tuz Okçan glanced from time to time towards their companion to see if they were required to stay any longer. Aware of being the object of attention, at least at those moments, Çelebi took his time.

At last he turned on his heels and the others followed on behind him. They walked back over blood-soaked ground where the tumbrels were almost at a standstill. Some of them bore only one or two bodies, presumably those of officers. The torch of one of these carts had fallen on to the floor right next to the victim's head, and the spilled oil flared up in strange forms. A distorted reflection of the dead man's face could be seen in the smooth surface of the oil spill. Covered in hellish sweat, in glinting lamp-light, the face seemed to be grappling with a cruel dilemma — to wake, or to sleep for ever.

The janissary grabbed Çelebi by the sleeve.

"That man's going to catch fire," he whispered. "My God! I think it's my commander, Suleiman!"

The burning oil had in fact almost reached the man's body, but the chronicler insisted that even if it did catch fire, it would not be a great misfortune. The ancients, he added, considered it a duty to incinerate their dead.

Tuz Okçan turned his head away so as not to have to see the spectacle. He was sure the body had begun to burn.

"What can I hear now?" the astrologer asked. "Am I having hallucinations?"

"No. The watch has been reinforced," the janissary answered.

When they got back to the centre of the camp, the prevailing mood of anxiety seemed to have grown more intense. A few shapes moved about in the distance. Two horsemen with the insignia of the messenger corps on their tunics galloped past.

"They must be worried about Skanderbeg mounting a counter-attack," the janissary said.

"Look, there's another guard-post that has been doubled," the astrologer remarked. "Skanderbeg is supposed to be fearsome. Especially when he attacks in the dark."

"Everything is more terrible in the dark," the janissary replied.

"Our Pasha is his equal," the chronicler interjected. "In the capital he is said to be the most brilliant war leader we have."

"God be praised!"

To their considerable surprise they realised they were standing right next to the commander-in-chief's tent.

"Is the war council still in session?" the astrologer asked a passing courier.

The courier did not answer at first, but when moonlight made the astrologer's dress visible, he gave a curt "Yes".

"May you go cold!" the astrologer swore under his breath, uncertain whether he was cursing the sentinel, himself or the entire war council. He was worried. Whatever he did he could not stop his mind going back to his protector, the Mufti. Would the Mufti support him, or would he drop him at the council meeting?

Meanwhile, the emergency meeting went on. The leaders were seated on animal skins draped over a divan. Most of them were wounded and had bandaged legs or arms. Three members of the council had fallen in the battle, and the architect, seated at the other end of the room from the Pasha, was already sketching the hexagonal *turbes* which by custom had to be raised over their graves. During meetings he often took pleasure in sketching and drawing.

The Quartermaster General spoke. He asked for the astrologer to be stripped of his rank and sentenced to hard labour. Everyone knew that his onslaught, despite its measured terms, was really aimed at the Mufti. Saruxha, who had allowed himself to drop off from time to time, was now listening with rapt attention. At one point he even interrupted the Quartermaster to demand that the astrologer be put to death. Some of the sanxhakbeys who were in the sway of the Mufti attempted to excuse the astrologer's mistake. Others among them agreed only that he should be sacked. Kara-Mukbil was the only one of the divisional commanders who wanted the astrologer's head. The dreadful wound on his face made it difficult for him to speak, but lent great weight to the words he did utter. The Mufti himself, Old Tavxha and Kurdisxhi did not express an opinion. The Alaybey, for his part, went along with removing the astrologer from office, but did not suggest any further punishment. The Pasha listened to all of them in complete indifference. Whether or not to punish the astrologer seemed to him a matter of no greater importance than deciding whether to tread on an ant or not. He knew that was not the issue. The velvet-gloved fight between the two hostile factions within his own council, which in other circumstances might have agitated him, seemed trivial. Only one thing mattered to him: what was to be done?

He cut short the debate with a clear decision of his own: the astrologer would be removed from office forthwith and reallocated to grave-digging. While the secretary was transcribing the order, Kurdisxhi rose to speak. He asked permission, in accordance with tradition, to mount a punitive expedition to sack and terrorise the villages in the surrounding hills. He claimed that an action of that sort was especially necessary in current circumstances, so as to shatter the confidence that the Turks' defeat might have aroused among the rebels.

"Today, I shall avenge the blood we have spilled!" he yelled. "I shall lay waste to the whole country! I'll turn it into a living hell!"

Tursun Pasha looked at Kurdisxhi's flaming head of red hair

and thought to himself that the man would literally do what he said.

"Granted," the Pasha said, nodding to his secretary to transcribe the decision which he had taken, contrary to normal practice, without consulting his advisers.

"Pasha, sire," a barely audible voice whispered.

A curly redhead who was apparently attending the war council for the first time was requesting permission to speak.

"Tabduk Baba, Agha of the secret police," Tursun Pasha said, realising that most members of his council were eying the newcomer with astonishment. "Speak, Agha!"

The man pretended not to have noticed the disdain that could be read in the eyes of some of those present.

"Much has been said about the astrologer," he said, "but there are others who should be punished too. I have learned that attempts were made to steal the secret of the new weapon. I am also in possession of an anonymous letter that incriminates the spell-caster."

"What's an anonymous letter?" Aslanhan asked. "I've never heard of that before."

"It's a letter without a signature," Tabduk Baba explained. "I got a letter of that kind expressing grave suspicions about the damning of the citadel."

"Well, well," two or three men muttered.

Tursun Pasha gave a slight nod of agreement. The Agha of the secret police was like balm to his wounds when he felt depressed. The other members also perked up. So the defeat was not their fault.

"If that's how it is, let's not waste time. Cut off the spell-caster's head," Aslanhan said.

"Wait a minute," the Pasha intervened. "We must first be sure of his guilt. Isn't that so, Kadi?" he added, turning towards a small and wrinkle-faced man who was also attending the council for the first time.

"Punishing a caster of spells is no easy matter," the kadi said emphatically. "I would go so far as to say it is the opposite."

"That is not my view," the Agha of the secret police replied.

Tursun Pasha let them argue it out for a few minutes, and then cut in.

"That's enough! Put the caster of spells in chains, and investigate the matter with extreme discretion. We've got time to think about a trial. But I would suggest it be held in public."

"A public trial is always useful in these circumstances," the Quartermaster General said with a smile that was full of unspoken meaning.

Tursun Pasha pretended not to notice.

"I give you full powers to spy on suspect elements," the Pasha said to Police Commander Tabduk Baba. After a pause, he added: "To spy on anyone!" He noticed the glances across the room that his statement prompted and reckoned that all present had therefore grasped what it meant. "And now, let us get on to the main question, to the reason why the great Padishah sent us all here to the end of the earth. How are we going to proceed so as to take control of this citadel?"

Old Tavxha, Tahanka, the Mufti and a few others were of the view that a fresh assault should be launched without delay. The glorious army of the Osmanlis which had stormed dozens of supposedly impregnable fortresses should never, they said, be allowed to suffer the slightest humiliation, even that of remaining stationary in front of these walls. The whole world was expecting to hear that the citadel had fallen. They had to attack. However, most of the advisers were against attacking, especially in present circumstances. If they had a second mishap, their numerical strength could be seriously weakened, and, worse still, another defeat would certainly wreck the morale of the troops. So they were minded to try to devise other means that would lead to the result that had not been obtained by direct onslaught. They reckoned that, for an army, any victory is another jewel in its crown of glory, irrespective of the means used to achieve it.

The council went on arguing late into the night. Each spoke of all that he knew from long military experience about the means available for seizing a stronghold, from the most valiant to the least noble, not to say despicable. They included movable towers, infection with cholera, a feigned retreat followed by a surprise attack, the taking of hostages, throwing excrement over the ramparts, and a wide range of tricks, one of which would be to dress the *akinxhis* in Albanian costumes and to have them pretend to attack the Turkish camp.

Tursun Pasha tried to imagine Kurdisxhi in Skanderbeg's goat-head helmet, and thought, No!

Dozens of variations were suggested and each was gone over several times, with its pros and cons weighed against each of the others. One wounded council member fainted. The doctor was called, and he had the man taken back to his tent. In the end it appeared that the majority was in favour of digging an underground passageway that the architect had proposed right at the start. The Pasha nodded towards him. Giaour stood up in his corner, pulled a sheaf of plans out of his satchel, and came into the middle of the tent. Under the envious gaze of the secret policeman, who eyed him as a beast stares at prey within reach of its claws, Giaour laid out his plans on the kilim and started to explain. Nobody tried to follow what he was saying because they all knew that even if they concentrated as hard as they could they would not be able to understand. The only thing they could get out of the architect's gibberish was the word "shaft", which meant "passage", and for which Giaour also sometimes used the words "hole" or "underground", and even more often the term "tunnel", borrowed from the accursed language of the *giaours* themselves.

They contented themselves with watching the architect's waxen hand move over the strange shapes drawn on the paper, amazed once again that something as real, solid and huge as the citadel could be summed up in a few squiggles which represented not only the visible parts of it but also the parts that could not be seen from outside, such as the stairs in the turrets and the foundations. The Muslim religion had made them all aware of the diabolical nature of figurative compositions, but they were nonetheless obliged to rely on them, just as they had believed in the complicated diagrams which had given birth to Saruxha's monstrous cannon. The architect's index finger ran this way and that over the plan. He was describing the nature of the earth around the fortress, and explained that although loose soil is much easier to dig, and therefore an advantage, it was also subject to caving in, whereas digging through rock, though much harder to do, produced less risky results. He showed the depth to which the shaft had to be dug at the start, how deep it would then have to dip to get underneath the foundations of the outer wall, how it would then have to split into two to allow an escape if one of the exits got blocked. He finished off by calculating how long it would take to dig such a "tunnel" and the number of soldiers who could pass through it in a given period of time.

They didn't understand a great deal of the architect's talk. They didn't put much effort into understanding, anyway, since none of them could have suggested any useful amendment to the plan for the underground passageway. They simply stared at the red arrow which started at a spot outside the fortress, then moved on under the foundations like a man trying to wriggle under a door, and ended at a different spot in the cellars and dungeons. A single question could be read in all their eyes: would this sharp-tipped arrow really pierce the belly of the citadel?

During the architect's address the Mufti showed his disdain by not turning his head towards the drawings laid out on the kilim. Old Tavxha looked distraught as he gazed at them, thinking sadly that suchlike figures and inscriptions were rapidly taking over the profession of arms, which would very likely lose its holy ardour and gradually turn into a dreary succession of stratagems concocted by mysterious and cunning souls like the accursed architect with his incomprehensible blather. He vaguely foresaw that if the Empire put too much trust in such paperwork, it would slowly wither away, and if its roots ceased to be fed by the combative vitality of men of his kind but drew instead on dry-as-dust, intellectual formulae, it would perish from thirst. Old Tavxha kept his eyes half-closed. His face wound was hurting and he needed to sleep. While the head of the Janissary Corps nursed these thoughts in his weary mind, the Quartermaster General, keeping alternate watch out of the corner of his eye on the Mufti, Tavxha and Kurdisxhi, thought, for his part, that if the Empire wanted to endure, then it had better keep up with the times and gradually move men such as these away from decision-making roles. But perhaps it was they, in fact, who maintained the spirit of war. Maybe he and his kind, for all their knowledge, would achieve nothing without the help of the others' ignorance. Maybe a learned man and an unschooled one, when they serve the same cause, produce an alloy far stronger than two learned men or two unschooled men, just as bronze is harder than either the copper or the tin from which it is made.

It was past midnight when the discussion came to an end. Before closing the meeting, the Pasha urged all to maintain the strictest confidentiality. Each would answer with his head, without distinction of rank or role. He rose, and said calmly:

"If we have not succeeded in taking the fortress by pouncing on it like falcons, we shall now take it from below, like the snake, and will bite it in its sleep."

The Quartermaster General felt a shiver run through his entire body.

Their huge camp has changed its appearance these last several days. It looks more like an enormous fairground than a military camp. We who first saw it cover the earth like a glacier, then keep us from sleeping during its night of orgy, then glower, grow angry and spill forth horror and death on the day of the attack, we do not find it easy to get used to this new state of affairs. We could easily believe that it is not the same army at all, but some other force from another time and another power that has suddenly emerged at our feet, God knows how.

At first we watched with amusement as regiments marched off to exercises and marched back again to a chorus of orders and songs amid a jolly patchwork of brightly coloured banners and toy-like, hastily built wooden minarets, and as flutes, drums and cymbals played heart-rending tunes while horsemen ran races or competed in equestrian games.

Quite a few of us were bemused by it all. Some even went so far as to wonder whether the Turks had given up the idea of making war on us. Perhaps they had received an order — a firman, as they call it — from their monarch who lives at the other end of the earth? People began to pray. May they vanish from our sight as speedily as they can!

In short, after seeing much that was truly unbelievable, we noticed dozens of soldiers going about in flower-patterned robes and feminine adornments bought from the stalls set up in the camp. We thought either we were having a bad dream, or the Turks had truly gone out of their minds. We gathered our men and told them they would do better not to look down on what was happening in the plain. We also pointed out that an army capable of taking on the appearance of a horde of mercenaries, then of an iron monster, and then of a loose woman, must surely be a satanic force such as is rarely seen on earth. God alone knew what shape it would take on tomorrow, whether it would turn into a raging tiger or a dead vixen.

Many of us recalled the stories of our ancestors about ogres, many-headed dragons, witches with changing faces, about the Evil One and the horrible Horned Man. All those fantastical creatures had some resemblance to this wizard-army that now laughs and now cries, now spits smoke or else grows moody and silent. The noises it makes can't be trusted. Even less trustworthy is its silence.

CHAPTER SIX

The *akinxhis* were leaving. Their vanguard was already on the march. Thousands of men came out of their tents to watch the departure. Many did so to say farewell to their friends.

Seated on a short-legged horse, like all of the *akinxhis*, the chronicler, wrapped in a woollen blanket, cast a forlorn glance at all he saw.

The colour had quite gone from his cheeks. He had barely slept since the Alaybey had ordered him to accompany the expedition. At first he had hardly believed his ears. At his age! Join the *akinxhis*! What fault had he committed to warrant being sent to these desolate parts?

The Alaybey had explained that sending him on the expedition into the hills was not considered a punishment, but, on the contrary, as a favour granted him, so he could become better acquainted with war and describe it more faithfully, et cetera. Fearing he might otherwise be taken for a coward, the chronicler objected that his health was not up to it — his spine couldn't take it, for sure, but there was also his spleen, which stopped him sleeping. The Alaybey pretended not to hear and went on with his speech, stressing that henceforth history would be written differently, on the battlefield itself and not in the cushioned comfort of the capital, and so forth, and in the end Mevla Çelebi dropped his original intention of complaining about jealous rivals who wished him ill, and finally thanked the Alaybey and his colleagues for the great honour being done to him by this wonderful opportunity to see the famous *akinxhis* in battle with his own eyes.

And now that he was there, on horseback, waiting for his unit to fall in, he was picking up snatches of conversation from all around.

"Who knows how many captives they'll bring back?"

"Ullu, don't forget what I asked you to find for me."

"They'll come back with loads of gorgeous girls for us!"

"Wait and see."

"Why do you say that? A plague on your tongue!"

"The plague on yours, too! May you lick the earth with it!"

"Hey, you two over there, will you shut up? Today's a holiday. Can't you hear the drums? Come on, lads, get into the swing of it!"

"I'll buy one at any price, as long as she's blonde and a decent size."

"Even if she costs six hundred aspers?"

"Yes, I'll go up that far."

"You arsehole, you let the *azabs* bugger you."

"Shut your face, you venomous snake! Can't you see how beautiful the world is today?"

"And where are you going to find money like that?"

"Don't you worry. I'll manage."

"But in your unit you only get paid two and a half aspers a day. So how are you going to do it?"

"I'll find a way."

"I'll be surprised."

Çelebi was intrigued and turned around to look. The conversation was coming from a generously mustachioed, mounted *akinxhi* and a sapper standing next to him and leaning on the horse with his hand.

"Six hundred aspers is beyond your means," the *akinxhi* said with deliberation, staring suspiciously at the sapper with his black eyes. "But tell me, would you perchance have been . . ."

The sapper's face went crimson from the neck up.

The *akinxhi* showed his repulsion with a shrug.

"So that's what it is! I never thought you would fall so low."

The sapper said nothing.

"Have you heard? The caster of spells was thrown in irons this morning. Apparently he didn't do his curse properly. When he put up his hands with palms facing outwards, he got the direction wrong and covered only half the citadel."

"What are you saying?"

"When he was being chained up, he yelled: 'Careful with my hands! They're my working tools!' It's like worrying about your hair when you're having your head cut off! There's a rumour going round that all the suspects are going to be arrested."

"They'll only get what they deserve."

"You'd have done better to steal or pillage instead of . . ."

"You have to understand me: I'm just dying to have a woman."

"The way you're going about it, you'll end up losing your taste for the opposite sex."

"Why?" the soldier asked in a worried voice. "Why?"

Their unit's drum then began to roll, and the men formed into a column. Kurdisxhi went right past them on his imposing mount. He had an escort of soldiers accompanied by the Mufti. When they had almost passed by, Çelebi suddenly recognised Tuz

Okçan. He was talking to an *akinxhi* who seemed to be making some kind of promise to him. Did he also sleep with his "mates", as people called them nowadays? The chronicler looked up automatically towards the citadel and saw the ramparts streaked with long, funereal drapes of congealing pitch.

"*Bon voyage*, Mevla!" the janissary's voice rang out, once the soldier had recognised the chronicler. Çelebi waved a thank you. His heart was almost melting with gratification. It seemed that a warm wish of that kind was what he had really needed. "May luck be with you too," he mumbled to himself.

Tuz Okçan stood for a while, watching the dust cloud raised by the horses. When the last unit had set off, he walked back to the camp. On his way he overheard groups of soldiers talking about the *akinxhis* they had just seen off, and going over the booty they had requested from them. Tuz Okçan was well aware that many of them had done deals with the marauders, involving the purchase of captive women. He'd heard tell by army veterans that when expeditions of that sort make it back, the camp usually turns into a great slave market, especially of women, for a period of days. With their crude tastes, soldiers would hurry to buy flowery dresses to drape over their prisoners. When they had slaked their desire, they would sell their captives on at the best price they could get and use the proceeds to buy another one. The departments that set up military campaign plans well in advance never forgot to include in the list of supplies, alongside food, cannon, blankets and camels, a few thousand flowery dresses for captured women.

The janissary had also been told that the trade in slave women was both a delight and a risky activity for novice soldiers. There was no such thing as a fixed price; the value of a girl fluctuated by the hour, usually depending on the number of women taken.

There were no precise criteria for estimating the relative value of the slaves, either, since tastes in women were as varied as the origins of soldiers coming from many different parts of the Empire. Some liked them plump, with ripples of flesh around their midriffs, whereas others preferred them as skinny as rakes. Some were driven to ecstasy by a copious bosom, whereas others couldn't stand the sight of such a thing. There was just as little agreement about height, eye colour, age, neck, arms and especially about the thickness of pubic hair.

The only preference almost universally shared was for blondes. Their price sometimes went so high that only ranking officers, or at most the death squad soldiers, who had the highest pay among troopers, could afford the luxury of buying one.

Prices were high when the expedition got back, but sometimes had fallen sharply by the next day. Soldiers who had spent the night with their new slaves tried to sell them on in front of their tents, regretting they had paid so much. Weary and disenchanted, they were prepared to let them go at half the price. Crafty traders who knew the game would then snap them up in great numbers, well aware that dark and sultry nights would soon return and drive the price back up again.

But prices fluctuated wildly even after initial needs had been satisfied. Sometimes they went up steeply. That happened when girls died from exhaustion on top of each other before they even got out of the soldiers' tents, or else when they lost their minds.

As he re-entered the camp Tuz Okçan felt a shaft of regret in his heart as he remembered that he would not be able to take part in the exciting trade in captive girls. Members of the Janissary Corps were not allowed to own girls. He tried to console himself with the thought that, with his modest pay as a new recruit, he wouldn't have been able to afford one anyway. Despite that, he thought, he could have managed, if he had gone shares with one or even two comrades. He'd been told it was common practice.

He strode in leisurely fashion among the tents. Other janissaries went by with happy looks on their faces, for it was pay day. As he sauntered towards the tent of his unit's quartermaster, he worked out in his head how many months of his pay of forty-five aspers a month he would have to save up to accumulate two hundred, which was half the going price for a girl of average looks, and the third of the price of a blonde.

A girl's valuation also fluctuated considerably in the mind of Tuz Okçan. By day, when he was striding forth, as he was now, he reckoned it was crazy to squander a year's savings for a second-hand, no longer pristine woman. But there were stiflingly hot nights when he would have spent not a year's pay, but all his life savings, to be able to enjoy the pleasure of the swallows' nest. When he was aroused, he recalled a risqué song that he'd heard an old janissary recite: "It's snowing, the wind's howling/ A friend is yelling to find his friend" in which, to Tuz Okçan's amazement, the first occurrence of "friend" was replaced by a word for the female sexual organ, and the second by the name of the male organ. So it was a woman's sex that howled like a she-wolf on a snowy winter's day, Tuz Okçan mused. But in his own mind there was nothing in the world that could be likened to a male organ gripped by wild lust. He had felt its fury. When it was blindly excited and foaming at the brim, it seemed to him that an erection could smash right through a woman's belly, and it made his testicles hurt, hurt like mad, as they tried to slow him down, as if he was no more than a puking drunk.

Sometimes he was overcome with panic at the thought that he might perhaps never again have an opportunity to enjoy a woman, and at such moments he would have given not just his life savings, but several years of his life to escape such a fate.

He sighed a deep sigh and tried to think of something else.

For the second time in a week he noticed the new bread oven that had been set up on a platform not far from the ramparts. He was intrigued to see as he went past that several sentries had been detailed to guard it. In two or three places there were signboards prohibiting access to it. A rumour had gone round a few days before saying that an enemy agent had tried to poison the dough. That was apparently the reason for the heightened security. In addition, that must be the oven where bread was baked for the high-ranking officers, and so it was only natural it should be watched over with special care.

He was walking away from it when he heard the sound of horses' hooves coming up behind him. He turned around and was astonished to see a senior officer with an escort of three other officers trotting up to the oven. He stopped to watch. A few other soldiers did the same, and soon more joined them.

"The Pasha!" someone whispered.

Tuz Okçan opened his eyes wide. He had heard a lot about the commander-in-chief but had never seen him before. He stood up on tiptoe. There was whispering all around.

"How gloomy he looks!"

"Yes, he really does."

"Who's the other guy, on his right?"

"Don't know. The one on his left is the Alaybey."

"It's the architect," someone said.

"What a strange head he has! His face looks like an egg."

"Now and again he has epileptic fits, apparently."

"But he has no rival in the whole Empire, as far as his job is concerned."

"I don't doubt that. Epileptics are either idiots or geniuses."

"Why are they going to the oven?"

"How should I know? That's Government business."

"People are saying that poison was mixed with the dough and they're supposed to have launched an inquiry."

"Poison?"

"Yes. Hadn't you heard? You must be on another planet! Listen here: the poison is obviously bad enough, but there's worse, so it seems. The caster of spells wasn't acting on his own."

"Well, well. The plot thickens . . ."

"That's right, chum. And who can clear it up?"

A sentry came up to the knot of gossipers.

"Move on there," he commanded. "Public assembly is forbidden in these here parts."

The soldiers went their different ways.

Meanwhile the Pasha, the Alaybey and the architect had gone into the bake house together. The Pasha's aide-de-camp and a sentry made up the rear of the party. Two guards stood watch outside.

The Pasha went down into the cellar behind a sapper carrying a torch to light his way. The search party followed behind. There was neither flour nor dough down there, for it was the secret entrance to the underground passageway. The bake house built over it was just camouflage. The chimney smoked day and night, but no bread was baked in it. Carts with their loads fully covered under canvas went in and out of the main door without interruption. Everyone believed them to be loaded with sacks of flour. Only a very fine ear could have worked out that they were in fact empty when they went in, but fully laden on return. What they carried was much heavier than bread: countless sacks of soil from the underground excavation, which they removed to a dump behind a distant wood.

The party plunged into the tunnel. Ventilation shafts had

been put in and hidden on the surface inside tents that were under twenty-four-hour guard, but they were few and far between, so the air in the tunnel was heavy and stale. As they proceeded, the Pasha found it ever harder to breathe, but he pushed forwards with his inspection nonetheless. Buckets of oil-soaked ash placed at long intervals provided feeble lighting. Now and again they crossed the path of men pushing barrows full of earth.

In the half-light the Pasha looked like a ghost.

"Up to point here, struts. From point here, no struts," the architect droned.

"He's saying we should go no farther because the cribbing ends here," the aide-de-camp translated.

They halted.

The Pasha looked up at the wide, sodden beams. He and the others could just hear the muffled sound of picks and axes being used a few dozen paces further on in the dark. The architect got a drawing out of his satchel. A guard brought a torch nearer to him, and Giaour tried to explain. The aide-de-camp provided a running translation:

"He says that the point we are at now is located twenty-five paces from the outside wall. The men at the cutting face are now no more than seven paces from the wall. Tonight they'll be up to the foundations."

The architect made a mark on his plan right next to the line that represented the wall.

The Pasha noted that the tunnel dipped downwards sharply from this point on. The gradient was so steep that men going up or down had to hang on to ropes anchored to the side walls. The light of torches could be seen lower down, as if at the bottom of a well, but it was all clouded by dust and made men look like the phantoms that whirling windstorms sometimes create.

Giaour the architect droned on and on.

"What he's saying," the aide-de-camp interpreted, "is that this slope is obligatory to allow the tunnel to pass under the foundations of the citadel with a clearance of at least half its own height. That way we will have to demolish only one span of the buried section of the wall."

The Pasha was still staring at the human shadows. The dust was so thick at the cutting face that the hole made you think of the gates of hell.

"How long have they been working without a break in the fresh air?" the Pasha asked.

The Alaybey did not answer straight away.

"Apart from the sappers, the men have all been sentenced, so . . ."

"I understand," the Pasha interrupted.

An acrid smell came in whiffs from the end of the tunnel.

"What's that smell?" the Pasha asked with a grimace.

The architect explained:

"It is the smell of the brine we pour on the foundations to break down the mortar."

The architect then pointed to another spot on the plan that the Pasha could not see very well through the smoke that was making his eyes sting. He waved his hand and the torch-bearer moved the lamp away.

"Once we have got through the foundations," the aide-de-camp reported to him, "the passage will slope back up to its original level so as to reach the surface at the spot we have set for it to come out into the open."

"How will you manage to hide the noise of the pickaxes?" the Alaybey asked.

The architect replied straight off.

"On the other side of the foundations the digging will have to be done by spading the soil."

"It'll be a long job," the Pasha observed.

"He says it's the only way to proceed without giving ourselves away."

"How many days?" the Pasha asked laconically.

"Twelve," the architect replied.

He filled out the picture by showing in which of the citadel's dungeons the tunnel would exit, and how dozens of soldiers could spill forth from it in a short space of time. They would have to be able to defend the tunnel mouth until hundreds of others had come through behind them, even if the besieged were to discover the tunnel *in extremis* and raise the alarm.

The Pasha walked back towards the entrance with his escort behind him. It was already dusk when they emerged. The Pasha had a dreamy look in his eye as he crossed the camp to go back to his pavilion. Officers and men stood still with their eyes fixed as he went past. He went out and about in the camp only on rare occasions, and most of the men, including some officers, had not had a chance of setting eyes on him before.

The image of the dust-filled cavern was still in his mind when he got back to his tent. The world truly was like a building with three floors. Men on earth lived on the middle floor, mistakenly believing they had knowledge of things or even some power over them. In fact all was decided on the upper storey, in heaven, whereas secrets lay in misery beneath the ground. Like the dead . . . All the same he didn't cease hoping vaguely that the dead would help them dig their tunnel right into the entrails of the citadel.

Once inside his tent he sat on the divan and skimmed through the day's reports, which were of many different kinds. The Secret

Service Agha's daily report came along with a statement from a patrol about a squabble between two sanxhakbeys that had broken out the day before. Others dealt with matters of lesser importance: there was a request from the kadi to sentence to death two quartermasters who had sequestered the pay of dead soldiers (he couldn't be bothered to read it all through, but satisfied himself by noting that the document was signed at the bottom by the Quartermaster General); four sentences for disobeying superiors; and other less severe punishments of soldiers and officers in the various different corps requested by the head of the camp on various grounds, mostly fist-fights and unruly behaviour. He hastily initialled the sentences but added in the margin, "Send below". As he scrawled those words, which meant "to the tunnel", he felt the well-known sensation of the powerful of the earth who can cast another man into the abyss. The idea that his own fate was also in the hands of another did not hold him back, but, on the contrary, put fresh energy into his view. He had long known that the world is but a pyramid of power, and the loser would always be the man who gives up the exercise of his own power before the other.

He set aside the two longest reports, to read carefully later. The first was from the Quartermaster General and dealt with the state of the reserves of food and cash. The second was the work of the Alaybey. It gave a picture of morale among the troops. It was detailed, and was based on a wide range of information provided by the numerous underlings of Tabduk Baba. Together with the Alaybey's own suggestions and conclusions, the report contained dozens of accounts of everyday events, and snatches of conversations overheard among soldiers gave substance to the Alaybey's views. There was even an appendix with the lyrics of a song recently heard around the camp. As he glanced through the report, the Pasha saw that this endless recitation of mundane actions and utterances expressed a lukewarm and resentful attitude that was utterly incompatible with the straight lines, rules, ranks, standards, cornets and everything else that constituted the grandeur of war. It was like rising damp, permeating and rotting the great edifice of his army. And although the Alaybey put it indirectly and with a great deal of circumlocution, the situation was obvious. His experience as a leader had taught him that during a siege such a state of mind always arises in the end if after a defeat men are left without anything to do. The besieged fortress towered over his huge camp every day, his men saw it at reveille every morning just as they saw it at dusk every evening. He knew it would weigh on their spirits ever more heavily. He also knew that in such circumstances faint hearts can be rallied by creating imaginary dangers, by launching allegedly secret inquiries (like the one targeting the caster of spells, which had everybody trying to divine what the man's fate would be), by setting up trials and by holding spectacular executions, or by prompting disagreements among the generals, to which most soldiers and officers were already accustomed. He was certainly able to do all those things, and he would have done them if there was not, deep down beneath the ground, the foundation of all his hopes — a tunnel snaking forwards every day. A quick victory on a calm night, without too much bloodshed or toil, would be doubly precious in the present apathy, now that the bulk of his troops were giving way to the insidious disease of war-weariness.

He skimmed through the Alaybey's report a second time and stopped to read the passages quoting soldiers' conversations verbatim. A distant rumble rising like sea-swell from a thousand tents sounded in his ear. It was his habit never to talk to his men. During their exhausting march he had watched regiment after regiment file past, with heavy packs on their backs and covered in the dust of two continents, but he had never even bothered to ask himself what might lie beneath those identical, indistinguishable shaven skulls. He would have been inclined to think there was nothing there, save a handful of ash, and maybe a few names, of a mother, a father, a family, except for the janissaries, who were not allowed such things . . . Nonetheless, on the first day of the assault, when he watched the men scaling the ramparts, with blood and ash dripping from their backs, he had felt curious for the first time in his life about what might have been going on in their minds. "You are a great leader," Tabduk Baba told him when summoned to have this task entrusted to him. No previous Pasha had ever bothered to find out what his men were thinking. That was perhaps the main reason why they had all fallen in the end.

And now he could hear their rumbling. He recalled that long-past summer when for the first time the sea had come into his view. This buzzing of the soldiery was a bit like the noise of the sea, except that waves made a sound that was heart-rendingly beautiful. If that noise goes on for very long, however, an army that seems flawless will lose its will and go to pieces.

He was still lost in thought, wondering whether he should act now or wait until the tunnel was finished, when one of his orderlies came in to tell him that the doctor, Sirri Selim, wanted to see him on urgent business.

The Pasha found this late-night call surprising. He put the report down and waited for the doctor to come in.

The epidemiologist came in bent double, not just because he was too tall to enter the tent standing straight, but also from a long habit of obsequiousness.

"Pardon me, Pasha, for disturbing you at such an hour," he said in a baritone voice that made a strange contrast with the long, thin body that he could not straighten up beneath the tent roof.

"It is very late, indeed," said the Pasha. "What is the matter?"

"There is urgent business I have to report to you," the doctor replied.

His eyes met the Pasha's quizzical glance. He raised his hand and pointed his index finger towards the tent door, and after a short pause, he asked:

"Can you hear them?"

The Pasha pouted. "What?"

"The barking."

The Pasha nodded.

"That's what I have come about."

Tursun Pasha scowled as if he thought this was a ridiculous joke to bring him so late in the night. This scarecrow is so tall, he thought, that I can't even have him sent down to the tunnel. The Alaybey had told him that not only the sappers, but the janissaries who had been infiltrated under the citadel had been selected for shortness.

Seeing that the Pasha's patience was very limited, as with any great leader, the doctor hastened to explain.

"The day before yesterday, the dogs you can hear barking and sometimes wailing even here dug down into one of the mass graves where our dead are buried."

The Pasha grimaced.

The doctor went on: "They've clawed up and dismembered the cadavers. A plague could break out."

The shadow of terror passed across the Pasha's face at the word "plague".

"Sire, the sappers did not do their job conscientiously. The graves were hastily dug, and when I went to inspect them just now I observed that in some places there is less than one foot of earth covering the bodies."

The Pasha cursed under his breath. He clapped his hands.

An orderly appeared at the tent door.

"Get Ulug Bey! I need him here this instant!"

The orderly vanished. The Pasha said nothing for a while. The doctor stood as if rooted to the ground. From afar, somewhere over on the left, came muddled sounds that sharpened into the barking of dogs.

"They barked all last night, too," Tursun Pasha observed.

"Yes, they did, Pasha. But nobody knew why. One of my men told me this evening, he'd got it from a carter during the afternoon."

The tent fell silent once again and the sound of barking seemed to them both to grow nearer. Then came the footfall of a man running. Ulug Bey, the captain of the sappers, burst in, panting heavily. Before he had even finished bowing low, as regulations required, the Pasha yelled:

"Can you hear them? Can you hear, you wretched man?"

Ulug Bey couldn't say a thing.

"The dogs are unburying our dead," the Pasha resumed, in a grating tone.

Ulug went pale. He had understood.

"Our heroes give their lives for the glory of the Osmans, whereas you can't even be bothered to put a spadeful of earth over their bodies!"

The commander's voice, broken by a kind of hiccup, fell mercilessly on Ulug Bey. The Pasha went on to call him a cur, even insinuating that the sapper had purposely left the graves in that woeful state so as to give the other members of his pack something to eat, and so forth. But Ulug Bey did not feel offended. He thought: It serves me right. Or else: May God protect me. He would have liked the Pasha to insult him even more gravely, to call him a jackal, a hyena, or even to whip him — anything to put a stop to the terrible barking of the dogs.

When the vituperation fell away and the yelping could be heard loud and clear, as if it was coming from just behind the tent, Ulug Bey thought his own end was nigh. He was tempted to prostrate himself before the Pasha or else to explain that as he had been incarcerated night and day in the tunnel with his sappers, he had been obliged to pay less attention to his other responsibilities. But as he was paralysed with remorse, he did neither of these things. He just lowered his eyes and waited. Perhaps it was to that posture that he owed his salvation.

"If all the graves are not covered with four cubits of earth by tomorrow morning, I shall have you buried alive. Dismissed!"

Ulug Bey bowed and went out. From the tent you could hear the sound of his steps, which were speedy to begin with, and then turned into a run.

"Sirri Selim," the Pasha asked when the footsteps had faded into the distance, "is there really a risk of plague?"

"No, not yet, Pasha," the doctor replied in a measured tone.

He thought he saw a gleam of scorn in the Pasha's eyes, and, fearing that he was perhaps suspected of having raised a false alarm, he hurriedly added: "No. This evening, we still have time. If we had waited until tomorrow it might have been too late."

The Pasha lowered his gaze. Sirri Selim took his leave, bowed low, and went out.

The Pasha stood for a while with his arms crossed. Barking and yelping could still be heard at intervals, from the same direction. Listening hard, he stared at a single spot on the kilim. It was only when the noise of the dogs suddenly ceased that he reckoned Ulug Bey and his men had reached the graves, and he sighed a deep sigh of relief. He lay down and leaned on a cushion, half closing his eyes. His weary mind ranged over the huge camp. He didn't linger on the myriad tents, but followed the *akinxhis* as they marched through these horrible mountains, then wandered back to the sentries, glanced along the ramparts, returned to the lilac-blossom tent, then alighted once more on the dogs and the graves, wavered for a while before the shady entrance to the blonde girl's vagina, then all of a sudden abandoned everything to plunge underground and crawl unseen along the dark, damp tunnel under construction. He dropped off to sleep. One of his orderlies tiptoed up to him and covered him with a soft cloak as he gazed with fearful veneration at his master's creased and weary face.

We came to understand the significance of the flowery dresses that the soldiers had been flaunting and to realise what was hidden by the Turks' ploy of silence. The dresses and baubles were the signal for an imminent raid by the akinxhis. Naturally, the soldiers had to be ready to purchase captive girls. As for the calm, it was a prelude to death.

Our first suspicions were aroused by the construction of what was supposed to be a bread oven bizarrely close to our ramparts. We had it watched. Carts were seen going in without interruption; smoke came out of the chimney. Trained eyes could see that despite their slow pace the carts going in were empty, while those that left were full. Similarly, observation of the smoke plume and especially of the time lag between the thickening of the smoke corresponding to the lighting of the oven and when it thins out again, which is when the baking begins, convinced our bakers that no oven in the world could work like that. It is therefore obvious that the carts do not bring in any flour and that the oven cooks no bread. But when they leave the carts are laden. What with? It can only be earth.

The Turks must be digging an underground passage, that's certain. It's a stratagem they often use in sieges. We lost no time and went down to check our dungeons and cellars, and posted observers in every corner. They lay flat out with their ears to the ground for nights on end. Many fell ill. Then we remembered that vessels made of beaten brass amplify underground noise. Our watchmen could thus keep their ears open for many more long nights. Sometimes the strain of concentration makes them hear banging. But at last we did spot where the besiegers were. They have already got several cubits' length inside the perimeter of the citadel. They are digging, or rather nibbling, at the earth with some difficulty. They sound like an animal scratching itself incessantly in the bowels of the earth.

Lying on the cold flagstones with their ears to the ground, our watchmen are following the hidden advance of the enemy step by step. The Turks are now digging with such caution that they could have faded away. But they are still there. They have split the tunnel into two branches, like a two-headed snake, forever slithering forwards beneath our feet. We are listening so hard that we have a constant ringing in our ears.

THE MIDDLE CHAPTER

The *akinxhis* had returned. We could hear their drums. The camp emerged from drowsiness and sprang to life. Soldiers rushed out of their tents, calling to comrades who were still reclining. Those who rushed the fastest were men who had done deals with the *akinxhis* for a woman or some other trophy. Some had already grabbed the flowery dresses they had bought at the army bazaar, with which they now hoped to drape their captives. As he navigated his way through the throng, Tuz Okçan regretted not having made such a purchase. At the time he had thought it was premature and might even bring misfortune, whereas now he was nervous that there would be none left to buy. On two or three occasions when he caught sight of the returning column in the distance he was tempted to rush towards the market stalls, but he held back from fear of being late and missing the *akinxhi* who had more or less promised to sell him a slave woman.

The crowd buzzed with excitement. Soldiers were laughing and joking, swearing and telling dirty stories. The black eunuch Hasan went by, carrying an empty pitcher in each hand. Soldiers gave each other nudges and winks as they pointed to the jugs.

"He's going to fill them with water for *them*."

"For *them*?"

"Sure he is. Can't you see the pitchers?"

"Them girls are hot! They'll need to cool down!"

"So the poor lasses are hot, are they? What about us? Aren't we just boiling as well?"

"We could melt steel faster than Saruxha's furnace!"

"Shush! Someone will hear you."

The eunuch strode among the soldiers with haughty disdain. For a while their blazing eyes followed a man who strangely reminded them of the mysteries of women. Often, on seeing him, men's eyes would flash and their knees would go weak, but this morning, their eagerness to see the *akinxhis* return was so great that they paid the eunuch hardly any attention at all.

The first columns were now coming into the camp. Kurdisxhi's big flame-red head swayed sleepily in time with his horse's trot. As he traversed the crowd with his escort at his side, men shouted out huzzahs, but his eyes remained half-closed and, without halting or even acknowledging the salutes, he guided his horse straight to the commander-in-chief's tent, dismounted, and went inside.

While the long columns of dust-whitened *akinxhis* slowly merged like a weary river into the mass of the *azabs*, the janissaries and other troops, in his tent Tursun Pasha snapped his long fingers as he listened superciliously to Kurdisxhi's brief report.

"Is that all?" he asked when the soldier had finished.

"Yes, that's all."

The Pasha sighed deeply, and restraining himself with difficulty from aiming at the ill-healed wound at the corner of Kurdisxhi's mouth, he spat on the ground. Kurdisxhi, as if he had guessed what was in his chief's mind, raised his hand to wipe that part of his face.

"Traitor! Dog! Son of a bitch! Shithead!"

Kurdisxhi held his peace. He strongly suspected that if his commander had possessed any rights over him, he would have had him executed. But, although nothing was written down about this, he also knew that the Pasha had no right to lay a finger on him, just as he could not discipline Old Tavxha, the Mufti or the Alaybey. However he was equally aware that if he answered back, the Pasha would fly into a rage and would request Kurdisxhi's head from a higher place, which would come to the same thing.

Meanwhile, in the main avenue of the camp, the harassed *akinxhis*, their turbans all dirty and torn (many soldiers had torn strips off them to bandage their wounds) were dismounting, walking over to their comrades or else going to their tents without a word. Tuz Okçan gaped as he watched the units arrive one after the other. He was trying to spy the black curly hair of the man with whom he had made a deal. He noticed that a lot of other people were as impatient as he was.

"So where are the captives?" someone asked from behind.

"They're surely on their way."

Suddenly he saw Çelebi.

"Mevla! Mevla!" he shouted for joy.

The chronicler put a smile on his sallow and horribly downcast face. The janissary held out his hand to help him off his horse.

"Are you sick?" he asked.

"No, but I'm wiped out."

"I can see that."

A voice in the crowd behind them was asking worriedly for news of someone called Ulun. Mevla recognised the handsome young man in the uniform of a sapper. An *akinxhi* with wandering eyes whispered the sad news into his ear, and the sapper put his head in his hands.

"Are there many dead?" the janissary asked.

Çelebi glowered at him and answered feebly, "Don't ask."

Apparently quite a few of the people waiting had asked the same question, because the jolly hum of the crowd gradually turned into an angrier noise.

"Were you up against Skanderbeg?" the janissary asked.

"Perhaps."

"What do you mean, 'Perhaps'?"

"We were harried, especially at night."

Çelebi was staring at his friend as if he was seeing him for the first time. For a brief moment the janissary thought the chronicler had lost his wits.

"Maybe, Tuz Okçan, as I said. It usually happened at night, and how can you know who is attacking you in the dark?"

"Strange. Did you bring back any captives?"

The chronicler smiled sourly.

"Around a couple of dozen."

"So few!"

"I reckon it's quite a lot."

Tuz Okçan now thought he had done well not to buy a dress in a hurry. Dozens of men were standing around nearby looking downcast as they twiddled with adornments they no longer knew what to do with.

"The captives!" someone yelled. "Here they come!"

People jostled to get a view. Voices cried out, "Here they are!" They were chained together in groups of four or five. Their clothes were stained with mud, and so was their hair.

A great tumult arose from all around. They've been spoiled, upon my word! The poor girls have been raped! Why? Did you think they'd wait for you to service them? If they did it, then good on their pricks. Look, there's a blonde. And look at that other one, what a beauty! A redhead, the way Suleiman likes his girls. But what a pity, she's been damaged. So what? They've left her little bird's-nest, it's still there! Look, I'd be willing to pay three hundred aspers. Look at that one over there, she's laughing, she's gone quite mad, poor thing. Well, that's a fine job you *akinxhis* have done! You can tell the hunter from his catch.

More and more men joined the crowd. Some were waving bulging purses under the girls' noses. Some muttered dirty words. Voices called out: "Give way!" but the soldiers did not stand aside. Most of them seemed to be drunk. For many of them, it was the first time they had seen women without veils over their faces. They found it odd that the girls were chained when their eyes were freely available. They would not have been more fascinated if they had been allowed to take their pick from a fistful of emeralds strewn on the ground. Some of the girls let out little screams. The men thought they were laughing, but they were actually sobbing. Unless it was the other way round. Those eyes have quite an impact, someone standing behind the chronicler said.

"Move back!" someone said. "Soldiers, give way! The captives will be sold at the market according to custom. Are there so few? Aren't there any more?"

"This is but a drop of water in the salty desert of our desire," Çelebi said, feeling more and more happy just to be still alive.

"They'll be gone in a few hours' time. They won't last beyond midnight," someone spoke out from nearby.

Tuz Okçan turned round and without thinking asked: "Why so?"

"What do you mean, 'Why so?'" a middle-aged *azab* answered. "That's what always happens when there's only a handful of girls. They last until the evening. At best, until midnight."

"Do you reckon everyone will get a turn?" Tuz asked.

"Of course we will. As usual."

Tuz Okçan noticed the eunuch standing not far off. He was on his way back from the river but had stopped to take a look at the *akinxhis*, or so it seemed. He had put his pitchers, now full, down on the ground, and with fearful eyes watched the captive women being led to market. The janissary was struck by the pleasant smell of perfume coming from the eunuch's body.

The chronicler also turned his head to look at the source of such an agreeable odour, then felt a hand on his shoulder.

"Effendi," someone said softly to him.

He looked round. It was one of the Quartermaster General's orderlies. He whispered something in Çelebi's ear, then the chronicler turned back towards Tuz Okçan.

"Please excuse me," he said. "A highly placed friend of mine wants me to go to his tent. I'll be back."

Çelebi felt new energy in his stride as he walked towards the tent where, in a few minutes' time, he would, almost unbelievably, be sitting on a soft divan beside his eminent friend, drinking pomegranate syrup, and discussing elevated, agreeable topics far away from the fear and frost of mountain nights. In fact, he hadn't talked to anybody for several days. His tongue had gone dry. But now Allah was compensating him for all that suffering. Suddenly the world around him, from the cropped grass beneath his feet on the side of the road to the rumble of a chariot rolling somewhere behind him, seemed more magnificent than ever.

"Heavens! You've lost weight!" the Quartermaster General exclaimed when he saw Çelebi come into the tent.

The chronicler recognised compassion in his friend's eyes and felt comforted by that.

"Sit down. You look shattered. Maybe you would like a bath?"

Çelebi could feel himself blushing. He must surely smell of

sweat, and the surge of warmth prompted by his interlocutor's kind words must have made the smell even worse.

"How can I say . . . Excuse me . . . for turning up in this state . . ." he mumbled.

But his host interrupted him. "No, excuse me for having had you brought here before you even had time to take a rest. I wanted to see you as soon as I could to find out how the expedition went. And then, I was worried about you, too."

The chronicler felt almost happy.

"The friendship you grant me is like a jewel in my life."

The Quartermaster gave one of those special smiles that lit up his face every time anyone mentioned money or precious stones.

"Go and have a bath," he told Çelebi. "It'll cleanse your spirit even more than your body."

The chronicler stood up and with lowered head went towards the sergeant who was holding out a bathrobe for him. The hammam had been fitted into a tiny area, but it was fully equipped. The chronicler was over the moon.

After taking a bath, he was confronted with a jug of pomegranate syrup and a silver platter of halva placed before him by the sergeant. It was like a dream come true!

"So, how did it go up in the mountains?" the Quartermaster finally asked.

Before answering, the chronicler raised his weary eyes and looked straight at his friend.

"You can tell me the whole truth," the Quartermaster reassured him. "Chronicles are for future generations or for the good ladies of Edirne."

There was a pause. Then without taking his eyes off Çelebi he asked again:

"How was it?"

"Awful," the chronicler replied with a sad shake of his head. The Quartermaster then asked questions about the mountains, and Çelebi replied by repeating almost word for word the passages he had already drafted for his chronicle.

The senior officer seemed distracted, but then suddenly resumed his interrogation.

"Did you see any Albanians?"

"Of course we did."

"Tell me about them."

Çelebi half closed his eyes before answering.

"Physically, they are slightly taller and slimmer than we are. They have light hair, as if it had been faded by sunlight. And unlike our children, theirs are almost all blond."

"What else? I already know what they look like."

"How can I say?" the chronicler muttered. "They're highly-strung, very fierce. You would never think such wishy-washy hair topped such hard heads."

"Are they brave?"

"I am planning to put in my chronicle that they are so resistant to any kind of domination that they rage like tigers at the clouds passing over their heads and spring up to claw at them . . ."

"Listen to me, Mevla Çelebi. If I told you I wanted the truth from you, not fancy phrases, it was for a specific reason . . ."

A lump came into the chronicler's throat.

"You mustn't hold it against me," he said in a squealing tone. "I am just a humble chronicler. I don't have . . . I don't know . . . In a nutshell, there are so many things I don't properly understand."

"Come on, help yourself!" the Quartermaster said, pointing to the halva.

Çelebi started giving a detailed account of the raid. He described in particular the mountain chill, the pillage, the slaughter on both sides, the stake. When the chronicler reached the end of his story, the Quartermaster offered him more halva. Çelebi was hungry but he would never have allowed himself to eat anything without being expressly invited by his host, especially as the Quartermaster ate almost nothing and just stared with his light, cold eyes at the reddish gleam of his pomegranate juice.

Çelebi realised he had perhaps gone on too long about the violent and bitter side of the story. Thinking his friend would perhaps prefer to hear more refined and philosophical reflections, he mentioned the language of the Albanians, which he had frequently heard spoken during the raid.

"Theirs is a strange dialect," he explained. "It's as if Allah had cast on it a cloak of fog to make it impossible to separate one word from the other, whereas in our language the divisions are so clear."

He was holding forth about the sounds of Albanian when he noticed that his friend had stopped listening.

"With a people of that kind we are not going to have an easy time," the Quartermaster concluded. "With them, or with any of the other Balkan tribes."

"We shall smite them and destroy them without remission until they are wiped from the face of the earth," the chronicler replied.

"Yes, yes, I know," the Quartermaster riposted. "But the question remains, how do we smite them, and where do we smite them, and, above all, to what purpose? You talked of annihilating them. But let me ask three questions. One: is it possible to wipe out an entire people? Two: if the first answer is yes, then by what means? Three — and remember this, Çelebi, third questions are usually the trickiest — I ask you: is it desirable to do so? Or to be more precise: do we still need to do it?"

Çelebi now had a sharp pain in the back of his neck from concentrating so hard on following what the Quartermaster had said. In all current ways of talking as well as in all of the ancient chronicles, exterminating the enemy was considered the crowning glory of victory. Whereas he was now being told the opposite! If the Quartermaster had not been such an important personage, Çelebi would have walked away without looking back. Now he had got aches in all his joints again and his arms felt as if they had been crushed by bludgeons.

"I can see I've startled you," the Quartermaster said without hiding his satisfaction. "But let's take a proper look at the points I've raised. So, the first is the issue of extermination, to which you seem so attached."

Good Lord! What a hornet's nest I've stirred up! Çelebi thought. As if all the paths and boulders that had torn him to pieces weren't enough, now he had to face a conversation fraught with snags and brambles.

"I didn't say I was attached to it . . ." he objected, timidly. "But . . ."

"Let me finish saying what I have to say," the Quartermaster butted in. "Let's consider the proposal to exterminate an entire people. Is it achievable?" He shook his head back and forth. "It's difficult, my good friend, very difficult to do . . . And you certainly can't ever do it by war. It's quite ridiculous to think that you could . . . Don't put on that bewildered face, Çelebi. I'll explain it all to you. Go on, have some more halva."

The Quartermaster General took just a few sips of pomegranate syrup. As for the chronicler, he'd lost his appetite.

"Now listen to me! Every people in the world goes on increasing at a greater or lesser rate. The annual increase is usually around twenty or thirty people per thousand."

It was the first time Çelebi had heard figures of that sort. The books he read didn't generally contain that kind of information.

"A rough calculation on that basis means that in five hundred years' time there will be around ten million Albanians."

The chronicler furrowed his brow as if he had a bad toothache.

"And that's a figure that could easily stop us from sleeping, my dear friend," the Quartermaster continued. "Do you now grasp what it means to halt the natural increase of the population of a given land? Numbskulls like Old Tavxha or Kurdisxhi, or even the Mufti who pretends to be cultivated, think that a war and a massacre suffice to eradicate a nation. But it's not possible! Let's suppose we have a great battle and leave twenty thousand dead on the field. That would count as a brilliant victory for our army, wouldn't it? Well, it's really depressing, isn't it, to have to say that a battle so carefully and strenuously prepared would chop off just one year's population growth, and no more!"

Çelebi felt like putting his head in his hands.

"In other words, their womenfolk can give birth to more men than our army can slaughter, even with Engineer Saruxha's famous cannon!"

Despite his revulsion the chronicler recalled the litany of vulgar expressions referring to a woman's sexual organ that he'd heard during the raid into the mountains. The soldiers often drew images of it in chalk or charcoal, never forgetting to show alongside it a man's sabre, as they called it, and it did indeed remind you of a yatagan or sometimes of the barrel of a gun.

"So we should not get drawn into such unrealistic dreams, and be satisfied with restraining population growth. With punitive raids and massacres, by laying waste whole cities and expelling or deporting their inhabitants, by kidnapping their children to make janissaries of them, we will also reduce a people's desire to multiply, to some extent.

Yet that is not enough. Nations are like grass, they grow everywhere. So we have to invent other, more stealthy means. I'm only in charge of the accounts. The great Padishah has other men working for him on problems of this kind. They're all specialists in denationalisation, like Saruxha is an expert in the destruction of castles . . ."

For a second he lost the thread of his argument. Çelebi found it a burdensome moment, for he feared that a halt in the conversation, a sneeze, a spilled glass, or just a longer pause than normal would be laid at his door.

"Yes . . . Craftsmen in the rotting and corroding of nations, if I may say. But, my friend, you should know that peoples don't only dilate, they also contract. When they receive a great blow from the outside, from us, in this particular instance, they don't necessarily go into decline, they can also emerge from it with added strength. On the other hand, damage from the inside, damage secreted from inside their own ranks, well, yes, that is the evil that can bring them to their knees . . . Do you grasp what I'm saying, Çelebi? On your raid into the hills, you had occasion to see large excavations ringed with stone steps and columns. Those are the famous theatres of long ago. And do you know why thousands of people sat for hours on those stone steps? To watch and hear four or five individuals, who were called actors, recite the reasons why men kill each other and how they had to kill each other . . . And how the man who performed such abominations the best even had a crown placed on his head, as a sign of general esteem . . . Now those are customs that can teach us an important lesson. They explain why those peoples never grew much in number but kept a more or less stable population, like those species of dogs which are always small — the *hanums* of the *giaours* in Edirne usually have them as pets. But do have something more to eat!"

It was the first time the Quartermaster General had spoken to him at such length and on such a sensitive subject. Thank God that he wasn't asking him to respond. Çelebi even got the impression that his host had forgotten about him entirely.

"But even that is not sufficient," he thundered, as if riposting in a debate. "We slave away down here spreading death and desolation, but the real fight is going on up there." He raised his hand. "You cannot call a country conquered until you have conquered its Heaven. What I'm saying might seem hermetic to you, like some nebulous declaration of a poet . . . But it's nothing of the kind!"

Çelebi felt the blood rushing to his face, because exactly that thought had been in his mind, but fortunately the high official went back to his peroration without taking the slightest notice of what his guest might actually be thinking. Rudeness has at least one virtue, the chronicler thought.

"So the fiercest battle happens up there, in heaven," the Quartermaster resumed. "Because, just as folk hide their treasures in places that are hard to get at, so peoples and nations store their most precious assets in the heavens — their divinities, their faith, all that they hold to be sublime and that nothing can alter. By that I mean things of a higher order, things that transcend the limits of human life, things that are sometimes roughly called apparitions, in a word, everything that has to do with the soul. One day or another we'll take possession of their castles; we're sure to overcome them in the end. But that won't be enough. In the final analysis they're just heaps of stones that can be taken from us in the same way we will take them ourselves. But victory in war is something altogether different . . . I'm not sure if you're following me?"

Not only had Çelebi stopped following the thread, he was

no longer able to make anything at all from the tangled skein of the Quartermaster's speech. But he nodded his head nonetheless, thinking of his own tent, the tent he had so often cursed but which now seemed to him like a corner of paradise.

"Have you ever wondered about how something to which you've never attached much importance can be fearsome — let's say, a song? The war that took place a month ago, for instance, has become the subject of a song. All over the world people know the ancient art of extracting a handful of verses from a pile of events and struggles, including those that happen in royal palaces, just like you extract wine from a bunch of grapes. The grape and even the vine die in the end, but the wine never goes off, quite the opposite in fact: it gets better and better as time goes on. Same thing for war. The war comes to an end, but the song made in its honour moves on from generation to generation. It moves on like a cloud, like a bird, like a ghost, whatever you prefer. And it engenders a new war. How can we kill that black bird . . . ? Or else, we could take their language. I don't know if you've ever reflected — but as a man of learning, you must have — that a language is a creation as magnificent as it is mysterious. Well, it is, and to such a degree that I've often thought — may Allah forgive me! — that many things in this world would be a lot quieter if language simply didn't exist. A part of the heaven that I mentioned just now is connected to it, because, more than any other faculty, language is in communication with Heaven. Have some more halva! When you told me a while back about their habit of speaking in a slightly nasal tone, it struck me how hard it is to change anything at all, even just the nasal tone you mentioned. That's something really difficult, Çelebi, much more difficult than knocking down gates or demolishing ramparts. And to do it you can't call in the cannon or architect Giaour's ground plans to help you out!"

To the chronicler's amazement his host now began to eat ravenously. It seemed his exhausting tirade had made him famished.

"In higher places there are two attitudes to this sort of thing," he went on after wiping his mouth on a napkin. "But apparently our side is winning the argument at the moment."

Çelebi was now even more bewildered. What were these two attitudes and these two sides? He was, moreover, unclear about where the "higher places" were.

"We had a long debate on the issue," the Quartermaster said. "What would we leave to the Balkan peoples, and what would we take away from them: their religion, or their language? Some thought we should take both away, others reckoned we had to leave them one or the other. Naturally, all sorts of arguments were put, until, in the end, our camp seemed to have won. Which means we will leave these peoples their faith. As for their language, for the time being we will only prohibit it being written down. It's too soon to ban the speaking of it."

Çelebi must have raised his eyebrows because the Quartermaster General bent over and brought his perfumed head close to his ear:

"I must have worn you out a bit, but I took the liberty because you are my friend, and it's a long while since I had a chance to get things off my chest. Now I'm going to tell you a secret which I hope you'll keep to yourself."

The chronicler felt so shaken up already by what he had heard that he thought that his beleaguered brain could hardly bear an extra burden.

"Well, here it is, my dear Mevla. I have to inform you that my job as Quartermaster General is for me only a secondary occupation. In reality . . ."

Allah! the chronicler muttered to himself. A suspicion of that sort had indeed passed through his mind, but he had banished it from his thoughts so as not to sink and drown. Throughout the camp there had long been speculation as to who was the real head of the army. All sorts of crazy ideas went around. Some said the real commander-in-chief was a ragged dervish, others thought the role belonged to deaf-mute Tahanka, who was of course only pretending to be deaf but in reality heard everything. Another group was convinced that it was neither of the above, but the Black eunuch who looked after the Pasha's wives. But the truth turned out to be something else.

"In other words . . . you . . . to put it differently . . ."

The chronicler was stuttering. The Quartermaster noticed.

"What's wrong with you, Mevla Çelebi?" he asked in a gentle tone. "Have a drink of syrup."

"No, I'm quite alright, thank you . . . My Lord!"

"What . . . ? Are you feeling better now? Alright. I was about to confide in you the secret of my main occupation. My function is not specifically connected to this army, nor to any other more or less similar entity. It's related to a much bigger action. The Padishah has set up a kind of semi-official supreme council, so to speak, and its task is to answer a major, difficult question: what will we do with the peoples of the Balkan Peninsula? That's why I'm here, Mevla Çelebi."

The chronicler felt his throat going so dry that he dared stretch out his hand and take hold of the goblet of pomegranate syrup without being asked.

"I am deeply touched by the confidence you show in me," he mumbled.

"So now I come to the third question, which, as I told you, is always the most diabolical. Must we, should we, debilitate these nations? Annihilating them, as I think you are now persuaded yourself, is just eyewash. What we have to do is to weaken them, render them bloodless. But the question that arises is: would that even be wise?"

This man will make me go mad! Çelebi said to himself.

The Quartermaster's gaze, flimsily, transparently veiled, bore down upon him like the eyes of an inquisitor.

"Our side is of a different opinion," he said. "We see the Balkan peoples as the new star that fate has put in the path of our empire."

The chronicler began to realise just what a scandalous turn the conversation was taking. In the midst of a campaign, with battle raging all around, the talk was of an alliance with the Balkan nations . . . ! Before his eyes flashed visions of a deep hole underground where the astrologer was allegedly serving out his sentence, of a man being flayed, of limbs sawn off, and then the question: so what did *you* answer when he declared that we should love our enemies? Each vision felt like another nail being driven into his skull.

"I have reason to believe that our side will win," the Quartermaster pursued. "At the present time people are still too excited and a thick pall of death shrouds the issue, but the picture will become clear in the long run."

This man has really lost his mind, Çelebi thought, and I'm even crazier to sit here listening to him!

"Aren't you feeling well?" his host enquired. "Your lips have gone quite blue. Should I call a doctor?"

"No . . . No. Just a bit dizzy. It'll pass."

"It's fatigue, my dear friend. Now, what was I saying . . . Ah, yes, about the turn of fate that put the Balkan peoples in our way. The Anatolian soldier is the best in the world. As unshakeable as the earth itself. And just as faithful and obedient. But he needs leadership. And the best leaders don't grow on placid ground, but in demented lands like these. Have some more halva!"

The chronicler was now trying to stop his ears . . . I wasn't feeling very well, your honour. That's why I missed a lot of what was being said, particularly all that venom he wrapped up so cleverly . . .

"We confronted the Balkans sixty years ago, on the plains of Kosovo. My father was there, and he never stopped talking about that battle. That's when we saw them all gathered together — Serbs, Albanians, Bosniaks, Croats and Romanians, all allied against us. The fight lasted ten hours, as you know. For the first time we saw our army based on land and obedience up against an opponent driven by pride and daring. Our soldiers, who had no titles or *noms de guerre*, some of whom didn't even have a family name, just their first name, overcame those proud counts and barons. Now, Çelebi, think what a marvel it would be to mix the noble earth of Anatolia with those rocks that spark! Do you see what I mean? We all need each other. They need our generosity and we need their hotheadedness . . . I guess you've read plenty of chronicles about that war in Kosovo?"

"Of course," Çelebi replied. "Especially because that is where our glorious Sultan Murad I fell as a hero."

He mentioned the heroic death of the sovereign in the hope that the conversation would take a different turn. But the Quartermaster General's eyes clouded over even more.

"That plain . . ." he drawled. "That's where the most tragic mystery of our empire is hidden . . ."

The chronicler didn't really understand what his eminent friend was talking about. He couldn't help thinking: He's going from bad to worse! The Quartermaster's eyeballs seem to have become opaque, as if they were steamed up on the inside.

"You're a historian . . . You have read many chronicles . . ."

"Yes, indeed."

"Well, what do they say on the subject . . . ? I mean, about the death . . . about the murder!"

Çelebi knew by heart everything that had been written about that fateful day, especially after sunset, when the victorious Sultan Murad had ridden with his escort among the corpses of the fallen. And suddenly . . . just there . . . a Balkan soldier . . .

He retold the tale, but the official's eyes got no clearer, they darkened even further.

"And then . . . ? What happened?"

The Quartermaster's voice was distant and muffled, and the chronicler realised he was undergoing a second interrogation, just as he had been fearing for a while.

"The Sultan's death was kept secret so as not to damage the army's morale."

"And then?"

"There then occurred another murder, that of Jakup, one of the Sultan's sons."

"And who did it?"

The chronicler wasn't sure why, but he found himself staring at his own hands. He had heard said that sometimes the whim of the gods makes bloodstains migrate to innocent hands.

"The Council of the Viziers did it, sir. To ward off disputes over the throne."

"You're hiding something, chronicler!"

Çelebi thought the tent was falling on his head. He stared at his hands again, and even did so in a way that made it possible for the Quartermaster to see what he was doing, as if to let him know that he was in no way responsible for those chronicles.

"You're hiding something!" the Quartermaster repeated icily.

"You mentioned the murder of one of the two sons without recalling that contrary to what might have been expected in such circumstances, the one killed was the elder brother."

"You are quite right, sir," Çelebi replied. "The elder son, the legitimate heir to the throne, was the one who was killed, and the younger, Bayezid, was declared Sultan."

"In other words, everything happened back to front, didn't it? Or to put it another way . . ."

The official drew his face unbearably close to the chronicler's.

"To put it another way, the other murder . . . the murder of the Sultan himself . . . wasn't perpetrated by a Balkan assassin at all . . . but . . . Ah! You poor man, you're trembling all over . . . ! But now listen to what really happened . . ."

It was too late. The chronicler had not time to wave it all away, to turn his head to the side, to block his ears or to puncture his eardrums. The Quartermaster had literally grasped him by the neck and was pouring into his auricle a poison so venomous as to send every historian of the Empire raving mad. O Allah! Make me deaf, so I may not hear these abominations! he pleaded inwardly, yet the bitter truths entered him willy-nilly. He was so flummoxed that he had no difficulty in pretending to pass out. It was probably only his accursed curiosity that prevented him from really losing his senses.

In the end something happened over his head. The lugubrious muttering of the Quartermaster General gave way to homelier words: "Mevla, my poor chap, what's the matter? Must be the fatigue . . . Yes, fatigue. Probably."

He felt a wet towel on his forehead and when he opened his eyes he saw it was the sergeant wiping his brow. The Quartermaster was leaning over him, looking like his old self, beaming and concerned.

"Don't worry," he was saying, "it's just a bad turn. I've sent for the war council's doctor . . ."

"Oof! What a crazy day this has been!" the doctor blurted out as he hurried into the tent. "So what's up, Kurt?"

The chronicler was astounded by the doctor's familiar tone, but even more by the first name, "Kurt", that he had never heard uttered before.

"I wouldn't have troubled you on a day like this for myself," the Quartermaster said. "But it's about my friend here . . . Mevla Çelebi, the army's historiographer, I imagine you've heard of him . . ."

From the doctor's lack of reaction to these words and especially from the way he pulled back Çelebi's eyelids to examine his pupils, the chronicler deduced that historians were not very high on the man's list of priorities. They're only accustomed to examining important personages, he thought spitefully. But the good smell of his own body that arose when he'd had his tunic undone to have his chest sounded filled him with some pride.

"It's due to two kinds of fatigue," the medical practitioner said, turning round to face the Quartermaster, as if the patient were a mere token. He repeated the words "two kinds" while tapping the side of his forehead.

Çelebi felt mortified again. I'd like to have seen *you* listening to all those horrors! he muttered to himself.

"He should drink a little of this," the doctor said to the Quartermaster as he took a vial from his satchel. The two began to confer in a whisper, as if the chronicler were not even present in the tent. Then, in response to a question from the host, the doctor said: "Fine, fine, go on using the balm I gave you. Right-ho. Farewell, Kurt."

No, I'll never be one of them, Mevla thought with despair.

Right-ho. Farewell, he repeated in his mind as if he were learning a phrase in a foreign language. In fact, he had noticed every now and again a slight foreign accent in the Quartermaster's diction, but like most people he had put such worries aside . . . Wasn't the name "Kurt" quite widespread among the Osmanlis?

Not in a thousand years could he learn to say "Right-ho. Farewell, Kurt" with ease. The Quartermaster had only made a friend of him so as to have someone into whose ear he could drip the poison that people cannot bear to keep inside themselves, just like he had been doing before the doctor's visit.

In any other circumstance he would have been proud to be the depository of a secret of such magnitude. On first hearing it, he had been scared out of his wits. Now, he thought it was just offensive. But who could know how he would view it over the coming days?

"What were we talking about when you came over queer?" the Quartermaster General asked. His manner was casual but in the man's eyes Çelebi could see the icy glint of a stalactite.

"I don't recall very well . . ." he answered. "About the Balkan peoples, I think. About Skanderbeg."

"Ah yes, Skanderbeg," his host said. His face lit up. "You didn't hear the rest of the story . . . ? So much the better!" he added.

Çelebi felt a wave of relief. His regret at losing the secret entrusted to him wasn't enough to disturb the peace of mind he had just recovered.

The Quartermaster also seemed relieved and in an excellent mood. He urged the chronicler to rest a while and then let the orderly accompany him back to his tent. In the meantime they could resume their interrupted conversation. Hi-hi! What they'd been saying about . . . Skanderbeg! The Quartermaster said that one of his friends had actually met him, at peace negotiations that had been held at a secret location. The Albanian leader had refused to go to the Turkish capital, even though the great Padishah, Murad Han, had begun his letter of invitation with the words "My son".

"What an ungrateful man!" Çelebi remarked.

The Quartermaster went on to say that during the said negotiations, Skanderbeg would speak only Latin, the better to mark his complete break with the Empire.

"The ungrateful man!" the chronicler repeated. "Renegade!"

"Worse than a renegade!" the Quartermaster insisted. "He broke one of the dreams of our empire. You know which one? The most beautiful dream of all: bringing the Albanian Catholics back into the bosom of Islam."

Their conversion had been a miracle. To be sure, there hadn't been many of them, only a handful really, but you mustn't forget they were ancient Christians, they had adopted the faith thirteen centuries ago and since then had been attached to the Church of Rome and under allegiance to it. So it was a sign that Islam was managing to make a breach in Christianity in one of its staunchest bastions. No better news had ever reached the heart of the Empire. But the dream was soon destroyed by that demon with a double name, George Castrioti-Skanderbeg . . . The chronicler's jaw dropped in astonishment.

"Everything about him is double. His name, the ram's horns he puts on his helmet, and the two-headed bird on his banner. And do you know what he did as soon as he had consolidated his power over the other local princes? He ordered the Albanians who had become Muslim to return to their original faith, or else die by the sword. And he kept his word. He forcibly re-incorporated into Christendom those new Muslims who had just donned their first thin cloak of Islam. So there, Çelebi . . ."

"He's a two-horned devil!" the chronicler exclaimed, then asked what the Albanian leader looked like.

"What he looks like?" the official rejoined. "I remember asking my friend the same question at the time he told me the story. According to him, Skanderbeg appears completely normal. On the day of the talks, his voice was hoarse, he must have caught a cold. All through the negotiations he kept a scarf wrapped around his throat.

"A scarf around his throat," the chronicler repeated mechanically, almost dropping off to sleep again.

"Normal-looking people are those I fear the most," the Quartermaster said.

His voice had a different resonance, as if the dimensions of the tent had suddenly altered.

Then came the first pause in the talking since the doctor had left. The Quartermaster's long fingers counted the beads on his chaplet faster than usual. One bead in particular seemed to have lost its brilliance.

"In the report I wrote, I reckoned the Albanians should be put alongside the Greeks and the Jews as the first peoples we should integrate." Unlike his hands, the Quartermaster's voice was slow and calm. "Only there's this Skanderbeg fellow in the way."

"I understand," the chronicler said.

In his mind's eye he could see the plain of Kosovo strewn with uncountably many corpses and Murad Han on horseback, at dusk, riding among them at walking pace . . . He had to wipe that vision from his mind, sweep it from his memory for ever if he wanted to stave off his own fall.

"Albania has to get rid of Skanderbeg. It's the only solution," the Quartermaster went on. "But he's doing all he can to prevent that happening. He knows full well that he'll lose the war in the end. But in spite of that, he's hanging on to Albania."

Skanderbeg and Albania can go to the devil! the chronicler thought, without daring to say so aloud.

"He's in the process of achieving an uncommon exploit," the Quartermaster continued. "An extraordinary exploit . . . Just now I was telling you about the heavens where peoples put their relics for safekeeping . . . Well, as from now, that man is aiming for the heavens . . . I don't know if you get my meaning. He's trying to create a second Albania, outside of anyone's reach, a kind of imma-terial Albania. So that when one day this Albania, the terrestrial one, falls to the Empire, that other, ghostly Albania, its shadow-self, will go on wandering among the clouds . . . Do you see what I mean?" (Actually, the chronicler was increasingly befuddled.) "He's devoted himself to a task which almost nobody has ever thought of before: how to re-use a defeat. Or, to put it another way, the eternal recycling of defeat in battle . . ."

Çelebi was in such a mental muddle that he wondered if his interlocutor was not trying to daze him so as to make him forget the Sultan's white horse on the Kosovo plain. But even if you don't ask me to do so, he promised silently, I will be sure to wipe it from my memory.

The Quartermaster was now almost tearing the beads off his prayer-string.

"You see, Mevla, he's trying to oblige us to fight his shadow. To vanquish a ghost, so to speak, the image of his own defeat. But how can you overcome a defeat, a rout? It's like trying to hollow out a ravine. It already is hollow! You would make no difference to it, whereas you could yourself fall into it . . . A while ago — I don't know if you happened to hear this — a strange rumour spread among officers that Skanderbeg didn't exist, and never had existed. At first this struck everyone as good news, but we soon saw that it was the opposite. Those responsible for the rumour were caught and punished. Why? Because, as I told you before, if there is no Skanderbeg, then we are fighting a ghost. It would be like struggling with one of the departed. What can you do if you are attacked by the dead? The dead already are what we fear for ourselves. So if you try to slay a ghost, all you do is bring it back to life. End of story. But I must have worn you out, my dear friend. Maybe it is time for you to go back to your tent. My orderly will escort you."

He did feel exhausted, to tell the truth. His head was a jumble of unclear ideas. It was evening. Life went on in its usual way in the vast camp. Men came and went, this way and that, like so many ants. He was walking along the main thoroughfares when he heard the sound of cartwheels from behind. He turned around, and on one of the carts he thought he could see the astrologer. He quickened his step so as not to be overtaken, but as he felt the convoy draw near him, he took a side path among the tents of a volunteer unit.

Once inside his own tent he threw himself fully dressed on to his bedding of animal skins. As he fell into sleep (at that moment the astrologer on the tumbrel was waxing indignant at Çelebi's faithlessness) he was gently overcome by a vague feeling that in spite of everything, life was beautiful. The same feeling, though mixed with bitterness, overcame the astrologer too as he got down from the cart and made ready to climb down underground with the detachment of sappers about to relieve the current detail. Before each journey into the tunnel he cast a sad glance at all around him, astonished that he had never previously noticed how beautiful the world was. All his life he had been dissatisfied with his position and had thought only of his own advancement by any means, but he had never fully tasted the satisfaction that comes from realising a dream entirely. Now fate had thrown him into a dark, damp hole underground, he realised that many of the days he had spent on earth could have been happy ones, had he not darkened them with his inextinguishable hunger for yet greater felicity.

Each time he went underground, the fear of never emerging cut through him like a dagger. Despite all the precautions they were now taking (they were barely digging any more, just gently scraping at the soil), they were obsessed by the fear of being located by the enemy. That was the first danger. The second was what awaited them when they came into the open. Those who had the bad luck to be the first to reach the exit were likely to pay for the privilege with their lives. And even if they didn't suffer a first bloody clash — if they managed to open the tunnel mouth without being seen by the defenders — then they would most likely be trampled to death by the surge of janissaries from behind. Indeed, the moment the mouth was opened, the janissaries were going to pour through the tunnel like a raging torrent, and they would push the harassed and unarmed sappers straight on to the lances of the besieged.

The nearer they got to the end of the job, the darker the astrologer's forebodings became. The camp was now drowsy but in the tents that had been pitched right next to the bakery hundreds of elite janissaries were standing by on full alert, armed to the teeth. The last two nights, hundreds of others had been posted inside the tunnel, ready to attack in case the roof collapsed accidentally. They stood stock-still like a row of statues in the dark, with sappers trundling past them as if they were part of the wall. Their presence in the tunnel had made the atmosphere even less breathable. The janissaries did two-hour shifts underground, whereas the sappers often worked until they passed out.

Everything indicated that the break-out was imminent. The astrologer plodded slowly through the darkness with a sack on his back, behind a former officer who had been punished for climbing back down a ladder during an assault, leaving his men in front of him. By interpreting the position of the stars in the constellation of the Snake (which obviously alluded to the tunnel), in a supreme effort to raise himself out of the mud into which he had been cast, he might try to forecast the most auspicious day for the break-out, accepting that if he failed he would bury himself in the mud for ever. But as he now found himself in the belly of the earth, he needed a few faithful friends to get his voice heard in high places. Çelebi was not among them. Maybe the poet Sadedin might have been his spokesman before he was mutilated, but he was now only a blind poet, and his words could hardly be taken seriously. The powerful Mufti who, by urging him to set the day of the assault, had been his undoing, had likely forgotten his very name.

The astrologer sighed deeply. There had never been as many janissaries underground as that day. With their backs to the wall they lined the tunnel on both sides, standing three or four paces apart. The glow of the oil-soaked ashes burning in buckets placed at irregular intervals lit their faces with ghoulish effect, as it illuminated only their chins, noses and forehead, and left their eyes and mouths as black shadows.

He came to the place where the passage dipped down steeply. Above it stood the foundations of the main wall, which they had tried to cross without disturbing them too much. Because this part of the tunnel was deeper underground, the air in this section was even heavier and damper than elsewhere. Then the tunnel climbed back to its previous elevation. The astrologer was now inside the perimeter of the citadel. Every time he came back here his heart slowed down. He hastened to fill his sack so as to get away as fast as he could, as if the fortress was weighing on his shoulders. He could see a knot of men at the face. The afternoon team was being relieved by the night shift. There was a lively discussion going on among them, with some men pointing to the walls, and others at the dripping roof. The astrologer recognised the architect and the Alaybey, talking to Ulug Bey, the captain of the engineering squad. The officer looked worried. The architect kept on raising his hand to make a gesture that looked as if he was drawing a circle over his head. They seemed to be trying to decide where the break-out point would be located.

The weak light of the torches made the shadows of their heads on the tunnel walls look as if they were shrouded by the kind of halo that the Christians put around the heads of their holy martyrs in their churches.

They were talking in whispers. The sappers, who had started to get down to work, were also digging noiselessly. They tore out the soil with broad-bladed daggers in complete silence. The astrologer began to fill his sack. It was obvious that the tunnel was not going to go any further. The sappers were currently widening it. That was no doubt in order to create a great crypt beneath the exit so that the largest possible number of janissaries could be assembled for the decisive moment.

The astrologer finished filling his sack and hoisted it on to his back. As he passed by the group of important people he could hear them talking in low and worried voices. Something was going to happen that night, that was clear. Expectation and anxiety could be felt all around. With his sack over his shoulder, he walked past the long line of soldiers standing against the wall, went down the steep slope and then back up again, until he got to the spot where the use of carts was allowed. As he did every time he got to this place, the astrologer uttered a cry of relief.

"What's going on down there?" a haulier asked him. "I reckon it's break-out tonight."

"I think so too," said the astrologer as he dumped his load in the cart.

The astrologer then walked off with his empty sack over his shoulder.

Visibly, the assault was going to be launched that night. When he got back to the cutting face he found the important people still there, still talking in whispers, and making the shape of a circle with their hands above their heads every now and again. Their presence gave him a feeling of security and confidence. They weren't as outcast as they had seemed, after all, since such elevated personages had come down there to be with them on this decisive night.

The astrologer was lugging his second sack of earth when two sappers came the other way carrying a short, wide ladder.

"It's the second one down," the haulier said when they met again.

"Is everything ready at the other end as well?"

"I don't know. I haven't been out yet."

When the astrologer got back to the face, the architect, the Alaybey and two unidentified officers were starting on the long walk back to the entrance. The feeling of safety that their presence had given the earth scratchers and sack carriers gave way to a sensation of emptiness and fear. But Ulug Bey, his deputy and a janissary officer had stayed behind at the tunnel face. The officer stood at a distance with his eyes glued to what was going on at the face. The sappers hadn't really been aware of him when the other VIPs had been around. Only now did they take note of this silent and immobile silhouette that had apparently emerged from the darkness. He seemed to be the man who would be in command of the break-out.

The sappers quickly expanded the area. The friable soil was easy to scoop. Like the other porters, the astrologer was drenched in sweat. On one side a low cavity was quickly excavated where more men huddled, as close-packed as figures in a bas-relief. The sappers were now clawing at the facing wall, so as to allow yet more men to be accommodated. The soldiers were petrified as they looked at the short ladders that would soon be the route to their fates.

No one knew exactly what time it was. All they knew was that up there, on earth, it was dark. Now and again Ulug Bey cast an anxious glance into the murky depth of the tunnel. He was waiting for the courier who was to bring the order for breaking out. He was late. Or maybe that was only the impression they all got from being underground.

Their senses were dulled, and even the flickering light from the torches seemed drowsy. But suddenly, they felt a shock, as if the entire earth had woken up with a start, and then they heard a roll of thunder. Everyone went rigid. One torch went out, another fell over. The muffled roar of a rockfall could be heard from somewhere near the middle of the tunnel.

They all kept on staring in that direction until the noise died away.

Ulug Bey and his deputy rushed towards the collapse. All the others — soldiers, sappers, porters — suddenly came to life as if they had been released from a spell. Someone yelled: "We're done for!" Another shouted out: "It's an earthquake!" A couple of men wanted to run after the captain of the engineers, but the janissary officer, who up to then had been as still as a mummy, abruptly drew his sabre and cried out:

"Silence! No one moves!"

They obeyed the command.

In the ensuing silence they could now hear quite clearly the sound of Ulug Bey's and his deputy's footsteps as they faded into the distance. Then that sound too disappeared. Other noises came into earshot, as if they were coming nearer, then moving further off, then staying still. A sapper came running from the other branch of the tunnel.

"Halt!" the officer shouted. "Who goes there?"

"Sapir, sir. What has happened?"

"I don't know, but we'll find out soon enough," the officer said.

"Allah! What has befallen us?"

"Silence!" the officer ordered. "Light the torches."

"Someone's coming."

They all pricked up their ears. The men could hear steps, but they were rather slow in coming.

"So what happened?"

Ulug Bey and his deputy were grey in the face and covered in cold sweat.

"We are lost!"

"Oh!"

"Silence!" the officer ordered. "What's up?"

"Tunnel collapse," Ulug Bey said flatly.

"They did it?" the officer asked, pointing his finger upwards.

"Yes, it was them."

"So they really got us!"

"They've buried us alive!"

"Silence!" the officer repeated, then turned to Ulug Bey and asked: "What can we do in a case like this?"

"Nothing," the engineers' captain replied.

"Nothing," one of his deputies confirmed.

The word echoed gloomily all around the tunnel. "No-o-o-thi-i-ing".

"Is there no way of cutting a shaft to let us out of here?"

"No, they're watching every move we make."

"Maybe the earth caved in under its own weight?"

"No. Can't you smell the gunpowder?"

"So all that's left for us to do is to die," the officer said in a composed tone, to no one in particular. "Allah chose this way for us to die, and we have to accept his will."

Some began to pray, but most of them started to wail.

The astrologer squatted on his haunches and put his head in his hands. In his mind he had already taken leave of this world.

"What if we surrendered?" somebody asked querulously.

"Be quiet, you wretch!" the officer said, putting his hand to his scabbard.

"So who thinks he can give orders? I'm in command down here."

"And I am in command of my men," the officer riposted.

"The only person to give orders down here is me!" Ulug Bey repeated.

"So you want to surrender as well, do you?"

"No," the captain answered. "What I want is for nobody else to issue orders where giving orders is my business."

"If we surrender, it will only be worse," the officer insisted. "They'll slaughter us like lambs."

"You never know," someone muttered.

"Silence!" the officer yelled. "They'll tear us limb from limb to avenge the slaughter perpetrated by the *akinxhis*."

Each syllable echoed around the group: limb . . . from . . . limb.

The astrologer leaned his back against a hump in the ground. He looked up to the roof of the tunnel which, in the crimson glow of the ash lights, looked like an upturned canal. So this is where you can now look at the stars, he thought to himself. Your Imperial Observatory, as the *giaours* call it, the institution he'd always dreamed of running . . . Blackish water dripped from its cupola. His befuddled mind could just about manage to gather a handful of loosely connected thoughts. He was aghast at the sad fate that had led him to end his days underground beneath a foreign fortress. Another thought took him back more or less to the stars which throughout his life had perhaps been closer to him than men, which had been his friends and partners in squabbles and reconciliations, and which now, as death approached, he would never see again. In their place he saw nothing but blackish earth with water dripping, dripping, dripping down.

Many minutes passed as the astrologer turned these thoughts around in his head. Then came another, even longer, phase. The big torches went out one by one. Then the lanterns also expired. And finally the oil and ash buckets ceased giving off their flickering light. Now and again they seemed to burst into life again, casting irregular flashes of bluish light all around, but then even that half-life fell away. Their last bursts lit faces marked by horror and exhaustion, with asymmetric features — eyes, noses and chins — on the verge of liquefaction, of melting like wax. They had all reached the threshold of eternal night.

Prayers and moans once again broke the long silence. Now and again a short scream or a hiccup rang out but was soon muffled by sobs. The astrologer imagined someone was crawling towards him. He suddenly felt hot breath on his cheek. "Do you want me to tell you the story of my life?" the supplicant asked in a whisper. The astrologer did not answer. "Yes, yes, I'm going to tell you the story of my life," the unknown speaker went on, and began to talk in an even, uninflected tone of a ladder whose rungs he went on climbing, on and on. The astrologer tried to move his ear away from the man, but the unseen speaker found where he had shifted every time. "May your tongue shrivel!" the astrologer said, using a traditional curse from his own language. Then, so as to stop thinking about the accursed speaker, he began thinking about forms of cursing in general. Most had to do with shadows and with earth: "May you smell of earth!" Or else: "May you be without your shadow!" But they had already lost their shadows without being cursed . . . For the first time in his life, he understood the deep meaning of the expression. I have no shadow, he thought, therefore I am dead.

"I am the alternate," a voice uttered somewhere close by. The astrologer then became aware of a struggle between two beings who were apparently trying to obtain sole access to his left ear. "What's an alternate?" one of them asked. "A body double," the other explained. "A man who for security reasons can take the place of Tursun Pasha." "Take the place of the Pasha? Where? When?" "Whenever it turns out to be necessary. Mostly during assaults, but also on other occasions, at meetings, for instance . . . Yes, but he didn't want to be replaced, and they shoved me down here." "Who did?" "They did . . . It seems the Pasha got suspicious, but they did too . . . and then so did I . . . One day, they said, you could be useful to us, but for the time being you must not be seen. They shaved off my goatee beard so I would not look like him, and threw me down here . . ."

"So you were his shadow?" the astrologer exclaimed. "That's why you were cursing so excitedly just now . . ."

"He didn't want me," the man said, "and that's why I'm moulding away in this grave. There are a lot of undesirables down here, that's to say, men who have been sentenced. Hundreds of others are under surveillance. Yet others are under interrogation. Not to mention torture . . ."

"Have you lost your senses?" the astrologer asked. "Where are all these people?"

"All over," the man replied. "Half of the field hospital is under Kapduk Agha's command. Many of the doctors are actually prosecutors. Behind the foundry workshop, on the waste land over there . . . there's a reign of terror. As for spies, they're all over the place, there are even some down here in this hole . . . I always keep on moving to cover my tracks. So I'm off . . ."

Yes, you can scamper away as fast as you like! the astrologer thought. But the double's voice was instantly replaced by that of a few moments before, the man with the ladder. The astrologer strove and strained to escape the voice, but it was no good. Eat me up! he moaned inwardly. Finish me off . . . ! The man spoke smoothly, as if to excuse his own persistence . . .

"The first time I thought of turning back, I was on the fourth rung," he was saying. "But I banished the thought and carried on climbing. At the seventh rung, a dead man slid down and landed beside me. At the eighth rung the wish to go back down attacked me once more with even greater force, but still I managed to repel it by thinking of what my soldiers would say about me. At the tenth rung I looked up and saw the scrimmage on the parapet. It was a dreadful sight. I looked around. My men were coming up behind me. They would have to make way to let me go down. So I went on up. At the eleventh rung I smelled burning flesh right under my nose. The nape of the man ahead of me was on fire. At the twelfth rung I reckoned that in such mayhem nobody would notice if I got lost. I pivoted round to the inside of the ladder, and hung on to the rung with my hands alone. With one hand I grasped the eleventh rung, and then swung in to grab the tenth with the other hand. I was on my way down. At the ninth rung my fingers were crushed by the feet of a soldier climbing up. At the eighth rung they were damaged even more. So I let go and fell on to the pack of men huddling at the foot of the wall. I thought no one had seen me. I was wrong. Every move I made had been watched. Nothing was missed. Later on it was all reported back to me, down to the last detail. To be honest, the idea of giving up came to me as soon as I had got on to the second rung. More precisely, by the seventh rung I had decided to climb down, but hadn't yet worked out how to do so. On the eleventh rung I thought of pretending to be dead and letting myself drop, but the height scared me. That was when I smelled burning flesh . . . Aren't you listening to me? Are you crying? Look, I would have told you the story of my life in any case. But I'd still like to add a few more details. Listen to me, but if you find it all too wearisome, I won't be offended . . ."

On and on he went, in his flat, even voice. He was still trying to work out exactly on which rung he was standing when he first thought of giving up and at what level he had taken the actual decision to go back down. Hesitantly, forever revising what he had said, trying as hard as he could to be utterly precise, the man seemed to go on for ever, saying again and again that he hoped to be as objective and as sincere as possible in his critical self-examination.

At times the astrologer imagined that a part of the man's life had now become inextricably tangled up in his own. He struggled like a man trying to run before a rising tide, but it was no use. Now and again the voice paused or else faded, and it grew ever more impenetrable as another sound began to rise over it. Things were quickly coming apart. Some kind of black, viscous ooze was rising inside everyone, or else creeping up on them. The astrologer was no longer sure his urine and sperm had any separate existence, and even his lungs and his spleen seemed to be dissolving. Everything became everything else. So here we are, melted down, in a single body . . . Skulls were sure to soften before long, and let their brains leak out . . . And that will be the end, the astrologer thought.

"Actually, the real Pasha is . . . me!" the voice declared.

"Are you back, you wretch?" the astrologer shouted, but the man pretended not to have heard.

"I suspected it for ages, but now I'm sure of it. I am Tursun Pasha! The other one up there is just my double. But as often happens with alternates, he's turned out to be the cleverer of us two, and he's ousted me! In other words, he did to me what I should have done to him!"

"What are you talking about?" the astrologer protested. "You've no right to go mad all on your own . . . ! Didn't we all agree to stay together until the end?"

"Don't interrupt me! My suspicions have been proved correct . . . One of us had to fall. But you should not be surprised at my misfortune. It's more or less the same as what has happened to all of us. We underground are the only real and authentic men. Those who are up there are mere nothings, they're just . . . wraiths and spectres . . . Anyway, I have to move on now . . . . Got spies on my tail!"

"Off you go! Go underground!"

The sounds of mumbling and praying grew more muffled. Occasionally, sobbing broke their even hum. Piercing screams became less frequent. The last one he heard came from far away, or so it seemed, from the very end of the tunnel. "I don't want to hear the story of your life!" someone was bawling. "I don't want to! My life is petering out. So why should I hear all about yours? No, I do not want to listen! I'm telling you, go away. Why are you clinging on to me like that? I do not want you, do you hear? I don't! I don't!" The speaker lost his temper, then was suddenly convulsed by violent sobbing. In a flash the weeping spread to everyone. Some added their own dirge: "Unhappy that we are!" Then in the midst of the moaning and wailing came a sudden cry: "The commander-in-chief!"

Tursun Pasha had indeed come down from the world of the living. By the light of a pit lantern that someone had somehow managed to get going again the astrologer recognised the commander-in-chief. He had the same voice as his alternate, and he had had time to let his beard grow back. How long have we been down here, O Lord? he wondered. Time enough for a beard . . . he answered himself. Up above everyone would have been terrified to hear such thoughts. Provided they reached all the way up . . . The Pasha greeted each in turn, showing more feeling for those he already knew. He asked Ulug Bey if there was a message he could take back to his mother and wife. He gave news of relatives to another man. Then as the light flickered out he said to nobody in particular, "Peace be with you!" They all answered: "May we meet again in heaven!"

Between his fingers the astrologer gripped his brass tag with its sign of the three stars. He tried to push himself through the earth and up into the light by the force of thought alone, but it wasn't possible: the darkness and the earth had already made him part of their empire. He began to cry. Images of friends, women, crowded noisy streets and doors he had bumped into struggled to form a more or less coherent sequence in his mind, but to no avail.

Among the wailing the laughter of a man demented fluttered about like a blind bird. Go on, the astrologer ordered his mind, leave this body, you are no use to it any more. Some spoke in drunken voices of the remorse that the people up above must be feeling. Others sobered up in a flash and burst into tears. But there were some men who refused to be downcast. They imagined themselves as conquerors of the Void, which made them stronger than anything else on earth. "We have Absence, the Queen of the Universe, on our side!" they said. The astrologer only just stopped himself from shouting out loud: "I am a foreigner in these parts, so leave me alone!" And he waved his identity tag in front of him . . . Admittedly, he had committed errors, but the celestial empire could surely have shown him more mercy. His only salvation now lay in madness. For pity's sake, he appealed to his mind, you have exhausted me, so now get out of my skull! But his mind would not go.

On July 26 we decided to make the tunnel collapse. We first made sure they had stopped digging. That meant that they were going to attempt to break out that night, or the next day at the latest. We chose to set off the landslip as close to the foundations as possible, at a spot where the tunnel was deepest underground, so that the greater weight of earth above it would ensure the fullest possible destruction of the enemy below.

After the collapse we carried on watching the surface over the whole length of the passage. But the men who had been buried alive didn't even try to cut a relief shaft, and no one came to their rescue from the outside either. In any case it would have been pointless to try anything of the kind.

To begin with we heard no noises at all, and we could hardly believe that dozens of sappers and soldiers armed to the teeth were right beneath our feet, no more than two fathoms down. But the silence lasted only a few days. Thereafter, and especially at night, when we put our ears to the ground, we could hear screams and wailing. But nobody will ever be able to say what really happened down there.

We considered that our best course was to let them die where they were. If we had got them out, we would not have had the means to keep them imprisoned, because even without them, we had limited supplies of food and water. In other circumstances we might have asked to exchange them for our own casualties who were in the enemy's hands and possibly still alive. Or else they might have surrendered our prisoners for a ransom. But after the horrors inflicted on those of our women that they captured, our men are outraged. Not only have we changed, it is likely we will never go back to the way we used to be. Most of us have been made bitter by death and have lost all inclination for forgiveness and mercy.

When their groans began to fade away our brothers nonetheless prayed for the souls of those unfortunate men. For several nights in a row we lit candles and burned incense over the path of the tunnel. Despite this we all lost our sleep, and even those who did manage to drop off woke up more exhausted than insomniacs, because of the horrors they had seen in their dreams. Some even began to suspect the Turks of having invented the tunnel with the sole aim of storing their own dead beneath our feet.

CHAPTER EIGHT

They were reclining on their camp-beds, leaning on their elbows. It was suffocating inside the tent. Despite their light garb, they found the heat unbearable.

"It must be cooler outside than in here," Lejla said. "It's always either hotter or cooler inside a tent than outside."

She was the only one of the women to have been on a campaign before. She had been taken by her master, a vizier, on the Thessalonian campaign, where he had been killed. Her first act as a young widow had been to disperse the harem, as custom required. She had sold the girls with unusual haste, and, as if that had not been enough to express her spite towards them, she set a price that was more or less equivalent to that of a she-goat.

Lejla had told the story to her younger companions on her first night in her new harem, which led some of them to call her "Goat Lady" or else "Nanny", depending on the warmth of their relations. In recent weeks, presumably because of the hostility all around them, the women had grown closer to each other.

"Phew! This heat is stifling!" said Blondie (so named for the colour of her hair), who was slouching next to Lejla. "Where's Hasan? Him to get fetch little water to fresh up!"

The others all laughed at Blondie's broken Turkish, knowing full well they would not find even that very amusing for long.

The youngest, Exher, said nothing and sat outside the circle, which was unusual for her. She was pale and hadn't put up her plaits very neatly.

"Are you already feeling queer?" Lejla asked.

"Yes."

"It must be that."

Exher stared hard at her.

"I had a hard time of it too," Ajsel said. "Oh! I miss my little daughter so! She'll be nearly two when autumn comes. Will we be back by then?"

"I don't think so," Lejla answered. "To judge by the way it's gone so far, this siege is going to last a long time."

"I had a difficult pregnancy, too," Ajsel said.

"But you got better looking after you'd given birth," Lejla pointed out. "When you were pregnant, we all thought, when we looked at you, that *he* would sell you afterwards. We were making a big mistake."

Ajsel laughed dreamily, looked around at each of her comrades in turn, then said, in a softer voice:

"Do you want to know why he loved me?"

They all turned round to look at her, with curiosity in their eyes. Even the blonde girl stopped staring at the carpet and cupped her chin in her hand.

"Well, it's because I had a lot of milk, and when he hugged me, he got a thrill from feeling his chest getting wet."

"Is that so?" Exher asked in wide-eyed astonishment.

"Yes, it is. On evenings when I was down to lie with him,

he had me instructed not to breastfeed my daughter so that . . ."

"Why didn't you tell us about this before?"

"I was embarrassed."

"Embarrassed? Among us?"

Ajsel shrugged.

"Will I have a lot of milk as well?" Exher asked.

They all laughed.

"Who knows?"

"You don't hook a man by your milk," Ajsel observed.

"So what do you think the trick is?"

"God alone knows . . ."

They looked at Lejla. Not only had she already been on a campaign, she was also the only one of them to have known another man. So she seemed to them all to be the wisest, in all circumstances.

"Men are the greatest enigma in the world," she said. "I . . . I . . . Honestly, my greatest dream has always been to talk to a man . . . To have a chat, I mean. Not to sleep with him, but to talk, for hours on end, until dawn . . . until you just can't talk any more . . ."

"What are you going on about?" Ajsel objected. "Didn't you ever talk to your first husband?"

"Never! He was as grim as night. As for *this one*, he's only ever spoken to me once. And do you know what it was about? I'm horrified even when I just think back on it. Well, what he asked was: 'Tell me how the other man did it with you.'"

"Really? Did you tell him?"

"Of course I did. I was shaking with fear. I thought he would kill me afterwards, but oddly enough, the opposite happened. He got more affectionate. Or maybe I just thought he was being kinder because I expected him to be angry."

"Fine," Exher said after a pause. "Tell us something else."

"What would you like me to tell you? I've already said all I know."

And indeed she had already told them everything, and more than once, especially about men's organs, which were sometimes as straight as a Christian's sword, and sometimes as slant as a Turkish yatagan.

They chatted on about other episodes in the life of the harem and were surprised to feel homesick so soon for their house in Bursa. They recalled their last night there; most of them hadn't got a wink of sleep. Some at home were sad to see friends leave, others disappointed at not having been chosen to go on the campaign.

"I knew it was war we were going to," Lejla said for the benefit of Exher and Blondie, "but I didn't want to spoil your joy. Exher, you were really over the moon. You kept on asking me, 'What's war like, then?' And you just couldn't wait for it to be morning."

"Maybe it's because he is born in pain and blood that man has a natural inclination to make his whole life a blood-soaked affair."

"What will you come up with next, Ajsel!"

"Who can say how this war will end?"

"How can you know?" Lejla answered. "May Allah's will be done. But whatever the outcome, it won't change things much for us. If he is victorious, he'll get promotion and acquire new riches, he'll buy more wives, and we'll have new friends."

"Ah! That would be fun!" Exher exclaimed.

"But if he loses, we'll be sold as well, and who knows what our fate will then be. Perhaps better, perhaps worse."

"Ah! That would be fun!" Exher said again. "I'd love to change master."

"Be quiet, you silly woman," Lejla said. "The eunuch might hear you."

"And where has Hasan got to?" the blonde girl wailed. "If he could bring us some water!"

"I think they're preparing to cut off the citadel's water," Ajsel said. "I heard Hasan talking about it with one of the sentries yesterday."

"Really? Then the war will soon be over," Lejla concluded. "In this heat, who can hold out without water?"

"But how are they going to cut it off?" Exher asked.

"How? They usually look for the watercourses, and when they find the channel, they destroy it," Lejla answered.

"That's right," Ajsel said. "They were talking about an aqueduct that they couldn't manage to locate."

"Thank goodness we have Hasan to bring us news from outside every so often."

"The day before yesterday, when he was walking around among the troops, he heard men say that the Mufti objects to us," Ajsel remarked.

"The Mufti? What has he got to do with us?"

"He claims we bring bad luck."

"That's typical!" Lejla exclaimed. "Soon they'll say it's our fault the citadel hasn't fallen!"

"Oh God, let us get away from here as soon as possible!" the blonde girl blurted out in exasperation.

"You're only yearning to get back to your Gyzel!" Exher said spitefully.

The blonde girl didn't react. She blushed slightly, and then turned away in embarrassment.

"Avoid making jokes of that kind," Ajsel said. "Hasan could hear you. Do you remember what happened when Kekike and that Greek girl were caught kissing?"

"I hadn't joined you yet," Exher said. "What's the name of the marsh where they were drowned?"

"Avdi Batak. That's where adulterous wives are usually dealt with. Apparently you can hear them screaming all night long."

"Adulterous . . ." Exher repeated thoughtfully. "What an odd word!"

"I shall never forget that night," Ajsel repeated.

"And I'll never forget this tent, where we are being cooked alive!" Exher shouted.

"Don't complain. There is worse," Lejla retorted.

"And what could be worse than this tent?"

"Oh! There are things that are much worse," Lejla insisted. "Being captured by the enemy, for example."

Exher's face lit up.

"I've never been a captive . . ."

"Be quiet, you nitwit," Ajsel scolded. "What if the eunuch heard you?"

"Would you really like to be taken prisoner?" Lejla remonstrated. "Have you forgotten what Hasan told us about the Albanian girls the *akinxhis* brought back two weeks ago? They only lasted one night in our camp. By dawn they were in the ground."

Exher lowered her head.

"Hasan saw them," Ajsel went on. "He'd got up before dawn and gone out for some air. As he came back in, he tripped over a basin and woke me up. He came up to me and said: 'Ajsel *hanum*, I saw them, they were all white, as white as sheets.'"

"Poor Hasan! His heart can't bear to see a woman in pain."

Exher suddenly burst into tears.

"That's enough, Ajsel," Lejla said. "In her state, Exher shouldn't hear that kind of story."

They fell silent while the younger among them went on weeping. Then the blonde woman spoke up:

"Ooof! I'm bursting!" she said as she put her hand through her hair.

The two other women were fanning themselves as hard as they could.

"Hasan told me other horrors," Ajsel whispered in Lejla's ear. "The next night the soldiers wanted to reopen the graves. Have you ever heard of men who enjoy raping corpses? I've forgotten what the word for it is. Well, in the middle of the night . . ."

"I think Hasan is coming back, I can hear the sound of his footstep," Exher said.

And the eunuch did indeed appear.

"Where have you been?" they all said, almost in unison. "How can you leave us alone in this oven?"

"I was watching our engineers trying to find the water line," Hasan said. "They've covered the plain with little holes, but the aqueduct is still in hiding."

"Maybe they aren't looking in the right place?" Lejla suggested.

She was the only one of the four to have heard of such things before, even though the previous campaign she had been on had not needed to take such steps.

"The sappers dig where the architect Giaour tells them," the eunuch said. "He's supposed to know all the secrets of earth and water."

"Talk talk, Hasan! Bring water quick!" the blonde girl shouted.

"Immediately, ma'am," the eunuch replied.

He went out, and the clatter of empty pitchers moved away into the distance.

Exher was leaning her head on her forearm.

"How are you feeling?" Ajsel asked her. "Do you want to vomit again?"

"Yes."

"You've gone white again."

"Does *he* know you're pregnant?" Lejla asked.

"Hasan must have told him."

"They have a weakness for children conceived on campaign," Lejla remarked.

She spoke as if in a daydream. She was on the point of adding something, but seemed to hold back.

"And why is that?" Exher asked.

Lejla didn't answer the question directly but said, "Especially if it is a boy . . ."

"So why do they have a special fondness for such children?" Exher asked again.

Lejla lowered her eyes. "I don't really know," she said. "Perhaps it's because they come into being amid devastation and death, on which their fathers' whole existence is grounded. Or else it may be because by spreading grief all around they incur a debt towards life, and are therefore glad to be able to return to it a tiny part of what they have taken away."

"*He* is very glum these days," Ajsel observed. "Haven't you noticed?"

"That's right. *He* never smiles."

"But I like men of mystery," Exher blurted out.

"*He* has ear trouble," Ajsel added. "A week ago, when I slept with him, he suddenly put his hand to his right ear. When I asked what was wrong, he told me he could hear buzzing in his head."

"With the din of battle and the banging of all those drums, how could he not have trouble with his ears?" Exher said.

"But I don't think that's what's making him grumpy," Lejla objected. "What's getting him down is the outcome of a battle that seems to have no end."

"And the collapse of the tunnel also upset him greatly," Exher added.

"The tunnel? Of course it affected him. Actually, I think that's where it all began . . ."

Rattling buckets could be heard coming nearer outside. It was the eunuch. They rushed over to him as soon as he came inside the tent.

"Hold your horses, you witches!" Hasan shouted at them.

He finally got them into the compartment of the tent that was used for steam baths. For a long while the women's laughter mingled with the sound of spilling water.

Once they had relaxed they came back into the main tent and started to do up their hair.

"Hasan, tell us all the news!" Lejla said.

The time after a bath was when Hasan was at his most fluent. He chatted about whatever came into his head, in no particular order, pell-mell. All over the camp people were talking of nothing but the imminent trial of the spell-caster. He was supposed to be mainly responsible for the failure of the first assault. Learned men from the Palace of Great Damnation in the capital had arrived at the camp, bringing instruments and little lengths of string that were to be used to establish the man's guilt. Proper measurements had been made, and had persuaded the estimators that the spell had been badly cast. A curse made with the palm of the hand had to be as precise as a shot with a bow, because the slightest error in aim increases in magnitude the further the arrow flies. So when the curse reached the citadel, it just glanced off the right hand wall and a great deal of its force frittered away in empty space and fell to ground on some far-off beech-wood or meadow, which would surely wither in a couple of years' time, but what good was that to anyone? The fortress would remain intact.

"Well, Hasan, that's all very complicated, isn't it?" Exher sighed.

"Wait a moment!" the eunuch said. "Things are even more complicated than they seem. To begin with, the spell-caster was suspected of having made a crass mistake, but what we're now learning is that none of this happened by chance . . . Under torture, his assistants, first of all, and then the man himself admitted they had acted knowingly, that they are in cahoots with enemies of the state, and there's even a rumour that they've got their own men planted in the council of war. If none of that was made public knowledge up to now, it was probably so as to lull the traitors into a false sense of security, and then — clack! — close the trap on them like rats."

"Come on, Hasan," Lejla said. "Why are you boring us with all this nasty business? Go get us some juicy fruit instead. We're parched."

"Tell us something more amusing!" Exher insisted.

"Amusing? The whole army is gossiping about Kurdisxhi and Karaduman! They've fallen in love with the same boy, and are at daggers drawn . . ."

Almost simultaneously the four women lowered their gaze with that touch of melancholy aroused by a revolting act that nonetheless retains something of the beauty it smothers.

Hasan chatted on interminably about trivia but the women were hardly paying attention any more, as their minds had been diverted to thoughts of a squabble of which they would be the object. They were well aware that if such a dispute broke out, it would not be settled in the field, to the sound of clashing sabres, but in the marketplace, over a matter of price, and to the tinkling of silver coins.

"Well! That's enough for now!" Hasan said. "Put your legs up one more time, because I didn't examine you properly when we were in the hammam just now. I've the impression that your little nests have gone darker already and that in a few days they'll be as black as the crows. Especially yours, Lejla and Ajsel. Get ready, we'll clean you up."

"Pfui!" Ajsel said. "So soon?"

"I've noticed that the little bush grows faster in summer," Hasan pointed out. "Come on, girls, let's get on with it. Otherwise Hasan will get the blame."

"And is she going to always be allowed to keep her forest?" Exher asked, nodding towards Blondie.

The foreign wife smiled mockingly as she listened to the conversation.

"On such matters, the decision is *his*," Hasan answered. "Orders are orders. You three: as smooth as a mirror. That one: don't touch a hair on her . . . head, as you might say. And do you know why?" he asked in a whisper. "Because she is fair. They all drool like dogs when they come across a blonde girl with dark pubic hair . . . If it were as fair as her head, you'd see me shaving away. But there you are: hers is black . . . I remember when I was working for a beylerbey, my master once bought a blonde girl of much the same kind as this one. He was dying to have her in bed with him. As I was washing and perfuming her inside the hammam, he called to me from outside the door: 'Make sure you don't shear her fleece! Otherwise you know what'll happen to you!' But he called me back after dinner. He was in a lousy mood and looked upset. He said grumpily: 'Shave her, like the others.' I guessed straight away what the reason for his mood was: unlike most blondes, she had pubic hair that was as fair as the hair on her head. I'd never seen a prettier little brush. Like a ray of sunlight had fallen between her legs. And I swear to you I had tears in my eyes when I shaved her, as if I was cropping fenugreek, and my teardrops fell like dew where my master's seed should have been sprinkled. I cursed him under my breath. 'Why the devil don't you appreciate this golden honey down? Why do you prefer a thicket as dark and frightening as a bottomless pit? Because all you are yourself is a crow and an abyss! That's why!'"

They were relaxed and ready to drop off to sleep after their bath, but that didn't stop the eunuch from prattling on. Silence even seemed to stimulate him. He told old stories about his former mistresses. He had fond memories of them all.

"In Izmir," he said, "I had one who was without compare. Her voice was as sweet as the *rahat loukoum* between her thighs. Anyway, I can read my mistresses' hearts the way I can read their sex, it's all the same to me. All of them were either completely angry with their eunuch, or else they had nothing but smiles for him. 'Bow, bow, Black eunuch, you son of the night,' I used to say to myself. The masculine power all around us was so implacable that I felt a perverse kind of pleasure in being mistreated by the women of my harem. 'Hit me, ladies,' I used to say, 'flay me, piss on my head while you chatter to each other!' It seemed to me that they would draw some comfort from doing so, that it would console them for their own fate. 'Why are you so sad, Hasan?' they would sometimes ask. That's what my ladies were like. They would notice if a passing cloud in the sky felt unhappy! Some of them now lie in their graves. Sometimes I go and visit them in the cemetery of the Lower Plain. And I would weep for them aloud if the whole place wasn't under surveillance. Because the world and its men are getting harder and harder. But God's punishment is also drawing nearer. In the camp no one sleeps peacefully at night any more. You can hear groans that are supposed to be coming up from underground. Last Sunday, towards dawn, the earth began to shake as if they were all going to come scrambling out, all covered in mud, out of the hole where they were buried alive. After forty days, forty more must pass, then forty weeks, for the earth to calm down again. Because everything happens at a slower pace for the earth than for men. True peace will only come back to it after forty years."

A blinding sun streams down, as if it had suddenly been aimed at us. No cloud to protect us, not even a smear of mist in the sky. It seems we have been abandoned entirely; our sentries no longer even see fairies or sprites. Maybe they are resting on a hill somewhere? From daybreak the sky seems to have been emptied of its heavenly substance.

Down below, on the plain, they are reaping the early wheat. Scythes and sickles sparkle in the far distance with a fierce and threatening glare, as if they were felling not ears of wheat but the heads of men. We who planted the seeds we were fated never to harvest are much downcast. For herein is that saying true, as is written in the Gospel According to St John, that "one soweth and another reapeth". The scythe we do not use ourselves has really fallen on the world as on the Day of the Apocalypse.

The plain all around our citadel is now pocked with holes and dark trenches dug in the search for the aqueduct. The leader of the search, an architect they call "The Christian", is sufficiently cunning to have guessed straight away, when on the third day they came on an aqueduct, that it was the old one, no longer in use, and he ordered the work to continue until the other one, the right one, had been found.

But nobody knows where the right one runs, not even we ourselves. All we know is that one of George Castrioti's first concerns was to build new aqueducts to serve all his fortresses. To keep their location secret, the trenches were dug by prisoners. Last year they ended up making such a labyrinth of ditches and tunnels that no one could tell which of these courses actually brought water into the citadel. And it is entirely possible that none of them does, that the one that fulfils the function is a completely different one, that cannot be seen. The enemy has placed all its hopes in discovering the true source of our water. But as we ourselves do not know where our water comes from or how it reaches us, we believe nobody else can find out either. The fearsome Christian appears in our dreams nonetheless, and so we have started to dig a deep well beneath the dungeons of our citadel, in case we have to face even harder times than these.

The siege has been upon us for nearly two months. The sight of the enemy has tired our eyes. They wander around in their tens of thousands all across the plain down below — an endless throng that is constantly on the move. Where can this vast horde come from? How do they manage to communicate with each other and act in concert? Where are they going? For what reason? People who have visited their land say that women are scarce in those parts, and are hardly ever seen. So who gives birth to them? Are they children of the desert?

CHAPTER NINE

Çelebi was jealous of the half-undressed men lying outside their tents. It was suffocatingly hot, and, if dignity and propriety had not forbidden it, he too would have liked to take off his clothes. In practice, none of the soldiers knew who he was. They were surely just as ignorant of the fact that among them was a historian whose task was to make the campaign immortal. Because of his costume he was sometimes mistaken for a doctor and sometimes for a soothsayer, but that was hardly surprising since most of the soldiers did not even know the word "history".

"What do those drums mean?" he asked a group of soldiers.

"A beheading," they answered without even looking up at him.

Men were crowding around the open space left between the tents where executions usually took place. Since he had nothing better to do, Çelebi joined the crowd. That morning he had been for a walk in the plain around the camp. The landscape was beautiful, but the ditches and trenches pitting the ground had spoiled his walk. Here and there in the grass he came across arrows, which had apparently come down in recent battles. He stooped to pick one up. He had never held a weapon in his hand before, and it seemed odd to him that a mere stick of wood with a little iron tip could cause anyone's death.

"Who is going to be beheaded?" he asked another soldier a little further on.

"No idea," the trooper replied with a shrug. "A pair of spies, I think."

The drum kept on calling men to assembly. The herald's voice could be heard in the distance. Çelebi noticed the tall shape of Sirri Selim coming towards him with someone else. The doctor greeted him.

"Well, how are you, Mevla? How's the chronicle going?"

The chronicler bowed down low.

"Don't you know each other?" Sirri Selim said with a broad gesture towards Mevla and the other man. "This is Mevla Çelebi, our historiographer."

The unidentified man gave the chronicler a supercilious look.

"And this is our new astrologer. He's just come in from Edirne."

Çelebi looked at him with the same curiosity he had for anyone coming from the capital.

"Any news from Edirne?" he asked in a gentle tone, pretending not to have noticed the newcomer's haughty air.

"No," the astrologer said. "It's hot."

The chronicler could see the new man wasn't keen on talking. In his mind's eye he glimpsed the old astrologer's corpse all covered in mud and rubble, and he thought better of giving way to his feeling of irritation with the new one. If he takes himself too seriously, he'll end up in the same state, Mevla thought.

"What's this crowd for?" the doctor enquired.

"Apparently they're going to execute a pair of spies."

"Really? Spies?" a passing janissary asked.

"And what did they spy on?" Sirri Selim asked as he moved towards the place where the drum-roll was coming from.

The other two followed in his footsteps.

"I don't know," the chronicler answered.

"I can tell you!" a dervish shouted out from behind them. "They are two spies who tried to steal the secret of our big guns!"

The chronicler then noticed Sadedin among the throng. He was being pushed and shoved. He'd often seen him wandering around the camp with a white stick, and most times he didn't speak to him, as he didn't know what to say, but this time, seeing the sturdy poet being knocked about like this, he felt sorry for him.

"Do you see the blind man over there being pushed around?" he asked Sirri Selim.

"Yes."

"That's Sadedin, the poet. He lost his sight in the battle."

The new astrologer still showed no interest in what Mevla was saying, and didn't even turn to look.

"I'll go and get him," the chronicler said. "I can't bear to see him being manhandled like that."

"In his condition, why doesn't he go back to Turkey?" Sirri Selim asked.

"He's composing a great poem about the campaign. He wants to be here when the citadel falls," Çelebi explained.

The chronicler went over to the poet and after a while brought him back.

"All around can be heard the feet of military men!" Sadedin declaimed in his thundering baritone. "It is an exalting sound!"

The astrologer cast a condescending glance at him.

"Many centuries ago, in Ancient Greece," Sirri Selim said, "there was a blind poet just like you."

Sadedin turned his blank sockets towards the doctor.

"His name was Homer, and he wrote a great epic about a garrison called Troy, which the Greeks destroyed," Sirri Selim went on. "Two months ago, Prince Mehmet, our future Sultan, said in a speech that God had designated the Turks as the avengers of Troy."

"I don't know anything about that," the blind man said. "My name is Sadedin. I used to be called Nightingale Sadedin, but the nickname never was to my liking."

"Wouldn't you have liked to be called Sarperkan Tol-Keleç Olgunsoy?" the chronicler suggested.

"I never had a chance to bear that name," Sadedin answered. "But this war has turned Nightingale Sadedin into Blind Sadedin. That's what everyone calls me now."

He swept his hand over his forehead as if trying to wave aside something that was irritating or terrifying him. When he'd finished, the chronicler saw something deathly in the gesture.

"I hear the feet of military men!" the poet said again. "We advance at night. Nothing can stand in the way of night with the crescent moon in its middle. The barren earth trembles beneath our boots."

Sirri Selim smiled. "I like you," he said.

Sadedin said nothing.

"Turkish blood will wet the dust of three continents," the poet went on. "It is written that our blood should course through our soldiers' veins no more, but should spring from their wounds until the earth is drenched with it!"

Sirri Selim frowned.

"An ocean of blood shall be spilled," Sadedin cried hoarsely, "an ocean of fine Turkish blood."

Sadedin then turned around abruptly and left without saying farewell. Çelebi watched him move into the distance, tottering along with the help of his stick.

"Is this execution going to happen or not?" the doctor asked.

"I don't think it will be long now," Çelebi said. "I just saw the chef-de-camp going by."

Meanwhile a group of officers were noisily greeting one of their comrades who had visibly just returned from a long journey. They were gossiping excitedly, and Çelebi strained his ear to catch what they were saying.

"So, what news from the capital?" a couple of the officers asked.

"What you would expect," the traveller replied. "The talk is all of this expedition. When people know you've come from Albania, the first thing they ask is whether you've set eyes on Skanderbeg."

"They fail to realise that if you do set eyes on Skanderbeg, you are very likely never to set eyes on anything else!" one of them quipped.

They all laughed.

"Look, here comes the Quartermaster General and Saruxha," Sirri Selim remarked. "They must be on their way to a session of the war council."

The two high officials nodded a greeting without stopping, but Sirri Selim waved at them.

"Heads are going to fall. Stay a while."

"And who is to be executed?"

"Two spies. Apparently they were trying to filch your guns' secrets," Sirri Selim said. Then he added in a whisper, "Do you really know nothing about this?"

"No," Saruxha said in a rasping voice. "What's all this spying business about?"

"Well, that's odd!"

"Who is that man?" the Quartermaster General asked under his breath.

"The new astrologer," Sirri Selim answered. "Just got here from Edirne."

The Quartermaster General looked the astrologer up and down.

"Do you really not know anything about the spies?" Sirri Selim asked the gun-maker once again.

"I already told you, no," the engineer replied.

"You've got a sore throat. Did you catch cold?"

"I suppose I must have."

Voices could be heard shouting from among the crowd. "Here they come! Here they come!"

People pushed and shoved to get a better view. Cries of "Death to the spies" rose from all around.

Two men with their hands tied were dragged on to the scaffold. The executioner climbed up behind them. The two convicts were almost naked and the marks of the torture they had undergone were clearly visible on their torsos.

The Quartermaster General looked at them with some care.

"I think I've seen those two somewhere else."

"Yes, they're a pair of snoopers we sometimes saw near the foundry," Çelebi said. "That one's the redhead. Do you remember?"

"That's right," Saruxha confirmed. "It really is them."

Men close by stretched their necks to listen in to the conversation.

"So that's why they went there every day!" Çelebi exclaimed. "The dogs! To think we treated them as good lads who were just being curious!" The executioner and his assistant were now untying the men's hands.

"No!" Saruxha replied. "It's not true! Twenty years ago, I too peered over a fence to watch and admire the great Saruhanli casting cannon in his foundry. These boys aren't spies any more than I was at their age!"

The chronicler was thunderstruck. "What, then?"

"Their thirst for knowledge, their curiosity has done for them," Saruxha said. "Of course I could save the pair of them, but my throat hurts too much."

The drum had stopped sounding the call to assemble.

"Why are you looking at me like that?" Saruxha went on in his hoarse rasp. "Can't you hear my voice? How can you snatch two people from the jaws of death without having to raise your voice at great length?"

"That's true," the Quartermaster General agreed. "And the fate of thousands hangs on your good health. You have every right to look after yourself."

The executioner's assistant laid the men's heads on the block.

"Look, there's the architect!" said Sirri Selim. "Rushing about like a whirlwind, as usual."

Giaour dashed on past them without looking round.

"We're going to be late," the Quartermaster remarked.

They turned on their heels and moved away just as the executioner brought his axe down on one of the two necks. There was a movement in the crowd, and then a great roar arose.

"They're in a hurry to get to the meeting," Sirri Selim muttered pensively. "I bet they'll soon summon me too."

Çelebi didn't dare ask the doctor what he meant by that.

The executioner raised his axe a second time. It was the carrot-haired boy's turn. And again the crowd shifted around, and again a thunderous roar arose.

"No, they'll surely not fail to call me in," Sirri Selim said aloud, and then suddenly went red in the face.

Çelebi was flummoxed. He didn't know what attitude to adopt — show interest in Sirri Selim's incomprehensible utterance, as politeness required, or else pretend not to have heard him thinking aloud. Although he was of a lower rank than the Quartermaster General, the doctor was a figure of some importance, and Çelebi cursed fate for putting him in his presence at such a delicate moment.

"No, no mistake about it," Sirri Selim added through his teeth, with his mouth in a twisted grin.

Çelebi felt the blood running cold in his veins. He turned towards the astrologer, but he seemed completely indifferent to everything, and just carried on staring at the crowd.

Meanwhile the Quartermaster and Saruxha were well on their way to the Pasha's tent. They saw the architect rushing into the pink pavilion a few feet ahead of them.

"It looks like he's gone a bit crazy," Saruxha observed.

"He certainly has a few things to worry about," the Quartermaster General commented. "The tunnel collapse was nearly the end of him."

"And you reckon he won't have any more luck in the hunt for the aqueduct?"

"I fear not."

"You're in clover, you really are!" Saruxha exclaimed. "You just don't have the same worries as we all do."

The Quartermaster General smiled.

"Superficially, you're right," he answered calmly. "But did you stop to ask yourself why, over the last two days, thousands of men are hurriedly reaping the last of the wheat?"

"That's true," Saruxha said. "I meant to ask you, but then it slipped my mind. What is going on?"

"I'll let you in on a secret only the Pasha and Alaybey are currently aware of."

Saruxha could barely stifle a cough, which always came to him when he was excited.

"Skanderbeg has attacked and destroyed the Venetian

caravans that were bringing our supplies," the Quartermaster whispered.

"He hit the Venetians? Good Lord . . ."

"That's right, it's tantamount to declaring war on the Serenissima," the Quartermaster said.

Saruxha looked at him with amazement in his eyes.

"He's gone out of his mind!"

"Maybe he has," the Quartermaster replied. "But don't forget, it may be a desperate act, but it's the act of a lion in despair."

"You can call it despair or a lion's anger, as far as I'm concerned, it's six of one and half a dozen of the other. Anyway, laying your sabre on a sack of grain or a skin of oil doesn't seem very leonine to me!"

The Quartermaster burst out laughing and then shook his head as if to make his laughter go away. "I'm of a completely different persuasion. A general who destroys your supply train before attacking you is a true soldier."

"I'm afraid we're going to be late," Saruxha said.

They went into the tent one after the other with bowed heads. The full war council had been assembled. The only empty seat was the commander-in-chief's. The captains and high officials were chatting quietly. Most of the others were silent, taking sips of syrup from a glass that was constantly refilled from a brass pitcher by a *chaouch* gliding among the council members like a shadow. Now and again they cast sidelong glances at the architect. But Giaour's blank face failed to give them the satisfaction they sought in such circumstances, when all the weight of a difficult meeting seems to bear down on one man, and, as they watch him writhing, the others feel immense relief not to be sitting in his place. The man's impassive appearance not only disappointed the council members who reckoned themselves deprived of a small pleasure to which they felt entitled, but irritated them, and thereby relieved them of all pity.

The Pasha came in and took his seat. Everyone stopped speaking, and only the familiar scratching of the scribe's writing instruments could be heard, less as a background noise than as a natural part of the silence of the universe.

Then the Pasha spoke. He was brief. He stated that on this day the council must determine whether or not to continue the siege. Then he mentioned the problem of the aqueduct. All efforts to locate it had failed. As everyone must have realised, hopes of finding it were diminishing by the day. He praised the architect for having realised that the aqueduct that was found was a decoy, and especially for not having allowed them all to rejoice prematurely. "As the great architect that you are, you spared us a great disappointment, in other words, you saved us from an evil." Nonetheless he refuted Giaour's hypothesis that there was no other aqueduct.

"You said yourself that the one you discovered was only a false lure, but now you tell us that there is no other. Well then, architect, tell us what the truth of the matter is. Is there a real aqueduct or not? I am asking you!"

Giaour's lips started mouthing words straight away.

"Aqueduct is real, aqueduct is semblance, yes and no."

The Pasha held both his hands to his forehead and motioned to the architect to stop talking. Looking at the man with his cold and weary eyes he begged him to wait until he had finished thinking. The architect closed his mouth.

"I praised you for those things in which you are praiseworthy, but all the same I am displeased with you," the Pasha continued in a serious tone.

As was to be expected, but only after hesitating for a while, he alluded, although not too insistently, to the tunnel. Without taking his eyes off Giaour, he observed that as far as the tunnel was concerned the architect, at a pinch, could be held to be not responsible for the collapse, since the sappers who were perhaps the reason why the tunnel was discovered were now, together with their captain Ulug Bey, buried under the ground, peace be to their souls, and could therefore not defend themselves; the failure of the search for the aqueduct, on the other hand, could only be imputed to him, and he had to answer for this to the war council. To finish off his speech, Tursun Pasha expressed the sour hypothesis that the architect Giaour had perhaps, "for some reason", lost his ardour to cut off the supply of water to the Christians.

The Pasha had spoken. In the utter silence that ensued all that could be heard was the scratching of the secretary's quill as he put down on paper everything that had been said. They were all accustomed to this sound which was always identical, whether the words being transcribed were sharp or smooth, scorpion bites or soft summer wind. Those among the council members who were familiar with administrative accounts realised that the secretary was making his quill squeal more than was actually necessary. To judge by the serious face he made at such times, it wasn't hard to guess that these silent pauses in which his pen scratching was the overriding sound gave him his sole opportunity in life to assert his own importance. Once someone started talking again, his very presence would be forgotten.

The architect stood up. He began to speak, in truncated words strung together without pauses or intonation. His tiresome, toneless diction was somehow reminiscent of the desert. As they listened to him members of the council imagined that this man had been specially created to dry up rivers and springs, as he had done in fact, and to great effect, in the many previous campaigns that had won him considerable glory.

He gave an account of his search. He explained to the council how he had based his work on a scrupulous examination of the surrounding terrain, noting the gradients of all the slopes, their degree of forestation, the composition of the subsoil, its level of humidity, and many other factors. This detailed survey was the basis for his orders to dig here rather than there ("dig where dig need, not dig where dig not need"). When these investigations led to the unearthing of a conduit which he immediately identified as a decoy (the trickle of water in it was so tiny that it would not have fooled anybody), he had insisted on going on until they located the real aqueduct. He had given orders for the river bed to be surveyed yard by yard so as to find some trace of it. His divers had been down, over a length of several leagues, but they found nothing. After that, and especially after Albanian prisoners had confessed under torture and until their dying breath that they did not know of any other pipe, he became convinced that the aqueduct they had unearthed was both the real one, and a false one.

"Stuff and nonsense!" the Mufti interrupted. "That's the second time we've been told such crazy rubbish. Pasha, sire, how can you tolerate this . . . this . . . making a fool of us? How can a pipe be both true and false at the same time? Are we to suppose that aqueducts have doubles, like human beings?"

"Explain yourself," the Pasha said to the architect.

"I not make fun nobody. I explain," Giaour responded.

He stated that the aqueduct could be considered simultaneously true and false insofar as it was no longer in use. A course which carries water, he continued, is an aqueduct, as its name implies, but one which has ceased to do that and to fulfil its role is merely a pipe. The citadel had been supplied with water through the channel they had discovered up until the day of the army's arrival. Then, for fear of it being found, they had themselves made it unusable.

"Did they now?" the Mufti shouted. "And for what reason did

they do that, Mr Architect? Why did they hasten to do what it would have taken us a great deal of trouble to do? Was it out of their deep respect for us and their desire to spare us toil and time?"

Several members of the council started chuckling. Others nodded approvingly, meaning that they found the Mufti's questions pertinent. One of the sanxhakbeys even declared: "That's just what I was going to ask."

The architect didn't blink. Only his mouth opened, and poured forth his usual blather of words as same-sounding as so many grains of sand.

"You want know what made demolish pipe? Only reason is, afraid poison."

He explained that it often happens that the besieged, once they have closed the gates and all other visible and hidden forms of access to their garrison, fill their cisterns with fresh water and, from fear of having their water supply poisoned, cut their last link with the outside world — their aqueduct.

A sly grin spread slowly over the wide expanse of the Mufti's face. The others were very curious to see how this duel would turn out, for it seemed that for the first time this immensely learned man might bite the dust. The Mufti asked to speak again.

"Let us suppose that is right," he said. "In spite of everything, what I cannot grasp is why they gave up their water supply three months ago, when they could have left the decision to cut it off until the fatal moment (fatal for them, that is) when we would find the aqueduct."

"The old fox!" Saruxha said quietly in the Quartermaster General's ear.

"He's not as dumb as he looks," was the whispered reply.

"It is obvious to all," the Mufti continued, "that a cistern fed by a water pipe cannot be replenished once the pipe is cut, and it is no less obvious that if it has to be cut, the besieged will try to delay doing so for as long as possible. But according to you, the besieged we're dealing with here are supposed to be mad enough to have cut off their own water before we even got here. That is what my poor brain cannot grasp."

"Your brain not grasp because your brain not know," the architect threw back at him.

"Don't insult each other, but answer these two questions," the Pasha broke in. "First: how do the besieged get their water? Second: why did they abandon their aqueduct prematurely?"

Old Tavxha, Kurdisxhi and some of the sanxhakbeys broke out in narrow grins. Tahanka's eyes were lit with a fierce glow. Kara-Mukbil's expression was as gloomy as ever. Tursun Pasha and the Alaybey, for their part, hadn't lost their grumpy expressions. As soon as they saw this, the sanxhakbeys wiped the smiles from their faces.

All eyes were on the architect. The sound of the scribe's scratchy quill seemed to make those glances even sharper.

Giaour's mouth went slack in a single movement, as it always did. He answered the first question simply: in his estimation, the defenders must have both a reservoir and a natural well inside the walls. To the second question he replied that the Albanians had disabled the aqueduct in advance out of fear that it would be discovered secretly, and not openly as had been the case. We could have kept our discovery hidden, he continued, so as to transmit poison or some horrible disease through the pipe. Indeed, that was how he had poisoned the defenders of Xhizel-Hisar, ten years before; the same method had been used at Tash-Hisar a year later, as it had been used at Aleppo, twelve miles away, to infect the fortress with cholera. He cited the names of other besieged garrisons and citadels that had been brought low by water, a weapon more fearsome than the sword.

One by one the members of the council were overcome by stupefaction. They had no idea that Old Eggface, as they called him behind his back, could be so tough. They had lost all hope of seeing him bite the dust, and they felt exhausted. Tursun Pasha's face also expressed weariness. You'll go back to prison, he thought, but you'll come out stronger, as you always do. Who knows what will happen to the others . . . But the Pasha could not believe his ears: the architect was now calling for an immediate assault.

"Next!" the Pasha said, not looking at anyone in particular.

The scribe took advantage of the pause to scribble away twice as fast.

"I'm in favour of an attack by stealth," the Quartermaster General said. "But what do you think, brother engineer?"

Saruxha shrugged.

"Makes no difference to me."

"But it is now or never!" the Quartermaster insisted.

Since the meeting began he had been thinking obsessively about a single thing: the destruction of the army's supply trains.

The Quartermaster General spoke again. Couching his views in elegant and well-turned phrases, he referred first of all to the disadvantages of an overlong siege and of its potential for blunting the army's ardour. Then he came to the point. He shared the architect's position: he was in favour of attacking.

"Apparently a new astrologer has arrived from the capital," a sanxhakbey said.

"That is correct," the Pasha confirmed. "Have him called."

A messenger stepped outside smartly.

"Since I have no special esteem for astrologers, I prefer to give my opinion before he comes in," Saruxha declared. "I am in favour of an assault."

They were all fingering their beads more and more slowly. They sought each other's eyes, trying but failing to understand the nature of the miracle taking place in the war council. Men who hours before had been reckoned as soft as city whores and derided as laid-back, do-nothing, cotton-arsed cowards had suddenly turned into hawks.

The astrologer came into the tent. He bowed low and then took the seat he was shown on the divan. The Pasha whispered a few words to the Alaybey, who was sitting beside him.

"The council of war would like to know what the stars portend," the Alaybey asked. "Do you have an answer?"

"I am ready."

"Then tell us: what do the stars say about a second attack?"

"The signs are not auspicious. The present position of the stars is not favourable."

The assembled dignitaries started whispering to each other.

"He seems to be smarter than his predecessor," Saruxha muttered to the Quartermaster.

The Quartermaster was furious and grunted under his breath, "Every time, we have to put up with ignoramuses who spoil things."

"He's understood that it's the only way he can avoid taking a risk," Saruxha observed. "Any other prediction could lead him straight to his predecessor, six feet under."

"The blockhead!" the Quartermaster went on.

Other members of the council gave their opinions in turn. In truth, they had never faced quite such a delicate juncture before. For one thing, they didn't understand why the experts had suddenly changed their usual position. But the Mufti's contribution made things even more complicated. The strong preference of the technicians for attacking now was enough to make him dubious, but when the astrologer came out against it, he had no hesitation in casting his own vote among the nays. The sanxhakbeys, who were next to speak, followed the Mufti. Old Tavxha and Kurdisxhi were totally confused by this upside-down state of affairs, and broke with their custom by showing no ardour for combat. As for Tahanka, who glared furiously at the technicians, he was prepared to join them provided they were in favour of attacking.

"What about you, Kara-Mukbil?" Tursun Pasha asked. "What do you think?"

"I don't know yet," he said. He cast his sad eyes around the assembly, trying to uncover the real reasons behind what was going on. The switching of roles frightened him more than the walls of the fortress.

"What if we tried our luck one more time with the aqueduct?" Old Tavxha asked.

They could hardly believe their ears. Nobody could have dreamed that the fearsome Agha of the Janissary Corps, a man who seemed to have been born for fire and blood, would start talking about pipes and water supplies. He realised that he alone could now bridge the abyss of silence that his words had created. He slowly rubbed his forehead with his stumpy, gnarled fist.

"Many years ago," he went on, "at the siege of Hapsan-Kala, we found the aqueduct by a most curious means. We didn't use any of that paperwork or those accursed drawings. We found the water with a horse."

"What was that?" the Alaybey asked.

"An aged *sipahi* showed us how to do it," Tavxha resumed. "It's very simple. We fed a horse very well for four days but didn't give it anything to drink. Then we let it roam free around the citadel. A really thirsty animal can find the trace of water in even the driest ground. Believe you me, a thirsty horse is more reliable than any architect!"

The Mufti and the sanxhakbeys burst out laughing. Tursun Pasha waved his hand to bring the council to order.

"So that's how we found the aqueduct at Hapsan-Kala," Tavxha concluded. "Why not do the same thing here?"

They began to discuss the idea. To begin with they were far from sure, but came to take it more and more seriously as the discussion proceeded.

"Every *akinxhi* knows from his own experience that a horse can find a hidden spring, especially if the animal is thirsty," Kurdisxhi declared. "But can it locate a water pipe? I've never heard tell of such a thing."

"There were thousands of us at Hapsan-Kala who saw it happen!" Tavxha exclaimed angrily.

Kurdisxhi stuck to his guns.

"However many you were, I'm still sceptical."

The Alaybey raised his voice to ask the architect if an aqueduct could at any point in its passage under the ground give off enough dampness to alert the nostrils of a thirsty horse. The architect replied that he had never dealt with horses in his life and knew nothing about their physiology, but as far as pipes were concerned, the amount of humidity they could leak depended on what they were made of. He explained that if the watercourse was made of sandstone, as was customary for aqueducts, then it could indeed seep, but that if it was a pipe made of lead, then obviously minor leakage was ruled out.

They talked about nothing else until the end of the meeting. When the council broke up, night had fallen. They came out of the tent one by one and went off in groups of two or three in different directions, except for the architect who, as was his habit, walked back to his tent on his own, with his bodyguard trailing him like a shadow.

A few paces away, a very tall man stood watching them emerge from the Pasha's tent. It was Sirri Selim.

For three days now they have been busy with a task that appears incomprehensible. Under the burning sun, thousands of shirtless soldiers are raising a high fence all around the citadel. We cannot imagine what use such a fence may have.

They have stopped all the other works in progress. They are no longer building their wheel-mounted towers, or their three-pronged pyramid ladders, and they do not seem to be looking for the aqueduct either. For the time being they are slaving away at their fence.

We have been racking our brains for two days trying to work out the deeper reason for what looks like a whim. Are they worried about our messengers streaking off somewhere in the dark? Are they trying to forestall a surprise attack from our side? But there are so many gaps in the fence that it wouldn't seriously impede our messengers, or an attack. So what does it mean? Is it something superstitious, along the lines of the curses and spells we have so much trouble understanding? Or is it just to make fun of us? The fence actually looks quite like a sheep pen. They may want us to think that as we are shut in like sheep, so we shall die, like lambs to the slaughter, and so on.

For some while now we have become very suspicious, even of each other. Our priests urge us to avoid sin and remind us of sackcloth and ashes, but to no avail. People fly off the handle for nothing and lose their tempers at the slightest pretext. Yesterday, our commander Count Vrana — Vranakonti, as we call him — had the Prela brothers thrown in jail for disobedience. It began quite stupidly. Gjon Prela was claiming that the sun had always been against us, and maybe that was why all the songs of the region begin, "The sun shines brightly but gives no warmth," when someone butted in, saying, "So maybe you prefer the Ottoman moon?" and from one riposte to another the swords came out.

In fact there are many here who do think that fate is against us.

CHAPTER TEN

In spite of the heat of the midday sun, throngs of curious soldiers wandered up to the great fence around noon. It had been put up so speedily that many of them had not yet had occasion to see it. The first sight disappointed them. It was just an ordinary fence, barely higher or sturdier than a garden gate. Nonetheless, they were expecting to witness a great spectacle. Even if the fence itself was nothing special, what was about to happen on the other side, in the no-man's-land that lay between fence and fortress, was going to be out of the ordinary. Rumours galore had been doing the rounds for the previous couple of days, and had reached their peak that morning. There were forecasts in abundance, but solid information was unobtainable. Some men said it was all to do with the hunt for the water pipe, but they were unable to explain the connection between a fence and a buried watercourse. Others maintained that the citadel was going to be struck with a spell, and prayers and holy water sprinkled on the fence would limit its effect to the closed-off area. Yet others offered different explanations based on the songs and legends of their homeland or of the places where they had done long service.

But when they saw a squad of senior officers come from the main camp and then a detachment of desert warriors followed by the commander-in-chief's personal guard, and when finally the Pasha himself came and took up his position on the little podium from which he had observed the initial assault, everybody was convinced that something exceptional was about to happen. Lined up behind the Pasha, in order of precedence, stood the Alaybey, Old Tavxha, the Mufti, the Quartermaster General, Saruxha, Kurdisxhi, Kara-Mukbil, the architect, Tahanka and the other members of the war council. Some way behind them stood the sanxhakbeys, the captains of the death squads and of the *dalkiliç*, the imams, the chef-de-camp, the head of intelligence, the chief kadi, Sirri Selim, the astrologer, the new commander of the sappers, Saruxha's assistant, the head gunner, the drum major, the first dream-interpreter, the keeper of the seals, and so forth. Still further back stood an even denser mixed group in which you could make out scribes, doctors, hoxhas, *sipahis*, technicians and officers of various ranks. Çelebi was among the latter set. He stretched out his neck towards the group in which Sirri Selim was located, and wondered if he would be better advised to go over and join him, or if such a gesture on his part would be taken amiss. He was wary of the jealousy of officials. The thought of such pettiness had often spoiled the pleasure he took in his walks with the Quartermaster General and with Saruxha. That was why in the end he decided not to budge from where he was standing.

Meanwhile the crowd began to stir, despite the crushing heat of the sun. There was talking, shuffling, standing on tiptoes. Then all of a sudden a shout of, "A horse! A white horse!" could be heard from all quarters. "Why is it white?" someone asked. He was told it was a holy steed. For a few moments the word "holy", as it went from mouth to mouth, drowned out the word "horse".

At that point a staccato neigh that sounded more like a sob confirmed in the minds of those who had not yet seen the beast that what was about to happen did indeed have something to do with a horse. Then everyone, or almost, saw the animal dart out on its own, beyond the fence, into no-man's-land. It had no rider. No one was running after it. The horse galloped around for a bit, then stopped, snorted, and, as if it was looking for something invisible in the air, rushed off towards the river.

"She's looking for water!"

"She's dying of thirst. That's obvious."

"She's been kept from drinking for days on end."

"They must have given her salted oats to eat."

The horse neighed a second time. A plaintive, majestic sound that wafted through the air. A voice said: "Have you seen how she's foaming at the mouth? Some people are saying she'll find the aqueduct!"

When it got to the fence, the horse reared up on its hind legs. Everyone noticed that on that side — the river side — the fence was higher and better made. Then the animal galloped around the entire length of the fence, visibly looking for a way out. As there was none, the horse turned on its tail and began to canter across no-man's-land again.

"The poor animal! Will she find the channel?"

"She surely will. Horses aren't as short-sighted as we are. They notice things that pass us by. For example, they can see the dead under the ground as easily as I can see you. Haven't you ever wondered why horses never step on a piece of ground where a man has been buried? Well, it's because they can see the corpse! A layer of earth doesn't stop a horse from seeing. So that's how she'll find the aqueduct, however well hidden it is."

"Yes, you must be right."

The beast stopped at one or two places, snorted, shook itself, and then began running again, this time towards the ramparts.

From the back, the Pasha issued a command:

"Make a precise note of every place where the animal stops."

The horse went up to the foot of the ramparts, lowered its head to sniff the ground, and then ran all the way round the wall.

Tavxha broke the silence to say to the Pasha: "Some people claim snakes are more alert to the presence of water. At Hapsan-Kala we tried to use one, but we weren't able to keep it to the area we were interested in, and we were also afraid it would slither away down a hole. So we gave up."

The Pasha's eyes were glued to the horse and he watched every movement the beast made. He seemed fascinated by it. In his tired gaze the horse seemed whiter and whiter, more and more ethereal. He was so tense that after a while, he could feel his own forelegs and neck muscles aching with fatigue, as if he was the one who was galloping round the ramparts and putting his head down now and then to sniff for a spot of damp in the scorched earth. At one point he even imagined he was foaming at the mouth, and he put up his hand to wipe his jaw clean.

Meanwhile defenders appeared on the parapet.

The horse ran around ever more wildly. For the fourth time, it came up to the moat, and turned tail.

The thousands of men surging against the fence had now almost all understood why the animal was behaving like that. Every one of them saw it as related to the outcome of the war, and consequently to what lay in store for them individually. The tenseness of the situation had moderated the noise of the crowd. Its tumult had sunk to a rumble, but it was still loud, since it was made by tens of thousands of voices. Against this thunderous background din — now more like a muffled last groan, now like a rasping breath — the clip-clop of the horse's hooves made a lonely sound.

Sirri Selim beckoned the chronicler to come over to him.

"The ancient Greeks seized Troy by using a wooden horse," he said, as he leaned his head towards Çelebi's ear. "Looks like we're going to seize this fortress by means of a horse of flesh and blood! It's true times have changed. Except that poets are still blind. By the way, where is your friend?"

The chronicler shrugged his shoulders to say he had no idea.

"Will the horse do it?" someone asked for the tenth time.

"I doubt it."

"The beast's worn out. I really think it's going to collapse."

"Look, look up there! There are girls on the parapet!"

"Girls? Where?"

"Up there! To the right of the second tower. There are several of them. And two more a bit further on."

"Well, well, so there are! I can see them now."

"Odd!"

"How dare they show themselves unveiled in front of thousands of men?"

Several young women had indeed come to watch from the crenellations. In any other circumstance their appearance would have attracted everyone's attention, but all were so absorbed by the progress of the horse that very few of them raised their eyes, and then only for a second.

"The horse looks like it's on its last legs!"

The beast was running round the main wall as if possessed by the devil. Three times over, it stopped dead in its tracks, pawed the ground furiously, then set off again. All around the fence there was now such a silence that you could not only hear the horse's hooves quite clearly, but even its snorting breath. Once more it stopped dead a few paces from the wall, stamped hard on the ground with its forelegs and raised a cloud of dust, then galloped off again with its nostrils to the wind. It was running by the foot of the third tower when a defender drew his bow and took aim. The arrow whistled through the air and into the horse, and when the animal made a desperate leap to dislodge it, thousands of voices uttered a moan and a cry of anxiety. Many had already reached for their yatagans.

The high officials surrounding the Pasha turned towards him with a quizzical look.

"No matter," the Pasha said, though he felt a sharp pain in his left shoulder. "The wound will only heighten its thirst."

The horse whinnied pitifully. Everyone had their eyes on the third tower, expecting a second arrow to come whizzing out of it. But there was no second shot.

"They could kill the horse. If they are sparing the beast, then it must be to make us think there is no aqueduct," a voice whispered from behind the Pasha's back.

"So why did they let off the arrow?"

"An accident. Someone must have lost his self-control."

The horse ran on, ever more frantically. The arrow fell out of its flesh at the second or third pace. The wound in its shoulder and the diagonal trickle of blood across its shank could be seen from afar.

"At Hapsan-Kala they killed three of our horses, one after the other," Tavxha said. "We had to put heavy armour on the fourth one, the one that actually found the water."

The horse started neighing again. Its mane stood magnificently erect. It was shaking its withers and stamping on the ground more and more often. From the top of the castle wall the defenders watched in silence (at least, that was the impression that their unmoving heads produced) while thousands of soldiers pressing up to the fence held their breath. Some cried out wishes: "Let's hope she does find it!" Others gave encouragement in beseeching and desperate tones: "O sacred horse, go on and find it!" Dozens of hoxhas and dervishes had kneeled on the ground to pray, holding the palms of their hands one against the other.

The horse whinnied. It seemed to pick up the scent of the river, and rushed off towards it once more. But the fence was sturdy and forced the animal to turn back. You could see steam rising from its exhausted body, you could see its nostrils quivering. A narrow streak of blood led away from its mouth. The mare was now cantering parallel to the fence a few paces from the soldiers, staring at them with its demented eyes.

The parapet was packed with defenders. It seemed every one of them had climbed up to the top. Some were waving crosses and icons.

Suddenly the horse stopped, pivoted around, put its head down, and plunged its muzzle into the ground. Then it trampled its hooves into the same spot with furious energy, raising great clumps of earth. But this time the horse did not move on. Quite the contrary: it stamped and nuzzled the ground with ever-greater fury and desperation. It was quickly enveloped in a cloud of dust. It soon seemed that a miracle was taking place: just like in a fairy story, the mare seemed to have been seized by a whirlwind and to have vanished into the heavens in a puff of smoke. As the dust cloud settled, the horse was indeed nowhere to be seen. A groan of terror and awe rose from a thousand breasts. Then from the midst of the moaning rose shouts of "She's back! She's come back!" and they were all so carried away that many of them raised their eyes to the heavens, expecting to see the horse float back down. But once the dust cloud had cleared completely, the horse could be seen by all, with its legs in the air, waving its hooves ever more feebly, and rubbing its back into the ground.

"That spot is to be excavated immediately!" the Pasha called out. The sapper's captain, who had come closer in the expectation of just such an order, rushed over to his men, standing at the ready a few paces away, with their spades and picks on their shoulders. A breach was made in the fence and the captain led his sappers at the double towards the horse. When they got to the spot where it was still lying, they pulled it out of the way and started digging.

There was much ado among the defenders at the top of the high wall. Sinister curved shapes emerged from the battlements, then arrows whistled through the scorching air. Two sappers sank to the ground without a sound. The third to be hit was the captain.

Tursun Pasha closed his eyes. He felt worn out, but happy.

"At last!" he muttered. "At last."

"Give the sappers some cover!" the Alaybey yelled.

Someone darted forwards. Commands were bawled, the breach in the fence was reopened, and a detachment of *azabs*, carrying their shields high before them, ran towards the diggers who had begun to flee, leaving their tools behind.

"The pipe is definitely there," Tursun Pasha said. "The fact that they shot at us proves we are on to their water supply. But why are the sappers running away? Get them back on the job this instant! They must dig at top speed. We mustn't leave them time to draw water! Quickly!"

"About — turn!" the Alaybey screamed as he went to intercept the handful of runaways. "Resume digging! At the double! Go!"

Under the command of an officer the *azabs* turned about and led the troops at running pace back towards the horse. The sappers followed on behind. When they got within range of the enemy, the infantrymen raised their shields and advanced with caution. By the time they reached the place where digging had been started, they formed on the fortress side an almost solid wall of shields, and waited for the sappers to come up behind them. Nobody seemed to pay the slightest attention to the men who had fallen beside the horse.

There were a few more shots from the battlements, but then, strangely enough, the defenders gradually vanished.

"They've gone back down to fill their water tanks," a voice suggested.

The Pasha gave an order. Another detachment of *azabs* instantly advanced towards the sappers and gave them a second semicircle of cover from enemy fire.

The digging went on. People waited and worried. In the midst of the excitement, anxiety and sweat that afflicted everyone, only the architect's face remained, as ever, unmoved. Now and again the Mufti nodded his head and uttered curses.

The sappers had now dug deep enough to be quite invisible to the onlookers. All that could be seen were spadefuls of earth flying up over the edge of the hole. And the more the pile of dug earth rose, the more you could read sheer terror in the eyes of all.

"At the siege of Hapsan-Kala, we had to dig for half a day," Old Tavxha said, looking at one and then the other of his comrades as if to seek their pardon for this delay in the discovery of the water source.

Silence reigned. The hole was now very deep and earth was being hauled up in sacks. A man ran over with a ladder on his back. Some of the onlookers grew weary of waiting and drifted off, but their places were quickly taken by others. People you never usually notice in an army came to join the throng: kitchen workers, officers' laundrymen, water carriers, embroiderers, knife grinders, all those whose tents were pitched on the other side of the river and who had come to be called the "othersiders", and even the dwarves who had just been sent from the capital to entertain the troops.

The Pasha slowly cracked his knuckles. His right ear had started buzzing again. He took another look at the corpses lying around the sappers and leaned towards the Alaybey to whisper something to him. But just at that moment, from the place of excavation, a savage roar of joy could be heard. "Wa-a-a-ter!" yelled ten times, a hundred times, a thousand times over by the horde of soldiers who suddenly shook themselves out of the state of lethargy into which the cruel sun had plunged them. The cry snapped them out of it in an instant, as if the water itself had suddenly refreshed their scorched limbs and faces.

Tursun Pasha began to laugh. It was the first time he had allowed himself that pleasure since the beginning of the campaign. Everyone in his entourage was taken aback, and turned to look. It was unusual, even shocking. They had never imagined their commander-in-chief was capable of laughing, and like anything that overturns a generally held opinion, the Pasha's guffaw aroused a kind of anxiety, almost a feeling of fear. Their leader's face suddenly seemed strange, distant, and undecipherable.

Shouts of "the water, the water!" now rose on all sides in wild excitement. Soldiers kissed and hugged, picked each other up, bawled and howled like madmen. Dervishes began to dance.

The battlements were still deserted. The defenders had vanished. Only the look-outs could be seen moving slowly at the tops of the towers, like shadows quite alien to the world of men.

"Skanderbeg!" Tursun Pasha growled, as if he was drunk on revenge. "At last, I am going to crush you!"

He ground his teeth as if he was crushing the bones of his

worst enemy, whose name he had just uttered for the first time in his life. At meetings of the war council and in other discussions, the Pasha always avoided saying Skanderbeg's name and only ever referred to him as "that man".

"Skanderbeg!" he mumbled again with repressed glee, slowly turning each letter of the name over on his tongue.

The Pasha's smile slowly drained from his face like water on sand, and his expression resumed its familiar look which all around him understood. They cheered up as a result and the wave of joy that had come to them with a slight delay now overtook them entirely. They began to chatter noisily about this and that and congratulated each other heartily. The Mufti, Kurdisxhi and others kept looking towards the still imperturbable architect, and put on faces to make fun of him. Old Tavxha stood stock-still. Cursing under his breath, he was proudly waiting for the others to come over and congratulate him.

The water had now flooded the pit and a puddle had appeared in the field. But the parched earth drank it in and the puddle did not grow any larger. Mud-covered sappers were busy all around it among their tools, the dead horse and the corpses of the soldiers who had been killed and who didn't seem to matter to anyone.

Mission accomplished. Tursun Pasha turned around. Before leaving, he called out to the Alaybey, "Tonight, let there be feasting!"

His deputies followed in his wake.

"I don't think the siege will last much longer now," Saruxha said. "A pity, because we won't have a chance of testing our third cannon."

"I think you will," the Quartermaster General replied. "And you'll have time to test number four as well, if you intend to cast it."

"How can that be? They've no more water. They won't be able to hold out for more than a week."

"I don't know why, but I doubt that," the Quartermaster went on.

"Well, you've given me some comfort, at least," Saruxha said. "When I heard them shout 'Water!' just now, I thought I'd lost my third cannon already."

"Are the moulds ready?"

"Yes, almost."

They were wending their way through muddle and mayhem. Orders and cries could be heard all around: "Keep away from the pit!" "You'll be shot at from the battlements!" "Keep away from the fence!" Sappers were bringing in the dead on stretchers. A larger group was coming in behind them — *azabs* hauling a stone-barrow, on which they had laid the dead horse. Soldiers stood aside to make way for the barrow and craned their necks to get a better view of the dead animal with its mud-spattered mane hanging over the side.

"She'll be buried with full military honours, like the captain of the sappers," someone said.

"They were right to say it was a sacred beast."

"She'll have a *turbes*. I heard the Pasha giving the order."

"A mausoleum? That's only fair. She deserves one."

"Who's going to be appointed to lead the sappers now?" a young janissary officer asked.

"Who knows? He's the second one to fall. The poor lad hardly had any time to enjoy his job. He was in post for only three hours. Maybe his successor will have better luck!"

The Quartermaster caught sight of the architect a few paces ahead of him, walking alone, save for his bodyguard. Two young janissary officers also noticed him and burst out laughing.

"Maybe he knows a lot, but an old nag knows more than he

does," one of them said. "People like that are just leeches on the state. They're all the same! They get themselves paid sacks of gold for doing bugger all."

"They don't fool the high command, actually. They're taken on because they're the best of a bad bunch."

"Did you hear that?" one of the janissaries asked with a smirk. "The architect lost out to a knackered horse!"

The men guffawed. One of them turned round, but on catching sight of the Quartermaster and Saruxha, he whispered something to his comrades, and they all stopped laughing. Surprised at the sudden wave of silence, one of the officers also turned round, and guessed the reason for it. It was not to his taste. Wishing to show that a janissary is not afraid of speaking his mind, even to officials, however elevated their rank, he puffed up his chest and said at the top of his voice:

"Indeed, a horse may well be able to do things that a scholar can't!"

Some of the janissaries grinned hesitantly.

The Quartermaster General went pale.

"Officer! Say that one more time, will you?" he cried out in fury. "Go on!"

"I was not talking about you, sir," the officer said with hauteur.

"Lout! Boor! Stand still!"

The officer stopped walking and stared insolently at the Quartermaster General. The other officer and the men also came to a halt. The architect turned round and looked on at the scene impassively.

"Are you talking to me?" the officer sneered.

"Yes, I am," the Quartermaster General said as he came up close. "And here is my answer!" He slapped the young man in the face with his leather fan.

The officer reached for his sabre, but the Quartermaster's bodyguard leaped forwards as quick as a cat, and put his dirk between his master and the janissary. Saruxha's bodyguard had also drawn his dagger. A muffled hum arose from the crowd that had assembled, for they had all seen the insignia sewn on to the long tunics worn by the Quartermaster and the master caster.

"Disarm this man!" the Quartermaster ordered.

The two guards manhandled the officer and took away his sword. The janissary looked all around as if he was seeking help. But the only response the crowd gave was another wave of muttering. The guards, with their arms in hand, awaiting orders, looked to their masters, and everyone realised that the fate of the bold officer now hung on the lips of the two imperial dignitaries.

"Off to prison with him!" the Quartermaster said. Seeing a high-ranking officer in the crowd, he called out to him: "Put this scoundrel under lock and key!"

The officer nodded agreement, and ordered two foot-soldiers to take the janissary off to jail.

"You did very well," Saruxha said when they had moved on a few yards. "But maybe we should have told our guards to execute the man on the spot."

"It comes to the same thing," the Quartermaster replied. "The court martial will sentence him to death."

"How ignorant can you get!"

"He interrupted us as we were talking most agreeably. But what were we talking about? Supplies, I believe . . . Alright. Let's have a glass of syrup in my tent, there's going to be lots of noise and I can't bear that sort of thing."

Saruxha accepted the invitation.

The feast had already started. Night was falling, and the drums had begun to roll in every corner of the camp. Soldiers flocked to where they thought the best entertainment would be. The Quartermaster and Saruxha almost collided with half-drunk *azabs* many times. Dervishes were trying to make a space where they could start dancing.

As they passed in front of the Pasha's pavilion, they heard the delicate and velvety sound of cymbals, so different from the brutal roll of drums.

"A woman's hand," the Quartermaster said as he slowed his pace.

"Yes, it surely is."

The lilac pavilion was more brightly lit than usual. For a second, their eyes gleamed with yearning for the magical delights it held.

"The Pasha's having fun," Saruxha said.

"He doesn't do that very often."

"I thought I'd noticed that he doesn't enjoy distractions. That proves he's particularly happy tonight. In the circumstances, he has every right to be happy!"

The cymbals tinkled on at a jolly pace, with occasional pauses, as if to tease the listener.

"If he doesn't win this campaign, his star will dim for good," the Quartermaster said.

"Do you think so?"

"I'm sure of it. If he's beaten, the best he can hope for is banishment for life. As for the worst . . ." The Quartermaster drew a line with his forefinger under his throat.

Again they nearly fell over tipsy troopers. They were mucking about waving flaming torches, swapping dirty jokes, laughing out loud. Others were playing at leapfrog or else trying to balance on a kind of seesaw.

The Quartermaster didn't try to hide his disdain. "I don't like to see the army unbutton itself," he said.

His own tent was pitched away from the mass, in a quiet spot. Soldiers who didn't feel like taking part in the feast were sitting or lying in front of their tents, chatting among themselves. Somewhere, someone was singing a sad song. The lyrics were not easy to make out:

We're on a new campaign
In a distant land
In desolate terrain . . .

The rolls of all the drums had merged into a single thundering rumble which reached their ears in waves, and then swept on and was lost in the vastness of the night.

On the threshold of his tent, the Quartermaster turned round and looked for a moment at the huge camp spread out from one horizon to the other, interspersed with thousands of triangular outlines made by the dull mauve of the tents.

"What's on your mind?" Saruxha enquired.

"I'm thinking that we'll have to come back and pitch our tents many more times in this part of the world."

"Inevitable. We live in a time of war."

"Listen," the Quartermaster said, changing the topic suddenly. "At the war council I'm going to insist on launching the second assault without delay. And you are going to support me."

"Sure. But what's the hurry?"

"They are many," the Quartermaster explained with a wave of his arm towards the myriad tents. "The grain won't feed them all."

Saruxha blew his nose.

"So, three or four thousand fewer mouths to feed?"

"That's right," the Quartermaster said. "What's more, we might even win."

"But every day they're without water brings our victory closer," Saruxha objected. "Time is on our side."

"We've cut their water, but don't forget they've cut our food," the Quartermaster replied.

He gestured again towards the centre of the main camp where there was feasting and uproar.

"They're rejoicing tonight, but they've no idea that in a few days they'll go on half-rations."

"Poor men," Saruxha sighed. "There's so much they don't know."

"A soldier's lot."

They went inside the tent. As time passed, they spoke less and less. Eventually Saruxha stood up to take his leave, and his host walked him back part of the way to his tent. The party was still going on in the distance, but less noisily now.

"Listen!" the Quartermaster said suddenly as he was about to say farewell to his friend. "Are my ears deceiving me? Or is that not the alert sounding?"

"It's been drumming like that for a little while already," his orderly said.

"Yes," Saruxha agreed. "That is the call to arms."

They strained their ears. The great drum was beating somewhere deep inside the camp, each of its beats overriding the rattle and bang of the party drums.

"Skanderbeg!" the Quartermaster exclaimed.

They listened intently once more. From somewhere far away to their left could be heard the distant sound of uproar. From the darkness came sporadic echoes of different voices shouting "*Silah bashna!* Alarm!"

"Saruxha, come and spend the night in my tent," the Quartermaster offered. "This part of the camp is safe."

"I have to go and see what's happening at the foundry," the master caster said.

"Your foundry's not at risk either."

"It would still be better if I went back," Saruxha objected.

"I advise you to stay. This night we are on alert."

Saruxha wavered. The great drum carried on sounding the call to arms without a pause.

"Skanderbeg must have learned that we cut off the water," the Quartermaster said thoughtfully. And, after a moment's silence, he added: "The tiger has pounced!"

They finally cut off our water. To begin with, when the white horse started running round and round like a curse on our ramparts, we took it for irrational behaviour on their part — a magical practice or a primitive rite. Only the count, who stayed up late that night straining to decode the messages that are sent to us by means of beacons on the mountain-tops, knew what it was all about. The signals spoke of the fence, and obviously of water too. While we joked away on the battlements, he went to church to pray. Gossip spread, and though we carried on amusing ourselves, we gradually succumbed to anxiety. Although we did not yet know the whole truth, we were plagued by fear and came out in a cold sweat.

The count's face was yellow when he came back up to see us at the top of the wall, and he looked down on the enemy camp with desolation in his eyes. He had not been afraid of their new weapon, but he seemed terrified of that horse. Later on, when it was all over, he explained that the aqueduct had been designed to follow a paradoxical path that made it undiscoverable by human minds. But once men had stepped aside and entrusted the task to an animal, he was sore afraid. In this circumstance instinct would be more effective than intelligence.

When they saw water spurt from the pit and turn it into a brackish puddle, our daughters burst into tears, then they all went to the chapel together to pray to the Holy Virgin.

The other side celebrated the water cut-off late into the night. Trumpets, drums, flutes, bagpipes and who knows what other instruments made a diabolical noise and filled the night with a hellish racket. It went on and on until we heard their alarm drum banging. Having apparently learned that they had cut our water, our Castrioti finally set upon them.

It is past midnight. Their huge camp is in convulsion, it is gasping for breath as if it were being hacked to death. George is down there among them. He is striking and harassing them as only he knows how. The night is pitch-dark and we cannot see anything. We can only feel his breath. We have all taken up our positions behind our great gate, and are ready to open it and launch a counter-attack as soon as the order comes. From the battlements a woman has started to yell: "George, George, avenge us and kill them all!"

CHAPTER ELEVEN

The chronicler had only just fallen asleep when the first alarm woke him up. He had spent a gloomy evening. In a camp entirely given over to noisy merrymaking, he had tramped up and down without meeting anyone of his acquaintance. He gave up looking for a friend, went back to his tent and tried to get some sleep. But he couldn't. He felt painfully alone, and the sounds of carousing going on outside just made it worse. Two or three times he nearly got up to go out again, but when he remembered the fruitless walk he had taken earlier on, he decided to stay in bed. Then he just waited for the noise of the festivities to abate, hoping that once things had quietened down he would be able to get to sleep. But sleep actually stole up on him before the party was over. The white horse seeking out water kept on running round the fortress in ever slowing circles, wrapping his mind in its web of dream. Then the no-man's-land on the other side of the fence suddenly reminded him of the plain of Kosovo — except that the white horse now had a rider, and that rider was Sultan Murad. The monarch gazed with desolate eyes on the dead who lay all around when suddenly . . . "Good God! No!" he moaned out loud, and woke up in an instant. The noise in the camp had changed. He went outside his tent and cocked his ear. The great alarm drum was banging some-where in the heart of the camp. One by one, the other drums were stopping. Cries of "*Hazerol!*" and "*Silah-bashna!*" rang out all around. Mevla Çelebi got dressed in a hurry. He felt cold sweat on his brow. He went out. The party drums had now fallen silent, and the camp was swathed in terrifying darkness. All that could still be heard was the deep boom of the drum that signalled the alert. Çelebi could make out the sounds of running feet, of weapons being readied, commands and the clatter of hooves speeding away. Soldiers came out of their tents with their weapons in their hands and ran to their units' assembly points like fleeting shadows hastening to a meeting of conspirators. He was seized with fear. Why were they running around like that? Where were they going? He stood outside his tent, quite petrified, not knowing what to do. There was a suspicious calm in the space immediately around him. He could hear feet moving away at speed. Someone shouted "Quicker! Quicker!" Then silence again. Why was this part of the camp being evacuated? As the thought struck him like a shard of ice, he started running automatically behind the others who were fleeing. He had no idea how long he ran. He only stopped when he felt there were enough people around him. It was a veritable exodus. Janissaries, volunteers, *azabs*, *eshkinxhis*, all in arms, were trying to track down their units by torchlight. You couldn't tell whether they were preparing to retreat or to go on the attack. Raucous shouts, calls and orders bawled out by commanders rose on all sides.

"The fourth battalion has left!"

"Seems they've attacked the janissaries' quarters."

"Fifth *eshkinxhi* battalion, here!"

"Kara-Mukbil is fighting them to the death!"

"To the foundry! They're attacking the foundry!"

"Back! What is your unit? Second battalion? Then retreat!"

"The Albanians have opened the gate!"

"They can't have. Keep your mouth shut!"

"Bakerhan is dead!" someone screamed like a madman, at the head of the group that was falling back in chaos.

"Get back! Where are you going?"

"Skanderbeg!"

"Back, I said!"

"Skanderbeg! Skanderbeg!"

"What are you shouting about, you scoundrel? Here! Have this!"

The chronicler heard the dull thud of a blade entering a body, and then the sound of a man collapsing to the ground.

"The *akinxhis*! Here come the *akinxhis*!"

Kurdisxhi's great mane of hair, gleaming in the torchlight, flashed past at the head of a mounted squadron.

"Get back! Get back!" an officer screamed.

"Join your units!"

"The *sipahis*! The glorious *sipahis*!"

Sipahis galloped past and disappeared into the night on the tail of the *akinxhis*.

The chronicler's heart was ready to burst. The flower of the army was valiantly rushing to the front to repulse the enemy. He was ashamed of having yielded to fear a few moments before. He watched with admiration as the Moroccan *tabors* rushed towards the area where that beast Skanderbeg was wreaking havoc. But his joy was brief. The mass of men whose voices, arms and orders had dispelled his fear suddenly melted away before his eyes at incredible speed. The weapons, the voices and the commands were all swallowed up by the dark and very soon Mevla Çelebi realised that he was alone on a path that might very soon be taken by the marauding tiger.

He started running, not knowing which way he was going. He just had to get away from that spot which was being abandoned like a sinking ship. All around he could hear men calling and urging each other on, but in the black night he could not make out exactly where they were coming from. More like the voices of ghosts than of living men, the cries were carried off by the dark wind of the night.

He soon found himself once again in a crowd. He couldn't tell if this dense pack of men was running away from the fight, or looking for it. It too quickly dispersed and the chronicler once more found himself on his own. He could now see all over the camp that men were coming together like bees to a swarm, then moving around, then dispersing, without rhyme or reason, like fluffy white clouds on a windy day. On a night of panic such as this, there was nothing to rely on.

He ran on and on. His legs took him instinctively towards the middle of the camp, where the commander-in-chief's tent stood. He heard people calling and commanding, then from out of the darkness came an extraordinary, terrifying sound of heavy breathing which drowned out all other noise. Tahanka! the chronicler thought.

The Pasha's tent was dark. Yet he saw messengers coming and going. Çelebi reckoned the Pasha was inside, but that the lights had been shaded so the tent would not be visible. He had collected himself now, and noticed that all around the tent were hundreds of desert warriors standing silently with their long lances at the ready. They made him feel safer. He sat down on the ground beside an alleyway. All sorts of noises could be heard in the distance, but here, at least, it was quiet. Mounted messengers galloped up, stopped dead in their tracks, slid straight out of the saddle, then ran on. Praise be to God for having allowed him to find safe haven! But this relative calm did not last long. He felt as if something was crawling forwards and moving in the dark. More and more desert warriors were swelling the detachment. From behind him, someone shouted out an order. A distant rumble of thunder seemed to be drawing nearer.

Çelebi could feel the drops of sweat on his forehead. What if that tornado were to strike the tent of the commander-in-chief? He sat up straight. Yes, of course. The tent was obviously the target. Yes, it was aiming to get here, and nowhere else. He was overcome with terror once again. He started to run. Ah, if only he could find a spot to hide! A really safe place, a bolt-hole, a hole in the ground . . . His mind was working fast. The abandoned tunnel! The bread oven! (Mevla! Have you only just realised that the oven was camouflage for the entrance to the tunnel?) He hastened towards the broken-down building. The rumble behind him was getting nearer. Quickly! Quickly! Now he's got there at last. Nobody around. He goes inside. Feeling his way, shaking from head to toe, he finds the ladder. He climbs down. The rungs are ice cold. Further down. Pitch-black. A bitter odour of mud. He thinks of the astrologer. Suddenly, beneath his feet, in the dark, he felt something move. A snake! he thought, in terror, and he had already started to dash back up when from down below someone said quietly:

"Careful! You're treading on us."

He was petrified.

"You'd better sit down," the same person said in a placid tone.

Çelebi couldn't make sense of it all. He thought he felt something else move a little further on. He heard a sneeze.

"Where are you from?" the voice said.

"Me? From here . . . accidentally . . ." the chronicler stammered.

"It's alright," the voice replied. "I know the kind of accident you mean. But you had a bright idea. You're not stupid!"

Çelebi didn't answer.

"Have no fear," the man went on gruffly. "We're not hiding here so as to give you away. Crows don't pick out each other's eyes. I'm from the fourth *azab* battalion. Eleven years in the ranks. I worked out long ago that I'd lay low down here if Skanderbeg mounted a night raid. Dying on the walls is fine by me, but getting mown down in the crush really isn't worth it. So at the first sound of the alert I ran out of my tent. Off you go, old *azab*, I said to myself, time to find your hidey-hole. Then once I got here I found friends. They'd been even quicker off the mark than I had."

As if to confirm the *azab*'s explanation, someone nearby hiccupped.

"Sit down," he went on. "Make yourself at home. Nobody will bother you down here."

Çelebi found a little hump to sit on.

"You a sapper?" the *azab* asked.

"Yes," the chronicler answered.

"Thought so. You must have worked here, obviously."

By the time Çelebi felt like having a chat, as everyone does in due course once danger has passed, the *azab* had fallen silent. The chronicler didn't dare speak first. He was afraid his voice might be recognised. He was ashamed. At the very moment when battle was raging, he, the historian, the writer of the chronicle destined to immortalise the stirring deeds of the campaign, was crouching like a rat in a hidden tunnel waiting for it all to calm down.

"Up there it must be sheer murder," the *azab* muttered, as if he was reading Çelebi's thoughts.

The chronicler didn't know what to say. They could hear banging on the ground above them, sometimes quite clearly, sometimes less so. There was a long pause, then the noise began again, far away to begin with, then getting nearer and nearer.

"They're coming this way," the *azab* mumbled.

They held their peace and strained their ears. The banging was getting nearer, and was turning into the sound of horses galloping. They were even nearer now, right on top of them. The ground began to shake. The chronicler huddled up.

"They're right above us," the *azab* declared.

The sound of hooves above their heads became a terrifying din. He put his hand into his hair to shake out the earth he thought must have fallen into it and mumbled prayers until the thunder moved away once again.

Someone sighed deeply. Çelebi was relieved and was about to raise his voice when from the far distance the sound of trampling became faintly audible, and then grew steadily louder.

"Another wave," the *azab* said.

They all held their breath. The noise got so loud they thought the ground over the roof of the tunnel would collapse on them.

"Skanderbeg!" a voice cried out.

The chronicler thought that the latest wave would go on breaking for ever; worse still, it seemed to be besieging him ever more tightly, as a fever narrows a throat. Then when the noise abated and finally disappeared, allowing him to assume that there would be no further assault, Çelebi became aware of the calm and steady voice of the *azab*, who had probably been speaking for a while already without worrying whether anyone was listening to him or not.

"Eleven years in uniform. You reckon that's a lot, don't you? And who knows how much longer I'll have to serve? We're veterans, and it's about time we were given the land that was promised us. Before we left for this campaign we were told we'd be allocated the land around the fortress when we'd taken it. I come from Anatolia, but I've been far and wide. I've fought in the plains of Karabogdan, at Stara Planin and Tarabullur, in Bulgaria and Bosnia, and I've even been as far as Szemendre, in Hungary. There's good land everywhere, and each time we pitch camp, I wonder what could be grown in the area and what the soil is like, compared to the other places where we've fought. You're a sapper, so you shouldn't be surprised by all that. You're a man of earth and mud too, aren't you, except that you don't honour the land, you make it submit to outrage, like people say, and then you grumble when it takes its revenge, like it did in this tunnel when it caved in on your comrades. Anyway, what was I saying? Ah, yes, about land. So they promised us we'd be given plots around the fortress, and when we got here the first thing I did was to look carefully at the soil. I scooped it up in my hand, crumbled it and smelled it. It's good earth. Wheat ought to grow easily here. But what's the use? It's foreign soil. I don't know why it doesn't cheer my heart, but it doesn't, and it leaves a feeling of emptiness in my breast. It's foreign soil, after all. You know what I mean? It even smells different."

The sound of dragging feet could be heard coming from the entrance. Someone was climbing down the ladder. The *azab* stopped chatting. Everyone held their breath. A man was groping his way into the tunnel.

"Careful, chum, or you'll trample us," the *azab* said.

"Ah!" said the newcomer, scared out of his wits.

"No point moaning, sit down, you're fine just where you are," the *azab* said. "Where are you from?"

"Ninth *eshkinxhi* battalion," the man replied in a voice stran-
gulated by fear.

"What's going on up there?"

"Better not ask."

"It seems the Albanians have tried to break out. Do you know
anything about it?"

"No. All I know is that people are slaughtering each other."

"I can imagine."

"No, you can't. It's worse than anything you could imagine."

"How can it be worse?"

"Oh, trust me. It is worse."

He fell silent, but from his heavy breathing you could sense
he wanted to say something more.

"Come on, spit it out," the *azab* said. "Why is it so bad?"

"Because . . . As far as I could tell . . . there is no attack
going on up there."

"You're crazy. If we haven't been raided, what the hell is going
on?"

"I have no idea. Maybe it's a fake alarm. Or a mistake. At
any rate, it's a total mess, and nobody understands anybody else."

"And why would that be worse than a night raid?"

"Because . . . when you're attacked, you know what you're
up against. But this . . . it's impossible to give a name to it. It's
like fever, delirium. No Skanderbeg! That's what people are saying.
He hasn't been here for a while. Somebody else named Gjergj has
taken his place. And he is quite something."

"You are really crazy. But I am even crazier for listening to
you. Got that? So why don't you say something, you jerk?"

The stranger had left. What a bloody jerk he was, the *azab*
thought. He even pretended to be an *eshkinxhi*! How could they
have put such soldiers in a hole like this? Sod that!

There was another long pause. More thunder could be heard, but this time it did not grow any louder. It was whirling around somewhere on the outskirts of the camp, getting fainter, then getting clearer, then fading away entirely. These ebbs and flows of the tide of sound went on for an interminably long time.

"I'm going up for a bit to see what's happened," someone said.

He could be heard trudging through the loose earth and then climbing the rungs of the ladder. The others waited for him to return. He came back.

"Well?"

"Looks like it's calming down. It's not yet dawn."

Someone else moved in the dark.

"Are you leaving?" a voice asked. "As you like. I'm staying put a bit longer. We'll meet again. As soon as the alert is given, run back here, you'll find us where you left us."

Çelebi wanted to stand up, but overwhelming weariness kept him still. The thought that he might not find his own tent standing, that his present shelter was likely to be the best he would ever find henceforth, made him want to close his eyes. He couldn't have said whether he really was dropping off to sleep, or just seeming to do so. He could not stop seeing a white horse running round in his mind's eye but he no longer knew which one it was, whether it was the horse of noon or the ancient horse of Murad at Kosove Polye. It seemed as if an entire season had elapsed since the early afternoon. He thought of the sheets of his manuscript trampled by horses' hooves. But even they could not be more distressing or destructive than the Quartermaster's account of the murder of the monarch. He'd tried to forget about it, but it was no good. He first tried to coax the thought away, then he tried to order it to leave his mind, but neither method worked. Then he sought to transform the story to some degree and to soften it, but it serried its ranks into an impregnable position . . . The great Sultan, Murad Han, was not killed by Christians but by his own viziers . . . A trickle of molten lead in his ear would probably not have hurt him more. It was a horror, a space slashed open, and an intoxicating doubt all wrapped in one.

He couldn't work out why on a night like this his mind remained for no obvious reason firmly fixed on this vision. Then he thought he understood: he was on his own in the dark, in a quite unnatural place that was neither the ground, nor a tent, nor an office. A kind of nowhere place, a place truly beyond the reach of law, outside the world and the Empire. Maybe this was the first opportunity he had ever had to ponder at length on something he would never dare write down: the truth about the Battle of Kosovo! Hurry up! he told himself. Dawn will soon be breaking.

And that was how, in the bowels of the earth, he meditated the first canto: Sultan Murad Han on his white horse, when battle was done, towards dusk, inspecting the dead. Suddenly, a ragged Balkan with running sores rises up from the ground and tries to come close, supposedly to kiss his hand. The guards hold him back, but strangely the Sultan tells them to leave him be. Now the man approaches and, instead of kissing the proffered hand, he extracts from beneath the rags covering his otherwise naked body an even barer blade, then leaps up like a wild cat and plunges it straight into the Sultan's heart. That's the story you read in all the chronicles, but the Quartermaster cries out: Lies! How could you believe, you idiot, that on such a bloody day any infidel could have got so close to the Emperor? And how could you assume in addition that a wounded man could spring from the ground to the full height of a rider on horseback, and with a single blow get a knife through the Sultan's breast-plate?

First counter-canto: a murder really did take place, a strange one indeed, a little before sunset, in front of dozens of witnesses. The man on the horse wasn't Murad Han but his body double. And the man who knifed him wasn't a Balkan but a dervish who had been specially trained for the job and was wearing a disguise. Help me, O Muse, he begged, help me with the second canto!

Second canto: the Sultan's tent; the council of viziers surround the sovereign. A messenger runs up announcing the monarch's death. The Sultan laughs; but the viziers frown. Why have your eyes gone as dark as ravens? "Because it is an evil omen," the Grand Vizier declares. "When a shadow falls, its owner must fall too." At which point they set upon him and stab him to death.

Second counter-canto: that is how this crime has been told for many a long year. They wanted us to believe that the Sultan had perished at the hand of a Christian . . . The body double's guards and the killer dervish were slain on the spot to prevent the story being leaked . . . Come to my aid, O Muse, for the third canto!

Third canto: at the other end of the camp, a message reaches the heir to the throne, Jakup Çelebi. "Your illustrious father requests your presence." On his way over he can hear people shouting, "The Sultan has been killed!" But the messenger reassures the prince: "His double has been slain, my lord." Jakup nonetheless feels a sinister foreboding.

Third counter-canto: when they set off for Kosovo they had already laid plans to kill the monarch, whatever the outcome of the battle. The aim was to put on the throne not the elder son, in proper order of succession, but the younger son, Bayezit, for it was he who had the viziers' preference. Help me, O Muse, to write my last canto!

Canto the last: Prince Jakup Çelebi enters his father's tent. The Sultan's corpse lies on the kilim. "But that's my father!" the

prince cries out. "They told me only his shadow had been slain!"
"In this vale of tears we are all shadows," one of the viziers says.
Whereupon they slay Jakup as they had slain his father.

Counter-canto the last: the younger brother, Prince Bayezit,
buries his face in his hands. He pretends not to understand, but
he had actually known all about it for some time. They had promised to do it all without shedding blood, and he had pretended
to believe them. He contemplates the funereal field of Kosovo
stretching out before him and foresees that victors and vanquished
will both be cursed for evermore. Cries rise in the far distance:
"The Sultan has been slain!" The heralds again spread the false
news that it is only the Sultan's double who died, and, like his
brother before him, he walks to his father's tent. He goes in and
sees the two bodies on the floor. My father and his double . . .
he thinks. But at this point the assembled dignitaries bow down
low and call him "Padishah". He then realises that one of the
bodies belongs to his brother Jakup. "We didn't have a choice,"
the Grand Vizier murmurs. "It wasn't part of the plan." The new
monarch covers his tear-streaked face with his hands, but nobody
will ever know what the tears were really made of and why they
were shed . . .

"Forgive me, all-powerful Allah!" the chronicler sighed. He
felt washed out as if he had committed an unpardonable crime.
The same feeling he had had long ago as an adolescent when his
friends had taught him how to have pleasure on his own. He
played with himself all night long and by dawn he was emptied
out and completely exhausted. "Forgive me, O Allah," he prayed
again, and he wanted there to be someone next to him, to cuddle
and comfort him, like there used to be, but now there was nobody
at his side. Sheer terror at being on his own made him stand up.
He groped for the way out, and even managed to find it. Day was

breaking when he emerged. The dawn was an impenetrable, purple-flecked grey that hid the horizon all around, and made everything seem unreal. He felt soil falling from his clothes as he walked. Anyone who had seen him at that point would have taken him for a corpse that had just climbed out of the grave. He raised his collar so as not to be recognised and hurried on. The camp seemed to be sleeping peacefully. There was no visible trace of what had just taken place. Çelebi felt as if he really had returned from the grave. In it he had buried his only chronicle that was hostile to the State. He took a deep breath, happy to be relieved of it. On the slant sides of the tents you could just make out the dampness of morning dew, so alien to the hostility of men. Terror, screams, panic and thundering hooves had all been dissolved in millions of droplets, each one of which contained a sense of the end of night and the ineluctable dawning of day. But what he saw when he got a little further on was suddenly quite different. Laid out before him was a whole line of tents that had been knocked over, some of them slashed, with trampled banners on the ground among a dead horse and a human corpse lying face down. Çelebi shuddered. It was a sight of devastation that rent the heart. And further on there was another endless line of knocked-down tents looking as if they had been swept over by a gale. *He* came this way, he thought, as he hurried to leave the area and get back to his own tent. Then he heard the sound of irregular footsteps. Someone was limping towards him. It was the tall figure of a man leaning on a walking stick, of the kind blind men use. As he got nearer he made out who it was: Sadedin. He was muttering through his teeth. From time to time he waved a club, threateningly.

The day after they cut off our water, they sent a deputation to nego-
tiate with us. Clad in their formal attire, the envoys waited outside the
great gate for us to let them in. One of them held the flag of peace in
his hand, another beat softly on a drum. From the battlements we
shouted down to them to move away, or else our arrows would pierce
them. Then the drummer shouted back at us:

"You benighted ones! Do you not hear this drum? The Padishah
had it made from the skins of his enemies!" He struck it a few more
times, then said: "We shall make more drums like these from your
skins. Madmen! If you only knew the fate that awaits you!"

That was all the negotiation there was. It is still unbearably hot.
The well we dug is almost dry. We are digging another one. We suffer
from thirst. So this is the siege by thirst they so often mentioned in the
negotiations that were held before the fight. You can build up stores of
food, they told us, but you can't stock water!

Fearing further attacks, they are digging trenches all day long and
driving stakes into the ground all around their camp. Rumour has it
that Gjergj hasn't actually attacked. Oddly enough, their own chiefs
are trying to quash such rumours. If they had an explanation for the
chaos in the camp, then it would be to their benefit if such rumours
turned out to be true. But if the only explanation for the mess is a
general panic among the troops — that would hardly be to the army's
credit.

Black smoke rises all the time from their foundry. Apparently they are casting more cannon. Their engineers and technicians are just as fearsome as the janissaries that scale our ramparts. They want to deliver a fatal blow. They are taking advantage of the great heat and of the thirst that is devouring us. As if the moon were not enough for them, they think the sun is also on their side, and thus they reckon they are masters of the universe.

They are in a hurry. They want to have it over before the first rains. Because if it begins to rain . . .

We often look carefully at the sky. Not a cloud to be seen. An azure desert. Solitude.

CHAPTER TWELVE

They were on the attack again. Contrary to usual tactics, they had launched the action on the stroke of noon, when the heat was at its peak. A great horde of assault troops drenched in blood and sweat pressed up against the entire outer wall of the fortress, gesticulating, climbing ladders, climbing back down, retreating, rushing forwards, whirling, panting, and screaming over the thunderous noise of their cannon and the hundreds of drums that went on banging without a break. A thick pall of yellowish dust obscured parts of the tableau from time to time, just as it revealed others more horrible as it slowly moved away on the wind.

The sun beat down without mercy.

Disobeying the rules of war, Tursun Pasha had decided to attack at midday for an obvious reason: the besieged would be doubly punished by thirst. In the architect's opinion (he had noticed that the Pasha, oddly, paid more attention to his views when he was angry with him), seven days with no external supply of water should have exhausted all the cisterns, however large they may be (under torture, prisoners had given varying numbers — some said there were four, others three). As for water from the well, it could not possibly be enough to meet the needs of the besieged and allow them to care for their wounded. In weather as hot as this, the architect emphasised, wounding them is even more useful to us than killing them. Tursun Pasha had to make a great effort not to scream back at Giaour: "You're not going to start proposing yet more ill-advised stratagems, are you? Maybe you'll try to persuade me to order my troops to take care when they're fighting not to slay the foe, but just to wound him?" In the event, he did say something like that to the architect, but not roughly, only as a joke. Giaour replied: "Do as you think fit, sire."

In spite of everything, it was the architect who had given the canniest advice about the timing of the attack. Most of the council had wanted to put it off even longer so as to let thirst do part of the work of the scimitar. Delay might seem sensible, he had said, and thirst will indeed assist the task, but they should not forget that it was past the middle of August and that people who knew the region reckoned that the rains would come very soon. A sudden shower could put everything in jeopardy.

The objection was enough to convince the Pasha to act on the architect's advice. Moreover, even if the rain should hold off, he had his own deadlines for this campaign. He had put a ring of iron around the fortress, but he was as much in its grip as the defenders were. They may lack water, but he was short of time. The campaign could go on to the middle of the autumn at the latest, but no longer. The first frost usually brought the order to withdraw, and for him that would be the end.

He kept his eyes glued to a single spot, the main gate, where the surge was fiercest. The *azabs* had managed to erect another scaffold which they had covered with wet animal hides. The great reed screens hovered over the attackers' heads, like rafts on a stormy sea. Sheltered by these devices, the soldiers had started battering the heavy door with their gigantic iron rams.

"The hinges are giving way already," the Alaybey observed. "They don't seem to have been properly repaired."

"Repeat the order not to enter the inner courtyard," the Pasha said.

An officer rode off towards the ramparts.

At the council of war held the previous night, someone had put the view that, since the attempt to batter down the main gate had failed first time round, it would be wiser not to try it again. But the Pasha objected that forcing open a main gate, even if it was of no practical use, served most of all to raise the attackers' morale. Moreover, in consultation with Saruxha, he had devised a stratagem which required the main gate to be open in any case.

"Your magnificence," the Pasha's aide-de-camp whispered as he leaned towards his master, "the doctor requests an audience."

"Now?" Tursun Pasha said without taking his eyes off the castle's main door.

"Yes, now."

"Bring him."

Sirri Selim introduced himself, bent his great length down low twice over, and, thinking that the Pasha had still not noticed him, bowed a third time.

"Speak," the Pasha said when a long shadow awkwardly darkening his feet alerted him to the presence of the doctor standing behind him. Speak, and may ill befall you if what you have to say is out of place, he added silently.

"Pardon me, sire, for disturbing you at such a moment . . ."

"Come to the point," the Pasha cut in.

Sirri Selim swallowed his saliva. "We must take a prisoner from among the besieged," he said, pointing towards the ramparts.

"Alive if possible, wounded or not." Realising he might be asking for too much, he paused, and then added, "But a corpse would do, just about. I will study the man's innards and find out whether he has drunk any water, and if so, how much."

A prisoner . . . During the first attack they had tried to capture one by every means at their disposal, but the effort proved extremely costly. It was not easy for a besieger to bring back a prisoner on his own down a burning stepladder. Twice already a wounded prisoner struggling on his captor's shoulders had made the pair of them fall to their deaths. A corpse was a different matter. You can throw a dead man down from the top of the ladder. A shattered body is much the same as one with a hole in its chest.

"An enemy corpse!" Tursun Pasha said without even a glance at Sirri Selim. "Bring me a prisoner, dead or alive, at any price!"

A few moments later he saw a handful of armed dervishes running towards the wall. They disappeared into the marauding throng. Then he caught sight of them again as they clambered up one of the innumerable ladders propped against the ramparts. But as his attention then became distracted by something else, he lost sight of the dervishes a second time. The battering rams pounding on the main gate were about to smash it open. A cloud of dust hung over the frantic scrum of soldiers ready to push through the creaking door. The cannon thundered in close sequence, and their missiles could be seen tearing down pieces of the main wall.

"That was gun number three," the Quartermaster General said to Sirri Selim after the final blast.

The great door was about to give way.

"Have it torn off its hinges and brought to me here!" Tursun Pasha ordered.

It was a rather peculiar order. He was well aware that from a military point of view the capture of the door had no value, but symbolically it would be as important for raising the morale of his troops as it would be for casting the enemy into despair. The mayhem at the gate rose to a peak. The defenders must have guessed the attackers' intention, because they now launched a shower of arrows on them. Without a door, nobody can sleep soundly, even in his own home, Tursun Pasha thought. He had a second messenger take the promise of a special reward to the attackers on the front line. The *azabs* and the mechanics, already fighting like men possessed, threw themselves even more wildly into the struggle. Many of them clung to the rungs of the ladders even in death, while others clambered furiously over them. Then, above the thousand noises of battle, there rose a great screeching that might have been a cry of joy or of alarm, and the gigantic wooden door fell on its back in a deafening clatter. Soldiers that had stepped aside as the door fell immediately rushed around it like ants. And in the end, by force of ropes, grappling hooks and dozens of bare brawny arms, it began to move slowly away from the wall. The infuriated defenders rained arrows and molten pitch on the men who were heaving the door away. The dead men whose fists were still clenched around its ironwork were dragged away along with it through the dust of the earth, but nobody took any notice of them. The captors — panting for breath, drenched in sweat, and covered in black powder-dust — hauled the ancient, heavy door out of the combat zone, shouting to the heavens as if they were carrying off a young bride.

The cannon again thundered in turn and after the last detonation the Quartermaster again turned to Sirri Selim and said, "That was gun number three."

"I recognised the noise myself this time," the doctor said, staring at a place on the parapet where a bunch of dervishes was fighting hand to hand with the enemy.

"He's aiming lower every time," the Quartermaster observed.

"So he is," Sirri Selim agreed, still staring at the dervishes.

In the vacant area between the camp and the assault troops, the messengers galloping back and forth seemed ever more sparse. Convoys of stretchers bearing the wounded dashed back from the foot of the castle wall. A small detachment of soldiers with drums set off from the camp side to replace the front ranks who had been pierced and torn by arrows and were now silent or else groaning more or less mortally depending on the gravity of their wounds.

"They've got one! They've got one!" Sirri Selim exclaimed softly as he narrowed his eyes to see better what was going on in the distance.

The Quartermaster General looked in the same direction.

"Ah, my eyes deceived me!" the doctor said a little later.

But again he shouted out, with a wild look in his eyes, "There he comes! There he comes!" but he was wrong once again. Finally, a dervish really did appear on the top of the wall with a body over his shoulder. With feline agility, the dervish grasped the top of a ladder and without dropping his load began to climb down. He must surely have been shouting out that he was carrying a prisoner on orders from the Pasha, because the janissaries on their way up swung to the side to let him pass. The ladder was burning in two or three places and *azabs* had already brought up another one to replace it, but the dervish managed to reach the ground just before it collapsed. He was lost to sight for several minutes, then re-emerged among the crowd of soldiers, with the prisoner still on his back.

"Here he comes! He's coming over!" Sirri Selim shouted out loud.

The Pasha and his deputies turned to look where the doctor was pointing. The dervish was running towards them, despite having a man on his back, and raising a cloud of dust beneath his bare feet. His swarthy face dripping with sweat came into view. His chest was heaving as he greedily sucked in the scorching air. Blood dripping from his neck streaked his naked torso, but there was no way of telling whether it was his own blood or the blood of the anonymous corpse he was carrying. The foreigner's fair-haired head lolled about on the dervish's iron shoulder.

"Put him down!" Sirri Selim ordered, sounding fierce all of a sudden. His long neck and face had turned purple.

In a final heave, the dervish raised the prisoner over his shoulder, bent forwards and dumped him on the ground. Sirri Selim kneeled over the body and rapidly examined his chest, his face, his mouth and his eyes.

"He is still alive!" he exclaimed.

"Alive?"

"Yes, but almost dead."

He opened the prisoner's mouth and looked at his tongue.

"Is he thirsty?" the Pasha asked.

"Yes, he is, sire, but now we're going to see just how thirsty."

Sirri Selim reached into his pocket, took out his paring knives, leaned over the body and set to work. Some of those present looked away. Most of them had witnessed great slaughters, yet they went pale at the sight of what the medic was now doing. For the first time they learned that the progressive, slow mutilation of a body can be a hundred times more affecting than the sudden impact of a lance or sword. Sirri Selim worked for many minutes on the naked corpse. When he stood up, his hands and forearms were spattered with blood. Holding them wide apart so as not to stain his tunic, he went up to the Pasha.

"They are fairly desiccated — dehydrated, as my colleagues say — but they are still drinking a little water," he said.

The exhausted Pasha blinked and took a deep breath. Then he waved his hand, and the body was taken away. The panting dervish was still standing around.

"Reward this man," the Pasha said, and then, with weary eyes, tried to get a view of the entire length of the walls where the assault was in progress. The overall picture had not altered. There was still unceasing and chaotic movement, hundreds of ladders, some with soldiers on them, some abandoned, others burned to a cinder, and still the same yellow dust whirling and whirling around and falling back on to sweat-drenched, cut and wounded bodies. The sun was beginning to decline but the heat remained merciless. The Pasha's eyes clouded over from fatigue. Every now and again he almost fell asleep, and only the roar of the guns brought him back to himself.

A messenger galloped up.

"Uç Tunxhkurt has been killed!" he announced curtly.

The Pasha turned his head towards the East Tower, where the *eshkinxhis* were massed. The troops looked as if they were moving clumsily, as in a dream, but the Pasha was well aware what was really going on over there and how much effort and determination lay beneath their apparent lethargy.

To reassure himself he took his eyes off the *eshkinxhis* and looked lower down towards the foot of the ramparts, where waves of *azabs* led by Kara-Mukbil were still bearing the brunt of the assault. He had once commanded that unit himself, and he knew what it meant to be on what he called the underfloor of an attack. To be forever pulling back burning ladders and raising new ones, often to fall off them and never rise again, to be shot by a stray arrow, to be hit by pitch or sulphur, and, last and worst of all, to get trampled by your own side, by *akinxhis*, janissaries, *dalkiliç*, death squadrons, and not only have no right to complain about it, but to be obliged to look on with admiration at those who were climbing up to glory while remaining down below, the lowliest of the low, to die a death which like the life you had led would ever be unknown . . .

Old Tavxha had moved his janissaries several paces back from the empty space previously occupied by the main door and which strangely seemed even more fearsome now. Crouching under the cover of screens, many of which were now alight, his men were waiting for the order to charge into the courtyard, towards the inner gate.

On the parapets the *eshkinxhi*s were furiously struggling to gain possession of the rampart walk, but had not yet succeeded. There were still not very many who had got up over the parapet. Most of them got knocked off the ladders on their way up, and those who managed to find a fingerhold in the stonework at the top were savagely beaten, but they hung on, until, as they finally had to loosen their grip, they pulled a dead or wounded defender down with them into the abyss. It was too soon for the *dalkiliç* to come into the fray, and by the same token much too soon for the army's true elite, the *serden geçti*, or soldiers of death.

As if to remind survivors of the existence of a higher plane where the blows struck were closer to those of the Lord, the cannon began to roar in sequence.

A cloud of dust burst from a breach made in the inner door.

"Saruxha's going to try to use his cannon-balls to smash down the whole doorway," the Quartermaster said to Sirri Selim.

The doctor said nothing. He seemed to be deep in thought.

"He'll have a hard time doing that," a one-armed sanxhakbey muttered.

"It's hard to do, surely, but our gunners will pull it off splendidly," the Quartermaster replied. "They have a new kind of cannon, which they are using for the first time."

The sanxhakbey shook his head dubiously.

"There's nothing more tricky," he objected. "They have to aim very low, and that's dangerous."

"I know that," the Quartermaster said.

There was another barrage of fire. Gun number three hit the walls above the inner door, a few cubits to the right, enlarging the breach that had already been made there.

"The next shot will be a bull's-eye!" the Alaybey trumpeted to the world at large.

After the last round, the janissaries had again moved up towards the gaping entrance to the castle, keeping themselves under the cover of their huge reed screens.

"Tavxha's getting ready," the one-armed sanxhakbey observed. "Get on with it, you old blockhead!" he muttered to himself.

"They'll launch an attack more terrible than a tidal wave!" someone standing behind them said, raising the stakes.

The handful of dignitaries watching the battle shuddered. They were waiting for the next cannonade. None of them now cared what was happening all along the wall. Collapsing ladders, sudden surges and retreats: all that had happened a hundred times already in the deafening racket of the battle drums. Everyone's attention was on the area around the main gate, where Tavxha's men, drawn up in squares, were waiting for the right moment to attack.

The mortars fired, one after the other. Their projectiles rose up over the battlements and fell on the other side, in the heart of the citadel. Then big guns one and two roared, and everyone held their breath, waiting for the now familiar thunder of gun number three. It hadn't been fired yet.

The janissaries were now jostling up to the main entrance through which a part of the courtyard could be seen. It was completely deserted. Javelins, arrows and rags soaked in flaming pitch and oil fell uninterruptedly on their testudos, but the janissaries did not yield. Apparently guessing that the enemy were readying themselves to attack the inner door, the defenders raised the tempo of their efforts to repulse them. But at other points around the wall, *azabs*, *eshkinxhis* and volunteers were maintaining terrible pressure and making it impossible for the besieged to pull any of their men back from the front line.

The Pasha still did not give the go-ahead for the *dalkiliç* to advance, nor did he yet send in the last remaining death squadron. He was waiting for the blast of the third big gun. It had still not been fired.

"Why doesn't he fire?" "What's Saruxha up to?" Questions like these, spoken not shouted, were being repeated all around with increasing impatience. The Pasha sent an officer on horseback off to the battery. But the messenger had barely gone a hundred paces when the roar of gun number three shook the ground. They were all so wound up with expectation that they thought the explosion had been louder than it really was. It was immediately followed by an unusual screeching whistle tearing through the air very low, just above their heads. They were anxiously watching the outcome, expecting the cannon-ball to burst through the inner door, when they saw it crash down right in the middle of the Janissary Corps.

"Oh . . . !" the Pasha exclaimed in a tone that was not at all customary.

The janissaries, who had been standing in serried ranks up to that point, suddenly pulled apart in all directions. Total confusion reigned in front of the main entrance. Officers ran up from every side trying to assess the exact level of losses.

Old Tavxha galloped back on his black horse, raising a great cloud of dust. From afar he started yelling. Two bodyguards closed in on the Pasha to protect him. The Agha of the janissaries slid off his horse as if he were in a state of collapse. He was yelling at the top of his voice, spluttering and muddling up Mongolian with Turkish, so that his meaning was, at first, more to be guessed at than properly understood. The gesticulations he made with his stubby hands to accompany each expression made it look as if he wanted to strangle someone. When he stopped shouting quite so loud, people had to admit that he had more or less said what they all expected to hear from him.

"We've been taken for a ride by those pigs, those traitors, those Christians!" he started yelling again. "You see? Now they're mowing us down from behind with their cannon-balls! Can we put up with that? No, we cannot, a hundred times no!"

"How many dead?" the Pasha asked.

Tavxha was so incensed with anger that he could hardly breathe.

"Dozens, hundreds of dead! I want revenge for my janissaries, the sons of Kara-Halil. I want the guilty man. Yes, Pasha, sire, I demand the head of the guilty party. My janissaries call for the guilty man!"

"They shall have him," the commander-in-chief replied.

"This instant!" Tavxha boomed. "They want him now! They are beside themselves. They want to judge the man themselves. Give him to me!"

"Let the man responsible be found this instant," the Pasha ordered. "Summon the *chaouch-bashi*!"

The chef-de-camp came running.

"Find the guilty party and arrest him forthwith, whoever he is," the Pasha said. "You will give him over to the janissaries. It is their right, they can do what they will with the man."

"Pasha, sire," the Quartermaster interrupted, looking as white as a sheet. "What if . . . what if the man is . . . none other than Saruxha?"

Tursun Pasha raised his eyes to the sky as if to say, I can't do anything about that.

The *chaouch-bashi* led a detachment of *azabs* off to the gun battery to arrest the guilty man.

"The Devil himself sabotaged this action," Tursun Pasha said aloud, as if he was talking to himself. He knew there was no point carrying on with the assault without the janissaries. He gave the order to beat the retreat.

The harassed battalions withdrew in turn beneath the still powerful sun and the Pasha turned away and went back to his pavilion. The Quartermaster General promptly made his way to the gun emplacement. On the way there he came across a group of janissaries led by Tavxha and the chef-de-camp, all of them howling like a pack of wild dogs. In their midst he saw Saruxha's assistant, tied hand and foot, and looking quite livid. Three or four officers were dragging him along the ground. The young man raised his terror-stricken eyes to the Quartermaster, imploring him to come to his aid. But the group was walking fast and the Quartermaster was not tortured by that look for very long. His attention was quickly caught by the sound of a furious voice that he knew well. It was Saruxha, running behind the janissaries, with his own orderly behind him.

"Stop, you lousy brutes! Let him go, I tell you! You will answer for this with your lives!"

"Saruxha," the Quartermaster said to him gently as he grabbed his sleeve. "Listen to me for a minute."

"Let go of me! He's got nothing to do with it! Stop!"

The Quartermaster General almost had to run to keep up with the master caster.

"Wait! There's no point running after them. Don't you see that you'll achieve nothing? Listen to me!"

"No! Stop, you lousy brutes! Tavxha! *Chaouch-bashi*! You're no better than animals, you disgusting vermin! Stop, I tell you!"

The janissaries just kept on going at a spanking pace and not one of them even turned his head. The Quartermaster reckoned that if he didn't restrain Saruxha, he would launch into them with his fists and have to pay a high price.

"Saruxha, my brother, calm down, please."

He tried to hold him back and signalled to his guard to help him. The guard came up but did not dare lay a hand on a member of the council.

"Tavxha Tokmakhan, you filthy pig, you sinister fool, you pile of shit, I shall smash your fat head! I'll fire a cannon at your janissaries as soon as I can! I'll demolish the lot of you without mercy! I'll do in the whores who are your mothers, every last one of them!"

With great difficulty the Quartermaster finally managed to control the master caster. Saruxha was foaming at the mouth. His pupils were fixed wide open. "Rub his forehead," the Quartermaster told his orderly. He himself wiped the spittle from Saruxha's lips. Saruxha's attempts to get free were gradually weakening. But his head with its protruding veins remained turned in the direction where the janissaries had dragged his assistant, and his words had now become incomprehensible because his voice had gone completely hoarse.

When the detachment passed out of sight, Saruxha began to moan as if he had been wounded.

"How will I manage without him?" he sobbed. "Those animals are going to kill him. Tell me, how can I manage without him?"

"We'll take counsel," the Quartermaster said. "We'll try to save him."

"What door will you knock on? To whom can we turn?" Saruxha whimpered. "It's like a desert here."

"We'll have a think about it," the Quartermaster said again.

Saruxha shot a dark look at his friend, trying to fathom whether he really had some hope, or was just consoling him.

"They'll be sorry for killing him, but by then it will be too late," he added sadly.

The Quartermaster wondered who might be capable of interceding with the Pasha to save the deputy caster. He was certainly willing to plead the case, but he wouldn't pull enough weight, since his close friendship with Saruxha was no secret. Someone more distant was needed. Kurdisxhi would have been just the right man, but he was mouldering in his tent recovering from two serious wounds he had suffered in the course of Skanderbeg's last raid. Kara-Mukbil would not be well received because of his known mistrust of Old Tavxha. Anyway, after this exhausting attack in which he and his *azabs* had taken the brunt of the fighting, it would be absurd to speak of saving the life of one man to someone who had just seen hundreds lost all around him. As for the Mufti, that was out of the question: he would probably rub his hands with glee at the death of an expert. There was only one man of influence left who might just be approachable: the Alaybey.

"Let's go and see the Alaybey," the Quartermaster said. "Maybe he can help us."

As they walked towards his tent they saw endless columns of soldiers returning from the ramparts. Dreadful fatigue was written on the faces and in the weary movements of these men. Many were supporting wounded comrades-in-arms, whose singed heads lolled strangely on their shoulders. The Quartermaster turned away his eyes two or three times so as not to see the ghastly wounds that metal, pitch and stone had combined to make.

They tried to get there by way of a side alley, but it was a waste of effort. The combatants were streaming back towards their tents from all directions, and in gloomy silence. As the sun sank towards the horizon and bathed the sky in an orange glow, the great camp looked like a giant sponge imbibed with sweat and blood.

"The time is not particularly favourable for an approach of this kind," the Quartermaster said, "but let us try, all the same."

The Alaybey was alone in his tent. He listened attentively to what the Quartermaster had to say, without changing his sombre expression in the slightest. Saruxha did not say a word. When the Quartermaster had finished, the Alaybey went on staring at the same spot on the kilim. They guessed there was nothing they could expect from him. Then he told them that he would have considered it a great honour to be able to come to the aid of eminent men of science such as they were. He understood completely that the execution of such a skilled metal-caster was contrary to the true interests of the Padishah and of the Empire in general, especially as an age of new armaments had dawned, and that the number of gunsmiths in the entire Empire could be counted on the fingers of one hand. However, he considered that he would not be well advised to plead this case with the Pasha. They must know that themselves. He asked them to imagine the state of mind of men who had spent hours on end desperately attacking inexpugnable ramparts, getting slashed by lances and scorched by pitch, and had then been mown down from behind by cannon from their own side, cannon in which they had placed such high hopes. It would not be easy to reason with those men at a time like this, especially as many of them were also suffering from sunstroke — even leaving out the fact that Tavxha was involved.

At the name of the hated captain of the janissaries, Saruxha spat out a curse.

As they were leaving, the Alaybey advised them to seek an audience with the Pasha themselves, though for his part he did not hold out much hope of success.

Once they had left the Alaybey's tent, Saruxha declared excitedly: "Let's go to see the Pasha! Let's go straight away, because if we don't that scum is quite capable of executing the lad on the spot!"

They almost ran to the tent of the commander-in-chief. Two sentries with their axes at the ready stood outside the door.

"We have to see the Pasha," the Quartermaster said curtly to an orderly who came out to deal with them.

"The Pasha is tired," the orderly said. "He has given orders not to be disturbed."

"Tell him it's an urgent matter," Saruxha insisted. "I am the Chief Engineer and my friend is the Quartermaster General."

"I know who you are," the young officer said with a bow, and he went back inside the tent.

The two sentries looked at the visitors out of the corners of their eyes. The blades of their axes gleamed in the last light of the setting sun.

The orderly came back after a few minutes had passed.

"The Pasha has a sore throat and cannot see you."

Saruxha reached for his throat as if he had just been attacked.

"Tell him that we . . . we . . ."

But the orderly had gone. Saruxha caught the sidelong glance of one of the sentries.

"We'd better go," the Quartermaster said.

They went away. They walked slowly. They no longer had any reason to hurry. The flat ground in front of the ramparts, which had been but a few hours earlier the scene of horrendous uproar accompanied by hundreds of war drums, lay abandoned and silent. All that was left there was the useless debris of the great iron gate that had been hauled as far as the outskirts of the camp.

As they walked they came across a long line of tumbrels setting off to gather the dead.

Their steps took them unthinkingly towards the quarter of the camp where the janissaries had pitched their tents. They walked in silence, as if they did not ever want to get where they were going.

They shuffled hesitantly, even when they came across a large crowd of janissaries among whom something still seemed to be going on. But now the men were beginning to disperse in two and threes. So it must be all over. They wandered nonetheless towards the assembly even as it broke up. The men who were still there all had blank and distracted expressions on their faces. Some looked dazed, and held hatchets or yatagans in their hands. The Quartermaster General and his friend Saruxha noticed the wide shoulders of Tavxha who was in the process of departing, with his men in his train. They came closer, and as they looked for the victim's body, they saw sappers spading something on to a stretcher. That something was no longer a body, nor was it limbs, or even parts of limbs, but earth, flesh, bone and stone pounded into a pulp by the demented thrashing of yatagans and hatchets.

They could not take their eyes off the stretcher as the horrible mess was shovelled on to it. A few janissaries who were still standing around gazed with astonishment at the two council members. Hatred had left their eyes. They now looked only stunned, and immensely tired. The Quartermaster General stared at them. A few moments earlier they had been beating the caster with all the disgust and all the fear that the mystery of science, which so tortured their minds, inspired in them. In dismembering the technician they believed they were freeing themselves from the grip of the terror of the unknown. They would only be free of it for a while, for the same terror would soon seep back into their minds and preoccupy them once again. For the sake of mental peace they would then set off to find another head to smash . . .

The Quartermaster General and Saruxha walked away without saying a word. The sun was setting. The first tumbrels bearing the dead were now coming back into the camp. In some cases, there was blood dripping through the planks on to the wheels. The camp was virtually lifeless. A battalion of sappers, bearing shovels and picks, passed by. Presumably they were off to dig graves.

A voice greeted them from behind, but neither man paid any attention to it at first.

"Hail there, effendis," Sirri Selim repeated, for it was he, striding hurriedly along.

"Hallo," the Quartermaster answered.

"What is the matter?" the doctor asked.

No answer.

"I'm going straight to the Pasha," Sirri Selim answered without having been asked. "I've thought of another way of robbing them of their water."

They didn't respond to that remark either. The doctor was now beside them and his shadow, distorted by the evening light, seemed monstrously oversized. Bizarrely, his face and long neck had gone purple.

"You think war is made only with cannon and calculations!" he blurted out bitterly, accelerating his pace. Then, when he was already several strides ahead of them, he turned around to confront them with a question.

"What about rats, effendis? Haven't you ever thought about rats?"

"He must have had too much sun," the Quartermaster muttered.

Saruxha said nothing.

They were now in the heart of the camp. They had never seen it so empty. A team of doctors was just coming out of Kurdisxhi's great tent. Another squad of sappers was on its way to the mass grave.

They launched a furious attack on us, like the first time, and, like the first time, we repulsed them. We were dazed by the merciless heat and were dying of thirst. But in spite of that we held on.

At the worst point of the battle, fate decreed that one of their cannon — the most fearsome of all — not only failed to shatter our inner gate, but fell in the midst of their own men. Upon which, the attack was abandoned.

For some days now jackdaws have been circling above the ramparts and also lower down. The dead have been removed from the field, but apparently the smell of blood still hangs in the air. The sight of these birds and their screeching disturb us, but we have too little water to use it to wash away the blood.

From here we can see their exercise grounds where their men are trying out new kinds of ladders. They run up and down, wave their arms and hang on the rungs with a diabolical sort of grappling-iron. They sometimes do their training with a torch in one hand. It looks as if they are preparing for a night attack.

For our part, we have thought about all possible eventualities. We have had the remains of our fallen incinerated. Their ashes have been placed in urns, which we have buried deep underground, so that, whatever happens, our enemies will not be able to find them and desecrate them, as is their wont.

They know we are agonisingly short of water, but to increase our suffering they have installed a kind of fountain at the spot where they cut the aqueduct. Naked soldiers splash and play shamelessly in the water all the scorching day long.

To undermine our morale, or else to boost their own, they sometimes use childish tricks. For example, yesterday they came up to what is now the open space in front of our main gate bearing a white flag. They stopped as if the gate really was still there in front of them, and they pretended to knock at the door, but obviously they were knocking on thin air. When our sentries drew their bowstrings, they closed the visors of their helmets, and the way our arrows bounced off them told us that under their silken tunics they were wearing chain mail.

CHAPTER THIRTEEN

The Pasha paid no attention to what they were saying. Each spoke in turn of the losses their own units had taken, then gave his opinion of the appropriate means to be used to carry the fight forwards, and also his view of the latest suggestion from Sirri Selim, who was attending the war council for the first time. But the Pasha's mind was exclusively occupied with the Alaybey's latest report, which had reached him that very morning. As he read the close-packed lines of the scribe's small, neat hand, he thought he could hear rising from them the deep-throated, rousing swell that his army had made but two months before, but with a sound that was now more rough and resentful, and beneath the cheering he could make out more clearly what he had only dimly perceived at that earlier stage, and that was the sound of what people call war-weariness. His long experience of campaigning had taught him to lend an attentive ear to that chord. On all the many expeditions he had led, he had always waited for it to emerge, like an old but fearsome acquaintance. Nothing frightened him more: not the failure of his attacks, nor acts of indiscipline, nor the insubordination or the infighting among his captains, nor blasphemy against the name of Prophet, nor insults hurled at his own person, nor fear itself, nor even the first symptoms of plague — nothing scared him more than this black cloud silently closing in and raining down on the faces, eyes, hands, voices and weapons of his men. Of course he knew it would come, on this as on all campaigns, even though he had done everything in his power to keep it at bay as long as possible. The first signs had appeared some six weeks before, straight after the failure of the first attack, but had dissipated fairly quickly. Summary judgments, rumours about secret investigations, the discovery and sentencing of the spies who had had their eye on the new gun, the squabbles over the women captives, a ghost said to be prowling late at night by the river bank, the arrival of performers from the capital (the star dancer had fallen in love with a soldier in the death squadron and both of them were in despair that they could never marry) and especially the hunt for the aqueduct and its final discovery — all these things had no doubt helped to put off the black cloud. But the Pasha knew that the weariness in question could not be held at bay for ever. It was always in the offing, somewhere near, all around. He had never feared its coming so much as he did now. And it was indeed upon them. He hadn't seen premonitory signs of the sort he had noticed six weeks earlier. He could now see war-weariness before his eyes, an all-pervading dust as ancient as war itself.

They were talking about the next assault. The Quartermaster General declared himself emphatically in favour of renewed and repeated assaults so as to give the exhausted and desiccated Albanians no opportunity to recuperate. The Pasha was well aware that the Quartermaster's main worry was that their own supplies of food were running low. Skanderbeg's night raid had spoiled some of their stocks, particularly their vats of honey and rice. The Quartermaster spoke scathingly about those among them who, though they were surely right to consider it important to protect the part of the camp where the cannon, the elite troops and the leaders' tents were located ("my own included", he added), were criminally indifferent to the fate of the storehouses, as if they belonged to nobody. On the night of the raid, he went on, the honey had been spilled on the ground and it broke his heart to see it all messed up by horses' hooves.

"May I presume that this was not a clever ploy invented by one of our commanders to slow down the enemy's advance?" he asked in a clearly sarcastic tone.

The officer in charge of camp security went pale. In a confused and sour attempt at self-justification, he declared himself amazed that members of the war council put the same price on a mere foodstuff such as honey as they did on the blood of Turkish soldiers. With an expression of disgust on his face, the Quartermaster told the man they were at a meeting of the war council, not at a hot-air contest. Since he looked as though he was about to say something even harsher, the Alaybey stepped in and declared that never before had such parallels been made at a council meeting. He added that seeing that the rules of the Empire required the allocation of a ration of honey to every soldier immediately prior to an attack, to give him strength, it was clear that this mere foodstuff was of military value, and that was the point that the Quartermaster had intended to make.

Tursun Pasha urged them to get back to the issue of the attack. Someone mentioned the astrologer.

"And what does the man of magic say?" the Pasha asked with unhidden irony.

No one answered. The Pasha repeated the question, turning to the Mufti, who was normally in close contact with astrologers.

Silence.

"Our troops are getting torn to shreds on the battlements," the Pasha said in a voice that was beginning to become hoarse. "And that man can't even be bothered to make predictions! Have him flogged in public and then sent to work in the mass graves, like his predecessor."

They weren't much surprised by sudden outbursts of this kind. The Pasha was openly resentful of all the inspectors and function-aries dispatched from the capital. He reckoned that most of them were only there to observe his fall, and so he took any pretext for getting his own back on them.

After a short pause for the scribe to note down the punish-ment meted out to the astrologer, the members of the council resumed their deliberations. Some were against repeat attacks on the fortress. In their view it was better to wait until Sirri Selim's plan had had its full impact and the wells and the defenders were infected. The Pasha followed the discussion for a while, but then his attention was once again distracted.

Someone mentioned clouds.

"Alas, our great Padishah cannot give orders to the clouds," the Quartermaster said, as a way of countering Kara-Mukbil, who had spoken against the proposal to attack again straight away. "One fine day they can come over the horizon and a sudden shower may then quench the defenders' thirst, despite all our long efforts to make it unbearable."

Rain! Never had rain been so constantly on the Pasha's mind as it had these past two weeks. He excoriated it and tried to banish it from his thoughts, but to no avail. Looking at a clear, majesti-cally blue sky under the command of a blazing sun, he sometimes thought that rain had disappeared for ever from the entire surface of the world. Yet he knew that at that very moment, while they were being stifled by heat, somewhere else, in other lands, rain was falling quietly, steadily, as depressingly as death itself. It was far away for the time being, but perfidious clouds did not need many hours to bring it to them and drown their efforts in hateful spittle.

"They're hoping for rain," the Quartermaster went on. "On one of their towers they have set up rotating tin plates by means of which they can predict the weather. That means they are near the end. We have to hurry."

At these words, the meeting collapsed into confusion and everything sank once again into muddle and dispute. The first targets of attack were the sanxhakbeys. All eyes were then trained on the Mufti, who looked overwhelmed and knocked out. He had taken the punishment of the astrologer as a personal affront, and was choking on his own anger. Suddenly, he asked to be allowed to speak.

"Everything that has happened has a sole and single cause," he declared gravely. "Licentiousness! The army has fallen prey to licentiousness. Apparently that evil cross is doing its devilish work. Our religious spirit is being weakened. Atheism is spreading. During the last attack a large proportion of the *eshkinxhis* were drunk. Degeneration can be seen all around, but our officers are turning a blind eye."

The Mufti urged them all to get a grip on things before it was too late. He requested that reading the Koran be made obligatory, that alcoholic beverages be banned, and that the sale of captive women and the presence of prostitutes be similarly forbidden. He wanted no more performers to be sent from the capital. Ottoman soldiers had no need of bottom-waggling whores or of strutting young perverts showing off the latest fashions.

"There is one more thing," he continued, looking straight in Tursun Pasha's eye. "It is in the army's interest, and in yours, too, to get rid of the wives you brought here with you. That is all."

Such a heavy silence ensued that even the scribe did not dare break it with the noise of his quill.

"Snake in the grass!" the Pasha hissed silently. His eyes gleamed more brightly than the ruby on his ring. Everyone held their breath. They knew that of all possible conflicts within a war council, outright hostility between the military and the religious commanders was the one that could have the direst effect. It was as if the great Padishah, who held both temporal and spiritual power, was tearing himself apart.

A viper and scorpion rolled into one! Tursun Pasha muttered silently between clenched teeth. The Mufti must have known that he was no longer at the peak of his favour at the Sublime Porte. That's how he can dare to flout my authority. But there was one thing the religious head did not know: if the commander-in-chief scored a victory, all the Muftis and imams of the entire Empire would be toothless against him. On the other hand the Pasha was well aware that if he was routed, he could be knocked over by an ant.

Vermin! he sputtered silently once again. He wished he could heap on the Mufti's head all the insults that Saruxha had thrown at Tavxha a few days previously and that Kapduk Agha had told him about in a private report. But as he was not in the habit of using vulgar language he couldn't remember the words. "You piece of trash!" Saruxha had once said, on another occasion, "I'll pull off your beard and wipe my arse on it!"

Even before he opened his mouth to respond, all present had grasped that he considered himself to have the upper hand, and that was enough for most of them to take his side.

"I have heard what you said, O Mufti," he said, speaking each word separately. "I have heard you speaking ill of our glorious soldiers and officers in action. Now it is your turn to listen to me. Captive women are allowed, artistic performers from the capital are allowed, the Koran will be read neither more nor less than at present, and soldiers, when off duty, are allowed, as I am, to amuse themselves as they see fit. And if you don't like it, you can get out. Right now, if you want!"

Tahanka made a noise that seemed to come from a severed neck. While the outcome of the conflict remained uncertain, the gargle, by the fact that its meaning was impenetrable, aroused the envy of all present. Anyway, they all knew that Tahanka's contributions to their debates were written up by the scribe as "Sounds from Tahanka". Moreover there was every likelihood he would take the Pasha's side, since the latter had come to the defence of Tahanka's *eshkinxhis*.

"Pasha, sire, weigh your words carefully!" the Mufti shouted without rising from his seat. "It was not you who appointed me to the post that I hold."

"But I am he who is in command here," Tursun Pasha threw back at him. "And from this moment I strip you of the right to speak."

The ensuing silence seemed charged with new meaning, such that the piercing screech of the scribe's quill seemed the most appropriate way of recording the ban on the Mufti opening his mouth.

"Now let me warn you all. Any rebellion, from whatever quarter, including any of you, will be dealt with by putting the instigator in irons. And I shall answer to the Sultan himself for all such actions."

The Quartermaster General requested the floor.

"After all that we have just heard, we should assume that a state of emergency has been declared."

"Yes," the Pasha said. "That is precisely what has happened."

"Then I understood you correctly, sire," the Quartermaster said before sitting down.

"You may now discuss the doctor's report," the commander-in-chief resumed. "Keep it short."

With the obvious intention of clearing the air, the Alaybey addressed Sirri Selim in a completely relaxed tone of voice, as if nothing had happened, and asked him how many days it would take for the epidemic to break out.

"At the second siege of Aleppo," the doctor answered, "the epidemic began fifteen days after the infected animals had been introduced. But we should not forget that only dead rats were used at Aleppo. Live animals move around and spread the disease faster."

"Do we not need authority from the high command to use this technique?" Saruxha enquired. As two or three voices could be heard muttering, "What does he mean to say?" he continued in a sharper tone:

"I don't see why my question should surprise anyone. The permission of the high command is required for the use of any new weapon. I know dead rats are allowed, but I'm not sure the same is true of live animals."

"Previously, the use of live animals was forbidden for safety reasons," the doctor replied. "But the Grand Vizier sent us authorisation three months ago."

"Were there any conditions?" Saruxha asked.

All present followed this exchange with interest. It was the first time that experts had had a row of this kind.

"Yes, there are conditions," the doctor answered. "We are not allowed to use catapults to get them inside the fortress, in case the animal cages burst in mid-flight."

Sirri Selim then laid out the paradox that confronted them. If the cages were strong enough to stay in one piece during flight, they would not be weak enough to shatter once they landed. On the other hand, if they were designed to break open on impact, then they might . . . That was why they planned to have soldiers carry them up the walls and tip them over the ramparts.

"Have you thought about the soldiers?" Kara-Mukbil interrupted.

"Of course I have," the doctor said. "They will be equipped with leather gloves and hoods."

"Like executioners," somebody observed.

"Like executioners, or like ghosts."

"Hangmen or ghosts, what does it matter?" the medic riposted. "What matters is for them to have protection from bites when they open the cages."

Still suffering from the high tension of the earlier exchanges, they were all relieved by this relatively normal interlude. Even the commander-in-chief seemed to appreciate the respite.

"Anyway, it's a better idea than using catapults," Old Tavxha broke in. "I remember that at the first siege of Szemendre we spent a week flinging rats, dogs and even dead donkeys into the fortress. Then they took to catapulting the corpses of prisoners, and the minders of the machine got so carried away that they started hurling vats of waste water, night soil, and god knows what else over the walls. Sure, the defenders caught diseases and finally surrendered, but what was the point? The stink was so sickening that our soldiers wouldn't go into the place once it was ours. The risk of infection cooled their ardour! So there was no booty, no captives were taken, and the victory was a miserable one. I think I'm right in saying that it's since that occasion that we've not been allowed to catapult filth. But as for live animals, that's a different question. I'm not against it."

Then each spoke to give his opinion, and after that, they all felt easier. Only the Mufti remained in the doghouse. It was clear that the resumption of normal conversation had made him angrier still and increased his isolation.

With the exception of Saruxha, who voted against for reasons that nobody understood, there was unanimous approval for the doctor's plan.

Finally the Pasha himself took the floor. He spoke slowly, for longer than usual, in a voice that was going hoarse from the cold he had caught. He decided that they would try to contaminate the besieged by means of infected animals, along the lines proposed by Sirri Selim. The doctor blushed with pleasure down to the nape of his neck. The attack would be resumed, and they would make repeated assaults to stop the enemy even catching his breath.

"We're here to take the castle, not to think deep thoughts," he said. "The assaults will be daily, or almost, and no account will be taken of losses or obstacles." He said that with deep conviction, because he knew from experience that only uninterrupted attacks, leaving soldiers no time to think, and barely enough latitude to save their own skins, were the best cure for war-weariness. Then he added, stressing each word individually, that he expected them all to put extra effort into preparing troops for combat. Also, and this was the essential point, he wanted them all to take part in the fighting themselves. Then he stared at each of them harshly in turn, as if to select those who should not be there at the meeting, reclining on the long stack of cushions, but ought instead to be lying six foot under, or at least on their beds, brought down, like Kurdisxhi, by battle wounds. In the ensuing silence the scratchy quill of the scribe felt like the fine point of a dagger scoring their skins. They realised that the commander was getting tenser by the day and that you could no longer tell what a man so overwrought was going to do. Lastly, Tursun Pasha ordered them all to treat the plan to contaminate the enemy as top secret, so that the soldiers handling the animals remained unaware of the nature of their charges. That was absolutely necessary if they were to avoid an outbreak of panic over plague.

The meeting came to an end. As the commander-in-chief had suggested, the Alaybey, Kara-Mukbil and the Quartermaster General accompanied Sirri Selim to the pavilion where the doctor kept his sick animals. On the way they encountered soldiers flocking to the central square where the flagellation of the astrologer was due to be held.

The trial of the spell-caster which had been taking place a little further on under a canopy had been going on for so long as to have stopped interesting anyone. People were waiting only for the sentence to be carried out — specifically, the amputation of both the man's hands, or, in the most favourable case, of the hand that had made the fatal error in the act of casting the spell.

The place where the doctor kept his infected animals — "Death Row", as he called it — was on the same hillock as the cannon foundry, behind a waste tip piled high with ash and other unusable material from the foundry. It looked just as sinister as the workshop, and was enclosed by the same kind of plank fence with a sign forbidding entry, but unlike the foundry there was a second enclosure behind the fence supporting a canopy that sheltered the whole area.

The guard attached to Sirri Selim took out a key and opened the gate in the fence, while the lord of this strange manor called out to all and sundry, "Welcome to Death Row!"

"Here is my kingdom," Sirri Selim continued with a smile and waved his long arms at the lines of hutches, some of them double height, that ran the whole length of the enclosure. Inside them creatures shivered and mewled, or else lay lifeless on the floor. "Have no fear! There's no risk of contagion for the time being."

He told them that at all the sieges he had taken part in as army doctor he had the habit of setting up these kinds of cages and of collecting various animals on which he tried out the effects of various drugs and microbes.

Kara-Mukbil looked with disdain at the small cages mostly containing rats. But there were others with small dogs, cats, rabbits and some grey beasts he hadn't seen before, as well as hedgehogs, grasshoppers and even, in a water-filled urn at the bottom of one of the cages, frogs. The Alaybey listened with all seriousness to the doctor's explanations, whereas the Quartermaster General seemed to have his mind on something else.

"The use of sick animals in warfare is not a new idea," Sirri Selim declared. "The Carthaginians, in ancient times, the Christian armies in later centuries, and more recently the Mongols all knew how helpful they could be. But the practice is not as widespread as it should be. Previously, cadavers were projected by catapult into besieged fortresses, but the use of live animals now looks set to become the norm."

Aware of Kara-Mukbil's look of disdain, he went on: "Some people may possibly find the tactic unworthy of a glorious army like ours, but that can't be helped. Sometimes the principle of contagion can be more effective than sword or cannon."

Kara-Mukbil said nothing. He carried on looking at the rat cages with distaste.

"Just look at this green grasshopper over here," the doctor said, pointing to one of the cages. "It's a little gem, if you know how to appreciate it. Local people call it 'the witches' horse', and not without reason, it seems. It can lay waste to whole fields of crops, but if it is infected, it can be ten times more damaging. The Devil's own horse!"

The Alaybey looked carefully at each one of the cages and then asked the doctor a series of questions. Sirri Selim provided all the clarifications he sought, ranging from details of the various diseases with which the animals were infected to the means of getting them into the fortress. He said that he would leave the sick animals without food or water for several days and then, just prior to the attack, place them in wicker hampers that the soldiers would strap to their backs for the climb up the walls. When the attackers got to breaches in the wall or to the battlements at the top, they would slash the cane with their knives and let the animals escape. In the mayhem of combat the defenders would not easily notice the trick, and anyway, even if they did, they would not be able to track the animals, especially the parched and famished rats, who would scurry straight off towards the food stores or to the water well.

Sirri Selim gave many other details about the extraordinary ability of rats to spread disease and the great future that lay in store for this new instrument of war.

They were about to leave the compound when Sirri Selim got excited all of a sudden, and, gesturing towards the ramparts, proclaimed solemnly:

"These people, who are said to have been born of eagles, will probably die of a rat."

He had honed that sentence for months, intending to come out with it at the meeting of the war council, but he hadn't had the opportunity.

The Quartermaster General easily guessed that the doctor was well acquainted with Mevla Çelebi.

Sirri Selim walked back with them for a while, then they all took their leave and went their separate ways to their own tents. The Quartermaster General saw the chronicler walking in the opposite direction, which confirmed his intuition about the relationship between him and the medical man.

"Are you off to see Sirri?" he asked.

Çelebi thought he detected a touch of irony in his friend's voice.

"Yes, I am," he replied. Under his breath he muttered: "May my legs shrivel up on the spot!"

"I've just been there," the Quartermaster went on. "Walk with me a while. I'm bored."

The chronicler furrowed his brow. "You aren't ill, are you?"

"No, thank you," the Quartermaster said, smiling gently. "I was at Sirri's for a quite different reason. How's your chronicle going?"

It was Çelebi's turn to smile. "Quite well."

The pathways they took were full of soldiers returning from training or else from the spectacle of the astrologer's punishment. They made way for the Quartermaster. Many men were lying flat on the ground beside their tents.

"They're stressed," the Quartermaster said. "The last attack drained them."

"They must be at their wits' end over there, too," Çelebi said, gesturing towards the apparently deserted castle wall, now pock-marked with breaches and draped with streaks of pitch that reached down almost as far as the ground.

The Quartermaster did not answer.

"They say their pupils have gone dark from peering day and night from the battlements at all the paths along which help might come," Çelebi said.

The Quartermaster seemed to be thinking about something else.

"Look, here comes our blind poet," he said sarcastically as he pointed at Sadedin. "Isn't he another one of your friends?"

This time Çelebi said nothing.

Sadedin was on his own, tapping the ground with his cane. In any other circumstance the chronicler would have been sorry for his unfortunate friend, but on this occasion he felt as if the man had appeared on purpose in order to discredit him, and he felt cross. Other officers hailed the poet as he passed. And as the blind man turned round to return the greetings, the Quartermaster slackened his pace so as to hear what the poet was going to say.

"What is there to see in the world?" Sadedin cried out in a rough voice as he turned his empty sockets towards them. "If I still had my eyes, I would pluck them out so as not to see such shame."

Seeing the Quartermaster General, the officers bowed obsequiously, wishing they had not prompted the poet. But it was too late now.

"May the bread of the Padishah choke you!"

Sadedin turned his empty eyes all around, apparently astonished at the sudden lack of response.

"What is there to see in the world?" he boomed again. "An orphanage for fallen stars and nothing else!"

He turned around and walked back, tapping the ground with his cane as if he was afraid of an abyss opening up before him at every step.

The officers stood still and silent. The Quartermaster didn't so much as glance at them as he walked on his way with the chronicler at his side.

"It's hot," he said. "It would be nice to be at the seaside."

"Apparently the coast is not far from here."

"Yes, there's a very beautiful sea quite near, though it has a complicated name."

"Ka-dri-a-tik", Çelebi spelled out. "I think that's what it's called."

The Quartermaster burst out laughing.

"At least you managed not to say 'Ka-dri-bey'! Now listen carefully: A-dri-a-tic, the Adriatic . . ."

Çelebi was mortified.

"Yes, it really would be lovely to be at the seaside right now," the Quartermaster went on. "They say the Padishah has gone to take a rest at Magnesia, in Anatolia."

Çelebi didn't know what to say. His friend was talking quite casually about people and things he wouldn't have dared let himself think about.

"Apparently he's spending his time on religious questions, on important points of doctrine."

"May Allah give him long life," Çelebi said, regretting having used up the only phrase he had in store for circumstances of this kind.

He cheered up when he saw the Quartermaster's great tent not too far off. He was hoping that once they had got there his friend, feeling on home ground as it were, would drop his ironical tone, which he found disturbing.

"Sit down," the Quartermaster said once they were inside. "Now I'll tell you a secret."

He revealed to the chronicler that diseased animals were going to be released in the castle during the next assault. Çelebi listened in astonishment, but he also felt reassured that he was once again being treated as trustworthy. In spite of himself he recalled the treacherous words of people he would gladly trample to death like snakes. So now their war-hardened lions and tigers were going to rise up against the citadel accompanied by fleas, grasshoppers, toads and rats . . . Ah, you mangy dog, he said to himself, don't complain if you're subjected to torture afterwards!

"It's our last try, Mevla," the Quartermaster said. "We have done all that was in our power, but fate has hardly smiled on us. This is our last chance."

There was not a trace of irony in the Quartermaster's words that Çelebi could make out. The declaration seemed deadly serious.

"The fighting season is near its end," the Quartermaster mumbled, almost melancholically. "Like your chronicle, there are not many pages left to write."

"What then? What will happen if . . ." Çelebi didn't dare add: if we don't take the citadel.

The Quartermaster looked at him with his calm expression in which the chronicler could never make out the respective proportions of coldness and honesty.

An orphanage for fallen stars: Sadedin's phrase came back to his mind as if in a dream.

"Then a new expedition will set out next spring," the Quartermaster replied in a strange voice. "Battalions without number will march in line, with drums rolling and banners flapping in the breeze just like before," he went on in the same odd tone. "They'll advance day and night, on foot, on horseback, on camels, in carriages, until they reach these ramparts. Here" — the Quartermaster pointed to the ground — "they'll see the traces left by our camp, all muddled and muddied by winter, but visible nonetheless. They'll pitch their tents in the same places, and the same story will begin all over again."

The Quartermaster's eyes gleamed evilly as he stared at the chronicler.

"Don't you want to know what will happen if the citadel doesn't yield next year either?"

The chronicler was in a cold sweat. He was certainly not crazy enough to ask such a scandalous question, but he also didn't dare contradict his illustrious friend.

"If the citadel does not fall next spring," the Quartermaster said, "then another expedition will be launched in the spring of the year after next."

Çelebi didn't know where to look. Sadedin — may the poor man go to the devil! — would have had an easier time with his glazed sockets!

"Only this time it will be a much bigger army, and maybe the great Padishah himself will lead it."

The chronicler could feel sweat dripping from his brow.

"The expedition," the Quartermaster went on, "will be far more imposing, as is fitting for one led by the Emperor himself. It will have many more units attached to it and their commanders will be of higher rank. Our war council will be replaced by an assembly of viziers, pashas and emirs, Kara-Mukbil and Kurdisxhi will disappear in favour of the beylerbeys of Rumelia and Anatolia, Old Tavxha's seat will go to the Grand Agha of the Janissary Corps, the Sheh-ul-Islam will take the Mufti's place, the astrologer who was flayed today will be supplanted by the astrologer of the Porte, and in your place, Mevla Çelebi, there'll be the famous Ibn-Suleiman himself."

After a short pause the Quartermaster resumed his speech.

"The thing is, the men will be the same and so will those walls. And death will still have the same colour and the same smell."

Çelebi's blood ran cold. What if the Quartermaster started answering another question of his own making which his partner never had the slightest intention of asking? He waited in terror for a moment; then, as his host seemed disinclined to resume the conversation, he drew the conclusion that even highly placed people, however powerful they may be, know there are boundaries that may not be crossed.

Gradually the cruel and candid look in the Quartermaster

General's eyes blurred and softened, and his face slipped back into its customary expression, save that it now betrayed a little weariness.

The orderly brought in two glasses of syrup.

"This war will go on for a long time," the Quartermaster said. "Albania will be drained of all its energy. This is only the beginning."

He took a sip and gave a deep sigh.

"Every spring," he continued, "when the green shoots re-appear, we will return to these parts. The ground will shake under our troops' marching feet. The valleys will be burned and everything that grows or stands in them will be reduced to ashes. The prosperous economy of the country will be ruined. Thereafter the people round here will use the word 'Turk' to scare their children. And yet, as I've already told you, Çelebi, if we don't overcome them on this first campaign, then we'll need twice as many men to win at the second attempt, and three times as many at the third attempt, and so on. If they escape from this hell, then it will be very hard to annihilate them later on. They'll become accustomed to sieges, to hunger and thirst, to massacres and alerts. Meanwhile their first-born will be children of war. And the worst of it is that they will become familiar with death. They will get used to it the way an animal that has been tamed no longer causes fear. So even if we do conquer them in battle, we will never overcome them. In attacking them, in striking at them without mercy, in throwing our boundless army at them without succeeding in laying them low, we are unwittingly doing the Albanians a great service."

The Quartermaster shook his head in bitterness.

"We thought we were putting them to death. But in fact, we are making them immortal, and by our own hand too."

Çelebi was dazed.

"Once, if I am not mistaken, I told you about Skanderbeg," the

Quartermaster went on. "He's much talked about. He's said to be the greatest warrior of our era, and he's been called at one and the same time a lion, a renegade, a traitor to Islam, a champion of Christ, and who knows what else. As far as I can see all these epithets do apply to him, but I would prefer to describe him differently. To my mind he's a man ahead of his time. We are striking at his visible part, but there is another part we can do nothing about, absolutely nothing, because it has escaped us already. For the moment he is dragging Albania into the abyss, believing that he is making his nation unattainable, in his own image, by making it also pass out of its own time into another dimension. He may well be right. It would be pointless for us to try to separate Skanderbeg from Albania. Even if we wanted to we would not be able to do it."

The chronicler strove as he listened to seize on a pause or a sigh long enough to allow him to change the topic and direction of the conversation. But as the Quartermaster General allowed himself to be carried away on the wings of his own words — a habit Çelebi was now familiar with — the chronicler could not get a word in edgeways.

"What he's working towards," the Quartermaster continued, "is to give Albania a cloak of invulnerability, to give it a form which casts it up and beyond the vicissitudes of the present — a metaform, if I may say, which makes it able to resuscitate, or to put it another way, he is trying to prepare his nation for another world. I don't know if you follow my drift . . . He is trying to crucify Albania, as their God was crucified, so that like Christ, Albania will be resurrected. He doesn't care whether it is on the third day, the third century or the third millennium after his death that Albania rises! What matters is his vision of the future . . ."

The Quartermaster sighed profoundly and lowered his eyelids, as if he too had had a vision.

"Mevla, your chronicle is going to be long and gloomy," he went on. He looked at the historian's grey hair, and his glance gave comfort to the chronicler, as it seemed to him to be full of sympathy. "This siege has gone on a long time," he added. "Autumn is nearly upon us. The assaults will get even more violent."

They chatted for a while about the change of season. For the moment there was no telltale sign of autumn, which existed only in their minds. But within the next few weeks, the plain would wake one morning and find itself spattered with thousands of puddles, big and small, blinking at the sky like so many worried eyes.

"What's Saruxha doing? I haven't seen him for ages," Çelebi asked, seizing what seemed like a good opportunity for redirecting the conversation.

The Quartermaster stared at him for what appeared to be the time it took him to remember who Saruxha was.

"He is still very upset. He spends his days at the foundry."

"He was very fond of his assistant."

"Yes, he was badly affected by the man's death. He stays on his own these days."

"Is he working?"

"Oh yes. He has conceived an implacable hatred for the human race, and it keeps him chained to his work. He's planning a monstrously large new gun."

"Really?"

"Yes. But I'm afraid this campaign will be over before he has a chance to try it out."

"Perhaps the next expedition . . ." The chronicler didn't finish his sentence.

"Of course," the Quartermaster agreed. "Next time, and the time after that, the gun barrels will get bigger and bigger."

The direct and evil glint came back into his eye.

"By the way, Giaour the architect has apparently been summoned back to the capital. He's been appointed to another job. Guess what?" The Quartermaster whistled through his teeth. "He's been appointed architect to the siege of Constantinople!"

"Why? Are we preparing for yet another siege?"

"Yes, we are. And it seems that it will be the last of all. Byzantium will fall."

"May Allah hear your words!"

"Yesterday we took delivery of the new war-cries to be uttered during the assault. What are you gaping at? Oh, of course, you didn't know that the wording of the main slogans yelled during an attack are worked out up on high . . ."

"That really is the first time I heard speak of such a thing," the chronicler confessed.

"Well, for decisive battles, the slogans come from the Centre. This time, one of the cries, which happens to be the most important one, is rather odd. The attackers are supposed to rush forwards chanting 'Rome! Rome!'"

"Really?"

"I guess you understand the significance of that word. What it means is that while the Empire is girding itself finally to destroy the Eastern Rome, Constantinople, here it is refining the details and performing a dress rehearsal for its onslaught on the Western Rome, that is to say, on Europe . . . And when that happens, this field will be turned into a blood-soaked hammam . . ."

When the clouds first appeared in the sky, as if waking from long slumber, the enemy attacked us even more furiously than before. We had been waiting impatiently for those clouds, and when they began to breast over the line of mountains surrounding us, we rushed to our church in great joy and rang the bells. But the clouds left as they had come, without bringing us rain, hail or anything at all. Those fitful, teasing clouds had only served to arouse the dragon.

We knew that the most awesome army in the world was camped beneath our walls, but none of us imagined that its ability to attack us was inexhaustible. Like an avalanche or a roll of thunder coming not from on high but from beneath us, their army bears down on us and is set on grinding us to dust.

At each onslaught they use engines of war we have not seen before — new kinds of ladders, assault towers on wheels, iron balls clad with spikes like hedgehogs, and all sorts of other diabolical inventions. During the last attack we saw some of their soldiers wearing hoods, and we thought it was just some new stratagem of theirs, intended like so many others to strike fear into our hearts. But we soon found out what it was really about. The hooded soldiers had hauled repugnant vermin to the top of our wall. Rats were thrown into one of our freshly dug wells. Two other wells were better guarded. As soon as the guards heard the cry of "Rats! Rats!" they covered the wells with great metal lids. Our blacksmiths are working day and night to make rat traps which are being set in as many places as possible. They clack shut all the time, and the noise keeps us from sleeping.

They have tried everything to overcome us. God only knows what they will try next! But someone had to stand up and face this maniacal horde. As we have been chosen by history for this role, and we have accepted it, that means it is our fate and our cross.

Day is dawning. The sky is overcast. But this time the clouds are of a different kind. They are heavy and laden with rain. Our men have gone up on top to see what is going to happen. They are whispering, as if they were in a sanctuary. The heavens that seemed to have abandoned us for so long now appear to be filling up. Along with the clouds, the divinities are coming back to us too. With their thundering chariots, their lances and the scales of Fate. Among them, the Good Fairy of Albania has apparently been seen, with the Bad Fairy scurrying behind her. Arberia's hour is about to sound! Lord, do not abandon us!

CHAPTER FOURTEEN

Inside the tent the atmosphere was hot, humid and stifling. With some effort, the chronicler penned a few more lines and then laid his head in his hands. He wasn't in the mood for writing. The rumble of the cannon scattered his thoughts like a flock of crows. He read over his unfinished sentence for the tenth time: "In the raging storm of battle the crocodiles charged the ramparts again and again, but fate . . ." The raging storm of battle. It was a fair and fine image, but he wasn't too sure about "crocodiles". Raging storm evoked the sea most of all, but it's a well known fact that crocodiles only live in rivers, so that strictly speaking he should have written "crocodiles in the stream of battle". But the image of a river just wasn't as strong as "raging storm", which, by summoning up an image of the sea — of its constant noise, rolling waves and sudden fury — fitted a battle rather well. He would rather drop "crocodiles" than lose "raging storm". Anyway, when he'd started on this passage and sought an image for soldiers swimming in the waves, he'd hesitated between several fish and beasts of the sea, but none of them seemed to fit the glorious combatants. "Fish" seemed too soft and smooth, "shark" too treacherous and greedy, "whale" too heavy and "octopus" far too repulsive. Whereas crocodiles, because of their strength and killing power, could indeed be likened to soldiers crawling towards the walls of the citadel, especially as their impenetrable and scaly skins were quite like soldiers' shields.

"In the raging storm of battle the crocodiles charged the ramparts again and again, but fate . . ." It was a hard sentence to finish off, and he had a headache. He was tempted to write ". . . did not smile on them", but "smile" seemed the wrong word here. How could there be any smiles in the midst of such horrible butchery? He put his quill down and stared pensively at the pages he had written in a hand now weakened by age. One day, they would constitute the sole remains of all this blood spilled beneath a burning sky, of those thousands of dreadful wounds, of the roar of the cannon, of the yellow dust of forced marches, of the unending, nightmarish ebb and flow of assailants beneath the castle walls, of men clambering up ladders under showers of hot pitch and arrows, falling to the ground below, then clambering up again alongside comrades who don't even recognise you because you are already disfigured by your injuries. Those pages were going to be the sole trace of the soldiers' tanned hides, of these innumerable skins on which sharp metal, sulphur, pitch and oil had drawn monstrous shapes which, when the war was over, would go on living their own lives. To cap it all, these pages would also be the sole remnants of the myriad tents which, when they were dismantled, as they would be in a few weeks' time, would leave thousands of marks on a wide empty space, looking as if it had been trampled by a huge herd of bizarre animals. Then, next spring, grass would grow on the plain: millions of blades of grass, utterly indifferent to what had gone on there, with no knowledge of all that can happen in this world.

Çelebi tidied away the pages of his chronicle in a folder, got up and went out. The sky was overcast once again. There was a hot wind that grated on your throat. Now and again it raised a cloud of thick dust which it deposited on the tents. Soldiers lay on the ground outside not even trying to shelter themselves from the dust and wind. Resigned and grey, they were waiting for the roll of the big drum to call them to assemble in their units. It must be the fifth assault to be launched in a week. Even hardened veterans could not remember such a diabolical rhythm of attack. They all now knew that as the rain clouds gathered in density, they would be required to attack ever more fiercely, and more frequently.

The chronicler wandered around the camp for some time without meeting anyone he knew. He observed the faces of nameless soldiers and officers drowsing in the humid, suffocating heat. Their eyes expressed endless weariness. The dust that rose from the dry ground seemed to have cast a veil of indifference over everything. Neither the Pasha's pavilion, in front of which soldiers usually slowed their pace to stare with veneration at the tall metal pole topped by the brass crescent, the ancient emblem of the Ottoman Empire, nor the tent pitched next to it, the only one to be lilac in colour among the infinity of other tents, which tens of thousands of men had imagined as a shimmering purple cloud hovering over their stormy sensual desires, attracted anyone's attention any more.

The roar of cannon filled the air from time to time.

Everyone was waiting.

At last the chronicler saw someone he knew — Tuz Okçan. At first Çelebi felt pleased, but then he noticed that the officer's face was extraordinarily pale. Okçan was walking slowly and what surprised the chronicler most was that the janissary had an armed escort.

"Tuz Okçan, what's happened to you?" he asked.

"Nothing. I'm being taken to hospital."

"To hospital? Under armed guard? Wait a minute: weren't you in the last assault?"

"That's the point," the janissary replied with a bitter smile. "Somehow or other, when I opened the cursed rat cage with my knife, I got a graze."

A gleam of terror lit the chronicler's eyes. The janissary took him by the sleeve.

"Listen, Mevla," he said imploringly. "You're in touch with Sirri Selim. Honestly, what was the disease carried by the rats we released during the attack? He ought to know!"

The chronicler shrugged his shoulders.

"I swear to you by Allah that I have no idea."

"Could it be the plague?" the janissary asked anxiously.

"Plague? Have you gone crazy? Come on, now. How can you think of such a thing?"

"I feel dreadful."

Çelebi could not think what else to say. The janissary moved off with his guard without saying farewell. The chronicler was glad their encounter had been brief. He walked away in the opposite direction, fearing that the janissary might retrace his steps. The fact that he had an escort was a bad omen. He had heard what had happened to the first soldiers who had been infected with the scourge. They went first to Sirri Selim's "Death Row", then were taken to a set of long sheds surrounded by a ring of lime, and left locked up there until they died.

Another one down, the chronicler thought. Like Sadedin. Like the astrologer. He recalled the night before the first attack, when the four of them had drunk raki from the same gourd. It seemed so long ago now, as if it had been in a different world.

His feet led him to the open area in front of the Pasha's tent. As always, two sentries stood motionless with their lances at the ready beside the entrance to the tent. A gust of wind covered the guards' faces, their lances and the brass emblem with a pall of dust. The whirling, scorching, yellow cloud formed bizarre shapes reminiscent of ancient legends. Mevla Çelebi felt dangerous associations of ideas beginning to emerge in his mind and in order to dispel them he turned on his heels. At that point he saw several members of the war council walking towards the commander-in-chief's tent. Among them he could make out the Mufti, with a sanxhakbey beside him. Their orderlies, who had to stay outside, lay down on the grass a little way off.

Yet another meeting, the chronicler thought, and then halted. The Quartermaster General came along unaccompanied. He looked worried and passed without turning his head. A few moments later, Kara-Mukbil went by, looking glum. People said he'd been wounded again during the assault two days ago. Then along came Saruxha, a pair of sanxhakbeys, and Kurdisxhi, leaning on his two orderlies. Beneath his russet mop of hair, the latter looked stunned, sallow, almost wan, as he had never looked before. He had visibly just got out of bed, and in view of his serious physical condition, his attendance at the Pasha's tent meant that the meeting must be of utmost importance. The cannon were roaring without interruption.

The Alaybey came alone. In his wake, one by one came deaf Tahanka, then Karaduman, Kapduk Agha and, behind him, scowling as if trying to hide some great pain, Old Tavxha. All of them, or almost all, looked worn out. Only Giaour the architect, who marched in last of all with a particularly regular stride, looked his usual, imperturbable self.

The dust whirling about Çelebi's head failed to sidetrack the chronicler's mind. The Empire was powerful. It was a great Empire even in adversity. The crescent of the Osmanlis would live on down the centuries. Strong and competent men were making decisions. They would think it through. They would not give up the citadel lightly. Now their grave words were clashing like weapons striking each other in battle, and the scribe was putting them down on paper. A bitter pang of jealousy suddenly shot through him. He was on the point of leaving once and for all when his eyes fell on the long visage of Sirri Selim. The doctor was standing as still as a pikestaff a few paces from the pavilion. He didn't seem to have noticed the chronicler, which made the latter uneasy. He didn't dare go away without greeting Sirri Selim, in case Selim had noticed his presence. On the other hand he was hesitant about being the first to speak, because the doctor's elongated face and his bloodshot, insomniac eyes looked particularly intimidating that day. He decided to stay where he was until the doctor appeared to notice him. Selim looked petrified. The chronicler even wondered if he hadn't fallen asleep standing up, and might collapse at any minute.

At last the doctor became aware of Çelebi's presence. Blood rushed back to his pensive face.

"They're making a decision in there," he said, gesturing towards the Pasha's tent.

The chronicler nodded.

"They didn't ask for me," Sirri Selim went on. The blush on his face and neck had turned purple in blotches. "They're not pleased with me," he added in a louder voice.

Çelebi looked around fearfully.

"They want everything to happen in a flash, but nothing happens like that. To be honest, I didn't put much hope in the rabbits, the toads or the dogs. But the rats . . ." His voice almost broke with emotion. "I can't hide it from you, Çelebi, the rats really let me down!"

The chronicler could hardly believe his eyes. This frightful beanstalk who had cut a man into little pieces in front of everyone was on the verge of tears!

"Maybe it's not the poor dears' fault . . . The enemy sets traps for them, and who knows how much they suffer before they pass away! They probably did take in the disease I entrusted to them, but nonetheless . . ."

He pulled himself together. His voice grew clearer and one of his eyes went bleary.

"All the same!" he said again. "All that trouble for an ordinary disease . . . Çelebi, they're not giving me my head. Ah, if I could have things my way, you'd see what I can do . . . My dear friend, let me tell you a secret. I wrote a letter to the Padishah: 'Let me have the plague, O my master!' Yes, that's what I wrote to him!"

A shiver ran down the chronicler's spine. He recalled Tuz Okçan and the proverb about the two scourges, each more fearsome than the other.

"But the authorities are blocking it," the doctor went on. "They bring up a host of objections. They won't let me have either of the two sovereign maladies — neither plague nor cholera. I bet they're keeping them for themselves!"

The chronicler butted in during a long sigh to ask the doctor what other maladies he had requested from on high. Sirri Selim reeled off a list, but most of the medical names meant nothing to him. Some of them rotted the gut, two or three of them made you blind, and another one drove men mad.

"But what's the point?" Sirri Selim moaned. "Like I told you, those are common afflictions. The two sovereign maladies I mentioned are quite different. They wipe you out, they don't just raise your temperature and make you retch." He sighed once again, and his eyes began to gleam as if lit from within. "A plague-infested rat . . . Ah, if only I were given that . . . I would send that in, like a seven-tailed page, or pasha . . . Why are you making that face, Çelebi?"

"Oh no, I'm not making a face, Sirri Selim. How can you say such a thing?"

The doctor's face hardened. His blush darkened.

"Well, that's what you say, but I'm sure you'll manage not to write about the rats in your chronicle!" he shouted, raising his voice all of a sudden.

The cannons fired again, in close sequence, and for no obvious reason Sirri Selim turned his back on the chronicler and strode away on his long legs. A moment later, he stopped, turned his head round, and shouted from afar: "Shall I tell you what I'll do with your chronicle, Çelebi? Do you really want me to tell you?"

He then uttered words that left the chronicler quite flabbergasted . . .

Before coming on this campaign he had never heard so many or such varied expressions referring to the human posterior. He had often pretended not to hear them, even when raw recruits quite gratuitously called him an "old bum", or, worse still, when in the half-light of dusk shameful propositions were hissed at him. "Hey, old man, you want a feel?" He comforted himself with the thought that if they knew the work he was doing, and how he was watching over them for their own good, they would be sorry for saying such things. He took even more solace in hearing that a man as eminent as Saruxha was also prey to this common fever, and never missed an opportunity to exclaim that whenever he relieved himself all he wanted was to wipe his arse on the Mufti's beard. But now a cultivated man, a colleague, and a most learned one to boot, had told him to his face and without so much as a smile that he intended to use the chronicle for the same purpose as the one to which Saruxha wanted to put the Mufti's beard!

Feeling pained and unsteady on his legs, Çelebi walked away in the opposite direction.

Meanwhile in the Pasha's tent the council had begun its debate. The sanxhakbeys reported in turn on the state of their units.

Suddenly, in the pause that followed the end of one of the reports, Tavxha gave a little scream of pain and put his hand to his legs.

He wanted to say something, but the silence grew more complete, and all eyes turned to the Pasha. Everyone knew that Tavxha had rheumatism, and his wail meant that his short and crooked limbs felt rain coming on. The cry had a sinister echo.

The Pasha's eyes grew harsher.

"Speak!" he said.

The Mufti rose to take the floor. He spoke of the dead and of their souls now tasting the glorious nectar of martyrs in the gardens of paradise.

The Pasha was not really listening to anything they said. He only noticed the way his subordinates' eyes looked away each time his glance met theirs. He realised that this evasiveness was the first but infallible sign that, as from that instant, they were separating their own fate from his. There they were in front of him, sitting in a half-moon, cheek by jowl, with their worry-beads between their fingers, bearing their insignia of office and the decorations they never forgot to display. He thought back to the day last spring when he was planning the expedition and first looked carefully at the list of his general staff, which he had to submit to the Grand Vizier for approval. All their names were on it. Some of them he knew personally, others by repute; and others he had never heard of had been warmly recommended to him. All had been in and out of the Sultan's favour at different times, and had had careers filled with expeditions, hard campaigns, long-drawn-out sieges, wounds, garrisons taken by stealth or by valour, enemies vanquished and regions laid waste, where not even grass would ever grow again. At that time he had hoped they would all get along, which was always easier between men of quality. To begin with they had in fact had good working relationships. But now, rather sooner than he had expected, the days of shifty glances had come. Contrary to what might have been expected, he was now the one to be consumed with envy. The campaign was coming to an end, and whatever its outcome, their careers would go on, they would fight another day, they would pitch their tents before castles new, they would climb up or slide down the rungs of the military or administrative hierarchy. He would not. His own path ended at the foot of these ramparts. What awaited him now was either the peak of honour or descent into the abyss. This they knew, which was why their eyes kept racing towards the back corner of the tent, as far as possible from his own. And that was also why silence fell upon them all when Old Tavxha's limbs (which the Pasha found so short as to be deformed) foretold rain. It suddenly occurred to him that not only did none of them fear the rain any more, but that they actually wanted it to pour. They were weary and wanted to get back to their harems. In their eyes the commander-in-chief was getting more detrimental to their interests with every day that passed. Like a drowning man who clings to anything still afloat, he might drag them down with him to the grave.

Gradually and progressively, he formulated all that in his mind. They were trying to step aside. To drop him. But he was still their commander-in-chief and he was not going to let them get away as easily as that. He would show them what a real leader was capable of in a desperate situation. They were expecting a shower. Like idol-worshippers, they venerated the misshapen legs of Old Tavxha that had anticipated rain. They had their ears open for the sound of the rain drums. Fine and good. He would fulfil their wishes, he would give them rain! He would drench them with rain — of a kind they were not expecting.

The great muster drum banged away outside. Its muffled thudding blanked out all other sounds, overwhelming everything like a tidal wave.

The last speech was ending. The Pasha looked at all those closed faces. He announced that the attack would take place shortly. He said that the full complement of the entire army would be deployed in successive waves of attackers. He added that none should imagine that the start of rain would affect the assault in any way. Of course he knew that the first drop would finish everything off, irremediably, and he found it hard to hold back words that could not be easily spoken either. Instead, raising his head in a threatening manner, he announced:

"Today I shall take part in the fighting myself."

Nobody said a word. They all understood what that statement meant. It meant that all of them without exception, from the Mufti to the architect, had to join in the fighting. A smile lit up Old Tavxha's face.

"Tell the soldiery that members of council will join them in battle, in person," the Pasha said, and stood up.

All bowed low as they left the tent.

The great muster drum had stopped. One of the commander-in-chief's orderlies had brought him his white horse and was holding it by the bridle.

Meanwhile all the units had assembled. The great plain was covered with men, further than the eye could see. Never before had this army assembled such a huge number of soldiers for an attack. The hot wind that made the innumerable standards flutter and wave seemed intent on registering all the images that their emblems ever inspired in poets and chroniclers.

The Pasha came out of his tent. He raised his head. Low, pregnant clouds hovered uncertainly in the sky. He mounted, and with his orderlies and his aides-de-camp beside him, rode to the vantage point from which he usually observed the battles. A few moments later, he followed his custom of raising his right hand, the hand on which he wore his ring, and this gave the signal to start the attack. The air filled immediately with the sound of a thousand drums. With his weary, indifferent eyes he followed the first wave of volunteers as they went up to the wall, then the successive waves of *azabs*. It all went on in the ordinary way except that the battalions surging forwards were more numerous than before. The units reached the foot of the ramparts, and from their midst rose hundreds of ladders, like long wooden arms slowly falling (as in a dream, so it seemed) to lean against the walls. Then an impetuous flood of *eshkinxhis* overran the hacked and harried *azabs* in their rush towards the embankment. It was all proceeding as in previous assaults, and the thought that this was but a repetition plunged the Pasha into a mood of depression. He gave an order, then another. Then a third. The officer who had transmitted the first order came back. Then the second one returned. The third officer, on his return, looked very glum.

Over there beneath the wall, men could feel Death itself moving among them. The shiver that swept through the body of troops was a sure sign of the first blow of the reaper's scythe. Then the men grew more hardened. The army's reactions slowed down and became sluggish even as ever harsher blows fell upon it.

The Pasha understood all this, just as he instinctively respected the natural order of things and their necessary sequence.

The janissary units began to move, with their customarily grim faces and a whole firmament of stars and crescents waving above their heads. But hadn't he sent them forward too soon?

He shook his head from side to side as if trying to dispel something that seemed like a fit of drowsiness. Everything was taking place at the proper pace, but in his mind a certain number of fixed points emerged which allowed him to measure the acceleration of time.

He was almost astonished to watch the elite *dalkiliç* troops surge forwards, as if it had not been by his own order that they were moving up to the front line of the assault.

He rubbed his forehead and nearly shouted out aloud, "There's no need to hurry!" This impression of haste was prompted by a kind of sleepiness hovering in the air.

The death squad . . . They were still there in his mind, which was the starting point for everything. The squad, or rather, its anthem: "We are the grooms who wed Death!" That day he felt as he had never felt before how closely his own destiny resembled theirs. We have signed a pact with death, he said over to himself as he shouted aloud:

"The soldiers of death!"

After them, there was nothing left to throw into the fray, save the dome of the temple — in other words, himself.

He motioned to his orderly to hand him his breast-plate and his yatagan, then he lowered the visor of his helmet and cantered towards the rampart, followed by his aides-de-camp and a detachment of Moroccan desert warriors.

Every stride of his horse shortened the distance between him and the wall. He felt no fear. He just had a dry and sour taste in his mouth.

The wall came nearer. The nearer it came the higher it seemed to be, and the breaches looked ever more frightening. The battlements above, like the bared fangs of a monster, had begun crushing bodies. Between those implacable teeth his own bloody fate still struggled, and on them it hung.

The citadel came closer. It was the first time he had seen it so close up. Its shrouds of black pitch fluttered before his eyes. They covered whole stretches of wall and great lumps of stone, but they could not veil the entire body of the keep. Last spring, during the long march towards it, he had seen the castle in his dreams. It had come to him as a woman, maybe because the writers of ancient chronicles of war often tried to make their glorious captains' thirst for conquest more convincing by depicting citadels in terms and images usually reserved for women. So the keep had come to him as a difficult woman. He embraced it, sweating from head to toe, but still she refused to yield to him. Her walls, towers, gates, limbs and eyes obsessed him, but they slipped through his fingers and got him in their grip in the end, so as to strangle him. Oddly, her sexual organ was not the main way in, as might have been expected, but was somewhere lower down, and probably in the beyond.

The huzzahs of tens of thousands of fighters hailing his arrival at the foot of the ramparts jerked him out of his torpor. Surrounded by his guards and the detachment of Moroccans, he joined the assault force. The wall was now close by. Sinister black drapes of congealed pitch swung around his head. Hundreds of janissaries, *sipahis*, *azabs*, volunteers, *eshkinxhis*, *dalkiliç* and *müslümans* were scrambling up flaming ladders.

"Hurrah!" the Pasha cried out. "Forward!"

Nobody could hear him, but all saw him wave his hand, and from the foot of a hundred ladders soldiers fought each other to be the first to reach the top of the wall. They knew they were climbing the first rungs of their careers on these bloodied and already half-burned ladders. Upwards lay the path to promotion, wealth and a harem.

The Pasha felt the intoxication of battle. The drums, the banners, the smell of burning oil and hot pitch, the flaming ladders, the clouds of dust, the huzzahs, all this smoky, bloody riot enveloped him and went to his head like a strong drink. He rode along the wall with his escort of guards and aides-de-camp. Apparently the defenders recognised him, because they started aiming arrows and balls of flaming cloth at him, which fell all around with a piercing whistle. His guards put themselves at risk by forming a screen around him with their shields. One of the aides-de-camp riding close by him had a bloody neckband that grew steadily thicker. The commander-in-chief carried on galloping amid cries of "Long live the Pasha!" and invocations of the Prophet and the Padishah. Now and again he heard his soldiers shouting out the battle-cry of "Rome! Rome!" In a flash Giaour's new posting came back into his mind, or rather, the associated rumour that said that if he was victorious here, then he, Tursun Pasha, would be given the task of taking Constantinople.

"Onwards!" he yelled once more. "Victory!"

There was an ever more frantic crush of soldiers at the foot of the ladders trying to get to the top of the wall. Looking up at

the men climbing you sometimes saw shields, yatagans and occasionally human limbs fly up in the air and then fall to the ground,
all apparently discarded by the attackers so as to lighten their
load.

Suddenly the wall began to wobble, the towers slid terrify-
ingly over his head, the funereal drapes of congealed pitch with
their bloody fringes flapped in a strong gust of wind and seemed
about to engulf him. He fell. The sky went black. The guards
formed a roof of shields over him.

Someone cried out:

"The Pasha has been killed!"

One of his aides-de-camp, the one with the bloodied neck,
leaned over him.

"Help me up," the Pasha said. "I've not been hit."

"It's his horse that died," the other officer shouted out.

Tursun Pasha stood up. With his feet on the ground he felt
like he was in a hole.

"The Pasha has been killed!" the same voice screamed again.

He got on to another horse that someone had instantly
brought to him, and spurred it to a gallop. His guards followed.

"Pasha, sire, keep away from the wall," one of the aides-de-
camp shouted to him. "The *giaours* have spotted you!"

Arrows rained down even more thickly. But the Pasha did
not move away from the wall. Once again he cantered alongside
the wall at whose foot what people call a "war" was taking place.
On this occasion it took the form of a human mass rising from
below towards another mass of men overhead. Unseen like a
demon behind a screen of smoke given off by pitch, the latter
was doing all it could to prevent the former from climbing up. It
was hitting it without mercy, setting it on fire, burning it to a
cinder, chopping off hundreds of its arms and legs. But the rising

mass did not falter or turn back. It went on rising, rung after rung, slipping on its own blood, clinging by its nails to the stone, and when its limbs were cut off, it instantly grew hundreds of new feet and new hands that sought only to go on going up and up . . .

The nightmare went on until dusk. Then the fall-back drums rolled. Units beyond counting once again flooded back into the deserted camp and the Pasha waited in his tent for estimates of the day's losses. Though it had not brought victory, the battle could still not be considered lost. Never before had such a large mass of men reached the top of the wall. Usually only a small number of men who got over the parapet came back alive, but those who stayed up there did not give their lives cheaply. And today's assault must have cost the defenders a multitude of dead. Thirst had begun to do its work. A few more assaults of that degree of violence, and the decimated, thirst-tortured defenders would not be able to repulse the attack all the way along their wall. The Pasha needed a few more days of drought. Just a few days. That's what he told himself, but at bottom he knew that a few days without rain would not be enough. Exhausted by such long-drawn-out tension, he sometimes indulged in absurd daydreams. He imagined how easy it would all be if after September came not October and November, but July and August. He fantasised about a crazy wind that would suddenly come and muddle up the seasons like autumn leaves. At other moments he thought that so much time had elapsed since the start of the expedition that a pile of things had sunk into oblivion, that passions had dulled, and that forecasts of victory and the timescale set had all been wiped from memory. He felt that way especially at night, when he went outside and cast his eyes on the huge camp with its tents, its stars and its brass, bronze and golden crescent moons giving a lugubrious imitation of the night sky. He mused that a whole chunk of the heavens had been forcibly brought down to earth and set to work amid the bloody business of men. As he gazed at length at the desert of the night he began to doubt whether somewhere in the far distance, beyond the roads and the clouds, there really still were towns containing offices cluttered with papers explaining the ins and outs of every case, the merits and the weaknesses of officials, including his own. At such times, when he stood facing the night alone, facts became detached from their consequences, the linkage between causes and effects went slack and anything seemed plausible. But dawn came with its cruel rawness, and everything — things, facts and the order of the days — recovered its logic. And he knew that logic was against him.

His aides-de-camp brought him the first reports: three hundred and ten officers of all ranks killed. The number of non-ranking soldiers lost in battle was not yet known. He enquired about council members: all were safe. The thought that they paid too much attention to their own wellbeing made him feel downcast once again.

But over the next days he would set them a challenge in self-preservation. He only needed a few dry days, nothing more. He now feared one thing alone: the sound of the rain drums. Their rumbling had not been heard for several months. If they were to strike up again now, it would be the end of everything.

Sirri Selim sent him a short report. He had examined the innards of four Albanians who had fallen off the battlements and he could certify that they were suffering from lack of water far more acutely than the man captured during the previous attack. But no sign of disease. They were clearly not drinking the contaminated water any longer, so their thirst must have doubled, or even tripled. If only that could go on a little longer, dear God! he prayed. Still no figure for losses among the soldiers. Tursun Pasha ordered an increase in the number of sentries and put some battalions on alert. Night was falling, and a raid by Skanderbeg was to be expected. It was his usual time.

The Pasha sat down to relax and he noticed that his elbow was stained with dirt. He hadn't previously paid any attention to the soil of this place. He gazed at it as if in a trance. The aide-de-camp who came into the tent found him staring hard at the elbow of his sleeve.

"Excuse me, sire," he said, fearing he would be blamed for falling short in his duties, "I've only just noticed it myself. You must have dirtied your tunic when you fell . . ."

But the Pasha's mind was elsewhere. He was pondering the fact that soil is the same in any land on earth, the only difference being in what grows in it. His eyes were drooping, and the attending officer lowered his voice to a whisper. The commander-in-chief was nodding off to sleep. The officer quietly placed a light blanket over his master and tiptoed out of the tent.

After the troubled nights he had had, the Pasha at last sank into deep sleep. An orderly brought him his supper, then aides-de-camp came to give him the figures for the day's losses, but they all found him fast asleep. They did not wake him. One of them tucked the blanket over his master's shoulders, then they all carefully closed up the entrance to the tent and silently went their way.

He spent several hours in calm and dreamless sleep. Later on, he did have a dream. He saw the rain drums all lined up on parade. Then they suddenly began to beat by themselves. He ordered them to stop, but they did not obey his command. They carried on beating a muffled beat. Then he ordered them to be punished.

His guards launched into them, tore them to shreds with their lances and daggers, but still the drums kept on beating. The Pasha woke up. It was pitch-dark inside the tent. He moved an arm that had gone stiff and realised he had fallen asleep in his battle dress. He felt he was not yet properly awake because his ears were still buzzing with the thump of the drums he had seen in his dream. He threw off the blanket and sat up straight. What was that? The thudding noise had not stopped. So it wasn't the afterglow of his dream. Far away, deep inside the camp, someone really was beating a drum. He heard a gentle swishing on the sloped sides of his tent, and then it all became clear in a flash. Rain.

He stood up and stayed still for a moment at the foot of his divan. Then, stepping on the animal skins laid on the floor, he went to the entrance, pulled back the oilskin curtain, and went outside. The first glimmer of dawn threw a white haze over the horizon. The sentries who had been huddling by the side of the tent to keep out of the rain stood to attention as soon as they saw him and presented arms. But he didn't even glance at them.

A rich, thick smell of earth wetted by rain after a long drought rose from the ground. The sky was entirely overcast by heavy, stationary, grey-black clouds releasing a steady, even stream of rain. Regular autumn weather.

Dawn was breaking.

He gazed at the dark sky, then at the huge camp with its thousands of grey, triangular tents looking like funeral mounds erected over thirty thousand sleeping soldiers. He turned his back on all that and went inside. Then he woke one of his orderlies. The man was shaking.

"Fetch Hasan," the Pasha told him.

A moment later Hasan was beside him. He was shaking as well.

"Bring me Exher."

The eunuch bowed and left. He was back a moment later, holding the Pasha's young wife by the hand. She had puffy eyes with horrible black bags underneath.

"Listen," he said. She wasn't properly awake and he had to shake her roughly by the shoulder. "Listen!" he said again, pulling hard on one of her plaits to bring her terrified face closer to his. "If it's a boy," he said, jabbing a finger at the belly beneath her fine chemise, "if it's a boy, you will name him after me."

The girl stared at him in terror.

"Do you understand?"

"Yes, sire."

"Now go away."

The eunuch came in and took the girl out.

The Pasha stood still for a moment in the half-light. Then he asked his orderly to bring him a glass of water, which he did.

"I'm going back to bed," he said.

He took a vial of sleeping draught from a casket by the head of his bed and poured it into a goblet.

He thought how the powder, when it dissolved, would make the water go cloudy like a section of sky. There was sleep in that powder that would last one night, maybe two. He emptied another vial into the goblet. A thousand nights, he thought, a thousand years. He brought the goblet to his lips and drank its contents in a single gulp.

He was still standing upright. Far away outside, the rain drums carried on with their mortal pounding. When he started feeling dizzy he reclined on the cushions and closed his eyes. Thoughts crowded into his mind untidily. He would have liked to have thought a sublime thought, but he could not. So that's it, then, Ugurlu Tursun Tunxhaslan Sert Olgun Pasha! he said to himself.

Then, before asking God for his mercy, he reflected on his life and wondered if it was really necessary to invent such a long name for a life that was so short, then he thought of the man for whose greater glory he had worked so hard — but in vain, alas, in vain! — and then, as if in a feverish delirium, he thought of this noisy world standing well back while his own soul wandered off in the rain.

It began to rain at dawn on the first day of the month of Saint Shenmiter. I was about to relieve the sentries when the first drops began to fall, as heavy as tears.

Day was breaking. I wanted to shout out loud, ring all the bells, wake up all our men, but I only thought about doing such things. All I did was lean my head on the stone wall and stay still in that position for a while. As they wettened, the granite blocks sweated out all the heat they had stored up through the summer and they also seemed to release, so to speak, all the anguish of that long season. They seemed to be coming alive, and it struck me that at any minute they would begin to breathe, moan and sigh.

Somewhere in the heart of the Turkish camp the drums that speak of rain are beating. From up here we can see soldiers wrapping equipment in oilskins. Thousands of lances and emblems stick up like the spines on a hedgehog's back from that huge dark camp that stains the land as far as the eye can see. Unusual activity can be seen around the tent of the commander-in-chief. Torch-bearers go in and out incessantly. It surely signals some important event: an urgent meeting, a sacking, or a death.

O Heavens! Do not let up too soon! I hear myself praying. Thou who art ending this season of war, do not abandon us now, great Heaven of ours!

THE LAST CHAPTER

The closed carriage transporting the women of the harem moved along the road on its own. At the start of the journey it had travelled almost in convoy with another vehicle loaded with the deceased commander-in-chief's arms and chattels, but after two days on the road the harem carriage had had to slow down because one of the women, Exher, was in pain, and so it fell back.

It was drizzling. The women gazed dreamily at the muddy track dotted with the first puddles.

"Look," Ajsel said as she pointed to the right. "Up on the mountainside, you can see the small villages we noticed on our way here. Can you make out the church and its bell-tower?"

"What a god-forsaken hole!"

"What about the fortress? It can't be far from here. Do you remember when we saw it? It was dusk, and the flag on top looked completely black."

"The fortress is a long way yet."

"Do you think so? I remember it being very near those villages," Blondie said.

"You're getting it all muddled up. Let's ask Lejla. She's doing this trip for the second time."

"Don't wake her up!"

The carriage wheels kept up their monotonous creak and screech. Through the gently fluttering silk curtain they could see the silhouettes of Hasan and the driver.

Ajsel carried on staring at the empty road and the dreary autumn landscape. Lejla was asleep and each time there was a bump in the road her head lolled so far to the side that it looked like it was about to come off her shoulders.

"Look! Sappers!" Ajsel exclaimed. "They're making a new bridge."

"They're setting things up for the retreat," Lejla blurted out.

For a few minutes they watched men working in the rain.

"Yet *he* will never go home!" Ajsel said.

"*He* must have been buried today."

"Yes, that must be so. And now all this rain is falling on *him*."

Blondie raised her head slightly and then let it fall back. It was the first time they had spoken of their master after the event. They could still not quite get their tongues round it.

"It was you who spent the last night with him, wasn't it?" Ajsel asked. "Tell us, did *he* speak in his sleep?"

"Yes," Blondie said without moving.

"And what was *he* saying?"

"I couldn't make it out. I don't speak Turkish very well."

"Didn't you catch anything at all? Perhaps *he* hinted at the reason for *his* act. Did you talk about Skanderbeg?"

"I can't really remember. Maybe *he* did mention that name. But *he* was constantly talking to the Sultan. *He* was explaining himself, awkwardly. *He* was saying *he* was innocent. *He* also spoke of Skanderbeg, but under his other name, the name of . . ."

"The fearsome name of Geor-ge Cas-tri-ote?"

"Yes, I think that was it."

"*He* always used to speak in *his* sleep," Lejla mumbled.

Blondie was about to say something more, but she changed her mind and lowered her gaze to the floor.

"Girls! Look at the hanged men!" Ajsel shouted as she pointed out of the little carriage window.

They all leaned over to get a look.

"Are they the ones we saw on the journey out?"

"Yes, the same."

"They're nothing but skeletons now."

A flock of crows startled by the noise of the carriage flew off down the road.

"When we came the other way, their bodies were still whole, so they must have just been hanged."

"How long will they be left up?"

"Who knows?"

"Further on we'll see heads on stakes."

"No, we won't, we must have gone past them during the night. The next landmark is the monastery with the three crosses."

"That's right. I get it all muddled up."

"Maybe because we are going backwards."

The carriage shuddered to a stop. Rough voices shouted, "Halt! Give way!"

"What's going on?" they asked, in fear and trembling. It took them a while to grasp that a military convoy was coming past. Scouts had come ahead to clear the route. Their helmets and packs were soaked right through and slowed their pace. Their tired eyes looked as if they had gone blind.

"They've got new equipment," Lejla whispered. "Do you see

their short swords? And the green helmets? It's the first time I've seen ones like that."

They kept quiet as the seemingly endless line of soldiers went past, leading their pack mules by the bit. Then came long six-wheeled tumbrels, making a hideous din.

"They're the field canteens," Lejla explained. "They're usually the last vehicles in a convoy." She sighed. "I suppose it's all over now."

The harem carriage slowly got back on the road.

"So what are we now? Young widows?" Exher wondered.

"What nonsense!" Lejla exclaimed. "Young widows! Mind you, I wouldn't object for myself, but . . ."

"We mustn't grumble. I feared the worst after *he* died."

"What do you mean?"

"They might easily have done away with us all," Lejla observed. "My blood ran cold when the war council met that morning. I was terrified they would give the command to Old Tavxha. Hasan had heard the sentries on duty at the time saying that if Tavxha was appointed commander-in-chief, he would have us beheaded. He and the Mufti blamed us for all the army's misfortunes."

"Idiots!" Ajsel exclaimed.

"Only when the meeting ended and I learned that the high command had been handed jointly to the three senior captains," Lejla went on, "only then did my blood begin to thaw."

The conversation petered out, as it had so many times before. Ajsel propped her chin on the ledge of the carriage door.

"Does it still hurt?" Lejla asked Exher as she leaned over the pregnant girl.

She nodded. Her lips were pale and her eyes were clouded.

"I think I've started to bleed again."

They said nothing for several minutes. Eventually Exher

seemed to find some relief. Ajsel turned away from the window. Blondie ran her slender fingers through her hair.

"There's a winter pasture," Lejla said. "Are there any in your part of the world?"

"I don't know," Ajsel replied. "I've never been in this kind of country before."

Now and again they noticed storks' nests, and shepherds wearing black hoods over their heads. And identical steep, rocky slopes without end.

"Is that what a state is?" Exher asked, pointing to the countryside. "I mean: is a state the same thing as the land, or is there a difference?"

They burst out laughing, but none of them could really answer the question. Lejla said that the State was actually the Empire, whereas Ajsel opined that the difference between a land and a state was that the latter could not be seen by the naked eye.

"Good God!" Blondie suddenly shouted, her eyes bursting out of their sockets. "Just look at the vehicle coming up behind . . ."

Through the wire-netted porthole at the rear of the carriage could be seen a closed carriage, of a colour and bearing insignia that they knew well.

"Could it be his coffin?" Lejla asked.

"That's all we need! To be pursued by his coffin!"

The wagon was gaining on them, making a dreadful racket. It was easy to see that it wanted to overtake them. They slumped back into their seats and waited to see what would happen. Their driver and Hasan were also worried, and turned round to look.

For a few moments the two carriages drove abreast of each other. The girls had put their hands over their eyes, save for Lejla, who carried on staring out of the window. What she saw seemed to scare her even more than the idea of having the Pasha's coffin on her tail.

"Good God!" she wailed. "The architect Giaour!"

The rattling of the wheels was so loud that none of the others heard what she said. She had to wait until the other wagon had pulled some way ahead to describe what she had seen. Hunched forwards and poring over his maps with eyes as bloodshot as Satan's, Giaour was drawing!

"There's a rumour that he's planning the seizure of Constantinople," Ajsel said.

They kept their eyes on the shrinking black square of the architect's carriage until it disappeared into the mist ahead, and then gave a sigh of relief.

"There's a bird that only comes with the snow," Lejla said. "Tweet, tweet, come here, little bird!" she said in a girlish voice as she tapped on the window. "Those birds are never wrong," she added after a while. "Winter is coming on."

"Woe is me!" Exher moaned. She had gone quite livid, and her whole body was shaking. The women looked into each others' eyes. "This cursed road is killing me. I can feel I am going . . ."

"Should we ask Hasan to stop for another rest?"

"What's the point?" Lejla said. "She's going to have a miscarriage anyway."

Exher was weeping.

"And he hoped I would give him a son!" she blurted out between her sobs.

"Lie flat for a bit," Lejla told her. "It might stop the bleeding."

Exher lay down and raised her legs. She seemed to get a little better after a while.

The carriage shuddered to a halt again.

"Another convoy," Ajsel said. "Just look at it!"

The unending caravan seemed utterly monstrous. The soldiers were covered in armour — and so were the horses. With just two little eyeholes, their helmeted heads looked terrifying.

Soldiers sat like statues in packed rows on the backs of long six- and eight-wheeled carts, propping their chins on their weapons. Then even heavier vehicles came by. You could make out the black barrels of cannon.

"Every day brings a new invention," Lejla observed. "Lord, why can't they just stop with what they've got?"

They said nothing more until the entire convoy had passed by. Then they could see out of the window again, and looked at the breast of the mountain passes, a cross standing crooked by the wayside, and trees draped in hoar frost. Here and there they came across signboards nailed to posts, saying "To the capital, 113 miles" or "To Constantinople, 300 miles", with finger-arrows pointing in the right direction.

"Who will buy us now?" Ajsel wondered aloud.

Blondie raised her eyes. It seemed she was about to work out what to say.

"Can we ever foretell our own fate?" Lejla asked without taking her eyes off the landscape. "If a soldier buys us, maybe we will have to travel this same road again."

"Ah, give me anything but this journey again!" Exher wailed. "It's the road to hell!"

Blondie lowered her eyelids and began to hum softly. It was a sad song, with incomprehensible lyrics in the language of her homeland.

"More villages," Lejla said, to break the silence that had overcome them. "We must have left Europe behind us by now."

The carriage went on rolling through the rain.

Tirana, 1969–1970
Paris, 1993–1994

AFTERWORD

In 1968 Soviet tanks overwhelmed Czechoslovakia and put down the liberal government of Alexander Dubček. Albania, the only European ally of Mao's China, felt the icy breath of the colossus on its doorstep, almost as close to its borders as the decadent bourgeois world of the West. In a mentality of siege, Enver Hoxha, the country's dictator, ordered the construction of hundreds of thousands of concrete pillboxes across the countryside to defend his tiny country against all imaginable (and imaginary) aggressors. In such a context of national paranoia, Ismail Kadare, then in his early thirties but already a celebrated novelist and poet in his own country and abroad, imagined a novel about a great siege — a siege as evocative of the present as it was radically disconnected from it.

The Siege tells the story of a generic siege of an unidentified Albanian fortress by the Ottoman Army in the earlier part of the fifteenth century. The siege fails. As a result, Kadare's story had at least two meanings when it appeared in the last days of 1969. It could be read as a politically correct assertion of Albania's impregnability; but because everyone knew as a matter of historical fact that Albania had been overrun by the Turks and incorporated into the Ottoman Empire by the end of the fifteenth century, Kadare's novel is also the story of an insignificant victory which only delayed the inevitable breaching of the walls. Critics were therefore not too sure what to make of this double-edged sword.

Kadare does not count *The Siege* as a historical novel, a kind of writing which in his view does not really exist. His imagination of the past was nonetheless fed by a well-known source, the Latin chronicle of the 1474 siege of Shkodër (*De obsidione Scodransi*, Venice, 1504) by Marin Barleti, one of the earliest works to come out of Albania, prior to any surviving literature in Albanian. Barleti's first-hand account implies that chronicles of earlier sieges had been written in the vernacular, and Kadare reproduces imaginary fragments of just such a lost chronicle in the "inter-chapters" of *The Siege*, which seem to come from the pen of a cleric within the besieged community.

Barleti was also the historian of George Castrioti, known as Skanderbeg (or "Lord Alexander", in Ottoman dress, Iskander Bey), who led Albanian resistance against the Turks until his death in 1468. In *The Siege*, Kadare does not portray Skanderbeg directly, but by alluding to his presence in the mountains, he sets his novel in a time which Barleti could only have known from Albanian chronicles. Skanderbeg defended Albania against the Ottomans in the name of Christendom. Credited with having saved Western Europe from Islam (in part thanks to Barleti's biography, which was translated into every European language), Skanderbeg was treated as a hero in Rome, where he still has his statue in a piazza bearing his name. From the time of the *rilindja*, the Albanian national renaissance in the late nineteenth century, and throughout the pre-war monarchy of King Zog, Skanderbeg was promoted as a national hero, and the cult persisted even under the Communist regime of Enver Hoxha. Tirana's central square was renamed Skanderbeg Square, and the fortress at Krujë where the warrior made his last stand was rebuilt as a national museum. This explains why Kadare stops short of portraying Albania's national hero in a novel set in Skanderbeg's time. The only acceptable portrait of the Dragon of Albania would have been an encomium, a genre entirely alien to Kadare's repertory.

The Siege was first called *Duallet e shiut*, "The Drums of Rain", but the Albanian publishers decided on a more heroic title, *Kështjella*, "The Castle", which also served to redirect attention to the Albanian side in the struggle. When the novel appeared in French in 1971, in a fluent translation by Jusuf Vrioni, the original title reappeared "as if by chance", according to Kadare. The name of *Les Tambours de la pluie*, "The Rain Drums", has thus remained attached to the book in France, but not elsewhere. The third of Kadare's longer works to reach a wide international audience through the medium of French, after *The General of the Dead Army* and *Chronicle in Stone*, *The Siege* confirmed Kadare's rising reputation as a universal storyteller.

Kadare left Albania for France in 1990 and set about revising all his novels for republication in a bilingual *Complete Works*, of which sixteen volumes have appeared to date. *The Siege* was partly rewritten for this definitive publication. Many references to the Christian beliefs of the Albanians, cut by the censors in 1969, were restored, some politically motivated passages were deleted, and the dialogue and descriptions were tightened up in many places and in other parts expanded. This new English translation is of the *Complete Works* text. (An earlier translation by Pavli Qesku, published in Tirana in 1978, reflects the Albanian text of 1969.)

Ismail Kadare asked me to invent an English title that would collectively signify both the besiegers and the besieged. Alas, despite its huge vocabulary, the English language cannot oblige. Like *The Castle* and *The Rain Drums*, "The Siege" is not exactly what the author wants this book to be called: it is just the least unsatisfactory name that he and I could find.

Kadare's story is more focused on the world of the besiegers than on the vestigially pagan mindset of the Catholic population of the city under siege. It is the first room in the sumptuous wing of Kadare's own castle of stories devoted to the Ottoman past of his native land (*The Three-Arched Bridge*, *The Blinding Order* and *The Palace of Dreams* are not sequels to *The Siege*, but other rooms in the same wing). Kadare provokes wonderment at the coloured ceremonials of the Ottoman Army at the peak of its splendour, and also horror at its "oriental" inhumanity, especially towards its nameless foot-soldiers and the women of the harem and of the surrounding countryside. Using a central character whose role of chronicler provides a writerly perspective on events, Kadare assembles a cast of the Ottoman elite, from the Pasha to experts in logistics, artillery and medicine, who slowly come to resemble figures out of modern rather than medieval history. The intentional anachronisms in tone seek to achieve a two-sidedness characteristic of all Kadare's fiction. The use of show trials, of banishment to "the tunnel", the unquestioned authority of the Pasha and the shifting chain of command beneath him — all these details make the Ottoman world, ostensibly the very image of Albania's Other, merge into an evocation of the People's Republic that Kadare could not possibly tackle directly. In a magical way that perhaps only great writers can achieve, Kadare's Turks are at one and the same time the epitome of what we are not, and a faithful representation of what we have become. *The Siege* is therefore not a simple transposition or blending of medieval and modern history, but a complex symbol of a divided and suffering nation besieged by itself. The miracle is that this exotic tale, translated twice over from an obscure Balkan tongue and dealing with a far-off and largely forgotten past, echoes on every page with the clashes and issues that burden us today. Kadare's chronicle of ancient battle is not a historical novel, as he rightly claims. It is an anti-historical one.

David Bellos
Princeton, NJ
11 September 2007